THE SHADOW CURSE
THE SHADOW ENFORCER SERIES BOOK FIVE

N. M. THORN

THE SHADOW CURSE

THE SHADOW ENFORCER SERIES BOOK 5

N.M. THORN

The Shadow Curse

By N.M. Thorn

Copyright © 2022 by N.M. Thorn. All rights reserved.

nmthornauthor@gmail.com

This book is a work of fiction. Names, characters, places and incidents are products of the author's imagination or are used fictitiously. Any resemblance to actual events or locales or persons, living or dead, is entirely coincidental. Reproduction in whole or part of this publication without express written consent is strictly prohibited.

Cover art design by Original Book Cover Designs

Edited by Spirit Editorial

PROLOGUE

* * *

Village of Gus-Zhelezny, Russia.
End of Eighteenth Century.

A TINY FLAME danced on the wick of a candle carried by a man dressed in a ceremonial suit made of silk and velvet. The candlelight could barely illuminate the room with its warm, flickering glimmer, but shadows slithered away from it and gathered in the corners, patiently waiting for the light to vanish so they could rule once again. The wooden floor moaned and squeaked under the man's shoes, and the mellow scent of smoke followed in his wake.

He halted in front of a large painting and raised his arm to touch its frame, but then pulled his hand away, and his fingers gathered into a fist as if he had second thoughts, his heart beating heavily against his ribcage. Throwing a wary glance over his shoulder to make sure no one had followed him here, he lifted the bottom of the painting a little and found the small lever hidden behind it.

With a groan, he pushed down on the lever and let go. Something clicked, the jarring sound echoing through the silent room, and a small door hidden beneath the wall tapestry cracked open. He slipped under the thick fabric and pushed the door, bending down to pass through the low doorway into a small area with a spiral stairway leading up. He cursed quietly at his creaking old joints as he started to climb up the narrow stairs, carefully placing his feet on the steps. When he finally made it to the top, he halted in the doorway, bracing his arm against the doorframe.

The room at the top of the stairway was small enough for the single candle to illuminate it fully, the flares of fire reflecting on the polished surface of a round table supported by short, curved legs resembling the thick paws of a lion. He crossed the room, heading toward the door at the other end. As soon as he reached it, he put his hand on the door handle, but then jerked it away, cursing colorfully.

"God damn his black soul, his magic and his turn-away spell," he grumbled, taking a deep breath to calm down. "Why, in God's name, do I need it here? No one in their right mind would ever dare follow me into my secret chambers."

He closed his eyes and took a deep breath, fighting the fear inflicted by the turn-away spell. Then he pushed the door open and stepped into the darkness of hidden passages. As soon as he crossed inside, the door closed behind him, and the heavy influence of the spell dissipated, allowing him to fill his lungs with oxygen and relax to a degree.

The flame flickered and almost died as a cold breeze came from the passage on his right, carrying a musty, stale odor with it. Andrey Batashov glanced down, thinking about the personal mint he had built under his estate, and all the counterfeit gold and silver coins that had been crafted there by his workers. Together with these thoughts came a troubling one, reminding him why he was here in the first place.

Stifling a sigh, Batashov turned to the second door and headed toward another staircase leading to a secluded platform on the roof of his mansion. Luckily, this stairway wasn't as steep as the previous one, and he quickly made it to the top. The crisp night air enveloped him, and he sucked in a deep breath, leaning heavily against the railing. For a few minutes, he gazed down, enjoying the view of his enormous estate, the Eagle's Nest.

My brother and I started all this years ago... Look at it now... The thought surfaced in his mind, and a proud smile lifted the corners of his lips.

A six-meter high, massive brick wall surrounded an enormous property, running for over two miles. Complete with watchtowers and embrasures, the actual mansion looked more like a medieval fortress than a regular Russian estate. Encircled by a fence and a moat, a beautiful park, decorated with gazebos, pavilions, and bridges, spread across a large part of the property. Despite its beauty, quite a few dark secrets were hidden among the trees.

The *terrible garden* was one of them. This obscure area within the park instilled fear into the hearts of local workers and villagers. No matter what happened in the Batashov's estate, they refrained from asking questions or saying anything in fear of getting tortured and killed somewhere in the depths of the garden.

Batashov's eyes darted in the direction of the "pavilion of love" hidden within his park, and an uneven smile curved his lips. Everything here was his. He had built his wealth and fortune from nothing, achieving his goals with sweat and blood, and even though the blood wasn't always his, it didn't bother him in the slightest. After all, gold was the only thing that mattered in this world. Gold and power. And he had them both.

At least for now.

Taking a deep breath, he turned around, reached into his pocket and pulled out a small vial filled with a shimmering, purple liquid. Raising it to his eyes, he stared through it at the bright disk of the full moon. As much as he didn't want to do it, he had no choice. Trying not to dwell on the consequences, he made his way to the wall across from him and smashed the vial against it. Thin shards of glass flew in all directions as the potion splashed all over the wall, thick drops trickling down from the place of impact.

As a large portal rotating with bright purple sparkles opened in the place where he had smashed the vial, he took a few steps back and halted by the railing. A few seconds later, a tall man wrapped in a black cloak from head to toe stepped out of the portal and stopped, a purple glimmer igniting in his deep-set eyes.

"*Goi esi*, Iron King," the man said, his soft voice filled with sarcasm, and even though the bottom part of the man's face was obscured by his cloak and darkness, Batashov was positive a mocking smile was playing on his thin lips. "What can I do for the mighty industrialist?"

"I need your help," Batashov rasped and cleared his throat, the mere idea of dealing with this eerie man again sending deep shivers down his spine.

"Oh?" The man cocked his brow. "You could not bribe or kill your way out of this situation yourself?"

"If I could," Batashov said through gritted teeth, "we would not be having this conversation."

The man snickered, his laughter dry like old parchment. "In that case, what can I do for the mighty Iron King?"

"Destroy it all," Batashov exhaled and turned away, leaning heavily on the railing.

"Pardon me?" The man halted by his side and also leaned on the railing, turning halfway toward him.

"I do not want to spend my last days as a convict of Emperor Pavel, rotting for the rest of my life in His Majesty's dungeon," Batashov muttered, looking straight ahead at the dark monolith of the wall surrounding his property. "I am seventy years old, and I have more than enough money for myself and to leave behind for my children." He chuckled icily and finally looked at the man. "I want you to help me destroy the mint and any witnesses of its existence."

"Curious," the man muttered, cocking his head. "Why do you think Emperor Pavel is after you?"

"I was betrayed—an anonymous denunciation. I hope their souls burn in Hell," Batashov grumbled, anger shaking through him. "I received a note from one of my people in St. Petersburg about my imminent arrest. So, I do not want to take any chances. When the Emperor's inspectors arrive here, they should find absolutely nothing incriminating."

"I see," the man murmured, his long fingers drumming a complicated rhythm on the railing. "I can help you, but as you are well aware, my services are not cheap."

"What do you want? My soul?" the old industrialist huffed, a crooked smile on his lips.

The man gave a derisive guffaw, which he cut off abruptly and shifted closer to Batashov, towering over him. "You seem to mistake me for one of your Christian habitants of Hell…" He took the hood of his cloak off, his long gray hair billowing in the night breeze. "Lucifer I am not, and I do not care about your soul." He measured Batashov with a scoffing stare. "Or whatever is left of it, anyway. All I want is your wealth, your money. You give me your gold and silver, and I will conceal your… um… indiscretions so well, no one will ever find any traces of your underground venture."

Batashov staggered back, thousands of uncontrollable thoughts and doubts racing through his mind. Making a quick decision, he met the man's blazing eyes.

"You can have all the gold and silver coins I have in my possession—real and those we minted in the underground basement—but only after I pass away," he said icily. "Leave the

Eagle's Nest estate and *Gusevsky* iron plant to my children. Everything else is yours."

"We have a deal then." The man's lips stretched into a sinister smile, exposing his yellow teeth.

He offered his hand to Batashov, and as he took it, something sharp pierced his skin. Batashov hissed, yanking his hand back. He flipped his hand over and peered at his palm, noticing a dark spot of blood.

"Now our deal is sealed with blood," the man said dryly, his voice making Batashov's hair stand on end. "Meet me tomorrow at midnight in the chamber under the tower the villagers call 'scary' and make sure all your workers are inside the underground room next to your mint. I will take care of your little problem." The man waved his hand and opened a dark portal, which rotated counterclockwise slowly. "See you tomorrow, Iron King."

Throwing one more glance filled with mockery at Batashov, he stepped through the portal and vanished.

* * *

THE FULL MOON disappeared from the sky, veiled by low, stormy clouds, and the dark park was submerged under the cloak of darkness. The evening was uncharacteristically cold, but Andrey Batashov didn't feel the chills, his mind set on what he needed to do next. He left his chambers, slipping through the hidden door into the underground corridor leading toward the Scary Tower, and didn't stop until he reached the end of the tunnel.

The man in the black cloak was waiting for him already, slowly pacing in front of a low iron door. In his hands, he held a wooden chest reenforced by iron and decorated with gold embellishments and red gemstones. As soon as Batashov walked in, he halted and cocked his head, glowering at him.

"Is everything ready, Iron King?" he asked, his voice cold like a winter blizzard.

"I've done everything as you said," replied Batashov through clenched teeth. "All my workers from both the morning and night shifts are inside the mint. There is no one else who knows about my side venture." He glanced at the chest in the man's hands and frowned, pointing at it. "What is that?"

The man cocked his head, the ugly sneer on his lips making his sharp, skeletal features look ghastly.

"You are not the only one who wants to hide something," he replied, venom dripping from his words. "Wait for me here. I will be right back." He waved his hand and vanished in the dark swirls of his portal.

Cursing quietly, Batashov leaned against the wall, crossing his arms over his chest. He wasn't having second thoughts, strongly believing he was doing what needed to be done, but he hated to wait for people—no matter who they were and their social standings—and this unexpected delay was driving him crazy with aggravation. When the portal manifested next to him and the man walked out of it, he could barely contain his irritation.

"Are you ready now?" he asked, tapping his foot. "I am not paying you for taking care of your own business at my expense."

A dark smile crossed the man's face, his bone-chilling purple eyes igniting brighter. "No, you most certainly do not," he said quietly. "Are you ready, Iron King? Are you sure this is what you want to do? Once I start, there will be no way back."

"Do it." Batashov threw a glance over the man's shoulder at the locked iron door behind which all his workers had gathered, none of them the wiser about the terrible fate he had doomed them to. Something twitched in his soul, and tightness gripped his chest, but he waved his hand, gesturing for the man to proceed, and repeated, "Do it, God damn your twisted soul."

"As you wish…" The man's words ended in a low hiss as he bent his tall frame in a ceremonial bow.

When he straightened, a strange purple mist surrounded him, wrapping around him like swirls of smoke. He muttered a few words that sounded like gibberish to Batashov, but before he could say anything, the ground trembled and the wind rushed through the underground passages, raising clouds of dust in the air.

Batashov coughed, burying his face into the crook of his elbow, and staggered back until he hit the wall. Even though they were deep underground, real thunder boomed somewhere above his head, the clamorous sound echoing through the endless corridors and tunnels running under his estate.

The man shouted something, raising his arms, and deep tremors ran under his feet. Horrified voices and cries for help reached Batashov's ears from behind the locked door, but the sound was quickly swallowed by the grinding noise of the quaking earth, the howls of the winds, and the low rumbles of thunder. Batashov pressed his back against the wall and pressed his hands over his ears, blood running cold in his veins.

Suddenly, the man waved his hand, opening a portal, and before Batashov could ask anything, he seized his shoulder and pulled him through the rotating swirls, leaving the underground passage behind.

When Batashov stepped out of the portal, he nearly fell, his heart beating in his throat, cold sweat covering his forehead. When he could finally take a breath, he looked around, recognizing his personal chambers. The man in the black cloak stood next to him, his face showing no signs of distress.

"Our business has concluded, Iron King," he said calmly, as if he hadn't just buried alive hundreds of people. "Your coin factory is sealed forever, and all the chambers and dungeons are either flooded or buried under a thick layer of dirt."

"Are you sure—," Batashov started, but cut himself off as he caught the man's furious gaze.

"I swear on my power," he growled, "the emperor's inspectors will find neither any signs of your underground mint nor any witnesses who could confirm its existence. Even hundreds of years in the future, no one will ever discover them. In addition, I placed a powerful turn-away spell on every entrance into your underground tunnels, so even if someone finds a door, they will run from it screaming in fear. Rest assured, Iron King, your terrible secret has been buried forever."

The man bowed and vanished from the chamber in a swirl of purple mist, leaving the horrified industrialist alone in his enormous estate.

CHAPTER 1

~ DAMIAN BLAKE ~

Superstition Mountains, Arizona

Despite the late hour, the night was warm, bordering on hot, the waves of heat rising from the rocks. Free from the brightness of the city lights, the sky was speckled with bright dots of stars, and the crescent moon shone cheerfully among them. The crickets and cicadas led their endless concert, and night birds screeched somewhere in the distance.

A few small stones slipped from under Dallas' foot, rumbling down the narrow mountain path. Damian, Cole and Atticus halted at the same time, throwing a reproachful glance at the young man. He shrugged with an apologetic smile and caught up with them.

"Cole, are you sure Dallas is ready?" Damian asked through their blood bond. *"He's young, he's human, and you barely started his training."*

Cole didn't reply right away, climbing silently up the hill. *"I'm not sure about anything, Dima,"* he replied after a while, a vibe of unease following his words. *"I wish I could talk him out of going* deeper into this rabbit hole, but you know how it is with human hunters. Once they set their mind on something, there is no way back."

"Did you introduce him to Sam?" Damian asked, thinking of River's father. A pureblood human, he'd been exposed to the World of Magic when he was in his early twenties. After his wife passed away, he stepped on the perilous path of a human hunter and hadn't stopped since. It's true what they say—once a hunter, always a hunter.

"I did." Cole all but rolled his eyes. "And a lot of good it did me. I invited Sam over, hoping he could help me deal with Dallas. Instead, they sat in my living room for five hours, drinking coffee while Sam was telling stories of all his heroic deeds. Do you think Sam's boasting about his adventures helped me talk Dallas out of becoming a hunter?"

Damian snorted, trying to suppress his laughter. "And where was Ruslan all this time? I'm sure he doesn't approve of you mentoring a human."

"Are you kidding? He's having too much fun with the whole idea of me teaching a human how to slay vampires to say anything." Cole huffed. "Ruslan sat on the couch with his legs crossed, blinking at them with his cat-eyes and trying not to laugh too loud."

"Sounds like Ruslan, alright." Damian stepped on a hard, rocky plateau and stilled at the edge, probing the area with his magical senses. "Hmmm..."

It was a small flat area ending in a tall, nearly vertical slope. As far as he could see, the wall was solid and there was nowhere else to go from here.

"What?" Cole asked warily, his hand reaching up to the hilt of the sword sheathed behind his back.

After the battle under Old Ladoga, Mara had vanished, and Cole had had no choice but to keep both swords in his possession. Besides, during the confrontation, a few Slavic deities had witnessed his unusual abilities, so the proverbial cat was out of the bag, at least partially. With that in mind, keeping his swords close by was probably the safest way to go, anyway. Since the blades were as short as a Roman gladius, Cole had ordered a dual sword back scabbard, and now he always carried both of them securely strapped to his back anytime he expected the need to use them.

Damian turned around and seized Atticus' arm, pulling him closer. "Are you sure this is the place Hawk was talking about?" he whispered into the young werewolf's ear.

"I'm sure." Atticus gave him a short nod, the orange light of a predator igniting in his eyes. "The fanged leaches retreated here after the fight my pack put up. My brother and I followed their scent all the way to this plateau."

"Jesus Christ," Dallas exhaled, wiping the perspiration off his brow with the back of his hand. "Must be nice to have all these magical powers." He chuckled softly. "None of you even broke a sweat climbing up here." He glanced around, taking in the view of the midnight mountains and the endless desert. "I thought I explored every inch of Lost Dutchman Park and the Superstition Mountains, but I never knew about the existence of this place."

"Shh…" Damian held his breath and sharpened his hearing. A consistent buzzing noise touched his senses. "There is something here. Cole, can you hear it?"

The vampire nodded. "A soft buzzing, like a giant beehive."

"Wards?" asked Atticus.

"Maybe. Maybe not." Damian channeled his magic and moved his arm in a wide arch to make sure his spell covered a larger area. *"Latentius revelare."*

As the glass-like layer of his spell manifested in front of him, Damian observed the area through it and stroked his chin, narrowing his eyes. A barrier constructed out of magical energy spread before him. It vibrated slightly, producing the buzzing sound they'd heard earlier. While it did resemble a layer of some kind of protection magic, it didn't have the usual shining lines characteristic to wards. Also, the even shine of the barrier had strange, pale-purple swirls and inclusions, suggesting the presence of a spell other than just wards.

"What is it?" Dallas' whisper sounded behind him, bringing him out of his thoughts.

"Good question," Damian muttered. "But whatever you do, don't touch it. You may activate something we won't be able to deal with…"

He took a step forward and squatted a few inches away from the energy barrier, careful not to touch it. Placing his palms flat against the ground, he channeled his elemental power and magic, sending both toward his eyes to reinforce his second sight. His magical sight, however, didn't help him uncover anything new, so he rose, stepping back carefully.

Suddenly, a soft movement of air brushed his skin, and the vibration of the magical barrier increased, the buzzing noise morphing into a high-pitched shrill. A blinding light ignited somewhere behind the wall, hurting his eyes adjusted to the dark of the night and making them water.

"Get down!" Damian shouted, realizing a second too late what was about to happen.

The vibration quickly turned into a wobble, and the wall exploded outward, a powerful blast wave striking Damian square in his chest. Other than the shrills of the wards, no sound accompanied the explosion, but the power of the impact lifted him off the ground and propelled him a few yards backward. He hit the mountain slope hard with his back, getting the wind knocked out of him, and kept rolling down, unable to stop for what seemed to be forever. Ignoring the pain, he called to the elemental power of Earth. A few long vines broke through the rocky surface and wrapped around his body, finally breaking his fall.

With a strenuous groan, he pushed himself into a sitting position, coughing and gasping for air with his mouth open.

The stinging pain of cuts and bruises all over his body intensified as he moved, and he had to focus on blocking it.

"Goddammit!" Damian cursed, his chest shuddering with short breaths. He rose to his feet and glanced around but couldn't see his brother or his friends anywhere. *"Cole? Are you okay? Where are you?"*

"I see you." Cole's reply followed almost immediately. *"Look up."*

Damian raised his eyes, looking uphill. Cole stood just a few feet above, his eyes glowing with the furious scarlet glow of his vampiric energy.

"Are Dallas and Atticus with you?" Damian asked, starting on his way up.

"I have Dallas with me. I was able to catch him before we started to fall," Cole replied, a wave of anger rushing through their bond. *"But I don't see Atticus anywhere."*

Damian reached his brother and halted by his side, quickly checking both Cole and Dallas for any visible injuries. Aside from a few minor scrapes and bruises, the young hunter was fine, and Cole's wounds were superficial enough for the speedy vampiric healing to take care of them almost immediately.

Slowly turning in place, Damian explored the surroundings with his magical senses. "I see Atticus." He pointed a few feet down and to the left.

The young werewolf was walking toward them, nursing his left arm. He reached them a little while later and stopped, breathing laboriously. Blood was trickling down his arm, spilling between his fingers. His pants and shirt were torn in a few places, bruises and lacerations visible through the cuts.

"What the hell was that?" he growled, partially transforming. His bleeding slowed down after the partial transformation but didn't stop completely, and he cursed through gritted teeth.

"Wards on steroids," Damian muttered, going through everything that had happened but couldn't figure out what had triggered the defense mechanism of the spell. He knew for sure he didn't touch anything. "If Hawk is right, and this is the place where the rogue vampires who attacked your pack are hiding, they can't be working alone. Vampires don't wield magic, so someone had to conjure these wards for them."

He channeled his elemental power, redirecting its flow toward his right hand. Then he approached Atticus and moved his arm out of the way.

"Damian, it's okay," the young man objected softly. "I'm a pureblood werewolf. I'll heal on my own. Your healing magic takes too much out of you."

"I know," he replied, forcing Atticus' hand down. "But I need you to be able to fight, and with this wound, you can't."

He channeled a small amount of the healing energy of Earth through the cut on Atticus' arm, careful not to overuse it. The werewolf closed his eyes and exhaled, his tense face gradually relaxing. Damian waited until the bleeding stopped completely and the laceration closed before he stopped the healing process.

"What now?" asked Dallas, rubbing his shoulder where a giant dark bruise was forming.

"Now?" Damian raised his eyes at the plateau, and a dark smile appeared on his face. "Now that I've seen what we're dealing with, I'm going to break these wards, and we're going to kill every single one of these bastards." He glanced back at Atticus and Dallas and added, "Stay with Cole." Then he gave his brother a short nod and headed back up the narrow trail, anger searing through him.

Damian stopped at the edge of the plateau and channeled his magic, opening his other sight at the same time.

"*Veritatius revelare,*" he whispered a different revealment spell, which was supposed to be a lot more potent.

Staring intently at the barrier of wards glowing with a dim light, he froze in place, taking in every new detail he discovered. An entirely different view unveiled behind the wall of protection magic. He stood at the edge of a relatively large open space, the wall of a mountain rising at the other end of it. A dark opening, most likely an entrance into a cave, was clearly visible even from this distance.

"How clever," he muttered through clenched teeth, realizing the true purpose of the pale swirls and inclusions he had noticed in the magical barrier before. "Not only do they have powerful protection magic, but they added an illusion to it as well." He reached out to his brother through their bond and projected, *"Cole, get closer, but stay below the level of the plateau. You'll know when the wards are down."*

Focusing on the barrier, he glanced up, noticing thin, vertical lines rising from the ground and disappearing into the dark sky high above his head. A chain of small runes, sigils and strange glyphs ran parallel to the ground at about chest level. Most of them never overlapped the vertical lines, perfectly fitted between them, except for one sigil that looked more like a monogram than a single glyph. Slightly larger, it was drawn right over the line closest to him, glowing just a little brighter than the rest of the symbols. Undoubtedly, this sigil was the key, supporting the entire spell.

"I got you now..." Damian extended his arms toward the key-sigil and whispered, *"Exitius."*

Two blinding rays of pure magical energy escaped his palms, hitting the glowing glyph. The wards shrilled and wobbled, gathering energy for the next blast, and Damian knew he had just a few seconds to break the spell.

"Zhulik!" he yelled, his voice trembling with strain. "A little help would be nice!"

With a light pop, the gargoyle materialized next to him in his puppy form. "I'm here, Commander. What—," he started to say, but cut himself off and assumed his natural form. Stepping closer to Damian, he focused on the wavering barrier. Two rays of brilliant blue light erupted from his eyes, impacting the key-sigil.

Damian channeled more of his energy into his spell, increasing the potency of his strike. Under their joint assault, the purplish shade of lines and symbols started to morph into white as his magical energy invaded the wards. The ruckus of the failing protection spell echoed through the desert, and a group of dark figures rushed out of the maw of the cave, forming a single line in front of it.

"A welcoming party?" Damian laughed icily and tapped into the full power of a Destiny Enforcer, reinforcing his spell. *"Exitius Amplio!"*

With a thunderous bang, the wards finally collapsed, taking down the illusion with them. For a brief moment, the key-sigil expanded and grew brighter, but then quickly dissipated, vanishing in a swirl of purple mist.

"Cole, now!" Damian projected.

A soft whisper rushed through the line of his opponents. Their eyes ignited a bright scarlet, and they charged toward him, swords in their hands. Damian wasn't sure how many vampires were there, and he didn't care to count.

In his peripheral vision, he saw Cole, Dallas and Atticus appear on top of the plateau, and he gave them a quick nod. Summoning his daggers, he ran toward the rogue vampires. A giant black wolf fell in step on his right, and Zhulik stayed on his left, his solid-rock paws hitting the ground with loud bangs.

"Keep an eye on Dallas. I'll watch out for Atticus," he projected to Cole as his daggers collided with the sword of the first vampire he met on his way. Sparks flew in the air, and the magical energy of his daggers grew brighter. With an explosive mix of anger and adrenalin charging through his system, Damian pushed back his opponent and then quickly closed the distance, decapitating the vampire with one swing of his blade.

The black wolf rose high in the air, crushing the next

vampire with the weight of his body, his fangs ripping his throat to shreds. The vamp howled in pain, his eyes widening. Once Atticus lifted his head, blood dripping from his fangs, Damian swung his dagger, decapitating the second monster. Atticus inclined his furry head and charged the next attacker.

"Dallas, on your left!" Cole's voice boomed somewhere next to Damian, causing him to snap toward the sound.

Two vamps charged Dallas at the same time. To Damian's delight, the young man didn't blink an eye. Moving with the speed and fluidity of an experienced martial artist, he spun out of the direct line of attack, successfully avoiding the weapons and claws of both monsters assailing him. His machete whistled through the air, cutting through the vamp's neck with unexpected ease.

Dallas didn't look back to see if the vampire had turned into ash, his eyes already set on the second assailant. As the vamp roared and charged him, he met him with a powerful sidekick. The monster staggered backward, running into Cole. His brother laughed, and his clawed hands ripped the vampire's head off with ease, turning him into a pile of ash.

Way to go, little bro... Damian watched Cole reach behind his back and unsheathe both swords in one swift move.

A blinding white light enveloped him, and Cole screamed, throwing his head back, pure joy in his voice as his magic filled his entire being. He moved forward, fast and deadly, every strike of his terrifying weapons leaving behind piles of ashes.

A few minutes later, everything was over. Damian lowered his bloodied daggers and opened his second sight, probing the area inside the cave as far as he could reach. The cave seemed to be empty.

"Zhulik, come with me," he said and headed toward the entrance.

Followed by his gargoyle, he walked inside and halted at the entrance, quickly surveying the area. The cave was large enough to hold at least twenty people with ease, but it didn't give off the vibe of an old vampire's nest, nothing there suggesting these vampires had used it as a hiding place for longer than a couple of days.

"Hmmm…" Damian rubbed his forehead, feeling the slickness of sweat and blood under his fingers. Turning to Zhulik, he petted his head, the roughness of the stone grazing his fingertips. "Can you do me a favor?"

"Just tell me what you need," the gargoyle replied, rolling his enormous, glowing eyes. "They call you Commander for some unexplainable reason, so command."

Damian chuckled. "I don't want to command you, Zhulik. I much rather treat you as a friend."

"That's because you're a Child of Earth. You can't help but love all animals." Zhulik morphed into a German Shepherd puppy, a wide, doggish grin splitting his face. "And I'm the cutest doggy in the entire world. Right? Right?" He pushed Damian's hand with his wet nose.

"Absolutely," Damian agreed, lowering to one knee next to him, his fingers threading through the puppy's thick fur. "Now, can you please check those passages?" He pointed at the two dark holes at the opposite end of the cave. "I want to make sure no one's left there."

"Your wish is my command!" Zhulik vanished with a light pop. He reappeared a few minutes later, shaking the dust of his dark fur. "There's no one there, Commander. I went as far as I could. Everything is dark and empty."

"Hmmm…" Damian shook his head, nibbling on his lip.

"You've been saying that a lot today." Damian heard Cole's soft voice next to him and turned to his brother. "What's going on, big bro?"

"Not sure." Damian headed out of the cave, motioning for Cole and Zhulik to follow him. "I need to speak with Hawk. This group of rogue vamps attacked Hawk's ranch. I understand that part. But why would Hawk assume they had been around for a long time? This cave doesn't look like a vampire's nest. Nothing suggests that these vamps had been living here for a while."

"I think I can answer that question." Atticus had already transformed into his human form, his face, chest and arms covered in blood, his clothes ripped to pieces. "During the attack, we managed to capture one of the vamps, and he kindly volunteered some information. He said his team was hired by someone to attack local packs, and they nested in the Superstition Mountains, waiting for their boss's next command."

"I'm sure he lied… I wonder if he allowed you to capture him so he could deliver this information…" Damian muttered, his mind working on overdrive. Something didn't add up, and since he trusted Hawk completely, a dark sense of dread coiled in the pit of his stomach. "Did he say anything else?"

"No. He swore up and down that it was all he knew," replied Atticus, spreading his arms a little. "Of course, my father didn't take his word for it. Just like you, he suspected some kind of trap or deceit. So, after the attack, he sent Griffin and me to follow the scent of these vamps while it was still fresh. At the same time, he mobilized a few more groups of scouts from local packs to check the entire Phoenix Metropolitan Area. They found absolutely nothing out of the ordinary."

"Ahh…" Damian exhaled, lowering himself to the ground next to Dallas. "Why do I feel as though we are missing something important here?"

"Commander, do you want me to check the entire park? Just to be on the safe side?" Zhulik asked out loud, placing his paw on Damian's knee.

"Holy shit!" Dallas yelped, jumping to his feet. "Your dog can speak? English?"

"Not a dog, dumbass," Zhulik snapped, a tiny growl rumbling in his chest. "I'm a great and terrible gargoyle." He bared his tiny fangs and puffed out his chest, trying to look intimidating, but quickly gave up on it and added softer, "Of course, I can speak English, and maybe five or six hundred other languages, some of which you don't even know exist. And I bet your skinny ass my English vocabulary is a lot richer than yours." Zhulik stuck his tongue out at Dallas and turned to Damian. "Commander, is that your new recruit? You really need to raise your standards." He glanced at Dallas, cocking his head, one of his ears flopping.

"Sorry?" Dallas mumbled, looking so lost that Damian couldn't help but laugh.

"Dallas, this is my gargoyle, Zhulik," he said, giving the young man a light tap on his shoulder. "Don't worry, when he's with friends, he is a lot more bark than bite." Then he turned to Zhulik and nodded. "Good idea. Please check the park and the entire Phoenix Metropolitan Area for any unusual events, disturbances, or anything out of the ordinary. Report to me as soon as you're done."

"Yes, Commander." Zhulik raised his paw to his head in a semblance of a salute and vanished with a light pop.

As soon as the gargoyle was gone, Damian got up with a groan and looked down at his dirty, torn clothes, throwing his hands up. "Dammit! I don't think the Destiny Council pays me enough in human currency. I have to buy new clothes after every mission, and I hate shopping." The last three words he said slowly, spitting one word at a time. "Do you think they sell disposable clothes anywhere?"

Cole, Atticus and Dallas exchanged a quick look and burst out laughing. Damian pursed his lips, tilting his head reproachfully.

"It's not like any of you fared any better." He winked at Dallas. "Dallas, if you're planning to hang out with my brother, you should ask your boss for a raise."

Before either Dallas or Cole could reply, the shrill ring of a cellphone shattered the silence of the midnight park. Cursing under his breath, Damian reached into his pocket and pulled out his phone, silently thanking all the gods for the device surviving his fall down the mountain. The name of Luc de la Crosse displayed on the screen sent chills down his back, an expectation of trouble setting his nerves on edge.

"Luc," he said, answering the call.

Something cracked and fell, a loud grinding noise coming through the line.

"Damian…" Luc's voice was hoarse and shaky, sounding as if he had a hard time speaking. "Damian… please, help…"

"Luc, what's going on? Where are you?"

"The store… under—"

His voice broke off, and the line went dead.

CHAPTER 2

~ DAMIAN BLAKE ~

Dropping his hand with the phone, Damian met Cole's shocked gaze. He shoved the device into his pocket and turned to Atticus.

"I don't know what's going on, but I believe the local Wardens are under attack," he said quietly, his jaw set. "Before I leave to help them, I want to make sure both you and Dallas are safe. I'm going to open a portal to the gates of your father's ranch, and I need both of you behind those powerful wards at all times." He glanced from Atticus to Dallas and stifled a sigh. "I hope your father won't mind providing sanctuary to a human hunter... Tell Hawk I'll call him as soon as I can."

"Don't worry. Dallas will be safe with me." Atticus gave Damian a short nod. "My father won't mind."

Cole turned to Dallas, seized his arm and pulled him closer, concern shadowing his features. "Dallas, no matter what happens, you must stay with the pack. Do you understand me? You do not leave Hawk's ranch until either Damian or I pick you up."

"Yes, sir," Dallas replied, his face turning ashen.

Damian waved his arm, opening a portal. "Go now and stay safe. We'll contact you as soon as we can."

Once Atticus and Dallas were gone, Damian placed his hand on Cole's shoulder and snapped his fingers, leaving the dark mountains behind.

* * *

DAMIAN AND COLE appeared in a dark alley behind the Warden's bookstore. Since Damian had no idea what to expect, instead of materializing in front of the backdoor of the store the way he usually did, he teleported a few yards away from it. The alley looked as quiet and empty as always, yet something was different. He couldn't see, hear or sense anything out of the ordinary, but goosebumps covered his arms, shivers running down his back.

"Something is not right," he whispered, not sure he was talking to his brother or himself.

"Agreed," Cole replied, his swords already in his hands. "Can you smell blood and smoke somewhere in that area?" He pointed toward the door of the shop. "It's not strong, but I can still detect them."

"Do you hear anything? Heartbeats?"

Cole froze in place and closed his eyes, lifting his face slightly. "No," he whispered. "But it doesn't mean anything."

No heartbeats... Are Luc and Jamie... Damian cut himself off, unwilling to think about what this could mean. *Perun almighty, please, protect my friends, and I'll do everything I can on my side...* He clenched his teeth so tight they squeaked, his hands tightening into fists. "I guess we'll find out soon."

He moved his arm in a wide arch, whispering the most powerful revealment spell he knew. The glass-like layer of his magic materialized in front of him almost immediately, and when he glanced through it, the small hairs rose on the back of his neck.

"Holy shit," Cole muttered, looking over his shoulder.

The entire building was engulfed by a glowing dome of magical energy. Damian could see the runes and sigils of wards similar to those he had encountered just a short while ago, and this dome also had a powerful layer of illusion placed over it. It was so potent that even the revealment spell couldn't dispel it completely. Red and orange flairs of light shone through the layer of the illusion, dark shadows moving stealthily behind the wall of magic.

"I don't see it," Damian mumbled, narrowing his eyes at the magical barrier. He opened his other sight, reinforcing it with his magic and elemental energy.

"Can't see what?" Cole stepped closer, his vampiric essence spiking around him.

Damian glanced at his brother as if he saw him for the first time, his heart beating desperately somewhere in his throat. "The key-sigil," he whispered. "The one element that holds this monolith of magic together. I can't find it, Cole."

"Could it be upfront? This dome seems to be encapsulating the entire building."

Desperate to find a solution as soon as possible, Damian grabbed his brother's arm and snapped his fingers, teleporting them to the front of the building. It was past midnight, and at this point, he just couldn't care less if anyone saw them materializing out of thin air.

The plaza in front of the shop was mostly vacant, with a few unoccupied cars parked at the far end of it. The store looked dark and empty, the open sign shut down as always at this hour. But Damian knew better—what he saw with his normal sight wasn't even close to the terrifying reality. He whispered the revealment spell and opened his second sight.

The same flairs of light shone through the layer of illusion.

Something dark moved behind it, shifting from side to side. Trying not to focus on what it could be, Damian searched the dome of magic for anything that would help him break through but found no weak spots.

"If it's not there," Cole said, his voice ringing with fury, "we'll break it the old-fashioned way."

"Huh?" Damian glanced at his brother, having a hard time understanding what he had in mind, but he was gone already.

Halting in front of the glowing barrier, Cole swung both swords, slamming them on the surface of the dome. The magic he was wielding set his blades ablaze with a blinding white light, and a bright white splatter materialized in the place of the impact. The wards responded with an angry buzz and vigorous vibration, tremors running through the ground.

"That's right," Cole muttered, raising his swords again. "You should be afraid..." He slammed his swords down again, powering his attack with his magic.

"Dammit, bro... If the wards explode, we are both toast..." Damian channeled his power and magic toward his arms and shouted, *"Exitius!"*

Two eye-watering rays of pure magical energy escaped his palms, hitting the vibrating dome a foot away from his brother. Cole didn't even blink an eye. Using his vampire speed and strength, he kept assailing the dome, the area affected by his magic growing wider with every next swing of his swords.

Cursing under his breath, Damian reached his brother in one long stride and placed his hands directly against the shiny surface of the magical dome. He closed his eyes to protect his vision from the blinding light and whispered, *"Exitius Amplio..."*

The kickback from the strike of his magic was so powerful, he skidded a few feet backward, nearly falling. A thin fracture manifested in the place of the impact, glowing with a blinding white light. It ran upward and to the side, joining with the fractures created by his brother's relentless assaults. The wards howled, their shrilling sound so loud, it was unbearable to normal human ears, let alone the heightened hearing of a Destiny Enforcer or an ancient vampire.

With a groan, Damian pressed his hands to his ears, staggering back. Cole bent down and dropped his swords, his arms wrapping around his head of their own accord. The vibration became stronger, wide waves now running through the barrier, and Damian knew what was coming next.

"Nikolai!" A strangled scream escaped his lips.

In a heartbeat, he was back at the barrier, positioning himself between the wards and his brother. His daggers materialized in his hands, and he infused them with all the magic and power he could gather, including the purifying light of Creation. The steel shimmered with the swirls of brilliant light, vibration spreading through his arms, originating in his blades. He swung his daggers and slammed them down on the barrier with everything he had.

The wave of his magic spread around like an atomic blast. It hit him directly in his chest, throwing him over Cole's head and sending him flying a few feet back. The wards crashed with a deafening bang. The layer of illusion distorted like an old photo set on fire, and the last remains of the barrier dissipated, revealing the bloodcurdling truth.

The bookstore was engulfed in scorching flames, the swirls of dark smoke rising high in the air. Shoulder to shoulder, a few massive monsters stood silently in front of the blazing building. They looked like werewolves from some modern horror flick—half man, half beast. Thick, black fur covered the top of their bodies, their yellow eyes glowing with malevolence. Their hands still resembled human hands but were a lot larger and ended in horrid claws. Besides huge fangs that could crush a man's skull with ease and grisly claws, they were armed with swords, axes, and chains. The stench of dark magic permeated the air around them, leaving no doubt to what these monsters were.

Damian scrambled to his feet and stared at them. As he began to feel the state of his physical and magical exhaustion, fear for his friends rose in him, threatening to swallow him whole. His chest shuddered with laborious breaths, sweat running down his flushed face.

"Somebody..." he said in reply to his brother's troubled glance. He wiped his brow with the back of his hand, still holding a dagger. "They... went as far as to summon..." He paused, panting, struggling to equalize his breathing. "Each one of these monsters is an *oboroten...*"

"Whatever... How do we kill them?" Cole got up, swords in his hands blazing.

"Decapitation works, blade through their black hearts also works but not as effectively," Damian managed to say, gathering his magic again. "All these assholes are dark sorcerers who are powerful enough to shift into this monstrous form, or anything else they want, for that matter. So, beware of their magic."

"Any ideas on who sent them here?"

"Could be Koschei or his master... Could be anyone else who holds a grudge against me. Unless I'm sure, I prefer not to make any assumptions." He frowned, taking another deep breath. "But whoever runs this show has unlimited power and influence in the World of Magic and boundless creativity."

"Yeah, creative fuckers..." Cole vanished before Damian could say anything else.

Dammit, brother. Do you know how to wait?

The monsters responded to Cole's attack almost immediately. A deep growl rumbled in their chests, and their lips curled in a feral snarl as they raised their weapons. There were only six of them, but with their strength and magic they presented a power to be reckoned with, and soon the air was thick with the crackling discharges of dark magical energy.

"*Ignius Orbus,*" one of them roared, propelling a fireball at Cole. He spun out of the way, managing to avoid both the fireball and the energy strikes. His sword hissed through the air, catching the side of another monster who was trying to reach him. The wound wasn't deadly by any means, but the creature gasped, its eyes widened, and it fell to the ground, collapsing uncontrollably as it slowly dissolved into a stinky, disgusting puddle of black goo.

The rest of the monsters roared, fury surrounding them like a malignant cloud. Cole's diabolical laugher rose above their growls and shouts as he spun in place, trying to inflict as much damage as he could with his deadly blades. Damian stared at his brother in awe, unable to take his eyes off him.

With a thunderous bang, the windows in the shop exploded outward, showering them with shards of glass, and a surge of heat engulfed them. The hungry flames spread wider, devouring more and more territory. For a split second, Cole lost his concentration, but it was enough for one of the monsters to creep up on him from behind.

"Cole! Behind you!" Damian shouted.

Doubting his brother could respond in time, he propelled his dagger with all his might. The blade went through the monster's chest like a hot knife through butter, stopping the creature in its tracks. It seized the dagger, trying to rip it out with its claws, but Damian didn't give it a chance.

Pointing at his dagger, he hissed, "*Illucious.*" The blade lit up with the light of Creation, reducing the *oboroten* to a puddle of goo.

Cole swung his sword, decapitating the last monster, and turned to Damian, a faint smile on his face splattered with blood and black slime. "Thanks, bro," he mumbled, lowering his blades.

Damian nodded and extended his hand, summoning his

dagger, his eyes set on the burning building. As if hearing his thoughts, Cole halted by his side, shaking his head.

"I can hear three heartbeats inside," he whispered. "If Luc and Jamie are still alive there, why aren't they using their magic to get the hell out of this flaming inferno?"

"Good question... Stay here," Damian said and headed toward the fire, a shadow of grim foreboding lingering over him. He made a circular motion with his hand over his head, whispering a protection spell, and ran through the doorway.

Even though the shield of his magic protected him from direct contact with fire, the heat and smoke hit him like a sledgehammer, the putrid stench of burned plastic, wood and paper suffocating him. He groaned but kept moving forward, struggling to see anything through the gray screen of smoke hanging in the air. There was something strange about this fire, however. While it was raging throughout the store, the small area around the counter was untouched by it, and it seemed as if the flames were deliberately avoiding it.

His foot caught on something, causing him to look down. Two men dressed in the black attire of a priest lay on the floor by the counter, their hands still clutching their swords. It didn't look like they were killed by the fire, their skin and clothes unscathed by the flames. But when Damian bent down, he noticed deep lacerations on their necks.

If anything, they died fast... Dammit, I was too late...

Through the crackling of the fire, Damian heard a shuffling noise coming from behind the counter. He made his way around it and halted. In the limited space below the desk, a man in the black clothes of a priest sat with his back resting against the counter. Judging by his outfit and the medieval style sword lying across his lap, he was one of Luc's Wardens. His hand was pressed to his chest, blood spilling from a wound under it, running between his fingers.

Luc and Jamie lay by his side. Their clothes were torn and

covered in dark splatters of blood, but from a distance, it was impossible to tell whether they were alive or dead. Even without using his other sight, Damian could see the yellowish glow of a protection spell shielding the entire area under the desk, but he was positive it wasn't what kept the flames away.

The Warden raised his eyes, staring at Damian intently. "Save them," he whispered, his breath coming out in uneven gasps. "Maybe you can still—" A fit of cough interrupted him, and blood spilled from his mouth, bubbling up on his lips. He fell silent, pressing his other hand to his throat, his blood-coated fingers trembling slightly.

"God damn these evil bastards, whoever they are," muttered Damian.

With a strenuous groan, he lifted Luc and draped him over his shoulder while whispering a new protection spell. Once done, he headed out of the burning store, moving as fast as he could. Followed by a cloud of smoke, he rushed out the door and halted, gasping for air and coughing. Lowering Luc on the asphalt next to his brother, he rushed back inside, reinforcing his protective shield as he ran. He headed toward the desk, avoiding fallen shelves and burning books scattered all over the floor. Without slowing down, he lifted Jamie, placed him over his shoulder under the protection of his shield and took him out of the store. As he carefully lowered him on the sidewalk, the shrill sirens of the approaching emergency vehicles shattered the silence, and he threw his hands up, cursing colorfully.

Dammit! I broke the illusion, and the concealment spell came down with it. I'm sure someone must have noticed the fire and called nine-one-one...

Damian rushed back into the store and came out a minute later, carrying the last man in his arms. He lowered him to the ground just in time to see a few fire engines and an ambulance pulling into the plaza at the other end. Lowering to his knees, he checked Luc's and Jamie's vitals and exhaled with relief.

They were alive, but a heavy sense of dread coiled in his stomach as he took in their appearance. They were unconscious, their chests rising and falling evenly, and to a bystander, they would have appeared sleeping. But there was something about their faces that made Damian do a double-take, numbness settling in his limbs. A strange sharpness to their features, with dark shadows underlying their eyes and cheekbones, made them look as if they were one step away from crossing the veil. He'd seen death many times throughout his long life, and he could recognize the signs of the forthcoming demise, even if he didn't want to believe it.

"Commander Blake," the Warden whispered, and Damian turned around, trying to focus his attention on him. "I'm as good as dead…" He chuckled bitterly, more blood spilling from the corner of his mouth. He pressed his hand against the gaping wound on his chest and groaned, clenching his teeth. "I'm old enough to know when it's the end… But maybe you can still save them…" He jerked his chin toward Jamie and Luc.

"I'll do my best." Damian channeled his elemental power, redirecting the healing energy of Earth toward his hands, but the man raised his arm, shaking his hand.

"Don't bother, Commander," he objected faintly. "You can't heal either of us… at least that's what I've been told. Neither the vampire's blood nor the healing energy of Earth will work. Besides, humans are here, and right now your eyes are glowing like neon lights. You shouldn't expose the World of Magic."

"Told by whom?" asked Damian. He suppressed his magic and glanced back at the emergency vehicles coming to a screeching halt in front of the store.

"The man who is responsible for all this." He pointed at the burning store and then at Luc and Jamie. Sucking in a shaky breath, he closed his eyes for a brief moment before continuing. "He left me alive so I could give you a message."

"A message?" Damian echoed, cold sweat running down his back. "What message?"

"He told me to tell you his words exactly as he said them," the Warden continued in a hoarse whisper. "He said what happened today is just the beginning. He will not rest until every person and everything you hold dear to your heart is either dead or destr—"

A terrible coughing fit interrupted his words, and blood gushed down his chin, his fingers clutching spasmodically at his chest. Then his tense muscles relaxed, his eyes rolled to the side, and the last tortured breath escaped his lips.

Damian exhaled as if someone had just punched him in the gut. He shifted from a kneeling position, lowering himself heavily on the sidewalk, and covered his face with his hands.

"Dima, I need to leave for a moment. I'll be right back." Cole's voice sounded through their bond.

Damian raised his face to see the firefighters getting their equipment ready and a group of paramedics rushing toward them, but he could barely process everything that was unfolding around him, a single thought overpowering his mind.

Koschei the Deathless is back...

A month had passed since the fight under Old Ladoga, and Damian had spent every free moment searching for the location of Koschei's death but hadn't been able to find any information about it. Master Alliandr promised to check the Riders Library in Kendral and consult with the Riders Council, but so far, he had nothing to show for either.

"I wasn't ready," Damian whispered, bowing his head low, his fingers digging into the mass of his hair. "Goddammit! I was too late..."

"Are you okay, young man? Too late for what?"

Damian flinched and raised his head. A middle-aged woman in an EMT uniform stood over him, her attentive brown eyes gazing at him with sympathy.

"I'm sorry," he mumbled and pointed at the burning store. "My friends were hurt in the fire, and I was too late to help them."

"You pulled three men out of a burning building, risking your own life." Her eyebrows rose, sincere surprise in her eyes. "We'll take them to the hospital, and I assure you the doctors will do everything they can to help them."

Damian glanced back at Luc, Jamie and the body of the Warden whose name he'd failed to ask. A few paramedics gathered around them, checking their vitals and quickly assessing their state, their habitual moves filled with urgency.

The woman in the EMT uniform was asking something about the fire and his own condition, but he had a hard time processing her questions, sounds coming through dull and muffled. He tried to answer the best he could, struggling to keep up the layer of civil politeness while his mind was miles away from here. He had to speak with Magnus and Master Alliandr. He had to understand what was done to Jamie and Luc and find a way to heal them. He couldn't sit here answering mundane medical questions while anyone he had ever cared about was possibly in danger. He needed to be back home in Paradise Manor.

River... The train of thoughts came to an abrupt stop, and he sucked in a sharp breath, his hand reaching into his pocket for the cellphone.

The woman finished checking the cuts and bruises on his body and shook her head in disbelief. "You have a nasty cut on the back of your head. You really should go to the hospital and have it checked." She directed some light at his eyes, using a medical penlight. "Headache? Dizziness?"

"No… I'll be fine," he managed to say through clenched teeth, rising. "What hospital are you taking them to?"

"Scottsdale HonorHealth," she replied, giving him quick directions.

"Thank you," he muttered, following her with his eyes as she headed back toward the ambulance. As soon as she was far enough, he reached out to his brother through their blood bond. *"Cole, we have a huge problem. Where the hell are you?"*

"On your right." Cole's answer followed immediately. *"I couldn't walk around with two swords strapped to my back like some Renaissance Fair castaway, could I? Give me another minute to straighten things out with the fire department."*

Damian glanced to the right and saw his brother talking with one of the firefighters. He sat back down on the sidewalk and dialed River's phone number, his hands covered in blood, dirt and ash shaking a little. She answered his call after just a few beeps, but to him, it seemed like forever.

"Hello," she mumbled, her voice husky and thick with sleep.

"River," he said, exhaling with relief. "Where are you?"

"Where I'm supposed to be," she muttered. "Home, sleeping. Why aren't you home?"

"I'll be home soon," he replied, speaking urgently. "I'll explain everything when I see you. In the meantime, I need you to get up and go to the left wing of the house. Go into the bedroom the farthest from the entrance and wait for me. Take Gypsy with you..."

"Damian, what's wrong? What's going on?" Tones of concern sounded in her voice, and he heard a soft shuffling noise.

"River, please tell me you're on your way to the left wing," he said, his voice pleading.

"I am. Looking for Gypsy. Where the hell is that pesky cat?" she replied, her voice trembling slightly. "Here, kitty, kitty... Gypsy... oh, there you are..." She chuckled softly and added, "Okay, we're on the way to the left wing now."

"I'll see you soon." Damian disconnected the call and shoved the device into his pocket, heading toward Cole.

He wasn't sure his brother had finished answering all the questions yet, but judging by the amount of vampiric essence

Cole exuded, he could end this conversation any time he wished. Damian raised his hand to attract his brother's attention, and when Cole glanced at him, he tapped his watch, gesturing for him to get moving. A moment later, Cole shook the firefighter's hand, gracing him with one of his charming smiles, and headed toward Damian.

"What did you—," he started to say, but the loud ring of his cellphone interrupted him. He reached in his pocket and answered the call, his eyebrows gathering over his eyes. "Father, what—"

He didn't finish the question and froze in place, motionless like a marble statue, and by the look on his face, Damian already knew what Ruslan was telling him.

"Where?" Damian asked.

"My Court," Cole whispered, barely moving his lips. "Luciano's Mansion. I need to get my swords." He gestured toward the dark alley.

Dammit, I'm already so drained, I can barely stand on my feet... How am I supposed to—

Refusing to think of what was coming, he placed his hand on his brother's shoulder and snapped his fingers.

CHAPTER 3

~ COLE ADAMS ~

Cole found his swords in the same place he had left them earlier. Moving his unbending fingers as fast as he could, he fastened the belts of his back scabbard and sheathed his weapons. Then he glanced at his brother and his shoulders tensed, doubt gnawing at him. Damian hadn't had time to heal himself after the fall from the mountain, and the fight with assorted monsters as well as carrying three adult men out of the burning building had depleted his physical strength and drained his magical energy.

"Dima, are you sure you can do it?" he asked quietly. "You look like you can barely stand on your feet."

"Come on, bro." A faint smile touched Damian's lips. "It's your father… Of course, I'm going to do it."

He placed his hand on Cole's shoulder and snapped his fingers. The dark alley spun around them, disappearing in a whirlpool of colors and sounds.

* * *

They manifested at the far end of Luciano's property, next to a tall fence. Damian groaned and swayed, bracing his arm against the wall, but quickly recovered and gave Cole an apologetic smile.

The large house stood dark and silent. When Luciano was alive, he hadn't been a proponent of big gatherings and social events in general. He had liked darkness and solitude, and everything in his estate was designed to provide him with a place where he could relax and enjoy the isolation from the modern world with its information overload and invasive technology.

Seeing this enormous property submerged under the cloak of night wasn't something new to Cole. Yet as he observed the building from a distance, he couldn't get rid of the feeling that he was missing something. Something extremely important. He glanced sideways at his brother, noticing the orange glow in his eyes.

"Do you see anything?" Cole whispered.

"Nothing."

Damian waved his hand and murmured a revealment spell. As the glass-like layer manifested in front of him, Cole moved closer to his brother and peered through it, slowly shaking his head. The spell didn't show anything he couldn't see with his normal vision. There were no crazy wards or illusions. Everything he could see before him was real.

"What's going on?" he whispered, throwing a troubled glance at Damian.

"I don't know." Damian shrugged, exuding exhaustion with his every move. "Unless we go inside, we'll never find out." He turned to Cole and tilted his head a little. "Are you sure Ruslan called you from here?"

"Yes, I'm sure." Cole massaged the back of his neck, quickly going over the brief conversation he'd had with Ruslan in his mind. "I was supposed to be here tonight, too, but Ruslan thought you needed my help, so he promised to run the Council meeting instead of me."

Without saying anything else, Damian headed toward the house, stepping soundlessly on the walkway paved with cobblestones, and Cole followed him, searching for the keys to the backdoor in his pocket. He halted on the steps, his fingers fumbling with the key chain, and looked up at his brother.

"Dima," he said so quietly that he wasn't sure Damian could actually hear him. But Damian cocked his brow, staring at him quizzically. "Please, just this once, let me take the lead and do what I say, and not the other way around."

Damian chuckled softly, giving him a light slap on his shoulder. "Well, now you know how I feel when I ask you that and you don't listen." He winked but stepped aside, gesturing for Cole to go first.

"Doofus," Cole muttered under his breath, turning the key in the lock.

"I heard that, Dracula Junior," Damian murmured, but then raised his hands peacefully. "Don't worry, little bro. I'll follow your lead."

Cole pushed the door open and slipped into a spacious kitchen. For apparent reasons, this area of the house had never been used when Luciano was alive, and now that Cole owned the estate, it wasn't any different. He motioned for Damian to follow him and unsheathed one of his swords.

"I don't think there is anyone here." Damian's voice touched his mind through their bond. *"I do detect some vampiric essence though. It has strange deviations, but it could be because we're far away from the source, or because the actual vamps are long gone."*

"Maybe..." Cole murmured, not quite sure Damian was entirely right. Just like his brother, he could sense the presence of the vampires in the area, but there was something off about it, and it wasn't the time or distance as Damian suspected. Also, he couldn't detect Ruslan anywhere, and that set his nerves on edge.

He crossed the kitchen and stepped onto the soft burgundy carpet covering the floor of the hallway. Keeping his sword at the ready and all his senses at the highest alert, he ran forward, once in a while throwing a glance over his shoulder to make sure Damian was following him. He didn't stop until he reached the wide hall in front of the room he used for his Council gatherings. Carefully probing the area, he couldn't get rid of the feeling he was being watched, the small hairs on the back of his neck rising. The presence of vampiric essence was a lot heavier here, and now he could easily detect the deviations from normal in its energy signature.

As if hearing his thoughts, Damian touched his shoulder. *"Cole, do you feel it?"* he asked, daggers materializing in his hands. *"I know what that is, and you're not gonna like it..."*

"What is it?"

"Wurdulaks," replied Damian. *"Now that we're closer, I can clearly discern their stinky essence."*

"Are you sure?"

"Since we're dealing with Koschei the Deathless, I'm positive. If he's powerful enough to conjure volkolaks in packs, I'm sure conjuring a wurdulak is a walk in the park for him."* He placed his hand on Cole's shoulder, giving him an encouraging nod. *"Let me go first, bro. Trust me, it's the right thing to do."*

Too impatient and impulsive, Cole had never considered himself a great chess player, and thinking a few steps ahead while staring at a checkered board had never been his favorite pastime either. Ruslan, however, had been adamant about him learning the game and playing it right. At this moment, looking at the closed door of his Council Hall, he was trying to calculate all possible moves and outcomes.

"You're right," he said at length. *"You should go first."*

Moving as quietly as they could, they approached the

entrance and stopped. Giving his brother a quick nod, Cole seized the handle and cracked the door open, allowing Damian to slip inside. Since Damian didn't stop him, he followed him into the hall.

As soon as he crossed the threshold, the floor disappeared from under his feet. The room spun around him, the rotation becoming faster and faster, and before long, he could no longer see anything, feeling as though he were falling into an endless void. He screamed, struggling to regain control, but all his attempts were to no avail. Darkness embraced him, suppressing all his senses, quelling his desire to fight. He shut his eyes and let go.

* * *

THE FRESHNESS of night air touched his skin, a soft breeze ruffling his long hair. The delicate fragrance of roses entwined with the smell of grass and dirt touched his nostrils, and Cole kept his eyes closed, enjoying the aroma. A touch to his cheek, gentle and fleeting, made him open his eyes and look around.

He was sitting on a bench, surrounded by a most exquisite garden, the stars and moon gazing down on him. A young woman wearing a French empire style dress with opulent embroidery, high waistline and low décolleté sat next to him, her head resting on his shoulder. A deep blue vein pulsed under the pale skin of her long, elegant neck, her heart thudding loudly in her chest.

Cole froze in place and bit his lip, struggling to control his rising thirst, realizing that it wasn't easy when she was so close to him. He took her arm off his shoulder and tried to put some distance between them, but she resisted, wrapping her arms tighter around him, pressing her willowy body to his.

"Nicolas," she whispered his name in French, "do not push

me away. We do not have much time left, and I want to spend it with you."

She lifted her head and changed her position to face him. Then she cupped his cheeks and kissed him, a tender touch of her soft lips to his. A gentle fragrance of lavender invaded his senses, her heartbeat becoming faster and louder.

"No…" He seized her wrists, pushing her arms down to hold her at a distance. He remembered this moment. He knew what was coming next.

It's an illusion… One of my old memories… I must fight it…

In his mind, he understood what was going on but was unable to resist, going with the flow of the memory.

"I am dying, Nicolas…"

Her voice infused with pain and fear rang in his ears, and he couldn't help but look at her. Her large blue eyes, framed by long black eyelashes, gazed at him pleadingly, the tender pink blush barely coloring her pale, nearly translucent skin, characteristic of people suffering from consumption.

"Eloise…" he whispered in French, recalling her name. "Please, I have a hard time controlling my—"

"Do not control anything," she replied in a sultry whisper, her lips touching his earlobe. "I want you to do it… You are the only one who can save my life now, Nicolas…" Her hand slipped down his chest and stomach, moving farther south.

A hot wave of desire powered by the relentless thirst enveloped him, and before he could control himself, his fangs extended. She didn't get scared, her blue eyes igniting with excitement instead. She tilted her head and ran her fingers over her neck, offering herself to him.

"Do it, *mon amour*," she whispered, pulling his face closer to her neck. "Turn me, and we'll be together… forever…"

His lips parted as he touched her cold skin. The fragrance of her perfume mixed in with the fresh scent of her body was overwhelming for his heightened senses, dizziness assailing him. He felt the beating of her pulse under his lips. He could hear the blood running through her veins, her heart thundering under his palm rested over her firm breast. He groaned as his long fangs grazed her skin, and she sucked in a sharp breath, holding him tighter.

"*S'il vous plaît*, Nicolas… Do it… I love you…" she exhaled.

A low growl rolled in his throat as he sank his fangs into her neck. Her hot blood spilled from the two deep puncture wounds, trickling down her chest—scarlet on white. Its odor invaded his nostrils while its heavenly taste filled his mouth. The blood ran down his dry throat, instantly pacifying his thirst. The pure energy of life surged through him, invigorating all his senses while fogging his mind, making him forget about everything except the need for more.

"No, you do not!" A strong hand seized him by the scruff of his neck, yanking him back roughly. "Did I teach you nothing, boy?"

Cole fell to the ground, hitting the back of his head hard, blood still dripping down his chin. Ruslan stood over him, his angled eyes blazing with fury.

"You do not go around turning ladies of Napoleon's court into vampires," he hissed, leaning over him, his knee pressing heavily on Cole's chest. "You do not expose the World of Magic to humans."

Ruslan got up and approached Eloise, who stared at him without blinking, undiluted terror shadowing her beautiful eyes. He seized her chin and lifted her face, forcing her to look at him. His vampiric essence spiked, setting his eyes ablaze with a scarlet light, wrapping around her in gentle waves.

"*Mademoiselle* Eloise," he whispered, his deep voice sounding like the purr of a giant feline. "You went for a walk in the park alone. You haven't seen or spoken with my dimwitted son for quite some time. You know nothing about vampires or magic…" His fangs extended, and he punctured the tip of his finger.

Gently, he smeared his blood over the wounds Cole's fangs had left on Eloise's neck, and they closed almost immediately, leaving no mark. Then he reached into his pocket and pulled out a white, lacy handkerchief. Carefully, he wiped the red stains off her skin. "Now, darling, return to your friends and forget you've ever met us here."

Moving like in a dream, she got up and turned around. Ruslan followed her with his eyes until she turned the corner, disappearing behind tall, decorative bushes. Then he turned to Cole, his face clouded by anger.

"Father," Cole whispered, raising his arm in a defensive gesture. "Ruslan, please—"

Ruslan... I'm here because... It's all not real... The disarray of wild thoughts rushed through Cole's mind fogged by a powerful illusion, only one of them clear—he was here because Ruslan needed his help.

"Cole, wake up!" A familiar voice sounded somewhere at the edge of his consciousness. *"Open your eyes, little bro! Cole!"*

Cole screamed and woke up.

* * *

As soon as Cole opened his eyes, he saw his brother's gaze, his drained face dark with worry. He was supporting Cole with his arms, his hands trembling slightly, his daggers gone.

"Dima," he whispered, pushing himself up into a sitting position. He grabbed his sword from the floor, his fingers squeezing the grip until his knuckles turned white. "It was just an illusion, one of my old memories, but I couldn't break free."

"I figured." A sad smile touched Damian's lips as he helped Cole to his feet. "They tried it with me, too, but I was trained to resist external intrusions." He glanced to his right, and his features hardened. "There is something we need to deal with, brother," he said quietly. "Keep your cool."

Terrified of what he would find, Cole turned in the direction his brother was looking at and froze in place, unable to move. Ten chairs were positioned around a large office-style desk taking most of the space. A small glass box filled with a gray substance that looked like ash sat in eight chairs out of ten. A tall man dressed in black stood behind the table, his dark attire fusing with the shadows at the back of the room, his eyes burning with a sinister red light, a lot brighter than that of a vampire.

As Cole took in the containers with ashes, understanding dawned on him, and his stomach twisted with sorrow. Thousands of thoughts about what this could mean to him as the King of the Arizona Vampire Court flashed through his mind, chilling his soul. If he wasn't mistaken, every single member of his Royal Council was dead, and it was their ashes stored in the glass boxes and placed on display for him to see.

While the realization was painful and terrifying enough, it wasn't what shocked him the most, turning him into a motionless statue. A large, rectangular glass box—its shape resembling a coffin—sat on top of the table. Ruslan lay inside, his arms crossed over his stomach. His eyes were closed, and his lips were slightly parted, giving him the relaxed look of a person in deep slumber. His shirt was ripped open on his chest, and a thin wooden stake was pushed through the small hole in the glass. Positioned perfectly over his heart, its tip penetrated his skin and drew a few drops of blood but didn't go deep enough to kill him.

Feeling a touch on his shoulder, Cole flinched and turned toward his brother.

"We have to try to talk to this monster," Damian projected.

"Talking to a wurdulak?" Cole shook his head, and his lips curled into a snarl of their own volition, his eyes igniting with a furious scarlet light. *"I need to kill him, not talk to him."*

"Give me a chance." Damian gave him a reproachful glance.

"Before we go, swords swinging, we need to understand what's going on."

"Koschei is after you, and he does everything he can to hurt you. What don't you understand?" Cole shouted as anger took the best of him, but then he bit his lip, dropping his head. *"I'm sorry, Dima. That was uncalled for."*

"You're right. Koschei is after me and that puts everyone I care about in danger. You think I don't know that?" Damian said quietly, but a pained expression changed his strong features. "But I have to at least attempt to understand what his goal is... He has already given me his message. Why did he try to lock both of us inside an illusion? Why all this?" He waved his hand around. "Besides, we may still have a chance to save Ruslan."

Numbness suffused Cole's chest, and his limbs filled with lead, but he gave a nod to his brother, gesturing for him to proceed. Damian stepped forward, one of his daggers manifesting in his hand. He halted next to an empty chair and cocked his head, staring at the wurdulak.

"I will give you two minutes' head start," he said icily. "If I see you anywhere around this estate in two minutes..." His voice trailed off, and a pair of glowing handcuffs materialized in the palm of his free hand.

The wurdulak didn't acknowledge that he'd heard him, staring at him without blinking. Then he moved closer to the coffin and placed his clawed hand over the stake. Cole growled, his fangs extending, and took a step forward, but Damian seized his arm, holding him in place.

"Don't move," he ordered, the hold of his fingers tightening.

The wurdulak tilted his head a little, and his lips stretched grotesquely wide, showing off a set of four ghastly fangs.

"We're not here to negotiate with you, Enforcer," he said. The sound of his voice was familiar, but it didn't look like it belonged to this brawny man. It was too screechy and dry, like desert sand.

"Then why are you here?" Damian asked, the Destiny cuffs vanishing from his hand.

"To give you and your undead brother a message," the wurdulak said, staring down at them with derision.

"I think I've had all the messages I can handle for one day." Damian folded his arms in front of his chest.

The wurdulak ignored his statement with admirable consistency. His glowing eyes settled on Cole, and Cole couldn't help but wince inwardly from undiluted malice in the monster's stare.

"King, your Royal Council is dead." The wurdulak moved his hand, pointing at the small boxes filled with ash. "The rest of your loyal followers are scattered all around the state in a futile attempt to avoid the wrath of my master. But soon, they will all meet their true death."

A deep shudder rushed through Cole, but he willed himself to remain silent. The wurdulak cocked his head, his sinister eyes never leaving Cole's.

"But you can still save your maker," the wurdulak continued since Cole didn't say anything.

"Oh, yeah?" Damian asked, a corner of his mouth lifting into a dangerous, uneven smile. "And what kind of hoops do you expect my brother to jump through for that?"

"First, no hoops," objected the monster. "Second, we're not talking only about your brother." He snickered, and the sound of laughter coming out of this terrifying monster's mouth was more unnatural and darker than everything else he had said to them so far. "You must both choose a side. Choose wisely, and you can save all the people who are dear to your hearts." He glanced at Cole, a blood-chilling smile distorting his lips. "Not only this ancient leech." He drummed his fingers against the glass coffin.

"I'm getting tired of this friggin' game," Damian muttered and waved his hand, whispering a revealment spell.

Cole stepped closer to his brother's side, and his eyes widened, his eyebrows rising. Through the thin layer of Damian's spell, he could see a semitransparent visage of another man hovering over the wurdulak. He was tall and skinny, and his face, with yellow skin and dark circles around his deep-set eyes, resembled a skull. A malignant purple light glowed in the eye sockets, and his thinning gray hair fell to his shoulder in greasy strands.

"Koschei," Damian exhaled, a muscle twitching in his jaw. "Who didn't know that? Why don't you show yourself, and we'll talk like normal people do."

"Normal people?" The visage shook in silent laughter, the words coming from the wurdulak's mouth. "I already delivered my message to you earlier today. Did you like that little touch with the fire? I thought you might enjoy something like that. And do tell what happened to your favorite Wardens, Commander Blake. Are they still breathing?"

Damian didn't reply, but the fury radiating from him doubled, becoming almost palpable.

"That was *my* message to you personally, Commander Blake," the wurdulak, or rather Koschei, continued. "This message is from my master to the two of you. Listen carefully, boys, because I'm not going to repeat it twice."

The wurdulak leaned over the coffin, his fingers wrapping tighter around the stake, and Koschei's visage moved with him.

"War is coming," he screeched, the sinister glimmer in his eyes igniting brighter. "The ancient sanguinary feud is moving toward its peak a lot faster than anyone expected, and it must be resolved once and for all."

"He's repeating the words of the prophecy," Cole projected, and Damian gave him a tiny nod.

"We chose our side centuries ago," Damian replied calmly. "We've always stood on the side of Light, and we always will."

"It's no longer a matter of Light versus Darkness. At least not entirely." Koschei cackled, carnivorous gluttony reflected on his ominous face. "My master has high hopes for you two. For some unexplainable reason, he took a liking to you. Trust me"—Koschei's visage shifted closer, now hovering directly over the wurdulak he controlled—"if it wasn't for him, I would have killed you both a long time ago. Out of sight, out of mind, so to speak."

"I'm sure you'd have tried," replied Damian, the dagger in his hand igniting with the purifying light of Creation. "I'm done talking to you, asshole. Now, be a good doggy and run back to your master. Give him a message from us—we'll never change our side. Period!"

"Fine!" Koschei shouted, fury distorting his ugly features. "You're already three fighters down, Commander Blake, and this is just the beginning."

"So I've heard," Damian muttered with an indifferent shrug.

The wurdulak raised his arm over the stake, ready to hammer it deeper into Ruslan's chest. Damian responded to his move with lightning speed. His dagger hissed through the air and bit into the wurdulak's chest. The monster howled, and his elongated fingers squeezed the blade as he tried to pull it out.

It's not enough to kill this monster... Cole didn't wait to see what would happen next. Picking up his full vampiric speed in a time shorter than he had ever done it before, he zoomed toward the wurdulak. He wrapped his arms around his head, and with a strenuous groan, ripped it off his shoulders. Then he dropped the head, and it fell to the floor with a dull thud.

Damian pointed at his dagger protruding from the headless body's chest and whispered, *"Illucious..."*

As the light of Creation burned through the monster, he dissolved into a pile of dirty gray ash, and the dagger fell to the floor with a loud clatter. The image of Koschei shimmered with a purple mist and vanished.

Cole seized the stake and yanked it out of Ruslan's chest, but the ancient vampire didn't move, his face still relaxed. He found the edge of the lid and tried to pull it up, but even after he applied all his strength, it didn't budge.

"Let me try." Damian's voice sounded next to him, making him look up.

His brother placed his hand over the lid, and the soft glow of his magic spread through the glass.

"Recludius," Damian whispered. An invisible lock clicked, and the coffin opened silently, the lid rising on its own.

"Father…" Cole shook Ruslan, but the vampire didn't respond.

"Cole, stop." Damian placed his hand over his, squeezing it gently. "It's some kind of spell. I can see its energy with my other sight. You won't be able to wake him up." He lifted Cole's hand off Ruslan, forcing him to turn around. "The good news is that your father is alive. We both know if he were dead, he would have been a pile of ash." Cole nodded, feeling numb on the inside. "Spells are cast to be broken, little bro, and I promise you, I'll find a way to break this one."

Cole lifted Ruslan, holding him in his arms. His muscles responded with the ache of exhaustion, and he clenched his jaw, pressing his father's body tighter to his chest. Before he started to use magic, he didn't know what being tired felt like. Now, he felt like a human—sore and aching—and it just added to his overall level of aggravation.

"Promise me one thing, brother," he muttered through gritted teeth. "When you go after Koschei and his—" He cut himself off and looked away, nibbling on his lip. Then he turned back to Damian, meeting his steady gaze. "I'm going with you, no matter where this quest takes you."

"I swear," replied Damian. "In the fight against Koschei, you're the only person I trust fully. We're doing it together."

He placed his hand on Cole's shoulder, ready to snap his

fingers and teleport, when the loud shrill of a cellphone stopped him in his tracks.

"Dammit... It's mine." Cole let his brother take over Ruslan and reached into his pocket, pulling his phone out. "It's Dallas."

Cole answered the call and fell silent, listening intently. He hung up a few seconds later and dropped his head, pinching the bridge of his nose.

"I can't fucking believe it," he whispered, staring down at the marble tiles. "Dima, someone attacked Hawk's ranch, but the wards held. They're all fine." He raised his eyes, reading the reflection of his own fears on Damian's face.

"Go there. Make sure everyone is okay and update Hawk on everything that's going on," Damian said quietly, placing Ruslan's body over his shoulder. "I have to go back to Paradise Manor and make sure River is safe. I'll send Cossack to help you. If the attackers are still there, don't do anything until he arrives." Cole nodded, but Damian frowned, deep worry darkening his blazing eyes. "Swear to me you will wait for Cossack."

"I'm not an idiot, of course—"

"When it comes to a good fight, you are," Damian interrupted him in a no-nonsense tone, giving him a pointed stare. "Swear to me, you'll do as I say."

"I swear..." Cole threw his hands up, pursing his lips reproachfully.

"The portal will open in the desert, a few hundred yards away from the gates into Hawk's property," said Damian. "That should give you a chance to assess the situation from a distance, unnoticed."

He waved his hand, and a portal opened next to Cole. Giving his brother a reassuring nod, Cole stepped through the swirling mist, leaving Luciano's estate behind.

CHAPTER 4

~ DAMIAN BLAKE ~

As soon as Cole was gone, Damian punched the glass coffin, sending it flying off the table. It hit the marble tiles with a loud crash, shattering into hundreds of shards and slivers of glass. He placed Ruslan's body on top of the table and bit his lip, clenching his jaw so tight his teeth squeaked. Fighting to suppress the overwhelming anger fueled by pain and fear, he squeezed his head, his fingers digging into his scalp.

A short while later, he took a deep breath and lowered his arms, focusing on channeling his magic. It didn't come right away, his exhausted body refusing to obey the commands of his mind. Once he had collected enough magical energy in his hands, he drew a rune in midair and pressed his palm over it, connecting it with his Shadow Enforcer rune.

For a few endless seconds, nothing happened, but then a portal rotating with blue sparkles opened next to him, and his friend Cossack stepped out. He was dressed in the standard Enforcer's tactical uniform, and his face and hands were covered in splatters of demonic goo. He glanced around, taking in his surroundings, but once his gaze halted on Damian, his tense shoulders dropped, and he visibly relaxed.

"Dima, I'm glad to see you in one piece," he said, extending his dirty hand to him. "Your summoning call was a bit much. Intense, you know?" He chuckled, squeezing Damian's hand in a handshake. "You pulled me out in the middle of a serious fight. Some demonic gang in London…" He didn't finish and sighed. "Magnus was clear, though. If I receive your summons, no matter what I'm doing at the moment, I am to drop everything and answer your call." A wide grin split his face. "Music to my ears… But I'm sure Moore will have something to say after I return."

"Moore is still there?" Damian muttered, unable to conceal his aversion toward the other Commander of Destiny Enforcers.

Cossack smiled, gazing heavenward. "Yeah, you two hate each other, and everyone knows this," he said. "After the High Council restored me, I went through the entire Destiny Council realm, collecting the bodies of fallen Enforcers…" His voice trailed off, his gaze growing distant. "I found Moore and Ivor together, both dead. They fought to protect Ivor's lab. You know how many secrets are hidden there."

Damian nodded, his thoughts returning to the current events. As briefly as possible, he explained to his friend what needed to be done. Then he waved his hand, opening a portal to the gates of Hawk's property.

"I don't know if the pack is still under attack, but I trust you with my brother's life, Cossack," he said quietly. "Help him, and once you are done, I want you both in Paradise Manor."

Cossack pressed his fist to his chest, inclining his head. "Yes, my lord. I'm yours to command."

"I'm not your Commander, Cossack," he said with a sigh, throwing a reproachful glance at him. "I'm asking for your help as a friend."

"According to Magnus, you are." Cossack inclined his head with a sly grin on his face and walked into the portal.

Once the portal closed behind Cossack, Damian lifted Ruslan, placing him over his shoulder, and snapped his fingers, teleporting out of Luciano's mansion.

* * *

A THICK SCREEN of dust hung in the air, causing Damian to cough and spin around. Pieces of concrete and debris cracked loudly under his feet as he staggered away from the house. Under the cover of night, concealed by a layer of dust, the dark silhouette of Paradise Manor towered over him, but its outline was not the same as he remembered.

"*Ventius,*" he whispered, making a circular motion with his hand. A blast of wind spread around him, traveling in all directions, and a heartbeat later, the dust was gone, revealing a blood-chilling view.

The front yard looked as though a tornado had ripped through it. The driveway was destroyed, and the single saguaro cactus, River's pride and joy, lay on the ground, broken. The steps were gone, and part of the roof over the entrance was torn off. The door and the wall around it were demolished, and darkness stared at him through glassless windows.

"River!" A strangled scream broke from Damian's lips, and he took a step forward but then froze in place, holding his breath.

He lowered Ruslan to the ground next to the broken cactus and took one knee by his side, probing the building and the surrounding property with his senses, magical and mundane. His wards were gone, but that wasn't the worst. The wards that the Guardians had placed over the left wing of the house were down as well. An almost imperceptible layer of dark magical energy lingered over Paradise Manor, but as faint as it was, Damian recognized it right away, and fury roared through him.

"Koschei," he hissed, his hands clenching into fists of their own accord. *Dammit! I need to calm down. I can't allow anger to cloud my mind and impair my judgement...*

He closed his eyes and took a few deep breaths, slowly gaining control of his raging emotions. Then he moved his hand over Ruslan, casting a cloaking spell, and rose to his feet.

Taking into account all previous events, he was positive Koschei was gone by now. What he had left in his wake was a different story.

Keeping all his senses at the highest alert, Damian walked toward the house. Afraid to think about what he would find there, he crossed the threshold and stepped into the foyer, or rather what was left of it. The roof was gone, a patch of dark sky staring down at him through the enormous hole. The antique mirror lay on the floor, partially buried under the debris. The fallen support beams, pieces of concrete and other rubble completely blocked the entrance into the left wing.

It's good... The thought sprung in Damian's mind as he approached the barrier. *If River went to the farthest room of the left wing, as I told her to do, she should be safe. Doesn't look like anyone tried to take this blockage apart.*

He opened his other sight, probing the left wing as far as he could see, but didn't detect the glow of River's soul anywhere. Forcing himself not to draw any conclusions, he turned around and crossed the foyer. The entrance into the right wing stood wide open. Quickly surveying the right side of the house with his second sight, he didn't find any presence—human or supernatural. It appeared the building was empty.

Damian stepped over a pile of rubble and walked toward the kitchen, noticing that this part of the house hadn't sustained any damage. He reached the kitchen and peeked inside to find it cold and vacant.

"River," he called, his voice echoing through the strange acoustics of Paradise Manor. The sound of echo dwindled, leaving him alone in a silent mansion. He slammed his fist against the doorframe, the pit of his stomach twisting with dread, and called her again. "River! Gypsy!"

Except for the relentless echo, no one answered his call.

Damian turned around and marched along the shadowy hallway toward the living area, willing himself to stay calm and keep his mind clear. He stepped into the dark room and froze, his heart beating desperately in his throat, suffocating him.

"River… No…" he exhaled, his eyes burning, pain tearing at his chest.

I should have been here for you...
As soon as I received the message from the Warden, I should have...
It's my fault...

Illuminated by the silvery light of the moon, the space looked like a battlefield. The furniture was broken, and what was left of it was scattered all over the floor. The TV was ripped off the wall and lay on the carpet. Three bullet holes gaped in the middle of the screen, a web of fractures spread around them, and River's gun lay next to the couch. Someone had cleared the large area in the center, and a glass coffin sat on the floor, moonlight reflecting dimly on its surface. It was the same kind of glass box as the one Damian had seen back in Luciano's house.

Moving slowly, like in some terrifying nightmare, Damian crossed the room and peered inside the coffin. His heart gave a weak jolt and halted, bleeding with pain, guilt and despair. He couldn't breathe, his lungs burning. Bracing his arms against the lid, he dropped his head low.

River lay inside the glass box, her arms wrapped around Gypsy. They weren't dead, their chests moving with slow, shallow breaths, but they weren't asleep, either. Their condition was neither a natural slumber nor an enchanted sleep. Damian scanned both of them with his magical sight, and a howl of dismay and anguish broke off his lips. He staggered back, pressing his hand over his mouth, his chest shuddering uncontrollably as he struggled to fill his lungs with oxygen. He tripped over the pieces of the broken coffee table and fell, hitting his head against the wall. Scrambling into a sitting position, he stared at the glass coffin but could see nothing, his mind blank, his vision blurred.

Both River and Gypsy were alive.

Their bodies were intact.

Their souls were gone.

* * *

DAMIAN WASN'T sure how long he sat with his back pressed against the wall, motionless and dead on the inside. It could have been a few minutes or a few hours. Nevertheless, his mind cleared gradually, and his training took over, overpowering his crippling grief. He had to keep going no matter what, even if the members of his team were killed. He had been trained to do so for years, but now everything felt different. This wasn't a battlefield, and the person lying in the coffin wasn't a Destiny Enforcer, a trained warrior who wasn't afraid to die.

He scrambled to his feet and walked out of the room, heading toward the exit. Once he reached the broken cactus, he removed his cloaking spell and lifted Ruslan. Moving slowly and heavily, he returned to the house and placed Ruslan on the floor next to the glass coffin. With his mind still foggy, he started to clean the living room. He needed to think about his next step, and physical work always helped him focus.

He managed to take most of the broken furniture out of the house and placed it all in a neat pile next to the destroyed driveway. Grabbing a broom from the kitchen, he headed back to the living room when a slight fluctuation in the magical energy field touched his senses, and he halted, turning in the direction of the disturbance.

"Dima!" His brother's voice, filled with fear, rang through the house, and Damian relaxed.

"Living room," he replied and proceeded cleaning the floor, cringing inwardly at how empty and emotionless his voice sounded.

In his peripheral vision, he saw Cole and Cossack walk into the room. Cole gasped and froze with his hand clasped over his mouth. Damian turned his back toward his brother, unwilling to watch him crumble in grief. He just couldn't do it. Not now. He needed to stay calm, or he would fall and never get up again, turning himself into a literal no one for another five hundred years. Unlike Vita, River was alive, and he would do anything to see her back with her soul intact.

"Cole," he said without turning to his brother. "Luc and Jamie are in a hospital, in some type of a magical coma, so I can't count on their help. I need access to the Wardens Library. I'm going to summon the Master Warden of Florida, Raoul de Beaumont. I know him personally, and I hope he'll be able to assess Luc's, Jamie's and River's condition and tell me what I need to do to bring them back."

"Dima, are you sure—," Cole started, his voice hoarse with sorrow, but Damian snapped around, interrupting him.

"I know what I am doing, brother," he said flatly and returned to cleaning, his hands running the broom over the floor in long, even strokes.

"Cole, hold on, give him a moment." Cossack's voice, soft and a little apologetic, sounded behind him as his friend of many years spoke to Cole. "I know Dmitri is your brother, but I shared a small room with him for a few hundred years. I can recognize when he is… Trust me, the more he's trying to push us away, the more he needs us."

Damian ignored him, a chaos of thoughts storming through his mind. Two strong hands seized his shoulders, forcing him to stop and turn around. Cossack grabbed his wrist and pulled him closer.

"Dima, stop," he said firmly. "You need to slow down and give yourself a moment to process everything." He let go of his wrist and took the broom from his hand, throwing it to the floor. It fell with a dull thud, causing Damian to flinch.

"Cossack, you don't understand, I…" His voice trailed away, and he rubbed his eyes like a person who had just woken up after a long sleep.

Cossack sighed and took his arm above the elbow, ushering him out of the room. He walked him through the hallway into the kitchen and pulled a chair out, gesturing for him to sit down. When Cole joined them, he jerked his chin at the coffeemaker. Without saying a word, Cole grabbed two cups from the cabinet and placed them on the counter, getting everything ready to make coffee.

The bitter scent wafted through the room, and Damian sucked in a deep breath, hiding his face in his hands. Neither Cole nor Cossack said anything, and he was grateful for that. He focused on his breathing, willing himself to calm down, dispelling the sticky grip of rising panic. Little by little, his thoughts, driven by anger and sorrow, stopped hopping from one point to the next, the desperate chaos subsided, and calmness finally took over his mind. Once Cole placed the cup with the hot beverage in front of him, he lifted his face, his gaze darting from Cossack to his brother and back. He moved the cup closer and wrapped his fingers around it, ignoring the burning heat.

"You were right, Adrian," he said, barely meeting Cossack's eyes. "I didn't think clearly before." He took a careful sip of coffee and closed his eyes, savoring the bitter-sweet taste. He glanced at his brother, and his throat tightened, but he swallowed the lump and continued, "But I'm back now, and trust me when I tell you I am thinking clearer than I've ever done before."

Cossack and Cole exchanged a look, and while a cloud of concern shadowed both of their faces, they said nothing. Damian took another sip of his drink and got up, moving the chair back. Channeling his magic, he swayed a little and groaned, locking and unlocking his hands at his sides. Then he drew a complicated rune in the air and placed his hand over his Shadow Enforcer rune, connecting them. Cossack got up slowly, his lips parting, and he raised his hand in a warning gesture, shaking his head, but Damian didn't stop. Placing his palm over the rune, he infused it with his magical energy and whispered the summoning call.

"Magnus, I summon thee…"

CHAPTER 5

~ DAMIAN BLAKE ~

The oval communication window manifested in place of the rune almost immediately, and Magnus stepped into view, his white robes bright against the dark background. He met Damian's eyes, and his eyebrows rose.

"Commander Blake?" Surprise sounded in his voice. "You summoned?"

"Not like this." Damian shook his head slowly, folding his arms. "I need you here, Magnus. In Paradise Manor."

"Dmitri, you know I can't—" His gaze halted on something behind Damian, and he fell silent, his hand clutching at his chest.

Damian glanced back, but except for Cole and Cossack, there was no one there.

"Magnus, is everything okay?" he asked, observing the Head of the Destiny Council with concern.

Magnus didn't reply. Instead, he touched the communication window with two fingers and closed it. Damian threw his arms up, but before he could say anything else, Magnus manifested next to him with a light popping sound, causing Damian to flinch and jump aside, cursing.

Cole and Cossack kneeled before the Head of the Destiny Council, lowering their heads in a bow. Magnus smiled and gestured for them to rise. Giving Damian and Cossack a short nod, he circled the table, halting in front of Cole. His eyes moved up and down his body, as if sizing him up, but his lips parted, and his gaze fogged a little, a chain of emotions flashing across his face so fast, Damian wasn't sure of what he had seen.

"Nikolai," Magnus whispered. He lifted his arm, as if he wanted to touch Cole's cheek, but then dropped it and stepped back, a smile filled with both happiness and sadness playing on his lips. "We meet at last." He turned toward Damian, his smile growing wider. "Your brother is just as magnificent as you are, my boy." He glanced at Cole again and stifled a sigh, quickly assuming the look and posture appropriate for a member of the High Council. "What can I do for you, Commander Blake?"

Damian gestured at the exit, slightly inclining his head. "Please, follow me, my lord."

They made their way into the living room in silence. As soon as Magnus crossed the threshold, he froze in place, and his eyes lit up with the brilliant white light of his powerful magic. He didn't ask anything but lowered to his knees next to Ruslan and held his hand palm down over Ruslan's chest for a few seconds, moving it from left to right. Without saying a word, he got up and walked around the glass coffin, halting on the other side. He leaned down slightly, his unnerving silvery eyes quickly exploring River's face and body. Then he pressed his fist to his lips, and the troubled look that shadowed his features promised nothing good.

"Dmitri," he said, his eyes boring into him, "I need your full report. Don't skip any details. I want to know how it happened and what preceded it."

Magnus waved his hand, and four kitchen chairs appeared in the empty room. Gesturing for them to take a seat, he took one of the chairs and lowered himself onto it, his moves heavy, as if he were exhausted by hard, physical work. Damian pulled a chair closer but didn't sit down, leaning heavily on the backrest instead, worry and dread coiling in the pit of his stomach. Trying not to miss any details, he told everything that had happened in the last few hours. After he finished, Cole and Cossack added whatever they had learned from Hawk's pack to complete the report.

A heavy pause hung in the room after they were done. Magnus' glowing eyes darted from Ruslan to River, and his brows drew together, a deep line etched between them.

"You believe it's Koschei's handiwork?" he asked at length, turning to Damian.

"Yes," Damian replied, "but he's not working alone. He delivered a message from his master, and the more I think about it, the more I believe his master and Donna Luna's master are the same person."

Magnus nodded slowly. "I happen to agree with you, my child," he whispered, his eyes growing hollow. "Penny for your thoughts, Commander."

Damian lifted his shoulders in a half-shrug. "I'm not sure what to think anymore, Magnus," he said, averting his gaze. "Koschei hates me with a passion, and I believe this elusive 'master' is the only thing that keeps Koschei from killing Cole and me. If that's the truth, then things are even more complicated than I originally thought. The master has some kind of plan that involves both of us, but we have no idea what it is."

Magnus blanched, his eyes widening, but then he nodded again and got up with a strenuous groan, his expression becoming unreadable. He approached Ruslan, taking his hand in his.

"We need to find out who and what this *master* is... And we need to do it fast," he muttered, lowering Ruslan's hand onto his chest. "These spells are extremely complicated, and as powerful as Koschei is, I don't believe he could pull it off alone." He straightened and approached the coffin, throwing a veiled glance at Damian. "Koschei is known for abducting women and keeping them imprisoned in his old castle." He touched the lid of the coffin, sending a smidge of his magic through it, and it opened, moving slowly and soundlessly. A sad smile appeared on his lips as he brushed his fingertips over River's pale cheek. "He didn't take her. Instead, he took her soul." He closed the lid with a heavy sigh. "I wonder if he did the same to Luc and Jamie."

"Unfortunately, it didn't even cross my mind to check them for the presence of their souls. I was too busy making sure the injuries they sustained weren't fatal. I will confirm that as soon as I visit them in the hospital," replied Damian, fighting to keep the rising wave of sorrow under control. "My lord, the reason I summoned you is because I have no idea how to break the curse and restore them all."

Magnus chuckled, but there was no mirth in his laughter. "River's condition is not the same as Ruslan's," he replied, separating the long folds of his robe to shove his hand into the pocket of his pants. "Ruslan has been cursed, and curses can be broken. I will consult our healers. They know everything there is to know about these kinds of curses and how to break them."

"Thank you, my lord." Damian pressed his fist to his chest, glancing sideways at his brother. While Cole's face was shadowed by exhaustion and sorrow, a spark of hope ignited in his blue eyes.

"As far as River is concerned..." Magnus pursed his lips, his fingers stroking his beard absentmindedly. "Her soul is missing," he said after a short pause. "It's not a curse that can be broken. I'm sorry, Commander, but I don't know any way to find and restore a human soul. At least not off the top of my head..."

At his words, Damian felt as if the floor had vanished from beneath his feet. He stared at the Head of the Destiny Council without blinking, unable to say a word, a chaotic twister of thoughts and fears swirling in his mind again. He took a shuddering breath and exhaled slowly, silencing the disarray of thoughts in his head.

"How about the Wardens Library or the famous Destiny Council Archives? Is there anything there that can help us?" Cole asked, putting his hand on Damian's arm.

Magnus glanced at Cole, and a ghost of a warm smile flitted across his features. The blazing light in his eyes dwindled, making him appear worn out and pale.

"You're right. There has to be something," he replied at length and looked away, his eyes turning milky white. He stood absolutely motionless, and with each next second of his trance, hope was slowly abandoning Damian's heart, leaving him cold and empty.

Suddenly, Magnus swayed, and if Damian hadn't caught him, he would probably have collapsed. Carefully, Damian lowered him to the floor, placing his head on his lap. Little by little, Magnus' eyes returned to normal, and his mouth twitched just a little.

"My boy," he whispered, looking up at Damian, his voice frail like that of an old man. "There is a way, but you're not going to like what I'm about to say."

Damian laughed softly, shaking his head. "When did I ever like anything you said? You may as well proceed."

"Help me up." Magnus pushed himself off the floor and straightened, leaning heavily on Damian's shoulder. "Accessing the Destiny Council Archives from the realm of humans is quite taxing."

Cole moved one of the chairs closer, helping him to sit down. Magnus leaned forward, resting his arms against his knees, his hands dangling powerlessly. Then he looked up at Damian from under the strands of his gray hair and exhaled with a shake of his head.

"Koschei couldn't perform that kind of spell," he said, a

shadow of anger clouding his features. "It takes the power of a god to extract the soul from a living human being without killing them in the process. But it's not only the power…" He pinched the bridge of his nose, and a deep crease materialized on his forehead. "It's the goddamn know-how that is important. This spell is thousands of years old. It's older than some ancient gods that are still roaming this world. It's as old as Creation itself…" He slammed his fist against his knee and turned away.

"Where do I need to go? Who do I need to speak with?" asked Damian. "Rod? Svarog? Maybe Odin or Zeus? Celtic Annan? Who would know how to break this spell?" He stared at Magnus, but since he remained silent, he threw his hands up. "Come on, Magnus!"

"I don't know. I can't answer your questions," Magnus replied, staring down at his white shoes.

"Can't or won't?" Damian folded his arms. "Why do I have a feeling you're not telling me everything I need to know?"

"Both." Magnus got up sharply but swayed, grabbing the back of his chair. "By now, Commander Blake, you should be used to the fact that not all the knowledge I have can be shared with a Destiny Enforcer."

He turned away from him and walked to the glassless window. He halted there with his hands crossed behind his back and gazed at the mountains prominent against the ultramarine colors of the early dawn. Damian exchanged a look with Cole and Cossack but remained silent, hoping Magnus would add something to what he had already said.

"Here is what we're going to do," Magnus continued after a short pause, switching to a commanding mode. "I'm going to return to the Destiny Council realm and consult with the Board of Destiny. Once I know anything that can help, I'll summon you, Commander Blake. Don't do anything until I contact you. It's an order."

"Yes, sir," Damian replied, knowing full well that at this point, Magnus wouldn't say anything else on the subject.

"Adrian." Magnus turned toward Cossack. "You will return to the Destiny Council realm. I need you to gather a team of six Destiny Enforcers, including yourself, and position them in the hospital to protect Master Warden Luc de la Crosse and Jamie Coldwell." He gave a curt nod to Cossack and flicked his wrist. "You may go and start assembling your team immediately. Do not disclose anything of what you have seen here. I'll inform Commander Moore about your new assignment myself."

"I'm yours to command, my lord." Cossack pressed his fist to his chest, inclining his head in a bow, and waved his hand, opening a portal.

Once the portal closed behind Cossack, Magnus turned to Damian and Cole, his eyes darting between them.

"I have to go," he said, his hands clenched tightly in front of him. He looked out the window, furrowing his brow, and Damian couldn't help but notice how unusually nervous Magnus was.

"Is there anything else I need to know, my lord?" he asked.

"No. You know everything you need to know for now," Magnus snapped but then shoved his hair away from his face nervously and continued in a flat tone of voice, "I'm going to send Ivor here. Work with him to clean this mess and make sure the World of Magic hasn't been exposed by all the previous events. After that, restore the wards over Paradise Manor and sit tight, Commander. I mean it!"

"Yes, sir," Damian replied, pressing his fist over his heart. "I'm yours to command."

"Yeah, right." Magnus waved his hand dismissively and approached Cole, searching his face with his eyes. "You take care of your stubborn brother, Nikolai, and make sure he doesn't do anything stupid. I hope to see you again under better circumstances."

Without waiting for Cole's reply, the Head of the Destiny Council snapped his fingers and vanished.

* * *

AS SOON AS Magnus was gone, Cole kneeled next to his maker, casting Damian a pleading glance. He didn't say anything, but Damian knew his brother was begging for his father's life, and everything inside him twisted with pain. As a wild thought manifested in his head, he pressed his lips into a stubborn, straight line.

"Screw it. I'm not gonna sit and wait, twiddling my thumbs," Damian muttered through clenched teeth, answering Cole's silent plea. "Ivor is going to be here in a minute. I must take care of the exposure first, but as soon as Ivor is done, we're bringing Ruslan back. Trust me, a few hours are not going to make a difference in Ruslan's case, whereas possible exposure of the World of Magic can create quite a problem for all of us." He smiled faintly at his brother and offered him a hand, pulling him up once he grabbed it.

"But how?" Cole whispered, his face lighting up with hope. "I thought Magnus said he needed to consult with his healers to find out how to bring him back. Besides, he ordered you—"

A corner of Damian's mouth lifted, and he shrugged, interrupting his brother. "I know my orders, and I don't give a damn. We're bringing Ruslan back today. Period."

A soft knock on the doorframe interrupted their conversation, and Damian turned around, his eyebrows rising. An older man dressed in a long, navy-blue robe stood in the doorway, his slightly narrowed gray eyes twinkling with curiosity and warm humor.

"Ivor," said Damian, gesturing for him to come in. "It's nice to see you, old friend. I didn't notice your portal, though. How did you get here?"

"I opened a portal outside the house, and I've been here for the last few minutes, assessing the damage." He shook his head, pursing his lips. His gaze fell on Ruslan and River, and his weather-beaten face hardened, deep creases materializing around his tightly set mouth. "Magnus briefed me in…" He shoved his hands into the pockets of his robe. "You know he'll find a way to restore her soul. The Head of the Destiny Council would do anything for his Shadow Enforcer."

"I know he will," replied Damian. "I have to believe it or…" He didn't finish the statement and looked away.

Ivor approached the coffin and opened the lid. Then he took Gypsy out of River's hands and threaded his fingers through her long fur, watching the cat's chest moving up and down with quick breaths.

"Sweet kitty," he mumbled, passing her limp body to Cole.

"Yeah, very sweet kitty." Cole took Gypsy, cradling her in his arms, gently scratching her between her ears. "Especially when she's sleeping."

"Nice to finally meet you in person, Mr. Adams," Ivor said, giving Cole a quick once-over. "Over the centuries, I've heard so much about you from Commander Blake that I feel as if I've known you all my life." He winked at Cole, but before he could reply, Ivor switched his attention back to Damian. "Okay, Commander, first thing, we need to make sure River Evans is safe, and everything looks legit in the eyes of human authorities. She needs an explanation as to what happened to her and why she's not at work."

His gaze settled on River, and he scratched his chin, a thoughtful expression crossing his features.

"I need her in the same hospital where Master Warden de la Crosse and Warden Coldwell are being treated, so Adrian's team can keep an eye on all of them. I hope you agree with my plan?" Ivor raised his eyebrows, but then a corner of his mouth turned up, and he added, "In case you don't agree, I want to remind you how it works. I don't care what you think. We do as I say. When it comes to cleaning, it's my way or the highway."

"Oh, Perun almighty," Damian grumbled, rolling his eyes. "You don't change, do you?" He threw his arms up. "Of course, I agree. Do I have a choice? Besides, I need to know she's safe and protected before I start searching for—"

"You meant to say, you need to know she's safe and protected before you sit your ass firmly down in Paradise Manor and wait for Magnus' command? Isn't that what you meant to say, Commander?" Ivor raised his eyebrows, a layer of sarcasm in his words. "Magnus said hello, by the way. He asked me to kindly remind you not to go off half-cocked here."

"Yes, that was exactly what I was going to say," Damian replied through gritted teeth.

"Wonderful. We're on the same page after all." Ivor leaned over River, and his eyes lit up with the brilliant light of his magic. "While you're taking her to the hospital, your brother and I will take care of the little exposure associated with a tornado touching down in Blue Creek and the fire in the Scottsdale bookshop."

"Fine." Damian approached the coffin and lifted River, readjusting her position to make sure her head rested comfortably against his shoulder. "Ivor, just to be on the safe side, let me remind you that my brother is a vampire. You can't use your purifying magic around him."

Ivor sent him a glance filled with reproach. "Just go already. I promise, your brother will survive..." Before Damian could say anything, Ivor snapped his fingers, and the room spun around Damian, vanishing in swirls of white and blue sparkles.

* * *

As much as Damian liked Ivor as a person, he had to admit that as a professional cleaner, he had a bad habit. Ivor didn't think he needed to communicate all the details of his plans clearly, and Damian couldn't recall a single time when he hadn't ended up in the thick of things, figuring out Ivor's plan as he went.

"Holy shit," Damian mumbled, taking in his surroundings, and cursed under his breath.

He stood on the side of a road next to River's Charger. Her car looked as though it had survived a T-Bone crash with a rhino. The entire driver's side of the vehicle had been smashed, and the front wheel was positioned at an awkward angle. River sat in the driver's seat, her body leaning to the side, supported by the seatbelt, and blood was trickling down her face from a thin laceration on her forehead. The reek of burned rubber mixed in with pungent odors of gasoline and oil lingered in the air, and the dark tire tracks were visible on the asphalt road.

Damian ripped the door open, unlocked the seatbelt and pulled River out of the vehicle. He straightened, holding her against his chest, and looked around. The beige building of Scottsdale HonorHealth hospital towered across the road, the sign directing toward the ER visible on the opposite side of the intersection.

Praying to all the gods he knew, he snapped his fingers and teleported into the alley behind the hospital. The area was dark and empty, and Damian thanked Ivor, realizing that the Destiny Council's most famous cleaner had taken all the details into account and prepared everything for him perfectly. With River in his arms, he circled the building and burst through the doors of the Emergency Room.

"Help, please!" he shouted, running toward the woman at the front desk.

A few people in medical scrubs rushed to meet him. A man took River and placed her on a gurney, quickly checking her vitals as the others rolled it away. Damian moved to follow them, but a nurse with a digital tablet in her hand stopped him.

"Are you her husband?" she asked, craning her neck to look up at him.

He glanced at her, having a hard time focusing on anything. "No," he replied after a brief pause. "I am..." He swallowed and rubbed his forehead. "I'm her boyfriend. We live together."

"I need to ask you a few questions then," she continued, ushering him toward the front desk.

Damian barely paid any attention to the questions she was asking, cutting his answers short and dry. He knew nothing about River's medical history or her insurance, and all these questions were driving him crazy, setting his already stretched nerves on edge. When the nurse asked about what happened, he came up with a story about a hit-and-run accident, positive that Ivor would take care of it. Once the torture of the twenty-questions game hospital edition was finally over, he sighed with relief and sat down in the waiting room, hoping to hear from the doctors soon.

He wasn't sure how long he waited, time moving torturously slow. The Emergency Room was empty—probably cleared by Ivor—but he couldn't relax, bouncing a knee nervously. The cold smell of cleaning agents and disinfectants surrounded him, and he cringed, thinking how much he hated mundane medical facilities. He had never had to use them himself, taking care of all his wounds with his healing magic. The only time he had to visit a hospital was when someone he cared about needed medical attention.

The nurse visited him a couple of times to ask him a few more questions, promising to update him as soon as she heard anything from a doctor. Once she noticed the cuts and bruises covering his body, she suggested for him to get checked out, but all he wanted to do was find out in which room River was admitted and be on his way home, hoping to either hear from Magnus soon or start doing some investigating on his own.

"Mr. Blake?" Damian raised his eyes to find a man in a

medical uniform standing before him. "I'm Dr. Henley." The man proceeded with the update, but Damian already knew everything he was going to say. All River's vitals were normal, and they didn't find any injuries that could have caused her condition, yet they couldn't wake her up. A coma—that's what the good doctor called it.

I wish it was a regular coma... Damian nodded at the doctor, not meeting his eyes.

Once the doctor left, Damian asked for directions and walked briskly along well-lit hospital hallways, following the arrows on the floor and the signs on the walls. As soon as he stepped on the third floor, heading toward River's room, Cossack intercepted him. Dressed in medical scrubs and with a layer of illusion surrounding him, he was barely recognizable.

"Dima, we're in position," he whispered, falling in step with him. "I have two people watching River, and three people stationed by the Wardens' room. Don't worry, I'm not going to let anything happen to them."

"Thank you, my friend." Damian gave him a nod. "Give me a few minutes alone..."

Cossack opened the door into River's room for him, and Damian slipped inside. He halted by the entrance, his eyes glued to the single hospital bed taking most of the free space. River lay on the bed, her copper hair framing her pale face in gentle waves, her arms stretched out along her sides. Covered by a hospital blanket, she looked like she was asleep, and only the consistent beeping of monitors reminded him that she wasn't.

He halted by the side of the bed and took her hand into his, caressing her cool skin with his thumb. She didn't move and didn't acknowledge his presence in any way. He wasn't sure why, but the words she had said to him about a month ago surfaced in his mind.

"Every time you walk out this door, I can't breathe..."

Now he fully understood the meaning of her words.

Standing over her bed, watching her lying there, silent and motionless, he couldn't breathe, his chest constricted with torment beyond anything a normal human being could handle. He wanted to promise her that he would do whatever it took to restore her and make sure something like this would never happen to her again, but he couldn't say anything. Instead, he leaned down and pressed his lips against her cold knuckles. He stood like this for a short while. Then he lowered her hand by her side and kissed her forehead gently.

Turning on his heels, he headed out of the room without looking back. Cossack stood by the entrance, waiting for him.

"Show me to the Wardens' room," he said, barely moving his lips.

"This way. It's just down the hallway," replied Cossack, gesturing for him to follow.

Three more Destiny Enforcers clad in blue medical scrubs stood by the door, chatting with a smiling young nurse. They followed Damian and Cossack with their eyes but didn't say anything to them.

Damian walked inside the room and stopped by the bed, trying to ignore the monotonous beeping of the monitors. Cossack closed the door and moved his hand in a wide arch, whispering a cloaking spell. Giving him a quick nod, Damian opened his second sight and scanned Luc and then Jamie. As he expected, their condition was identical to River's. Even though both had a few scrapes and bruises, they hadn't sustained any visible injuries that could have resulted in a coma. However, just like in River's case, their souls were missing.

"Dammit..." he whispered, praying silently. *Perun almighty, give me the strength to save their souls... Please, keep them safe from all evil, magical and mundane...*

Turning around, he made his way out of the room, pulling Cossack with him.

"What did you see?" Cossack asked, escorting him toward the elevators.

"Their souls are missing just like in River's case," Damian replied, shocked by how lifeless and empty his voice sounded. "Most likely, the same type of magic was used on all of them. If I find a way to help her, I'll be able to save them, too."

Cossack pushed the button, and once the elevator arrived with a soft ding, he shook Damian's hand, a shadow of deep concern crossing his face.

"Be careful, Dima," he said quietly, watching Damian walk inside and press the button with the number one on it. "Godspeed."

The door closed with a soft hiss, and the elevator jerked, starting on the way down.

* * *

Forcing himself not to run, Damian walked out of the hospital building and marched around it in search of a quiet place where no one would see him vanishing into thin air. The sky was bluish gray, painted by the rays of the early sunrise, but the alley behind the building was still dark enough and blissfully empty.

Hiding behind a dumpster, he quickly surveyed the area and snapped his fingers, leaving the hospital behind.

He appeared on the broken steps of Paradise Manor and looked up at the demolished roof. A thought about how much work it would be to fix all that flashed through his mind, but he pushed it away and ran up the steps into the foyer. Without slowing down, he rushed through the dark hallway and into the living room.

His brother sat on the floor next to Ruslan. His arms were wrapped around his bent legs, his head resting atop his knees. In this position, he looked small and miserable, and his looks brought forth an old memory of a cold and hungry six-year-old boy sitting on the frozen ground, the first flakes of snow falling on his blond curls.

"Nikolai," he called, squatting in front of his brother. Slowly, Cole lifted his face, his lips twitching in a weak smile. "Are we alone?"

"Yes. Ivor left a while ago. Everything is taken care of." Cole unlocked his arms and got up, readjusting the straps of his scabbard. "What now?"

"Now?" Damian chuckled darkly. "We're going to bring Ruslan back."

CHAPTER 6

~ DAMIAN BLAKE ~

"Dima, are you sure?" Cole asked, a vibe of doubt surrounding him. "I love my father, but I don't want you to be punished for disobeying direct orders of the High Council."

Damian bent down and lifted Ruslan with a groan. Placing his limp body over his shoulder, he turned to face his brother. "I'm sure, little bro," he said calmly. "If I had a dime for every time I disobeyed direct orders from the Destiny Council, I would have been a millionaire by now, and as you can see, I'm still alive and kicking." He stifled a sigh, thinking about Magnus' displeasure, and headed toward the exit, nonetheless.

"Barely," murmured Cole, following him out of the room.

Damian walked briskly through the dark hallway, but as soon as he reached the foyer, he came to a sharp halt and glanced up at the rays of the morning sun shining through the hole in the ceiling. A bright flair attracted his attention, and his eyes darted in the direction of the light. The old mirror lay under a pile of debris, the sunlight bouncing off the silver embellishments on the frame. He lowered Ruslan to the floor and made his way to the mirror, carefully stepping over the piles of concrete and rubble.

"*Ventius*," Damian whispered, directing a light wind at the mirror to clear its surface of dirt and debris.

To his surprise, the actual mirror wasn't broken. He picked it up and placed it against the wall, wiping the dust off its surface with his hand. At first, he saw nothing except his and his brother's reflection, but then the silvery surface lit up with a soft light, and the image changed. Two feathers—one was snow-white and the other ultramarine, almost black—levitated in the air, lowering slowly, as if supported by a gentle breeze. Damian glanced over his shoulder at his brother, but Cole spread his arms, looking just as lost as Damian felt.

When Damian turned back to the mirror, the feathers were gone, and he could see nothing but his own reflection.

"Dammit, girl," he whispered, running his fingers over the slick surface of the mirror. "If you really want to help us, just speak plainly and stop with your goddamn riddles."

With a shake of his head, he lifted Ruslan, draping him over his shoulder, and headed toward the left wing of the house, barricaded by a pile of debris. Conjuring a protective shield over himself and his brother, he pointed at the blockage and whispered, "*Exitius.*"

A loud boom of an explosion rolled through the hallways of Paradise Manor, the sound reverberating for a few long seconds until it finally died down. The house shook, and pieces of wood and chunks of concrete bombarded Damian's shield, falling to the floor all around it. When the curtain of dust settled down, the entrance into the left wing stood wide open.

"I'm so glad Sam is not in Arizona right now," Damian mumbled, observing the foyer, a deep shudder running through him.

Cole chuckled humorlessly. "Sometimes, I have a feeling you're more afraid of River's father than of the High Council."

"You bet your ass I am." Damian's lips quirked up at the corners at the thought of the old hunter, but he sobered up quickly and bit his lip. "Sam would've killed me if he were here, and he would have been right." He choked on the last words and squeezed the bridge of his nose, his eyes tightly shut. "It's my fault, Cole... What happened to River... I knew my presence would put her in danger, but I was too selfish..." He cut himself off, swallowing with effort, and readjusted Ruslan's body on his shoulder. "Let's go. I don't know how to save River, but I sure know how to bring your father back, and I'm not going to sit and watch you bleed on the inside just because Magnus told me to do nothing."

Following the empty hallway, he marched all the way to the end and halted there, staring at the wide double door. When the wards still functioned, this door hadn't been visible, concealed by a powerful spell. Now anyone could see it, and this thought made his blood run cold, sending a chain of shivers down his spine.

As soon as I am done with Ruslan, I'm summoning Allerton.

He put his hand on the handle and pushed it open, unsure of what he was going to find behind it. The door opened easily, and he stepped inside, gesturing for Cole to keep back. He remembered the first time he had walked into this room and the mind-boggling space-like environment he had been thrown into, struggling against the hold of magic and unable to break it. Now, there was nothing here, just an empty room with white marble tiles and a tall white ceiling.

"Cole, you can come in but be careful," Damian whispered. As soon as Cole stepped inside, Damian lowered Ruslan from his shoulder and passed him to his brother. Cole took him over, carefully draping him over his shoulder. "I need you to hold Ruslan. If the shit hits the fan, I must have both hands free."

Damian crossed the room and halted in front of a small wooden door. He searched for a doorknob or a handle but couldn't find anything that could help him open it. As he reached for the door, however, he detected a sharp spike in the magical energy field around it and pulled his hand away, taking a step back. Channeling a little bit of his magic, he directed it toward his eyes and opened his other sight.

Despite the fact that all the Guardians' wards were down, a chain of tiny runes and sigils glowed around the perimeter of the door, shining with a dim white light. He squinted his eyes, sending more of his magical energy to enhance his vision. The runes and sigils surrounding the door didn't look familiar. Even though he wasn't a specialist in runic magic, he could recognize basic symbols used for different spells and incantations by any Order or Guild associated with the Destiny Council. These, however, were nothing like anything he had ever seen before, therefore they couldn't have been placed by Guardians. At least, he didn't think it was Guardians magic.

Making a mental note to ask Allerton about it, he moved his palm over them, feeling the soft touch of their magical energy on his skin. While he could detect the dangerous power in them, it didn't feel threatening for some reason. On the contrary, it felt familiar and welcoming, as if this magic was a part of him.

"Dima, what is it?" Cole pointed at the glowing symbols.

"You can see them?" Damian stared at his brother, not even trying to conceal his shock.

"Not only can I see them but I can also feel their presence with my very skin," Cole whispered, his eyes transfixed on the glowing runes. "They're calling to me..." Before Damian could stop him, he reached forward and touched the rune closest to him.

"Cole, no," he gasped, seizing Cole's arm and yanking him back.

Something clicked, and with a loud squeak, the door cracked open. A puff of cold air drifted from behind it, carrying a strange, slightly sweet odor.

"Damn..." Damian glanced back at his brother and found a familiar warm smile on his face. "Alrighty then. Ready?"

"Always ready." Cole winked and pulled the door open, allowing Damian to go through first.

As soon as they both crossed the threshold, the door behind them closed on its own, leaving them in complete darkness. Damian whispered a spell, conjuring light orbs, and once their shimmering blue light illuminated the space, he observed the area. They stood on a small wooden platform, its railings rising high enough to prevent them from accidentally falling. He turned to his right and peeked down but couldn't see anything except for endless darkness. A wide ladder was attached to the other end of the platform, and as far as he could see, this was the only way down.

"Watch your step," he whispered to his brother before he could stop himself, and then chuckled, responding to Cole's wide grin. Cole, with his vampiric vision, could see a lot better than he, and his reaction was a lot faster than his, too.

Damian stepped on the stairs first, carefully placing his feet on the narrow steps. Cole gave him a few seconds head start and followed him down. While the stairs looked quite old, they ended up being sturdy enough, squeaking softly under their feet. He wasn't sure how long they had been climbing down, but when he finally made it to the firm ground, he exhaled with relief and glanced around while waiting for his brother to join him.

He stood in what appeared to be an underground corridor, the red brickwork of the walls and arched ceiling looking quite old. The presence of the magical energy field here was elevated, which didn't surprise him in the slightest. After all, the lake hidden somewhere here was the essence of magic in its purest form.

Exchanging a look with his brother, Damian motioned for him to follow and headed along the corridor, running his fingers over the rough surface of the brickwork. As they kept walking, the passage became wider and taller. The same runes and sigils as he had seen on the door were drawn on the walls every few yards. They shimmered with a soft white light, flickering on and off from time to time.

The corridor moved down and curved to the left, going deeper and deeper underground, and soon it ended in a sold brick wall. Damian halted and narrowed his eyes, probing the barrier with his other sight.

"It's not solid," he exhaled, throwing a glance at his brother.

"I see it..." Cole nodded, his eyes glowing with a bright, scarlet light, but there was something different in their shine. It wasn't the color of his vampiric essence. His brother was encompassed by the glimmer of his magic, the stones embedded in the pommels of his sword shining as brightly as his eyes.

Damian reached forward and touched the wall. His finger didn't go through it, but circles of white light spread away from the place of connection like ripples in the water. The ripples started to move faster and faster, and soon the entire wall emitted a brilliant glow, too bright for his eyesight which was adjusted to the dark of the corridor. He blinked a few times, rubbing his eyes. When his vision cleared, the wall was gone, the last remnants of the light slowly dwindling out of existence.

Holding his brother back, Damian stepped across the threshold and froze in place, observing the view in awe. A cave, so large he couldn't see the other end of it, spread before him. Crystals of different shapes, sizes and colors covered every square inch of the walls, their smooth, polished facets reflecting the dim, bluish light. Damian looked up, but no matter how hard he searched, he couldn't find the source of it.

A small, round lake spread in the middle of the open space, its dark, motionless waters producing a soft, bluish glow just like everything else in the cave. Several stalactites grew from the ceiling above it, resembling crystal pendants of some intricate chandelier created by nature.

Feeling a touch to his arm, Damian flinched as if he had been awakened from a deep slumber. He snapped his head to the side to find Cole standing next to him.

"Is that...?" Cole asked, his eyes fixed on the lake.

Damian nodded. "The enchanted lake hidden under Paradise Manor and protected by the Guardians Order," Damian whispered breathlessly. "All I need to do is submerge Ruslan under its dark waters to break the curse placed on him." He gestured with his thumb at the lake. "Let's go."

He moved slowly down the narrow path surrounded by shimmering crystals on both sides. All of them reflected him in their wide facets as he passed them, creating a mind-blowing kaleidoscope of colors, movements, flairs of light and shadows. But one of them held his attention, causing him to halt and squat down, frowning.

Larger than the others, it shimmered with blue sparkles, producing a rainbow-like halo around itself. It didn't reflect him like the rest of the crystals here. Instead, a shadow moved beneath its surface, and a chain of images flashed, exchanging one view for the next so quickly he couldn't register any of them. He stared at the crystal, unable to take his eyes off, transfixed.

Suddenly, the flashing stopped, and the view of a dark street manifested inside it. Even though he didn't recognize the location, he was positive it was somewhere in the human realm. A deep crack ran across the road, spreading wider and wider. Shimmering crimson light erupted from the fracture, and the black silhouette of a tower ascended from beneath, illuminated by the blood-red flames rising from the crack in the ground.

The entire street—or at least the part of it he could see—quaked, and the buildings began to collapse, clouds of dust spreading around. Like in a silent movie, people struggled to get away, their mouths opened in voiceless screams, their faces contorted by fear and pain. The angry flames rose higher, and soon, he could see nothing but the scorching fire, swallowing everything in its way. Damian gasped, his arm rising of its own accord, as if trying to shield his eyes from the horrors of the vision.

"Dima, is everything okay?" Cole asked, concern shadowing his features.

"I think I've seen something like this before..." Damian exhaled a ragged breath and got up, turning to his brother.

"You've seen what?"

Damian frowned, closing his eyes, the terrifying images permanently imprinted in his mind. "Nothing," he whispered, ushering Cole toward the lake. "This place is infused with so much magic, I can't help it if my mind and body are responding to it."

The rest of the way, he walked in silence, staring straight forward to avoid looking into the crystals. The path ended in a narrow strip of sand surrounding the lake, a thin glowing line tracing its shape in the place where the motionless water touched the black shore. Damian turned to take Ruslan from Cole when the air behind his brother shimmered with bright white sparkles, and a new blast of magical energy rushed through the cave, throwing his hair off his face. Cole spun around and stepped back, halting next to Damian.

The light illuminating the space ignited brighter, and a giant beast materialized in front of them. It had the body of a bull and the head of a horse with a thick horn on its muzzle like that of a rhino, and its entire frame was surrounded by a pulsating glimmer of its magic.

Cole hissed, and his fangs extended as he took another step back, half turning his torso to shield Ruslan. Damian glanced at the monster, recognizing the Indrik-Beast, the protector of the enchanted lake, and lowered to one knee, pressing his fist to his chest in the habitual gesture of a Destiny Enforcer.

"Father of all Beasts," he said, inclining his head. "Mighty Indrik-Beast. I mean no harm to you or to the sacred lake you're guarding. I am here to—"

"Dmitri and Nikolai Chernov," the beast said, his voice sounding in Damian's head. *"I know why you're here, brothers..."*

"Does it mean you will allow us to use the healing power of the lake to revive my father?" asked Cole, making it obvious to Damian that he could hear the Indrik-Beast, too.

"Yes, Nikolai Chernov. Surprisingly, you do have the right to be here, even though you're nothing more than an unclean, unholy predator of the night..." Cole paled, his face turning blue in the unsteady light of the cave, but he didn't say anything, averting his pained gaze. The giant beast inclined its head, touching Damian's shoulder with its long horn. *"The last time I saw you, neither of you were ready, but now..."* The beast paused, fire igniting in the depth of its eyes. *"Now you both belong..."* It didn't finish the statement, its voice morphing into a low growl.

"We do?" Damian whispered, rising. "What do you mean? We belong where?"

The low rumble of icy laughter sounded in Damian's mind, and the Indrik-Beast's body shook, its eyes, which resembled the eyes of a human, glowing with mockery.

"It's for me to know and for you to find out, slave of the Destiny Council." The beast stopped laughing and tilted its head, drilling Damian with a heavy gaze. *"Do what you came here to do and leave this sacred place in peace."*

The air around Indrik-Beast shimmered, and it vanished.

"Don't ask because I have no idea," Damian muttered, taking Ruslan from Cole.

He approached the lake and kneeled by the edge, cautiously submerging Ruslan's body under the water. Unsure what to expect, he leaned forward a little, carefully watching his face, but the vampire remained motionless and silent. A few minutes passed, but nothing changed. Cole lowered to the ground next to him, dropping his hands in his lap, the spark of hope slowly dying in his eyes.

"I guess it didn't work," Cole whispered, making a move to bring Ruslan out of the water when the entire surface of the lake lit up with a shimmering white glimmer.

The light grew brighter and brighter, and soon it became impossible to look at it. When it finally dwindled, Damian still couldn't see anything, red and black spots dancing in his vision.

"My boy..." A deep male voice sounded on his left. Damian blinked a few times in the direction of the sound and pressed his fingers to the corners of his tightly shut eyes. When he lowered his hands, he saw Ruslan kneeling in front of Cole, his wide shoulders hunched. "I thought I would never see you again."

Ruslan pulled Cole into his chest, his hand finding its way into his unruly curls. Despite him being soaked with cold water, Cole wrapped his arms around his father and rested his forehead against his shoulder, an expression of relief softening his tense features.

Damian scrambled to his feet, brushing the sand off his knees. Ruslan let go of Cole and also got up, swaying slightly. Cole was on his feet at once, supporting him with his arm.

"We should go." Damian threw a wary glance around, the exhaustion of this endless night spreading through his muscles.

"Dmitri, thank you." Ruslan turned to face Damian, but his angled eyes focused on the crystals shining on the walls of the cave. "Why do I have the unpleasant feeling that you have broken a shitload of rules to save my life, Commander?"

"Because I have," Damian replied airily, starting on his way out of the cave.

* * *

No one spoke the rest of the way back. Climbing the wooden stairs all the way up presented to be a harder task than Damian thought, every step coming to him with a serious effort. The extreme use of his magic finally took its toll, but it was also his mental state that added to his exhaustion. He had never had a hard time suppressing his emotions before, trained to keep his mind clear no matter the circumstances.

Maybe it was because everything was extremely fresh in his memory, or because he had already lost the woman he loved to unspeakable evil once, but this time it was different.

It felt like some crippling, debilitating déjà vu, and he couldn't help but blame himself for everything that had happened to River, Luc and Jamie. He broke the oath he'd made to himself after Vita's death, and now people around him were paying the price. No matter how hard he tried to focus on the task at hand, this thought sat in the back of his mind, eating him from the inside. The pain was slowly morphing into blinding fury, which was even harder to control.

The door blocking his way back into Paradise Manor was locked and sealed, and just like on the outside, it had no handle or anything that could help him open it. Since Cole's touch activated the locking mechanism before, Damian placed his hand against the cold wooden surface, and the chain of runes and sigils lit up at his touch. Something clicked, and the door cracked open.

He let Ruslan and Cole out first and then followed them, closing the door behind himself. As soon as he crossed the threshold, he came to a sharp halt, staring at an older man standing in front of him with his arms folded over his chest. The man's eyes darted toward Ruslan, whose clothes and hair were still dripping with water, and he pursed his lips, gazing at Damian with silent reproach.

"Archmage Allerton," Damian greeted him, wondering how

the Archmage of the Guardians Order had ended up here before he summoned him. "I was about to call you."

"Was that before or after you broke direct orders and entered the sacred grounds?" the Archmage asked, his eyebrows rising. Despite his words, he didn't sound like a person of authority who wanted to intimidate him. If anything, he sounded a bit tired, tones of sadness breaking to the surface.

"I did what I had to do, sir," Damian replied quietly, meeting the Archmage's calm gaze.

"I know." Quinn Allerton nodded slowly, his shoulders lifting with a heavy sigh, and his eyes darted to Cole and Ruslan. "That's what makes you who you are, Commander Blake. The Destiny Enforcer unlike any other…"

His voice trailed away, and he rubbed his chin, a thoughtful expression settling on his features. Circling Damian, he approached the door into the underground corridor and touched it. Nothing happened. It remained sealed, and the runic magic didn't get activated.

"Works as expected," he murmured under his breath and turned toward Ruslan, inclining his head in a respectful bow. "Ruslan, I believe?"

"Yes, my lord." Ruslan returned the bow, his eyes never leaving Allerton's face.

"Could you please do me a favor and touch this door?" Allerton pointed at the entrance.

Ruslan threw a veiled glance at Damian and approached the Archmage. Lifting his hand, he brushed his fingers over the surface of the door, but nothing happened.

"Thank you, my lord." A faint smile played on Allerton's lips as he turned toward Damian. "So, Commander Blake, would you like to tell me who has the power to unlock this door? You or your brother?" Damian and Cole exchanged a look, and both stepped closer to the Archmage. Following their reaction with his eyes, Allerton chuckled. "Don't try to protect each other. I'm not a threat to either of you, Commander Blake. I'm just trying to understand what's going on."

Damian nodded, the tightness in his chest spreading into his arms. "Both," he said quietly.

"Curious, very curious," Allerton mumbled, cocking his head as he stared up at Damian. "Lord Magnus contacted me a short while ago. He wanted me to assist you with restoring the wards over Paradise Manor. He gave me some details of what transpired here…" His voice faded, and he shoved his hands into the pockets of his pants, sadness shadowing his gaze. "Knowing you, Commander, I expected that you'd try to restore Ruslan using the sacred lake. What I didn't expect was that you'd be able to open this door."

He glanced at the entrance into the underground corridor, rubbing the back of his neck. Since Damian, Cole and Ruslan remained silent, he sighed and continued.

"I'll be honest with you. I wasn't going to tell the Head of the Destiny Council of your little indiscretion. I'd do the same thing if I were in your place," he said. "But I can't keep from him the fact that you two can do more than you're supposed to. The High Council must know."

"I'm sorry, Archmage, but I'm extremely tired. Today, I'm probably not as fast on the uptake as you wish me to be," Damian muttered, crossing his hands behind his back. "I don't understand what's so special about this door. Isn't that the way all the wards and protection spells of Paradise Manor work? Anyone who lives in the house can open any door and access any area of the estate? Both Cole and I have lived here for a while. Why wouldn't we be able to open this door?"

"Paradise Manor's wards have nothing to do with this entrance," the Archmage objected. "Even though it looks like an ordinary door, it's anything but ordinary, and the runic magic protecting the entrance into the sacred grounds had been cast thousands of years ago by someone a lot more powerful than I am. Let me repeat it. It's the entrance that is protected by runic magic, not a door that closes it. You can replace the door, move the entrance into a different place, but the locking enchantment will follow it. I have no idea why you two can activate the runes, because you are not supposed to. As far as I know, you don't have what it takes to do it, and this is the reason the High Council must know about it."

"Goddammit," Damian whispered, but then met Archmage's gaze calmly. "You do what you must, sir. I'll deal with the repercussions."

Allerton inclined his head. "This is why I'm not going to report it to the High Council." He gestured toward the exit and started on his way there, pulling Damian with him. "I'll speak with Lord Magnus in private, and hopefully, that will minimize the consequences of your actions."

"My gratitude, sir." Damian inclined his head, realizing with shock how little he cared about the High Council finding out about him breaking Magnus' orders.

The Archmage stopped next to the exit and opened the door. He ushered Cole and Ruslan out of the room but held Damian back.

"Commander Blake, I need all of you to leave Paradise Manor for at least four hours," he said, leaning his shoulder against the doorframe. "Once you're gone, I'm going to summon a few of my high-level mages, and we'll place the wards over the entire building this time."

"Thank you, sir..."

Allerton shook his head, pursing his lips. "Damian, if I may..." His voice faded as he searched Damian's face with concern. "This is a suggestion of a friend, not a command. Take a step back and allow your body to rest and your mind to process everything. You need it."

Damian nodded. "I know."

"You're not going to do it, are you?"

Damian shook his head slowly, staring down at Allerton without blinking.

"I didn't think so…"

"I can't," Damian replied quietly. "The longer the souls of my friends are missing, the lesser my chances of ever finding and restoring them are. I have to do something."

Allerton stroked his gray stubble, but then nodded. "I understand." He looked up at Damian. "For what it's worth, you have my support if you need it."

"Thank you, my lord." Damian inclined his head in a bow and walked away, trying not to think of what he had to do next.

CHAPTER 7

~ DAMIAN BLAKE ~

Ruslan desperately needed blood, and despite his display of bravado, it was obvious. Severely affected by the curse and by the healing magic of the enchanted lake, he was becoming weaker and weaker with every step he took. Leaning heavily on Cole's shoulder, he barely moved his feet as they exited the gates of Paradise Manor, heading toward the Brown's Estate. Luckily, it was still early enough, and people hadn't started going about their business yet, so no one paid any attention to their small group walking at a snail's pace along the empty road.

"Are you sure you don't want me to teleport you home?" asked Damian, giving Ruslan a concerned once-over, but the ancient vampire shook his head.

"You're barely moving yourself, Dmitri. You'll teleport us into a wall," he muttered, stubbornly staring ahead. "I can walk on my own, thank you very much."

Once they reached the gates into Cole's property, however, Ruslan halted and dropped his head, closing his eyes. His knees shook, and he groaned, holding on to Cole for dear life, his fingers digging into his shoulder.

"Father, let me carry you," Cole offered, throwing a cautious glance at his maker. "God knows you carried me more than once."

Ruslan raised his face, and a strained smile stretched his lips. "Sure, go for it," he murmured. "If you're tired of living, that is."

Damian snorted, trying not to laugh out loud, and glanced around. Since the street remained blissfully empty, he placed his hand on Ruslan's shoulder and snapped his fingers, teleporting all three of them onto the steps of the Brown's Estate. Affected by the dizziness associated with the teleportation process, Ruslan groaned and slipped to the ground, falling heavily on his side.

Cole threw a desperate glance at Damian but didn't dare touch his maker. Damian gazed heavenward and lifted Ruslan, holding him against his chest. Ruslan's head tilted back, and his arms dangled powerlessly, but a dangerous growl rumbled in his throat. Damian snickered, ignoring his display of displeasure.

"You carried me into Paradise Manor against my will just a short while ago," he said, crossing into the house as Cole opened the door for him. "Consider it a payback."

Walking the familiar hallways, he made his way into a large room Cole used as his library and lowered Ruslan onto his favorite recliner. Ruslan relaxed and closed his eyes, the corners of his lips lifting just a touch.

"Give me a good glass of O Negative and a few minutes to rest, and I'll kick your behind, boy," he murmured, his smile becoming more defined.

"Dream on." Damian stretched out on a sofa, crossing his hands over his stomach, and shut his eyes. The sound of soft steps announced his brother's arrival, and then Ruslan's low, blissful moan told him that Cole had delivered some blood.

Damian didn't move, his eyelids so heavy, he wasn't sure he could open them even if his life depended on it. The fog of exhaustion obscured his mind, and little by little, he drifted off to sleep.

* * *

THE LIBRARY WAS Damian's favorite room in his brother's house. Everything here promoted tranquility and relaxation, starting with soft illumination and ending with the most comfortable furniture. The walls were lined with beautiful wooden bookshelves that stretched all the way from the floor to the tall ceiling, and every single shelf was filled with books. A few leather recliners and sofas occupied the middle of the space, each of them accompanied by a small table with a decorative lamp on it. The light scent of books and dust mixed in with the fragrance of an air freshener lingered in the air, adding to the general atmosphere of serenity.

When Damian stayed with his brother, whenever he'd wanted to take it easy or needed a few minutes of peace, he found himself here. Besides, Cole had the most amazing collection of books where anyone could find something for their taste and preferences in literature. Between his work and training, Damian hardly ever had time to relax and read, but when he had a moment to himself, he preferred reading to watching TV, just like his brother.

Damian wasn't sure what had awakened him. He pushed himself up, lowering his feet to the floor and looking around. Except for Cole, there was no one in the room, so he relaxed and leaned back, his eyes halting on his brother. Engrossed in reading, he sat sideways in a leather armchair with a book in his hand, his long legs thrown leisurely over the armrest. He didn't turn toward him, but the corners of his lips quirked up, and Damian knew Cole saw him rising.

"Good evening, sunshine." Cole put a bookmark into his book and closed it, placing it on the table. Then he turned around to face Damian and rested his arms against his lap. "So, did you come up with a plan while you were sleeping? What's our next step?"

"The plan is simple." Damian rubbed his chin, feeling the roughness of stubble under his fingers. "I locate Koschei's death. Then I'll find the evil bastard and save our friends."

"Simplicity is the ultimate sophistication." An uneven smile curved Cole's mouth. "But there is a chasm the size of the Mariana Trench in it."

"No shit, Sherlock," Damian murmured, leaning back with his arms folded behind his head. "But that's the best I've got for now."

"You've been searching for Koschei's death since the fight under Old Ladoga," Cole continued, speaking softly, as if he was voicing his thoughts out loud. "So did Master Alliandr, and Magnus, and Luc de la Crosse. None of you could find anything about Koschei or his death. What makes you think you can find it now? What's changed?"

Damian got up, stretching his shoulders. "I've changed," he replied quietly. "I'm done playing by the rules."

"Whoa, Commander, hold your horses..."

Ruslan's voice sounded behind Damian, and he turned around. The vampire stood in the doorway with his arms crossed, leaning his shoulder against the doorframe. He pushed away from the frame and strolled into the library, halting in front of Damian. A deep crease crossed his forehead as he stared at him without blinking.

"The Destiny Council doesn't take disobedience well, Dmitri," he said, tones of concern underlying his voice. "You've already broken the rules to save me. I'm sure you'll be paying dearly for that. How far do you think you can push your master's patience before you end up in one of the Destiny Council's infamous holding cells with no possibility for parole?"

"I have no idea," Damian exhaled. "The only thing I know is

that I can't sit and wait for Magnus to find something. I need to start searching myself, and if he finds a solution, he can reach me no matter where I am. As long as I carry his brand"—he brushed his fingers over his shoulder, setting the Shadow Enforcer's rune ablaze—"there is no place where I can hide from him or from the High Council."

Ruslan nodded, dropping his head to conceal the look of guilt on his face. "At least tell me what you're planning to do," he said, his voice unusually raspy. "Maybe I can help you."

"Shower and change first," Damian replied calmly, "and then I'm going to visit the local bar."

"A bar?" Ruslan repeated, his eyebrows rising. "I'm sure after everything, you need a stiff drink, but I'm afraid that's not going to help you find Koschei's death."

"No, of course not." Damian chuckled. "But divination may. All this time, I was searching for the information in books and archives. I've never even considered asking a seer. Kaleb, the bartender from the *Midnight Shift*, knows the supernatural community of the greater Phoenix area better than anybody. I hope he can point me in the right direction."

"I'll go with you." Cole got up, smoothing down his pants.

"You don't have to," Damian said. "I'm just going to the *Midnight Shift* and back. You and Ruslan should find out what's going on with the vampires of your court. Do you know if anyone survived Koschei's attack? They may need your help."

Cole nodded, his fingers fidgeting with the Royal ring on the index finger of his right hand. "I received a few calls. Except for the members of my council, most of them are alive but in hiding. I do need to deal with the situation in my Court, but I also stand by my word. We're doing it together, Dima."

"And we will," Damian promised, heading toward the exit out of the library. "I'm not doing anything special today. Just a peaceful chat with Kaleb and a quick drink… maybe." Damian winked at his brother and walked out of the room.

* * *

A SHORT WHILE LATER, he halted in front of the door of the *Midnight Shift* and quickly observed his surroundings—a habit he had gained over the centuries of dealing with assorted supernatural creeps. The evening was as hot as ever, but quite a few people promenaded down the main street under the yellow light of streetlights. The soft presence of the sanctuary spell touched his senses, but other than that, he didn't detect any unusual magical energy.

Damian pushed the door open and walked inside, stepping into the semi-dark atmosphere of the bar. The *Midnight Shift* was unusually busy, and the buzz of people's voices flowed through the wide space, filling every corner. An odor of beer blended with the smell of different spirits drifted through the air, overpowering the scents of air fresheners and cigarette smoke.

Noticing an empty stool by the bar, Damian made his way there and sat down, resting his arms on the counter. As soon as Kaleb noticed him, a corner of his mouth lifted, and he gave him a short nod. He finished serving his other customer and wiped his hands on a black towel, throwing it on the shelf behind the bar. Grabbing a few bills off the counter, he put them away and then halted in front of Damian, tilting his head.

"Damian, long time no see," he said, placing a shot glass before him. "The usual?"

Damian glanced at the glass, considering his options, but then nodded, lifting one finger. "Just one. I need to have a clear mind," he muttered and looked around, leaning forward a little. "I wondered if we could have a quick talk in private, when you get a moment, Kaleb."

The werewolf frowned, and his features hardened. Without saying a word, he grabbed a bottle of vodka and filled the shot glass, moving it closer to Damian. "On the house," he said quietly, his gaze swiping across the busy floor of his bar. "Give me a minute."

Once he disappeared behind the door leading into the kitchen, Damian took the shot glass and downed its contents in one large gulp. Placing the empty glass back on the bar, he exhaled, feeling the burning liquid rushing down his throat. Then he propped his elbows against the countertop, hiding his face in his hands, and closed his eyes, trying not to think about anything and just relax.

"Damian..." Kaleb's raspy voice made him lift his head.

The werewolf reached under the counter and pulled a box with cigarettes, shoving it in the back pocket of his pants. Then he lifted the flip-up countertop and gestured for Damian to come in.

"Let's go have that talk," he said, heading toward the back-door. As they passed through the kitchen, he tapped a young man's shoulder—also a werewolf, judging by his energy signature—and pointed at the front. "Leo, can you take care of the floor? I need a cigarette break."

He patted the back pocket of his pants where he had placed the case. Leo nodded, and Kaleb proceeded toward the exit, motioning for Damian to follow him.

As soon as Damian stepped outside, the usual Arizona hot air enveloped him. Kaleb jumped down from the low platform and headed in the direction of a dark corner behind the loading area. He circled a van parked in front of it and sat down on an empty plastic box, patting the unoccupied box next to him. Damian lowered himself onto it and rested his back against the warm wall, stretching his legs.

Kaleb lit up a cigarette, took a drag off of it, and exhaled a cloud of white smoke, blowing it away from Damian. "So, what's going on, Commander?" he asked, staring across the alley at the low fence.

"I'm looking for a fortuneteller," Damian replied. "But I need a real seer, not one of those human charlatans who are trying to make a few bucks, playing cheap parlor tricks on unsuspecting humans." Catching Kaleb's bewildered gaze, he shrugged. "You get all sorts of supernatural clientele here. Have you ever heard of anyone who has the real gift of sight?"

"A seer," Kaleb repeated in disbelief, taking another drag off of his cigarette. "Coming from a player of the Destiny Council team, it's a little strange. Can't you read the Board of Destiny or something like that?"

"No," Damian objected, staring down at the cracks in the asphalt. "As a Commander, I do have a connection with the Board of Destiny, but I don't know how to read it properly, and I don't want to ask Magnus to do it for me. This mission..." His voice trailed into silence, and he took a ragged breath. Meeting the werewolf's eyes, glowing with dim phosphoric light, he added, "It's personal to me, Kaleb. I need your help, my friend."

"Oh... wait..." Kaleb turned toward Damian, a tiny red spark igniting on the tip of his cigarette. "I've heard on the news something about a tornado touching in Blue Creek. Is Detective Evans all right?"

At Kaleb's words, pain took hold of him again, but he suppressed it, shoving it as far back in the darkest recesses of his mind as he could, and shook his head. "She's in the hospital, and so are Luc and Jamie, but human healers can't help them. Do you understand?"

Kaleb cursed and bit his lip, his cigarette burning out untouched in his trembling hand. "Are you saying all this tornado stuff and the gas leak in the Wardens' store are just that—some bullshit the local news is feeding us?"

Damian smiled weakly. "Well, the human authorities believe it to be the truth," he replied, his fingers finding the edge of his bracelet of their own accord. "But you know there are no coincidences in the World of Magic, right? Tornado in Paradise

Manor, a gas leak in the Wardens' store, and an attack on Hawk's property? All within a matter of twenty-four hours?"

"Damn." Kaleb threw his cigarette on the ground and stepped on it, extinguishing it. "Should I be worried, too? I was considering hiring a wizard to cast at least some protection spells over my bar. I doubt just a sanctuary spell will be enough with all the bullshit that's going on lately."

"I can't say it's a bad idea," Damian murmured, "but placing wards over a public place can be quite challenging, and a run-of-the-mill wizard won't be able to do it properly." He scratched the back of his head. "But I think I know someone who can do it for you. I'll put you in touch with him as soon as I can."

"Thank you." Kaleb smiled, his smile a little tired and sad. "As far as the seers..." He thought for a moment, nibbling on his lip. "From what I know, there are three of them in the greater Phoenix area. One of them lives not far from you, in Blue Creek. I'm not sure how powerful their sight is, but they're the real deal. Do you want me to give you their contact information?"

"Yes, please."

Kaleb reached into his pocket and produced his cellphone. He unlocked it and searched through his contact list for what seemed to be forever. Then he tapped the screen a few times, and Damian's phone jingled, making him flinch.

"I texted you their contacts," Kaleb said in a matter-of-fact voice, as if expecting Damian to know what he was talking about.

Damian pulled his phone out and unlocked it, staring at the messages Kaleb sent him. "What the hell is that?"

Catching Damian's confused stare, Kaleb chuckled, shaking his head. "Come on, man. You've lived in Blue Creek for how long now? And your brother is some tech guru. It's time you learned how to use modern toys, don't you think?" Then he rolled his eyes and extended his hand. "Give me your cell." He grabbed the cellphone out of Damian's hands and quickly saved the information into Damian's contact list before returning the device to him. "You're all set."

"Thank you." Damian got up and put the phone back in his pocket.

Kaleb also rose and waved in the direction of the bar. "I need to go back to work, but if there is anything I can do to help, you know how to find me."

They walked back through the kitchen and into the bar. Damian grabbed the flip-up countertop, ready to head out of the *Midnight Shift*, when his gaze fell on two familiar faces, and he froze in place with his mouth open. Atticus and Dallas sat in front of the counter with half-filled beer glasses in their hands. As soon as they saw Damian, they stopped talking and stared at him with widened eyes.

"What the hell are you two doing here at this time?" Damian leaned over the counter closer to them.

"Wait... what?" Dallas exchanged a bewildered look with Atticus and spread his arms. "I'm over twenty-one. I can drink, and Atticus also—"

"Do I look like a cop who's trying to ID you?" Damian lifted the flip-up countertop and approached them. "I don't care if you are of drinking age. Weren't my orders to stay behind the wards clear? What are you doing outside the protected area?" He switched his attention to the young werewolf. "Does your father know you are here, Atticus?"

"Yeah, kinda..." Atticus looked away, but then threw his hands up and continued in a firm voice, "My younger brothers were giving Dallas a hard time. You know how they can be toward humans... We just wanted to have a few minutes of peace and were going to return to the ranch after they had gone to bed." He glowered at Damian defiantly. "And what about you? You're also outside your wards. Or is it a 'do as I say not as I do' situation?"

"Perun almighty," Damian hissed through clenched teeth. "I'm a thousand-year-old Destiny Enforcer and a Child of Earth. You're a teen wolf with your milky fangs still intact, and he is—" Damian pointed at Dallas, but then just waved his hand dismissively. "Anyway, Atticus, the situation is a lot worse than I originally thought."

In so many words, he told Atticus and Dallas everything that had happened at Paradise Manor. Both men blanched and were about to say something, but he raised his hand, stopping them.

"Atticus, you need to return to the ranch as soon as possible. Please tell your father thank you for providing the safety of his home to Dallas. I'll call him as soon as I know anything new," he said in a quick whisper. "I'll take Dallas with me. He'll be safe with Ruslan and Cole until I figure out what to do next."

He reached into his pocket and pulled out his wallet. Placing two twenty-dollar bills on the counter to pay for the young men's drinks, he nodded to Kaleb and headed out of the bar, taking Atticus and Dallas with him.

CHAPTER 8

~ DAMIAN BLAKE ~

Damian made sure Atticus reached his car safely and watched him drive out of the parking lot. Then he walked out onto the well-lit boulevard and followed it all the way to the first intersection, where he turned onto a narrow suburban street. Dallas marched by his side silently, and Damian was glad he didn't have to talk. He turned a corner into a dark, empty lot and halted there, looking around to make sure no one could see them. Once positive they were alone, he put his hand on Dallas' shoulder and snapped his fingers, teleporting both of them back to the Brown's Estate.

They materialized on the steps in front of the entrance, but Damian didn't go inside. Instead, he lowered himself onto the warm marble tiles and patted the vacant space next to him, inviting Dallas to join him. The young man didn't ask anything and didn't object. With the guilty look of a puppy who had been caught with the owner's shoe in its fangs, he sat down by his side, barely meeting his eyes.

My brother trains him old style... Damian's lips twitched a little.

"Dallas..." he started but cut himself off, not sure what he was going to say to him. He raked his fingers through his hair, covering the scarred side of his face, and sighed. "Dallas, you have to be more careful, man. I know you're young and extremely inexperienced in everything to do with magic, but—" He shook his head, clenching his teeth.

The young man turned to face him, looking at Damian with his mouth slightly open, but didn't say anything and bit his lip.

"Everything that's going on now is my fault," Damian continued in a hoarse whisper, his throat dry. "Koschei the Deathless is targeting people who are closest to me, and I promise I'm going to put an end to it. But until I find his death and deal with him, you must be careful. Do you understand me?" He raised his eyes at Dallas, finding sympathy reflected on his youthful features.

"My lord—," Dallas started, but cut himself off as Damian snorted and pressed his hand over his mouth to stop himself from laughing out loud.

"Did my brother teach you to address me like that?" he asked, chuckling. "Do you call him 'Your Majesty'?"

"No, he didn't." A wide grin split Dallas' face, his tense shoulders finally relaxing. "Ruslan did…"

"That old pirate." Damian shook his head. "Ruslan is right to a degree, though. The World of Magic has archaic etiquette and a crazy set of rules that doesn't always make sense to people nowadays, but since you're neck-deep into all of this, it's a good idea for you to know it. Anyway, when it's only us, you don't need to address me like that. You're a modern man. You should behave appropriately to your age and century."

Dallas smiled again and nodded but quickly sobered up, his gray eyes turning a shade darker. "Damian, it's not your fault," he said, staring down at his shoes. "You shouldn't blame yourself for the actions of an evil, homicidal maniac."

A faint smile touched Damian's lips as he stared into the dark desert. "Sometimes, I think someone cursed me at birth," he said quietly. The old memories he'd struggled to keep in the darkest corners of his mind for years surfaced, playing in his head like some terrifying movie. "I was cursed to live my eternal life alone. Any time I get close to someone, they die…"

"You're not alone. How about your brother?" Dallas asked, reproach ringing in his voice. "Cole would kill for you, die for you, and go to the end of the world to save you."

"And I for him," Damian whispered, swallowing hard.

"You're not cursed, Damian." Dallas glanced at him but quickly averted his eyes. "You're blessed. How many people in this world can say they have what you and your brother have? I, for one, only wish…" His voice trailed away, and he took a deep breath, sadness suffusing his features. "You were right, though. It was reckless of me to leave Hawk's ranch without notifying you or Cole first. It'll never happen again." He looked over his shoulder at the massive double door of the house. "You know, I would do anything for your brother… That night, he saved my life and not only that…"

Damian looked at the young man with renewed interest, a strange tightness gripping at his chest. "Where is your family, Dallas?" he asked, half-turning in his direction. "You're spending most of your time either at Cole's company, working long hours, or here, training with him and Ruslan."

Dallas shrugged, not meeting Damian's eyes. "I don't have anyone," he replied at length. "I grew up in the system, going from one foster family to the next." A corner of his mouth lifted, forming a bitter, lopsided smile, and he added, "It's a long, boring and not very original story."

He glanced at Damian briefly, and there was so much sadness and longing in his eyes that Damian decided not to ask anything else, recalling the time when his mother passed away, leaving him and Cole all alone in this harsh world.

"Cole treats me like family," Dallas said after a short pause. "What he gives me is more than anything I've ever had."

Damian got up and offered his hand to Dallas. "I guess Cole

finally gets a taste of his own medicine." He winked at the young hunter, pulling him to his feet.

"Why?" Dallas tilted his head, curiosity twinkling in his eyes.

"Now he can feel what it's like to be the big brother to a little troublemaker." Damian opened the door, gesturing for Dallas to go in.

* * *

AFTER A BRIEF CONVERSATION with Cole and Ruslan, Damian went to his bedroom, still thinking about the situation at *the Midnight Shift* and the safety of the sanctuary. He sat down on the bed, pulled out his phone, and searched through his contact list for the right number. As soon as he found it, he pressed the green button and put the phone on speaker.

The dial tone rang a few times before Yakov Bruce answered the call.

"Commander Blake," he said, tones of surprise in his voice. "I've heard what happened to the Master Warden, Lady River and your young friend. I'm sorry, Damian. Is there anything I can do to help?"

"Thank you, Yakov. Yes, there is something you can do for me." Damian explained the situation, asking if it was possible to place wards or any kind of protection spells over the *Midnight Shift*. The wizard didn't say yes right away, and a long pause stretched across the line.

"That's quite a challenge, Commander," he said at length, but then chuckled in his usual lighthearted manner and added, "But I love challenges. They make life interesting. Text me Kaleb's phone number, and I'll call him tomorrow. Let's see if I still remember how to reinforce a sanctuary spell by adding a no-violence enchantment."

Once Yakov hung up, Damian texted him Kaleb's number and then stared at the three new contacts Kaleb had added to his list, wondering if it was too late to call them. Making a split-second decision, he decided not to call them at all and just go there tomorrow. He didn't think the psychic readers and spiritual advisors had people lined up in front of their doors, so making an appointment didn't seem important.

Putting his phone on the bedstand to charge, Damian grabbed a set of pajama pants from the closet and headed to the washroom. After a quick shower, he changed and returned to bed, sliding under the blanket. He turned to his side and wrapped his arms around a pillow, burying his face in it. Despite his physical exhaustion, he couldn't fall asleep, tossing and turning for what seemed like forever. The last thing he remembered before he finally drifted off was his clock showing five in the morning.

* * *

A RAY of bright morning sun danced over Damian's face, and he groaned, turning away from it, pulling a pillow over his head. A semi-conscious thought arose in his mind, struggling to break through the groggy fog inflicted by the lack of sleep.

Dammit... Damian threw the pillow off his face, and it fell to the floor. He sat up, rubbing his eyes to dispel the blurriness, but as soon as his gaze fell on the clock, he jolted to his feet. Cursing under his breath, he quickly cleaned up, got dressed and headed to the kitchen to grab a cup of much-needed coffee. Even though his brother didn't drink coffee, he always kept it available for Damian.

As he approached the kitchen, the scent of fried eggs and bacon, as well as the bitter aroma of freshly brewed coffee, filled his nostrils. For the first time since Cole purchased the Brown's Estate, its spacious hallways smelled like home, comfort and unusual normality, and he couldn't help but wonder what was going on. Neither Cole nor Ruslan ate human food, using the kitchen only to store their blood bags in the refrigerator or to warm up a cup of blood in a microwave, which didn't smell nearly as good.

Damian stepped inside and found Dallas standing in front of the stove with a spatula in his hand. He had probably heard Damian, because he glanced over his shoulder, and a wide grin split his face.

"Breakfast?" Dallas gestured for Damian to take a seat, and once Damian pulled a chair out and lowered himself onto it, he turned back to the oven and continued cooking, raising his voice over the splattering and hissing of bacon in the frying pan. "Since I'm spending so much time here, Cole told me to buy some normal food for myself."

"Where are they?" asked Damian, his stomach giving a twinge of hunger.

"Dealing with the Vampire Court affairs," Dallas replied. He poured two cups of coffee and placed one of them in front of Damian. "Cole asked me to assist you if you need my help. But if you don't need me, I should go to work. We have the next version of a game going into beta testing soon, so you can imagine the crunch before the deadline."

He filled two plates with scrambled eggs, home fries and bacon, and put everything on the table. Wiping his hands on a piece of paper towel, he took one of the chairs and sat down.

"I'll take you to work, and then either Cole or I will bring you back," said Damian between bites. "Until the situation is under control, you can't go anywhere alone."

Dallas nodded. They ate quickly and in silence, each in their own thoughts, and shortly after they were done, Damian drove the white Mercedes SUV out of the garage and onto the street, taking the road toward the highway leading to Phoenix. He dropped Dallas off at work but didn't leave right away. Instead, he grabbed his phone and after a momentary struggle, managed to enter the address of the Blue Creek's seer into the GPS, furiously cursing all modern inventions and technological advances of this century in general.

It didn't take him long to find the location, and soon, Damian parked his car in a small plaza located across the road from an old church. He glanced at his watch and frowned, observing the area without leaving his vehicle. The parking lot was vacant, which wasn't something uncommon, yet for some reason, he couldn't get rid of the feeling that something was off. The church stood silent and empty, its doors tightly shut, and it seemed as though this entire area was abandoned.

The door of the seer's shop was closed, horizontal shutters concealing the glass part of it. However, the 'open' sign shone brightly on its window, indicating that the owner was inside and ready to provide invaluable information about past, present and future to anyone who cared to pay.

"Astrologer and Spiritual Healer," Damian read the sign on the door and shook his head, wondering if Kaleb was mistaken about their gift of sight. Even though true seers, psychics and healers weren't unheard of in the world of humans, they were extremely rare, and to find them among numerous quacks and charlatans wasn't an easy task.

Just to be on the safe side, he scanned the plaza and the shop with his other sight. A barely noticeable fluctuation in the magical energy field touched his senses, making him do a double take. It was insignificant, like a left-over of some old spell, and normally, he wouldn't even pay attention to something like that. Today, however, everything set his nerves on edge, so he decided to proceed with caution. He stepped out of the car and headed toward the building, keeping his other sight open.

As he reached the shop, the presence of magical energy intensified enough for him to identify it, and he halted, an expectation of trouble coiling in the pit of his stomach like a poisonous serpent. Dark and sinister, the acrid stench of wurdulak essence seeped from under the door, slithering over the sidewalk in dirty gray swirls.

Closing his eyes, Damian extended his senses as far as he could reach but found neither wurdulaks' nor human presence inside the shop at this moment. He seized the door handle, feeling its cold, slick surface under his skin, but then lifted his hand and peered down at it, narrowing his eyes. The handle was silver-plated, and a few anti-vampiric runes were engraved into it.

I guess she's the real deal after all...

Damian opened the door and halted on the threshold as the metallic reek of blood hit his heightened sense of smell. The entire shop was one large room dimly lit by decorative lamps and candles. Most of the candles were either burned down completely or almost gone, tiny flames glowing faintly at the end of short wicks, drowning in puddles of melted wax. A few incense sticks were still smoking, their sweet fragrance entwining with the reek of blood and death.

A woman in her late forties lay sprawled on the floor in a pool of her own blood, her strawberry blonde hair soaked with it. Four deep puncture wounds on her neck in combination with the stench of wurdulak energy left no doubt as to what killed her. Nothing in the entire shop was broken or appeared to be out of place, and it looked as if the owner didn't put up a fight. Most likely, the wurdulaks were so fast, she was dead before she realized what was happening to her, and the regular anti-vampiric runes and enchantment hadn't been strong enough to stop these undead monsters.

With a slow shake of his head, Damian backed out of the shop and carefully closed the door. He spun around, checking the area, and even though the plaza remained empty, he couldn't be sure that no one had seen him going in and out of the shop. He returned to his car, unlocking it on his way there. Slipping into the backseat, he slammed the door shut, reached into his pocket and pulled his phone out. He found the phone numbers of the other two seers and dialed the first one.

Come on, come on, come on... Pick up the phone... he thought frantically as he counted the beeps, but the call went to voice mail. The third seer didn't answer her phone either.

"Dammit!" He slammed his fist against the soft seat, cold sweat covering his forehead as he realized they could be dead, too.

He pressed his hands to his eyes and stilled, carefully considering his next move. Then he channeled his magic and drew a rune on the back of the seat. Placing his palm over it, he connected it with the Shadow Enforcer rune on his arm.

"Ivor," he whispered, his voice hoarse, "I summon thee."

Always calm, Ivor had never been in a rush, taking his time answering the summoning calls no matter from whom they came. Ivor hated the teleportation process, resorting to portals, if it was possible. To Damian's relief, he didn't make him wait this time, and manifested next to him with a light pop, teleporting directly into the car. He glanced at Damian, and his brows knitted, his powerful magical energy spiking around him.

"Commander," he said quietly, "I thought Lord Magnus told you to remain in Paradise Manor and wait for his command."

"Ivor, I don't need a lecture. I need help," Damian replied, gesturing at the shop with his thumb. He told Ivor why he had summoned him and about the other two psychics who hadn't answered his calls.

"Heaven and Earth, Commander," Ivor exhaled after Damian finished talking. "I hate to say it, but most likely, you're doing the right thing by not waiting for Lord Magnus to complete his research. Sometimes what should be a simple Board of Destiny reading takes a few days to complete, weeks even. In the meantime, Koschei is trying to make sure you have no way of finding him, or his death for that matter. He's already ahead of you by a mile, so the faster you move, the better your chance of success."

Damian clenched his hand into a fist and looked out the window, staring into space over Ivor's shoulder. "I'll be honest with you, Ivor. This mission is deeply personal to me," he said and then added, slowly pronouncing every word, "I can't fail... I have no room for mistakes this time."

"I know." A sad, sympathetic smile touched Ivor's lips. "I do believe you're doing the right thing, so I'm not going to report anything to the High Council. But you know they will find out, anyway. They always do." He shrugged, spreading his arms a little. "Reading the Board of Destiny can do the trick, and then it's both our heads on the line."

"Thank you, my friend." Damian glanced at the psychic's shop and let out a harsh breath. "Can you take care of the exposure here and check on the other two seers? If they have indeed been killed by wurdulaks, the cause of death needs to be made legit in the eyes of the human authorities."

"I'll take care of it," replied Ivor, his deeply set eyes drilling into Damian as if he were trying to read his soul. "What's your next step, Commander?"

"I guess I'll call my old contacts in Florida and see if they can point me in the right direction. I met them when I still had my 'no one' status, so they're not connected with anyone at the Destiny Council," he said, not a hundred percent convinced it was the right thing to do.

What if by searching for another seer, he was signing their death warrant? His heart gave a painful jolt, and he dropped his head, fiddling with his bracelet. Ivor was right—in this twisted game, Koschei was far ahead of him. That was obvious. What he couldn't figure out was how Koschei knew he would be looking for a seer and had her killed before he got a chance to speak with her.

"If I may suggest, Commander..."

Ivor's voice broke the troubling train of thoughts, and

Damian raised his eyes at his old friend, gazing at him with expectation.

"There's one seer whom Koschei can't kill," Ivor continued. "She's so well protected and so powerful that even if he decides to abduct her instead, he most likely wouldn't succeed. She'll see him coming before he even takes a step in her direction. So, if you move fast enough…" He lifted his shoulders in a half-shrug, giving Damian a pointed stare.

Damian's heart sped up as understanding dawned on him. He opened his mouth to say something but then changed his mind. "Thank you, my friend," he said instead, giving him a short nod. "As soon as Cole comes back home, we'll leave to visit her."

Ivor opened the door and stepped out of the vehicle. Bracing his arm against the top of the car, he leaned down and looked at Damian. "Be careful, Commander. Just because she's not an easy target doesn't mean Koschei is not going to try to stop you from meeting with her."

"I know, and I'm ready." Damian got out of the car and opened the driver's door, slipping behind the wheel. "I'm also not a fluffy kitty-cat, you know?"

"I had no idea." Ivor chuckled and snapped his finger, vanishing from the plaza.

CHAPTER 9

~ DAMIAN BLAKE ~

As soon as Ivor left, Damian moved to the driver's seat and started the car. As he drove out of the plaza toward the freeway, he dialed Cole's phone number and didn't relax until he heard his brother's deep voice coming through the car's speaker system.

"Damian?" he said, unconcealed concern lacing his words.

"Cole, where are you?" Damian entered the freeway, quickly picking up speed as he moved toward the fast lane.

"My company. What's going on?"

"Ruslan and Dallas?"

"Ruslan is dealing with the affairs of the Court at Luciano's mansion," replied Cole, his voice growing softer—a sure sign of him being worried. "Dallas is with me. What's going on, Dima?"

"I believe all three seers are dead, killed by wurdulaks. I saw the body of one myself, and Ivor is going to check on the other two," Damian replied, cringing at how cold and hollow he sounded. "We need to get moving, and we need to move fast. You and I are leaving as soon as you come back home. Call Ruslan and let him know. Bring Dallas with you. We have to make sure they're safe while we're away."

He hung up the phone and pressed down on the accelerator pedal, increasing speed.

* * *

By the time his brother and Dallas finally made it home and walked into the kitchen, Damian was ready to leave. Dressed in his usual black jeans, shirt and combat boots, he sat at the table, a cup of hot coffee in front of him. The small black backpack Zabava had given him a while ago lay on a chair next to him, his fingers fumbling with its straps absentmindedly. He glanced at them, gesturing for them to take a seat.

"Where are we going?" Cole asked, taking his trench coat off. He draped it over the back of a chair and sat down, the red stone embedded into the pommel of his sword glowing with a soft, scarlet light.

"The only place I can find the answers I seek—the Land of Dreams," replied Damian, watching Dallas' eyes ignite with curiosity and excitement. He pursed his lips, giving the young man a reproachful gaze. "Don't even think about it, Dallas. Cole and I are going alone after I send you back to Hawk's ranch."

"But Damian—," Dallas started.

"No," Damian cut him off dryly.

"And why not?" A deep male voice boomed from the hallway, making Damian raise his head and look in the direction of the sound. Ruslan appeared in the doorway, his cat-eyes filled with a healthy dose of sarcasm and a touch of disapproval.

"How long have you been standing there?" Damian asked as Ruslan walked into the kitchen and leaned against the counter.

"I'm not a child. I don't eavesdrop, Commander." Ruslan folded his arms. "I could hear your voices as soon as I parked my car in the garage.

"I hate vampires with their sharp hearing," muttered Damian, shaking his head.

"You like me." A wide grin split Cole's face, his eyes twinkling with humor. "You really really like me."

"Shut up, little bloodsucker." Damian sent a heavy gaze to his brother, unable to help himself returning his smile. But as he switched his attention to Ruslan, he sobered up. "I'm surprised you of all people asked this question."

"Then let me repeat," Ruslan said calmly. "Why not? Dallas is a skillful fighter. I'm the one who trains him, so I know what he's capable of. Considering all, you and Cole will need all the help you can get."

"He's a human who is barely exposed to the World of Magic, Ruslan," Damian objected. "He's a child to boot, not even thirty! You seriously want me to take him to a land filled with monsters out of his childhood nightmares?"

"A child?" Ruslan laughed icily, his eyes darting to Cole and then settling on Damian. "Compared to me, you and your brother are infants. If age is the most important factor here, then maybe you two should stay home and I'll go to the magical nexus?" A dark shadow crossed his features, a deep vertical wrinkle materializing between his eyebrows. "To be honest, I wish I *could* go with you, but with the Royal Council destroyed, the Arizona Court is in a dangerous situation, and the throne is more unstable than ever. Either Cole or I must remain here to reaffirm Cole's rule and establish a new Council as soon as possible, and something tells me, Dmitri, you prefer your brother as your wingman."

Damian nodded, doubt tearing at his heart. "Fine," he said at length. "Dallas is coming with us." He raised his eyebrows at the young man. "Why are you still sitting? You have fifteen minutes to get ready. Except for a weapon of your choice, take nothing else."

"Yes, sir! I mean my lord… I mean… Ugh, never mind—" Dallas jumped to his feet, and a guilty smile crossed his face. "I'll be back in five, Damian." He rushed out the door, throwing a grateful look in Ruslan's direction.

"You should get ready, too, little bro. We need to leave as soon as possible." Once his brother collected his trench coat and walked out of the room, Damian turned to the old vampire, stifling a sigh. "I hope you know what you're doing, Ruslan."

"I always know what I'm doing. My intuition tells me you need to take Dallas with you, and with age, I learned to trust it." Ruslan's lips twitched slightly, sadness hiding in the depth of his eyes. He approached Damian, seized his arm and pulled him closer, his fingers digging deep into his bicep. "Bring my only child back home safe, Dmitri. I want all three of you back…" He brushed Damian's scarred cheek with his fingers, his fingertips barely grazing his skin, and dropped his hand. "Be careful, son. I'm sure it's not your first trip to a magical nexus, so I don't need to remind you to expect the unexpected and be ready for pretty much anything…" His voice trailed off, and he looked away, unease lingering around him. "But this time…" He shook his head, nibbling on his lip. "If Koschei could predict that you'll seek the help of a seer, he'll most likely guess your next move, too. Just be ready."

"Thank you, Ruslan." Damian smiled, trying to show assurance he didn't feel.

"How are you planning to enter the Land of Dreams?" Ruslan turned away and took a chair across from Damian, lowering himself onto it.

"Through a door," replied Damian. "Normally, I would have teleported there, but taking everything into account, I prefer to err on the side of caution and use a door. Teleportation always creates a spike in the magical energy field, so it will give away our location if someone is watching."

"Good choice." Ruslan nodded, but besides the approval, there was something else in his voice that made Damian do a double take. As an ancient warrior who had lived through the toughest and darkest periods of human history, Ruslan had seen it all and learned how to stare death in the eye without blinking. But the gloom of despondency was visible in the tight set of his jaw and in his dark eyes now, and that sent an icy wave of dismay through Damian.

"Am I doing the wrong thing by going after Koschei myself, Ruslan?" Damian asked, his throat dry. "Do you think I should wait for Magnus to finish his research?"

Ruslan turned into an unmoving statue, his shoulders tense. Then he slowly shook his head.

"No," he said after a moment. "You *are* doing the right thing. Time is of the essence. The longer you wait, the less your chances of saving the Wardens and the woman you love." He spread his arms, and a tired smile lifted the corners of his mouth. "I'm just concerned a little. Or maybe not a little…" He shrugged, and his smile grew warmer. "You don't have children, so you've never experienced what it means to be a father. Being constantly worried about your kids is part of every parent's job description. No matter how old your children are—one year old or one thousand—you can never stop being worried about them."

Damian nodded silently, a sense of yearning squeezing his heart. Being a Destiny Enforcer, he could never have children, and this fact had never bothered him before. His lifestyle didn't promote a healthy family environment, so having children was never an option. But listening to the words of the ancient vampire, he couldn't help but think what it would be like to have a child of his own, a family, a normal life.

He pushed these thoughts to the back of his mind and smiled. "I'll never let anything happen to Cole."

"I know, and as much as I like to hear you say this, it also scares me." Ruslan looked down at his hands, shaking his head. "It's amazing, you know?"

"What is?"

"You two had been separated for nearly a thousand years, leading absolutely different lifestyles, but the moment you're reunited, your codependent relationship sprung up to life as if those centuries had never existed. I hope one day your desire to save and protect each other won't kill you both." Ruslan chuckled humorlessly, shaking his head, and then gestured with his thumb at the door. "Your baby-bro is here, Commander."

When Cole and Dallas appeared in the kitchen a few seconds later, Damian got up and approached them. His gaze fell on a battle ax Dallas had sheathed at his belt, and his lips quirked up.

"An ax?" He gave Dallas an arched stare. "Not a sword?"

Dallas sighed, sending a veiled gaze in Ruslan's direction. "Ruslan said I don't have the finesse needed to wield a sword. I'm better off with an ax."

"Don't worry. Give it a year of training, and my father will beat into you all the finesse you need." Cole winked at Dallas and approached Ruslan, inclining his head in a bow. "Please, be careful, Father. Hopefully, we'll be back soon."

Ruslan pulled Cole closer, giving him a quick tap on his back, and then released him. "Good luck, kids. God knows you'll need it." He twirled his wrist, motioning his goodbyes, his eyes never leaving Cole.

Damian put the backpack on, readjusting its straps, and then placed his hands on Cole's and Dallas' shoulders, teleporting them out of the Brown's Estate.

* * *

THEY MATERIALIZED IN A LARGE, dark space. The air was stale, and a cold, musty odor suggested they were either in an underground cellar or a catacomb. Damian whispered a spell, sending a few light orbs flying toward the ceiling. Multiple dim flairs ignited all over the place, reflecting the unsteady, bluish glimmer of the orbs. Both Cole and Dallas spun around, their eyes widening in awe.

The walls and the ceiling of the room were supported by brickwork that looked old enough to date back to the eighteenth century, at least. The entire space of the cellar was filled with priceless pieces of art, religious relics, and weapons. Wooden chests reinforced by iron strips stood open, overflowing with jewelry and precious stones. Silver and gold coins were scattered over the floor, jingling under their feet as they moved.

Damian raised his finger to his lips, gesturing for them to be silent, and moved across the cellar toward the opposite wall. Once he reached it, he waved his hand in a wide arc, whispering a revealment spell. A thin layer of his magic materialized before him, and a door, filled with rotating blue light, shone faintly behind it.

"Quickly…" Damian mouthed, turning to face Cole and Dallas, and gestured at the door, but before they could make a move, something changed.

The transformation was so fast that even though Damian felt it, he had no time to react. The air became thicker and colder, grazing his skin with its glacial touch. He exhaled, noticing a white cloud of air forming in front of his lips. Electrical discharges crackled at the far end of the room, their dry sound echoing through the large space. Blinding zigzags of tiny lightning bolts sparkled in the dark corners, briefly illuminating the walls and the treasure stockpiled there.

Cold and menacing fear pervaded his soul, paralyzing him with its deadly embrace. The energy signature of Death invaded his senses, and he groaned, struggling to break its heavy influence. A group of dark figures materialized in the middle of the room, standing shoulder to shoulder like an ominous wall. Their semi-transparent bodies surrounded by dirty swirls of mist faded and then came into focus again as they slowly floated forward.

Shaking off the last influence of the spirits on his mind, Damian seized Dallas' and Cole's arms and pushed them through the door into the magical nexus. Throwing a quick glance over his shoulder, he followed them, and the rotating light of the portal embraced him just as a cold, ghostly hand reached for him.

CHAPTER 10

~ DAMIAN BLAKE ~

"What the hell was that?" Dallas spun around, looking at the rectangle of a door hanging in midair.

"What the hell is this?" Damian exhaled, taking in his surroundings.

It wasn't his first trip to the Land of Dreams, and even though he preferred teleporting here, he had used this very same door quite a few times. He remembered the beautiful field covered in tall, lush grass, the bright specks of the wildflowers, and the deep green forest surrounding it from every direction. The Lady Gatekeeper's house stood at the other end of the meadow, backing into the woods.

Now, however, everything was different. The field had been incinerated to the ground. The patches of yellow weeds that had somehow managed to survive the fire stood scattered around the black dirt, looking like the ominous eyes of a carnivorous monster. The acrid stench of burned wood and grass still lingered in the air, and a gray veil of either fog or smoke concealed the far end of the meadow.

"Where are we? What's happening to me?"

Damian heard his brother's constrained voice and turned

to him. Cole was down on all fours with his head dropped low, his clawed hands digging into the black dirt. Damian lowered to his knee next to him and gently lifted his face. Cole's eyes glowed a bright scarlet and his fangs were extended to full length. With his mouth open, he looked like a person who couldn't breathe, yet a vampire didn't need air to survive.

As understanding dawned on him, a sad smile touched Damian's lips. "You're okay, little bro," he said, helping Cole to sit down, supporting him with his arm. "Haven't you ever been to any of the magical nexuses?"

Cole nodded, swallowing. "I have but… never felt like this before… What's wrong with me?"

"Nothing. Just give it a minute, and you'll adjust." Damian glanced at him, noticing the glow in his eyes starting to dwindle. "Before, you didn't have magic, so the nexus didn't have this jarring effect on you." He pulled Cole to his feet, making sure to support him as he swayed a little. "The magical energy in the nexus is so concentrated that the senses of anyone with magic become overwhelmed by the sheer amount of it here. You feel" —he twirled his wrist, looking for a better word, but then shrugged—"as if you're drunk, intoxicated, right?"

Cole nodded, a slightly guilty grin splitting his face. "Feels good, though." Still holding his hand on Damian's shoulder, he pulled away from him to test if he could stand on his own. His eyes turned back to their normal blue color, his fangs retracted, and he was finally able to assume his human form.

"I don't feel anything," murmured Dallas, regarding Cole and his reaction to the nexus with curiosity.

"You're human," Damian replied airily, his mind already far from the subject. "I think we're too late…" He stared at the dirty veil obscuring the other end of the field but couldn't see the house, only some uneven, shapeless outline. "Dammit!" He punched the air with his fist and pressed the heel of his hand to his forehead. "This evil monster is ahead of me by a mile. Again!"

He pointed in the general direction of where the building was supposed to be and motioned for Cole and Dallas to follow him. As they moved briskly across the tarnished field, the veil of smoke slowly dissipated, revealing the terrifying truth.

The Lady Gatekeeper's house was no more.

Destroyed by the fire, only a few blackened logs and the chimney remained in the place where once the beautiful rustic building had stood. The windvane lay in the dirt, scorched and twisted, warped by the heat. The coals, still radiating the warmth of the recent fire, cast an orange glow on the dark land. Cracking under Damian's feet, they emitted fountains of sparks in the air, and flying embers slowly descended, dying down on their way to the ground.

Damian opened his other sight and scanned the area, but in the overwhelming cacophony of colors of magical and elemental energies of the nexus, it was hard to distinguish any traces of dark spells, even if they had been cast here. He didn't find any human remains among the wreckage of the house and that gave him hope that the Lady Gatekeeper escaped the place before Koschei's attack. He halted, shaking his head, still struggling to believe all this was real.

"Now what?" Cole asked quietly and looked around as if afraid someone could overhear them. "She was the last seer you could consult with."

"Now?" Damian turned to his brother, a hurricane of thoughts raging in his mind. "I need a moment to figure it out. I have to do something so out of character that even Koschei won't be able to guess my next move."

"What do you have—," Cole started to say, but a soft whistle interrupted him.

Damian spun in the direction of the sound and saw Dallas standing in front of a tall pine tree growing right next to the house. One side of its thick trunk was partially blackened by the fire and a few lower limbs were broken and burned, but the top branches had survived, still covered in long, green needles.

"Do you know what that is?" Dallas pointed up at the pine, but even after Damian halted by his side, he still didn't notice anything unusual there.

"Cole, do you see anything?" Damian asked, and when his brother shook his head no, he turned to Dallas. "Describe what you see."

"A small box or a chest, I guess…" Dallas took a step closer to the tree and craned his neck, narrowing his eyes. "It doesn't look solid, though, as if it's made from some kind of energy. I can see only its outlines and a strange symbol in the center, glowing a bright orange… You know what it is?" He turned toward Damian, spreading his arms with a light shrug. "Do you want me to climb up this pine and bring it down?"

"Hold on… A symbol? What kind of symbol?" Damian asked, a spark of hope, so tiny he was afraid to voice it, igniting in his heart.

"An upside-down triangle crossed by a horizontal line." Dallas picked up a stick and drew the image in the ashes.

"Yes," Damian exhaled, peering down at Dallas' drawing, warmth and wonderment suffusing his chest. "She truly is the best seer in all the worlds." He covered his eyes with his palm, whispering a short spell, and when he lowered his hand, he could see the box Dallas was talking about.

Channeling his magic, he opened his wings and rose in the air, lingering in front of the branch with the glowing box attached to it. He gathered some of his elemental energy in his hand and allowed it to flow through his fingers to the box. The orange light surrounding it grew brighter, and the chest vanished just to reappear in his palm.

Damian lowered to the ground and folded his wings behind his back. Then he touched the box with his fingertips and whispered a single word in Dragon tongue, making it visible to everyone. Lowering to his knee, he placed it on a tree stump and carefully explored it. The wooden chest was small, no more than two inches in width and length and less than an inch in height. He could clearly see the lid, but it was tightly sealed, and nothing suggested how to open it.

"*Recludius*," he muttered, sending a smidge of his magic into the box, but it remained shut and motionless. Damian scratched the back of his head, in his mind, going through other spells that could help him open the box. "*Rilekti Amnia…*" His last attempt was as fruitless as the previous one. He thought for a brief moment and decided to try a revealment spell instead. "*Latentius revelare.*"

An orange glimmer rose around the box, and when it dissipated, the lid still remained locked, but an engraving materialized on top of it. A picture inside a circle was so small and so incredibly detailed that no matter how much Damian strained his vision, he couldn't make out the image, seeing only a bunch of crisscrossing lines.

"Dammit," he muttered, pressing his fingers to his eyes. "I can see nothing."

"Getting old, are we?" Cole chuckled and took the box. "Allow me." His eyes ignited brighter, and his vampiric energy spiked around him. "It's a picture of a large oak," he said after a short pause, "and two birds. One on each side of the tree." He gave the chest back to Damian and cocked his head. "Do you know what it means?"

"It means…" With a half-smile, Damian took the box and touched it with his fingers, whispering a spell. The orange light surrounding it shone brighter and when it dwindled, the box was gone. "It means, I was on the right path thinking that I need to do something completely out of character to deceive Koschei. It also means the Lady Gatekeeper was expecting both Koschei's attack and our arrival."

"Sorry, but it doesn't make sense," said Dallas, his eyes moving across the burned field to the remains of the house and finally settling on Damian. "If she expected Koschei's attack, why didn't she protect her home?"

"She couldn't," replied Damian. "She's a seer, and as powerful as she is, combat magic is not her strength. But as a seer, she saw us coming, and she left a message only we could find." He glanced at the young man, and the corners of his lips lifted. "Dallas, only you could see the hidden box because you're human. She made sure nothing magical could discover it. The symbol she left glowing on it was the sigil representing the element of Earth, and only I, with my elemental power, could retrieve the box from the tree." He switched his attention to Cole. "Only Cole with his sharp vampiric vision could distinguish the details of the engraving on the lid." He shrugged and added, "Like I said, she's the best seer in all the worlds. She had seen all three of us coming and left the breadcrumbs for us."

"I'll never get used to all this magical stuff," Dallas muttered. "I mean, I know it's all real, and dealing with vampires, werewolves and other supernatural creeps back in Arizona doesn't faze me anymore. But every time I witness magic like this, I can't help but feel shocked."

Cole chuckled, tapping the young hunter's shoulder. "You better get used to it fast, pupil of mine, because you're standing in the epicenter of magic, and it's surrounding you in its purest form. The things you will see here and the creatures you may encounter on your way, you'll never see anywhere else." He switched his attention to Damian, giving him an arched stare. "To keep it on the safe side, I assume you're not going to say where we're going next."

Damian shook his head slowly. "No, I'm not. You just have to trust me." He placed his hands on Cole's and Dallas' shoulders and gave them a short nod. The world swirled around him in a tornado of colors, smells and sounds, and the incinerated field disappeared from view.

* * *

DENSE FOG SPREAD ALL around him, its silvery-white swirls obscuring the land. His shirt became damp almost instantly, and small droplets of water settled on his arms. Blinded by the fog, Damian sharpened his other senses. Somewhere in the distance, waves rolled onto the shore, the sound of their gentle whispers touching his hearing. The scent of water, wet dirt, and grass filled his nostrils, and he smiled with relief. Teleporting blindly was never his preferred method, and he was glad to know he made it to their final destination without dumping everyone into the World Ocean.

"Cole, Dallas," he whispered, reaching into the fog.

"We're here, right next to you," his brother replied right away, touching his hand. "By the way, where are we?"

"You'll see soon," Damian promised.

"Not in this fog," Dallas murmured on his left. "Do you have a magical fog-dispeller by any chance?"

Damian chuckled and whispered, *"Ventius..."*

A soft gust of wind rushed across the land, blowing some of the fog away, and now they could see some of their surroundings. They stood on a thin strip of beach encircled by a body of water so large that the opposite shore wasn't visible from where they stood. A narrow path surrounded by tall grass led deeper into the land, disappearing into the milky mist.

"Is there anything with fangs lurking in this fog? Vengeful spirits or pirates perhaps?" Dallas asked quietly, observing his surroundings with widened eyes.

"No, not here," replied Damian. "This place is sacred. Why?"

"Remind me to stop watching horror movies when we come

back home," Dallas murmured, eliciting a wild snort out of Cole.

"If you want to be a hunter, you shouldn't be afraid of things with fangs and claws lurking in the dark." Cole flashed him a wide grin, showing off his own deadly fangs.

"Let's get moving and stay close to me. You don't want to get lost in the fog." Damian moved forward, following the narrow path.

Although he had never been here before, he had learned so much about this place that he knew his way around as if he had spent his entire life here. Soon the strip of land became wider, the fog started to dissipate, and even though it wasn't gone completely, at least now he could see where he was going without the need to use his magic.

After a while, the path merged into a large meadow covered by dense green vegetation. Despite the patches of fog still remaining here and there, the entire place gave off a pleasant, relaxing vibe, and the soft light illuminating the area just added to its overall calming ambience. At the far end of the field stood a giant tree that resembled an oak, a hefty crown of its branches spreading wide around it. The top part of it disappeared into the clouds, and its trunk was so wide that ten people would have had a hard time circumventing it.

"This is where we need to be," Damian whispered, stepping onto the rich grass of the meadow. He headed toward the oak, gesturing for Cole and Dallas to follow him. "Now I can tell you where we are." He waved his arm around. "We're on the legendary Isle Buyan, the center of Creation in Slavic lore, and this is the World Tree, the center of the universe. The crown of this tree reaches the Prav—the realm of Slavic gods, and its massive roots are wrapped around the Alatyr stone, disappearing into the Dark Nav. The World Tree connects all three realms..." Damian trailed off, the memories of his initial training surfacing in his mind. "Look." He pointed up.

"Whoa…" Dallas exhaled, staring at the sky in awe.

The left side of the tree was completely submerged under the cover of night, the brilliant disk of the full moon pouring its silvery light down at the hefty foliage, and the bright speckles of stars shining all around it. The right side of the tree shone with the dazzling light of day, the sun showering the powerful branches with its warm rays. Busy bees buzzed in the air, and flowers bloomed in front of the Alatyr stone, creating a colorful canopy.

"This is amazing," Cole whispered. He reached forward to touch the root of the tree tightly wrapped around a large stone, but then changed his mind and pulled his hand back. "I've heard about this place, but as a vampire, I never thought I would see it…"

"Neither did I," said Damian. "One of the reasons we're here is that Destiny Enforcers are not welcome in this place. Actually, we're forbidden to come here, so Koschei won't expect me to venture to the Isle Buyan, breaking the Destiny Enforcers' code and a bunch of rules."

"But why?" Cole threw a bewildered glance at him. "As much as everyone hates Destiny Enforcers, your kind is not evil."

"It's not that." Damian craned his neck, looking up at the tree. "This place and those who dwell within the World Tree have a powerful connection with the Board of Destiny. As an Enforcer, part of my soul is fused with the Board, so coming here puts me at risk of…" His voice trailed away, and he just smiled, catching Cole's alarmed gaze. "Never mind. I'll be fine."

He placed his palm against the trunk, feeling the warm, rough surface of the bark, and whispered a few words in Dragon tongue. A light wind ruffled the crown, a soft rustling noise surrounding them, and a few leaves floated down, landing on the ground next to his feet.

"Would yah look at that," a pleasant female voice, laced with unconcealed sarcasm, sounded above him. "This one has some serious balls on him, showing up here."

Damian narrowed his eyes, trying to find the owner of the voice through the foliage but could see nothing.

"Aw, Sister, be nice," the second female voice sang over his head. "He probably got lost. Happens to the best of us." She tittered, and a few more leaves dropped from the tree. "Besides, I've never seen a live Destiny Enforcer. Can we go down closer? I want to check him out."

"Got lost?" The first voice snickered. "The only thing that got lost in his case was his brains. Look who he brought along. A vamp and a human boy."

"Aw, he's so sweet," the second voice took over. "He is an equal opportunity Enforcer, you know? Not like the others of his kind, from what I hear."

"Dima, what's going on?" Cole asked, using their blood bond. *"Who are these women?"*

"The only seers in the Land of Dreams whom Koschei can't touch," Damian replied. *"It's not easy to get answers from them, but I'll try. They're our last chance."*

He connected with his element and sent some of its energy through the tree. "My ladies, the sound of your voices fills my soul with hope," he said with a deep ceremonious bow. "Could you please show yourself, so we could have a word?"

"I told you," the second voice whispered, excitement breaking through in her words. "He's so sweet and so polite!"

"Yeah, sweet, alright," the first voice grumbled. "He wants something from us, otherwise he wouldn't be here."

"Pretty please…" the second voice pleaded.

"Fine, let's see what he wants," the first voice replied, not without a heavy layer of aggravation in her words.

The limbs of the World Tree trembled, sending a shower of leaves floating down, and two large birds descended from behind the clouds, landing on the thick bottom branches. One of them settled on the night side of the oak, and the other perched herself on the day side. Both were as large as an ostrich and instead of a bird's head, they had heads and faces of beautiful maidens.

The one on the dark side of the tree had long, ultramarine plumage, her tail feathers shining with an electric blue, reflecting the light of the moon. Her large eyes were as deep as a stormy ocean, and tears were running down her tender cheeks without stopping. Her sister had snow-white feathers, reaching halfway to the ground. Rich and fluffy, they sparkled and shone with all the colors of the spectrum in the sunlight, as if bedazzled with thousands of tiny diamonds and gems. Her beautiful cerulean eyes, the color of the morning sky, looked at them with kind attention, a friendly smile playing on her full lips.

"Holy shit," Cole whispered, throwing a bewildered glance at Damian. "Are these the Birds Sirin and Alkonost?"

Damian nodded without taking his eyes off the birds.

"Aw, Sister, look at that," Alkonost purred, spreading her white wings a little. "They know us. We're famous."

"Yeah, right," Sirin muttered, rolling her enormous eyes. "These two"—she pointed with her dark wing at Damian and Cole—"are so old, they were probably on first name bases with dinosaurs. Of course, they know us. Everyone who has an ounce of magic in them, or brains, knows us."

"My ladies." Damian raised his hands in a peaceful gesture. "Thank you for answering my call. I'm humbled by your kindness and beauty." He folded his massive frame into an elegant bow again, his eyes carefully observing the birds' reaction.

"Wow, big bro, you do know how to be eloquent and articulate after all." Cole snickered in his mind, but Damian ignored him.

"Aw, Sirin, come on," Alkonost whined. "He's humbled, you see? I like him, he's cute, and his two boys are just yum. Let's hear them out, at least. Pretty please?"

Bird Sirin frowned, tears starting to slide faster from her

eyes. "He's cute, alright. In a deadly and destructive kind of way. For the gods' sake, Sister, he's a Destiny Enforcer. He has a cold heart, and he cares for nothing but his mission." She shifted on her branch, spreading her wings, and peered down at Damian, her gaze heavy and indifferent. "Why are you here, Enforcer? This is the only place in the entire universe where your kind is not welcome. Spit it out and don't even try to lie to us. You know you can't."

"I wouldn't dare lie to you, wise Sirin... I'm here because seers are being killed all over the human realm, and the Lady Gatekeeper's home has been destroyed. I believe she escaped with her life, but not before she left me a message, sending me to seek your assistance."

Damian extended his hand and whispered a quick spell. The small chest, glowing with the bright orange light of his elemental energy, materialized in the palm of his hand, surrounded by swirls of a shimmering, orange mist.

"Look at this." Alkonost pointed at the box. "He's right. This is our picture engraved on the lid of this box. The likeness is just amazing."

Sirin huffed, ruffling her feathers, but didn't say anything, gesturing for Damian to continue.

"We're here because we need your help." Damian quickly explained the situation to the sisters, leaving out nothing. When he mentioned Koschei's name, Alkonost gasped and flew from her side of the tree to her sister's, hiding under her wide wing. After he finished, Sirin and Alkonost exchanged a shocked look, but both remained silent, staring down at them with an intensity that sent chills down Damian's back.

"You don't need our help, Enforcer," Sirin said after a long pause.

"The Lady Gatekeeper left you everything you need to find what you've been looking for..." said Alkonost, pointing at the glowing box in Damian's hand.

"In the chest with our picture on it, you'll discover the answers to all your questions," Sirin took over.

"But just because you know your path," continued Alkonost.

"Doesn't mean you can walk it," finished Sirin.

The birds exchanged a troubled look, and Alkonost wrapped her beautiful wing around her sister.

"We have to help them at least a little, Sister." Alkonost sent a veiled gaze to Damian and added, whispering in Sirin's ear. "He's a Destiny Enforcer, but his heart is not empty. His brother is a vampire, but he's alive. His friend is human, but he has the most powerful magic of them all… They are worthy of our assistance."

"The brothers have a terrible prophecy lingering over them. Their paths on the Board of Destiny had been set before they were born." Sirin shook her head. "No matter what we do, they can't avoid their future."

"But the future is not here yet," said Alkonost. "Let's help them with their present quest, and I'm sure when the time comes, they will both make the right choices in spite of the shocking revelation they may receive."

"You're so optimistic, Sister, it's disgusting," Sirin muttered, rolling her large eyes filled with tears.

"And you've been living on the dark side far too long, Sirin." Alkonost shrugged her wings, a tender smile gracing her face as her gaze fell on her sister. "You need to lighten up and look on the bright side of things." She pointed at the day side of the tree.

"You see, big bro? I've been telling you this very thing for ages." Cole's voice, filled with amusement, sounded in Damian's head, and he threw a heavy gaze at his brother.

Both birds spread their wings and flew up, disappearing in the hefty foliage only to return a moment later and land on a branch, positioning themselves exactly on the border between day and night. As they embraced each other, the bright light of their magic surrounded them like a shimmering veil. A large tear escaped from Sirin's eyes but didn't fall on the ground, lingering in midair in front of Damian. Both birds brushed the tiny droplet of water with their wings, and it started to grow until it was the size of a tennis ball. The brilliant light of the sun reflected on its surface on the right side, and the silvery glimmer of the moon touched its left side.

Two small feathers—a white one and a dark-blue one—hung inside the water-orb like in suspended animation. Slowly, they began to spin within the tear, moving faster and faster until the ball of water exploded into a fountain of mist. When the mist dissipated, a single feather hung in the air. One side of it was white, and the other was dark blue. A small stone shining with all colors of the spectrum was embedded at the tip of the feather.

"Young human," Sirin said, motioning for Dallas to approach. "Take this feather and touch the chest. The Lady Gatekeeper sealed the box with a powerful enchantment which can be broken only by one with a pure human soul, untouched by magic."

"Me?" Dallas threw a bewildered gaze at Damian and then at Cole, his eyebrows rising. Cole gave him an encouraging nod, and the young man reached for the feather, but then pulled his hand back, spinning toward Cole. "My soul is not that pure. I'm not a child, you know, and I haven't been..." His voice trailed, his chest rising and falling with short breaths.

Cole chuckled, shaking his head. "You *are* pure, Dallas, magically speaking. They are not talking about your purity in a religious sense. But even then, I believe you have a pure and kind soul. I saw it in you the first time I laid my eyes on you. Otherwise, I would've never agreed to become your mentor." He pushed the young man toward the feather. "Take it, and you'll see it for yourself."

Holding his breath, Dallas reached for the feather and took it, his fingers trembling slightly. Then he approached Damian and touched the box with it. At his touch, the chest shone brighter, and when the light dwindled, it was gone. A small silver saucer with a beautiful golden apple on it remained in the palm of Damian's hand.

"I believe you and your brother know what to do now, Enforcer?" asked Sirin, raising her black eyebrows. "You are Slavs, so go ahead and ask where you can find the help you need."

"Are you serious?" Cole asked. "That is such old school…"

"Define old, ancient vampire," Sirin retorted snidely.

Damian took one knee and placed the saucer on the ground. Then he put the apple on top of it and said, "Roll the golden apple on the silver saucer. Show me where I need to go to have my questions answered."

Nothing happened.

He raised his eyes at the birds, but both of them pursed their lips, glowering at him with reproach.

"No, seriously, Enforcer," Sirin muttered, turning toward her sister. "I told you, Alkonost, it's not his heart that is empty. It's his head."

"Aw, come on, Sirin, be nice. He just forgot. Old age and all." Alkonost switched her attention to Damian, smiling at him with the particular smile parents normally reserve for their silly little children. "The spells work only if spoken in their original language, Enforcer. You know how it is. Magic always gets lost in translation. Use your native tongue."

"Dammit," Damian muttered, facepalming. "Of course. I knew it, but I'm so used to speaking in English. I didn't even think…" His voice faded, and he switched his attention to the silver plate and the apple. *"Katis' yablochko zolotoe po bludechku seryabryanomu…"*

As soon as Damian whispered the spell in Russian, the saucer lit up with a bright, silvery light. The apple rolled around it, and as it progressed, the surface of the plate rippled and vanished, replaced by the image of an ancient castle surrounded by a tall wall, its watchtowers rising high over the land. The heavy gates opened, showing him the path.

Momentarily, the image changed, and now he could see a large room with tall stained-glass windows. A beautiful woman in ancient Russian armor sat on a massive armchair resembling a throne. As if feeling that someone was watching her, she lifted her face, and Damian felt as if she was staring directly at him. Her electric blue eyes widened, and a deep frown settled on her face, making her look harder. The fog rose, obscuring the image. The apple stopped moving, and the vision disappeared.

"Oh, Perun Almighty," Damian exhaled, a desperate look shadowing his features as he raised his eyes at the birds. "Are you sure there is no other way?"

CHAPTER 11

~ COLE ADAMS ~

Sirin leaned down a little, exploring Damian's face, and her pale lips twisted into a crooked smile. She cocked her head, sarcasm dripping from her every move.

"There are no other ways, Enforcer," she replied snidely. "I'm just curious. Why does a meeting with Lady Sineglazka bother you so much? Have you met her before?"

Cole glanced at his brother, noticing that all color had drained from his face, and he looked like he wanted to be anywhere but here.

"No reason," Damian muttered. "I've heard Lady Sineglazka doesn't favor my kind, and it's practically impossible for a Destiny Enforcer to get any answers from her. That's all." He averted his eyes, his fingers tracing the edge of his bracelet nervously.

"Well, tough." Sirin snickered. "You have your answers, Enforcer, whether you like them or not. We're done here." She turned to her sister, motioning up. "Let's go home. I don't want anyone catching us talking to a Destiny Enforcer, or we'll never hear the end of it."

Alkonost sent a reproachful gaze to her sister, shaking her head slightly. "Hold on, darling. Just one more thing."

She pointed at Cole, gesturing for him to come closer. He wasn't sure why, but there was something in her oversized blue eyes that made him wince as if from the touch of icy water. He took a short step closer, looking at her. Alkonost leaned forward, like her sister had done a moment before, and reached for him with her sparkling wing. She brushed his cheek gently with the tip of her feather, and an unusual sadness clouded her features.

"Handsome ancient vampire," she said quietly, her soft voice raising goosebumps on his skin. "With your vampiric speed, you can run so fast, the wind can't catch you. But you know what you can't outrun?"

"No, my lady," Cole whispered, transfixed by the sparkles dancing in those gorgeous cerulean eyes.

"Your past..." she exhaled with a light shake of her head. "No matter how fast you run, sooner or later, your past will catch up with you."

Alkonost glanced at her sister, and they spread their wings. The wind picked up, ripping the leaves off the World Tree. It made them dance in midair, swirling in an endless merry-go-round. Both birds flapped their wings and flew up, disappearing behind the thick canopy of foliage.

Cole staggered back, raising his arm to protect his face from the flying leaves, his mind set on the ominous words the Bird Alkonost had spoken. The wind died down, and Damian turned to him, a shadow of concern darkening his orange eyes.

"What was she talking about?" he asked, a muscle twitching in his tightly pressed jaw.

"I have no idea." Cole shrugged, searching his memory for any encounter in his past that would stand out. "I have over a thousand years of luggage behind my back. I've had it all—the good, the bad and the ugly. There are hundreds of people who hold a grudge against me or Ruslan, and who'd love to see me dead. Some of them are powerful witches, wizards or other supernatural types. How can I possibly distinguish the single person or occurrence she was referring to?"

"You realize she was warning you about something?" Damian asked, looking just as troubled as Cole felt.

"Of course, I do." Cole looked away at the breathtaking view of the Isle Buyan. Even though the night was settling over it, the brilliant light of the dayside of the World Tree illuminated the field, making it appear whimsical and mysterious. He returned his attention to his brother and smiled weakly. "If I think of something, I'll let you know."

"Where are we going now?" asked Dallas, sounding as if he wasn't sure he should be interrupting their conversation.

Cole smiled at his young friend, unable to shake off his concern. "I guess we need to find the castle of Lady Sineglazka." He turned to his brother. "Can you teleport us there?"

Damian massaged the back of his neck, the look on his face that of a person forced to do something against his will.

"Unfortunately, no." He suppressed a sigh. "I'll teleport us out of the Isle Buyan and onto the mainland, but from there, we'll have to follow the directions of the magical guiding device the Lady Gatekeeper gave us."

"Let's do it, then." Cole pulled Dallas closer, holding his arm in a tight grip. Damian placed his hand on Cole's shoulder and snapped his fingers. The world around him became blurry, and soon Cole could see nothing except for the rotating cacophony of colors.

A heartbeat later, they materialized in the middle of a forest, surrounded by ancient leafy trees, their crowns so dense that the light of the moon couldn't penetrate them. A barely visible trail led deeper into the woods, disappearing in the grass and thick shrubbery. While it was dark, the darkness didn't seem unnatural, at least not to Cole. A fragrance of damp moss, foliage and dirt enveloped him, the refreshing coolness of the midnight air caressing his skin. Faint whispers of wind and the rustling of leaves were interrupted only by the screeches of night birds, and everything seemed peaceful and serene.

However, somewhere far in the depth of the woods, Cole could hear the sound of beating hearts, the padding of soft paws stepping on the ground, and quiet breaths, and he knew the animals were all around them. But being in the company of his brother, the Child of Earth, he didn't think any encounter with nature would be a problem. The only encounters he had to worry about were those of a supernatural origin.

Damian took a knee and whispered a quick spell, holding out his hand. A soft orange mist enveloped his arm, and the silver saucer with the golden apple materialized in his palm. Watching his brother being so comfortable and confident in his knowledge of magic, Cole couldn't help but think how much he still needed to learn, unsure if his ability to wield magical energy was a gift or a curse.

Placing the saucer and the apple on the trail, Damian whispered the words of the spell in Russian, and the apple started to move. The ripples spread over the surface and a map of a terrain appeared before them, a red line ending in an arrow showing the path. Damian got up, muttering something under his breath, and the magical device vanished in the airy swirls of a sparkling mist.

"Let's go." He motioned for Cole and Dallas to follow. "We have a long trip ahead of us, so let's walk for as long as we can, and then we'll take a short break."

* * *

IT HAD BEEN a few days since they started their way through the Land of Dreams in search of Lady Sineglazka's castle. Surrounded by his element, Damian looked like he enjoyed and savored every moment of being here, almost as tireless as Cole, but it was Dallas who slowed them down. Being human, he was getting tired a lot faster than Cole and Damian, and despite the fact that the young man didn't complain even once, Cole knew every time his brother chose to have a short one-hour break to eat and rest or stopped earlier for the night, he did it to give Dallas a chance to regain his strength.

Zabava's backpack proved to be a priceless possession, and Cole was glad his brother hadn't forgotten to bring it along. Conjured by Baba Yaga herself, it had the unique properties of a *skatert-samobranka*, a Slavic magical item that could feed the owner better than any five-star establishment of the human realm. To Cole's surprise, the magical backpack could produce not only any meals of the human variety but also blood bags he needed to keep himself nourished in order to maintain his strength and sanity. All he had to do was ask.

Of course, the forest was filled with animals, and he could always go hunting to sustain his needs, but he didn't want to leave his brother and Dallas alone, especially at night. The fact that Damian could protect them all against the forces of nature better than anyone else didn't make any difference to him, and the idea of leaving them on their own while he wandered into the woods in pursuit of prey wasn't giving him a cozy feeling.

Today, they walked a lot longer than usual in search of a place suitable to stop for the night. They had passed a few small clearings, but Damian had rejected them all for reasons known only to him. As always, Dallas didn't say a word, silently following them, moving a few paces behind. When Damian finally stopped in the middle of a small clearing, exploring the surroundings with his magical sight, Dallas lowered himself to the ground with a strenuous groan.

"Dima, we must stop." Cole approached Damian and halted by his side, sharpening his senses. The shuffling sounds of animals moving in the darkness touched his sensitive hearing, tiny dots of glowing eyes shining with phosphoric light far in the distance. "The beasts are all around us, most likely wolves. They've been following us from the first moment you teleported us into the forest."

"I know," Damian exhaled and turned to face him, the orange glimmer in his eyes dwindling as he let go of his elemental energy. "Wolves, bears, foxes—you name it, it's there. We're in the middle of a freaking zoo." His lips twitched, but his smile was empty, void of mirth. "Animals don't bother me, brother. Something a lot scarier than a few hungry wolves has been following us for a while." He glanced at Dallas and frowned. "We'll stop here. Give me a moment to set up a protective circle around the meadow and conjure a fire." He took the backpack off his shoulder, shoving it into Cole's hands. "Make sure Dallas eats something and gets all the sleep he can. We leave at sunrise." His tired smile grew warmer. "You too, little bro. Eat and get some rest. I'll take the first shift."

Damian walked away toward the edge of the woods, and soon after, the bright orange light of his magic ignited around the perimeter of the clearing, quickly dissipating into the dark. Cole lowered himself next to Dallas and gave the backpack to him. By the time Damian was done conjuring the fire and finally sat down by Cole's side, Dallas was fast asleep.

"Sometimes, I wonder if we made a mistake by bringing him with us," Cole whispered, sending a sideway glance at Dallas. "He doesn't complain, doesn't ask us to stop and give him rest, but I feel how hard it is for him to keep up with us. I'm a vampire. If I don't use my magic and have enough blood, I can keep going forever." The corner of his mouth lifted a little. "You're surrounded by your element, and being in the middle of a magical nexus, you're as strong as you can ever be. Dallas… he's just a human boy…"

Damian nodded and pulled a blade of grass out of the ground, twisting it between his fingers. "I had the same reservations," he said after a while, "but Ruslan insisted, and over time, I've learned to trust him."

Cole nodded. "Yeah, Ruslan has this effect on people... and I don't mean his powerful glamor."

"Get some sleep, Cole." Damian leaned forward, resting his arms atop his bent knees. "Vampire or not, you still need rest. I'll wake you up in a few hours."

Cole smiled but lay down, folding his arms under his head. He closed his eyes, but as he did, he already knew he wouldn't be able to sleep, thousands of thoughts crowding his mind. He turned to his side and propped his cheek on his palm, squinting his eyes at the dancing flames like a giant feline.

"Still thinking about Alkonost's words?" Damian touched Cole's hair with the blade of grass.

Cole nodded without taking his eyes off the fire. "You have no idea, Dima," he whispered. "The amount of shit I went through after Ruslan turned me, the crazy monsters I had to deal with—human and supernatural." He pushed himself into a sitting position and shifted slightly to face Damian. "Any one of them could be *'the past'* Alkonost was talking about. I don't even know where to start."

Damian wrapped his massive arms around his bent legs, pulling them closer to his chest. A shadow of what could have been pain, or guilt, or a mix of both darkened his strange orange eyes as he regarded him.

"I wish I had been there for you all those years," he whispered. Then he turned away, and his Adam's apple moved in his throat as if he had a hard time swallowing. "When Koschei trapped me in an illusion back at Luciano's house, he showed me the same vision Mara used to show me all the time—the day I failed to save Vita." A painful wrinkle materialized between his eyebrows, a haunted look settling in his eyes. "But in Koschei's vision, I was able to see some new details I had never seen in Mara's. I was able to look into the eyes of the monster who took her life, Cole." Damian shuddered, his hands clenching into tight fists. He shifted slightly, readjusting his position. "Mara had no idea who the mysterious Beast Master was, let alone the color of his eyes. I can't get rid of the feeling that Koschei knows the truth… everything there is to know… Do you think Koschei's master and the Beast Master are…"

His voice trailed away, and he moved his gaze toward the fire, the red light of the flames coloring his face, making his scar stand out more than usual. As if feeling Cole's gaze on him, he dropped his head and ran his hand through his hair, covering the left side of his face.

"When we find Koschei's death, we should ask him about that. Maybe we'll even say pretty please." Cole smiled, tapping his brother's shoulder. "Something tells me when you're going to hold that proverbial needle in your fingers, ready to break it, he'll be a lot more receptive to the idea of answering your questions."

Damian didn't move and didn't reply, staring at the dancing flames for a while. "Cole, what did Koschei show you in that illusion?" he asked. "It could be the answer to Alkonost's riddle."

"Just one of my old memories. I don't think there is anything special about the actual moment in my life, and I'm not sure why he had chosen it to show me. Eloise de la Fontaine—an old fling of mine." He shrugged, thinking back to that time. "We dated for a while when Ruslan and I were invited to visit the French court. Before Napoleon decided to invade Russia, that is." He chuckled humorlessly. "Nothing special…"

"Let me be the judge of that," muttered Damian. "Describe the vision and don't skip any details."

"As you wish." It took Cole just a few minutes to describe the old memory Koschei had shown him with all the details. When he finished, Damian frowned, his eyes boring into him.

"What happened then?" Damian asked after a short pause.

"Did you ever meet with Eloise after the scene at Napoleon's gardens?"

Cole nodded, everything inside him twisting with the painful memory he didn't want to relive ever again. Damian straightened and reached for him, squeezing his arm.

"You have to tell me, Nikolai," he said, his voice quiet but firm. "The answer to Alkonost's riddle can save your life in the future, or at least prepare you for what's coming." He gave him an encouraging nod, raising his eyebrows. "Trust me, little bro. I can see how uneasy you are about it, and I would never ask you to relive it if it wasn't important."

Cole covered his face with his hands, rocking back and forth slightly, the old memory rising in his mind as if it all happened just yesterday. He lowered his arms and glanced at Damian, numbness suffusing his chest.

"Dima, you know what I am," he said, barely moving his lips. "I'm a vampire, and before I learned to control my urges, I hunted and killed hundreds of humans." Damian nodded, his face void of emotions as he motioned for him to proceed. "I killed to feed only when I had to, but with Eloise..." His voice trailed away, and he bowed his head, allowing the painful memory to take him over, transporting him back to the Paris of the early eighteen hundreds.

* * *

Paris, 1803

THE FETID STENCH OF WASTE, stale water, and God knows what else seemed permanently embedded in the walls, pavement and everything around him. Maybe for humans, this smell wasn't as pungent as for him, or maybe they had gotten so used to it that they had learned to ignore it.

Cole wrinkled his nose, trying to get away from the main

street as soon as possible. He turned a corner, stepping into a dark alley as he marched in the direction of the house his maker had rented for them when they first moved to Paris. Somewhere in the distance, a woman laughed, and a few drunken male voices joined her.

This is it, Cole thought, picking up his pace, aggravation spiraling through him. *I've had enough of Paris, France and Napoleon's court. I don't care whether Ruslan wants to join me or not, but I'm done.*

A slight movement of air brushed his skin, carrying over a concoction of odors, and he groaned, ready to speed up when the light presence of vampiric essence touched his senses, stopping him in his tracks. He surveyed the area, and his muscles tensed, ready to react at any moment.

A few dark shadows separated from the walls, moving soundlessly toward him. Even before he noticed the glowing scarlet eyes, Cole knew all of them were vampires. They closed the distance so quickly that he had no time to react, the speed and precision of their movements betraying their considerable age. Locked in a circle of deadly foes, Cole spun around, a low growl rumbling in his chest as his fangs extended.

They responded with derisive guffaws, exchanging looks brimming with mockery. Cole's hand jerked toward the sword sheathed at his hip in a habitual move, but in the back of his mind, he realized that if all these vampires were as old as he was, he stood no chance against them, whether he wielded a weapon or fought them the old style—fangs and claws.

The attackers tightened their circle, limiting his range of movement. Slightly lowering his head, he carefully assessed his foes, searching for a weak point in their wall but found none.

The rest happened so fast, he had no time to think and was forced to react on pure instinct. One of the vampires darted toward him and swung his massive fist, aiming at Cole's face. Cole ducked to the side to avoid the punch. His move, however, didn't work as well as he hoped. A few strong arms reached for him, seizing his shoulders, and someone pushed him back into the middle of the circle.

He staggered forward, falling to one knee, but quickly jumped to his feet just to find another giant vamp standing right in front of him. The monster threw a jab, and his fist connected with Cole's nose. A burst of white light and debilitating pain incapacitated him for a moment. Doubling up, his hands rose to his face of their own volition, and he felt the slickness of his own blood under his fingers, its odor making his head spin.

He groaned, forcing his arms down. With his eyes watering, everything around him was still shapeless and blurry. Through the shaky, unsteady vision, he distinguished a dark silhouette that appeared before him, and the next debilitating punch followed, sending him flying back into the line of his enemies. With his fading mind, he heard them laugh, felt his body—weak and helpless—thrown from side to side.

Suddenly, a pain so powerful it ripped him out of his dazzled state surged through him, eliciting a terrible howl out of him. He jolted, struggling to get free, but held in place by the strong hands of his enemies, all his efforts were to no avail. Following the pain, a wave of weakness spread through him, stifling his resolve to fight. He glanced down, noticing a dagger protruding from his chest, a dark stain of blood spreading around it, soaking through his white shirt. Moonlight reflected in the grip of the weapon, and an awful revelation dawned on him, explaining his crippling weakness. The blade of the dagger was silver.

The glowing scarlet eyes of his attackers, the black forms of their massive bodies, and the stinky, dark alley spun around him as his mind faded into sticky, mushy oblivion.

When he regained consciousness, he found himself on his knees in the same alley. Thick silver chains were wrapped around his wrists, his arms stretched to their full extent. Four vampires held the chains on either side of him, their hands clad in black leather gloves, and another two held his shoulders down. His shirt was ripped on his chest, and another silver chain encircled his neck and torso, pressed tightly to his bare skin.

"*Bonjour*, Nicolas..." A pleasant female voice sounded above him, causing him to raise his head.

Eloise stood in front of him, the moonlight reflecting on her pale complexion, making her look even more delicate and a little otherworldly, as if she were no longer among the living. Her weightless white dress shimmered and flowed in the evening breeze, adding to her resemblance to a bodiless spirit.

Ignoring the layer of dirt covering the pavement, she knelt before Cole and took off her red shawl with a decorative silver trimming running along its edges. In gentle strokes, she started to wipe the blood off his face. He groaned and tried to turn away from her touch, but one of the vampires seized his hair, yanking his head back.

"What do you want from me, Eloise?" he snarled, his jaw set.

The vampire holding his hair pulled it back harder and bent down, hissing into his ear. "Show some respect to the high lady of the court, *connard*..."

A growl rumbled in Cole's chest, his jaw clenched so tight that his teeth squeaked, but Eloise raised her hand, gesturing for the vampire to let go. He didn't release Cole's hair completely, but at least he lightened up his grip.

"Aw, Nicolas, *mon amour*..." She caressed his cheek with the back of her hand. "I already told you what I want. Nothing has changed since the time we spoke in the gardens. I want you to gift me life..." Her chest shuddered with quick breaths, interrupting her passionate speech, and she coughed, pressing her palm over her mouth. "Make me like you... Turn me, so we can be together forever... *S'il vous plaît, mon amour*..." She pulled her hand away, showing him the red splatter of blood on her fingers.

Cole met her bright eyes, his eyebrows rising. For a heartbeat, he just stared at her, unable to utter a single word, then a burst of laugher escaped his lips. There was nothing funny about this entire situation, and somewhere in the back of his mind, he realized that if he didn't submit to Eloise's demand, the vampire-mercenaries she had somehow managed to hire would kill him. Yet he couldn't stop laughing, his laughter so cold and hollow, he could barely recognize it as his own.

"I'd rather die..." he muttered between wild outbursts of uncontrollable chuckles.

She hopped to her feet, indignation coloring her cheeks a tender pink, and backhanded him with the strength he didn't expect from such a delicate lady. His head jerked to the side, white light flooding his vision, but at least he was able to stop laughing. He blinked a few times and raised his eyes at her.

"Why do you need *me* to turn you, Eloise?" he asked quietly, tasting the blood gathering in his mouth. "Obviously, you were resourceful enough to learn about the existence of vampires and hire all these undead mercenaries. Just pay a little more, and any one of them will gladly turn you."

"*Non.*" She shook her head, her lips pressed into a stubborn line. "Only you can do it. I want you—" She didn't finish her statement, and her mouth fell open, her eyes widening in terror.

Cole tried to look around but couldn't move, still held down by the vampires and the restraints. A sound of feet hitting the road followed by the noise of a short struggle and cries of pain reached his ears. Soon the grip on his hair and shoulders vanished, the chains dropped, and he fell to all fours, just now realizing that the chains had been the only thing holding him upright. Eloise squealed, her face distorted by fear, and turned around to run, but a pair of powerful hands yanked her back and threw her down in front of Cole.

"Hello, son." Ruslan's icy voice sounded like the dangerous growl of a wild beast, his eyes shining with a furious, scarlet glow. He pointed at the silver chains, and a snide smile tugged at his lips. "Having fun?"

Cole grunted and averted his gaze, not sure what to say to that. Ruslan sobered up quickly and pulled Eloise's head to the side, brushing her long, elegant neck with his fingertips.

"Hell hath no fury like a woman scorned," he said coldly. "You can't let her live, son. The Destiny Council will send Destiny Enforcers after you for exposing the World of Magic, and trust me, you don't ever want to meet one of those deadly bastards. Besides"—he glanced down at the young woman, shaking his head—"something tells me she'll never let you live in peace…"

Cole nodded. Burning his hands, he unwrapped the chains, and they fell to the ground with a loud clatter. With enormous effort, he rose to his feet, weakness assailing him once again. He met Eloise's tearful gaze as she stretched her hand toward him.

"Nicolas, *non*… I swear I'll never bother you again… *S'il vous plait, mon amour…*"

Cole froze in place, his lips curling in disdain.

"Do you want me to do it, son?" Ruslan asked, his fingers wrapping tighter around Eloise's neck, but Cole slowly shook his head.

"No." He took a step closer to her. "She's my responsibility. I must do it myself." Before Eloise could say anything, he assumed his full vampiric form and swung his arm, his sharp claws cutting across her throat like the blade of a dagger.

Eloise gasped, her eyes bulged, and her mouth opened as she struggled to breathe. Blood burst out from the horrid gash, running down her chest in thick rivulets. Her lips twitched, but only a senseless gurgling came out, blood spilling from her mouth. Her eyes moved up, staring at the space above Cole's shoulder. She swayed and slid down, falling to the ground in front of his feet.

Cole peered down at the red stain spreading wider on her white dress. For a moment, he couldn't take his eyes off the blood, but it wasn't his thirst talking. He felt nothing but internal torment, the pain of betrayal, and disgust. A gentle touch to his shoulder made him flinch, and he looked up at his maker.

"I'm done, Father," he whispered. "I'm leaving Paris today."

He turned on his heels and headed out of the dark alley without looking back.

After Cole finished, Damian remained silent for what seemed like forever. Staring at his clenched hands, his brother appeared troubled, and Cole wasn't sure if it was the Destiny Enforcer in him feeling appalled, or the story giving him some kind of disturbing hint. Then Damian glanced at him sideways, his eyes filled with the usual warmth and concern.

"Are you sure you killed her?" he asked, his voice below a whisper.

Cole nodded. "I saw her taking her last breath…"

Damian shook his head slowly and got up, stretching his shoulders. "Then death is just the beginning…"

CHAPTER 12

~ DAMIAN BLAKE ~

Damian took a step away from the fire, turning toward the forest. A slight fluctuation in the elemental energy field drew his attention, a strange sensation coiling in his chest.

My element... he thought, opening his magical sight. *It's calling to me...*

"Dima, what's going on?"

His brother's voice broke his train of thoughts, and he glanced at Cole, numbness spreading through his limbs. Alkonost's grim prediction and the memory Cole had just revealed set his teeth on edge, an expectation of something dreadful clouding his soul. The thought of losing his brother on top of everything else sent his heart into a wild frenzy, and momentarily, he felt as if the ground disappeared beneath his feet. His hand rose of its own accord, his fingers gripping at his chest.

"Dima, are you alright?" Cole seized his arm, making him turn and look at him.

Damian swallowed and forced a calm smile. "Not sure," he replied in a whisper. "My element is calling to me. I must go..."

He glanced back at the forest, and his jaw dropped. Bright

against the dark backdrop of the midnight forest, a shimmering veil composed of thousands of small, glowing orbs surrounded his protective shield. Weightless phosphoric lights, smaller than the magical orbs he used to conjure, were floating slowly in a continuous clockwise motion. They produced neither sound nor heat, looking like some kind of freakish ghostly apparition.

"Whoa…" Cole stepped closer to the protective shield, tilting his head. "Are these the swamp lights? Will-o'-the-wisp? I've never seen so many of them in one—" He cut himself off and raised his arm, pointing into the depth of the forest. "What the hell?"

At first, Damian couldn't see anything, but shortly after, he noticed a feeble golden glow. It grew brighter and brighter, and soon, a graceful stag with an enormous crown of antlers stepped out of the woods, halting a few feet away from his shield. The deer inclined his head and hit the ground with its hoof, bowing to Damian.

"Dima," Cole whispered, unable to take his eyes off the beautiful, glowing animal. "Did the deer just bow to you?"

"Yes," Damian replied and held his breath, realizing who this stag was. "It means I'd better go and talk to him."

"To a deer?"

Damian chuckled. "This is not a deer. This is Turosik, Leshy's little helper. He's one of the smaller spirits of the forest. Trickster by nature, he can be dangerous for humans, but he's no match for me." He glanced at Cole's troubled face and smiled, gesturing with his thumb at the golden stag. "Care to join?"

"You have to ask?" Cole's eyes ignited with excitement, but then he looked at Dallas and shook his head, twinkles evaporating from his gaze. "If you are not in any danger, I should stay behind with Dallas."

"Good idea." Damian glanced at his brother, trying to keep a straight face. Then he leaned down a little and whispered, "Enjoy being a big brother." He winked and waved his hand, creating an opening in his shield big enough for him to go through.

"Doofus," muttered Cole with a shake of his head. "Watch your giant back out there."

"Always."

Damian walked through the protective barrier, turned around and squatted, brushing his fingers over the ground. Responding to his move, the shield lit up with a bright orange light, illuminating the clearing. He whispered a complex spell, and a few glowing runes materialized on the surface of the barrier. Damian got up and touched one of them, softly chanting under his breath. A few lines separated from the rune he touched, connecting with the rest of them. Then he took a step back and checked the makeshift wards he erected in a matter of a few seconds, making sure he didn't miss anything.

"Well, this should be enough to keep both troublemakers safe while I'm away," he murmured, brushing dirt off his pants.

He glanced at the golden deer patiently waiting for him in the forest and headed in its direction. The phosphoric orbs stopped their rotation and followed him, showering him with their ghostly light. He made his way to the stag and halted, pressing his fist to his chest with a slight bow.

"Turosik," he said quietly, but somehow his voice was picked up by the echo, bouncing from one tree to the next.

"Hello, Brother in Element," the deer said, his words sounding in Damian's mind. *"My master would like to have a word with you in person. He's waiting for you not far from here, and he guarantees the complete safety of your friends while you're away. Would you mind following me?"* He gestured with his head toward the forest, his antlers leaving ribbons of golden glimmer in the air as he moved.

"Lead the way," replied Damian, approaching the stag.

Turosik turned around and headed deeper into the woods, its body shining brightly among the dark trees and bushes. Just to be on the safe side, Damian connected to his element and followed the spirit of the forest. The glowing orbs accompanied his every move, and Damian wasn't sure if Leshy sent the swamp lights to help him or to make sure his position was visible for miles around.

After a few minutes of walking, the wind picked up a little, and it seemed as though it was blowing in all directions at once. The silence of the forest was interrupted by strange knocks, squeaks and crackling noises, and while all these sounds weren't loud, goosebumps rose on Damian's arms.

Is Leshy trying to intimidate me? Why?

As if hearing his thought, Turosik turned its head toward Damian, and he could swear a sarcastic grin appeared on its face.

"Don't be afraid, Brother," the deer said, its golden glow increasing. "This is my master greeting you." He waggled his brows at him, mischievous twinkles hopping in its deep, round eyes. "Consider it an honor."

Honor my ass, Damian thought grumpily as he followed Turosik deeper into the woods, picking up the pace. *Leshy is trying to show me who's the alpha male here.*

After a few more minutes of a brisk walk through the deepest thickets of the forest, Damian finally stepped onto a small, round meadow. The moonlight illuminated it with its soft glimmer, igniting bright flares in every droplet of water and dew scattered among the tall grass. The trunk of a collapsed tree lay on the ground, dividing the opening in two. A layer of moss covered it, and a few strange mushrooms grew on top of it, glowing with a ghostly phosphoric light.

A man sat on the log, his fingers tracing the shape of the broken branches, leaving a trail of his elemental energy in their wake. His windblown hair had twigs and dry leaves stuck in it, and his skin had a slightly greenish tint. He was dressed in what appeared to be human clothes, but patches of moss covered his shirt and pants in a few places. The man raised his face, his glowing eyes halting on Damian, but he didn't get up to greet him.

"Leshy, Master of the Forest," Damian said instead of a greeting, inclining his head in a respectful bow.

"Child of Earth," Leshy replied in kind, and the noise behind him picked up a few decibels. "What are you doing in my domain?"

"Just passing through," Damian replied. "We don't upset the natural balance of the forest, and you should have no quarrel with us."

"And I don't," Leshy huffed, throwing his hands up, moss and dust dropping off his clothes. "If I was here to harm you, I wouldn't be having this conversation with you."

He got up with a groan and waved his hand, summoning the swamp lights. They came closer, circling their master, floating in and out of the grass.

"Then why am I here?"

"My master, the god of Nature himself, wants to send you a message, Child of Earth," Leshy said quietly. "Something is coming for you." Leshy looked around, and a shadow of fear crossed his face. "Something that doesn't belong in my domain. It's unnatural, malevolent and deadly. You need to be ready and try to leave my territory as soon as possible."

"Thank you for the warning, Master of the Forest," Damian replied with a bow, trying to sound calm, but a heavy sense of dread squeezed his heart in its iron claws. "We'll be ready, but can you tell me what it is?"

"No, I cannot." Leshy frowned, and the winds around him blew harder, howling among the trees. "Saying its name will bring it forth faster, making it more powerful. It's stronger within my domain and in Vodyanoy's kingdom. Try to leave the forest as soon as you can and stay away from any bodies of water."

Damian rubbed his forehead, quickly going through everything he knew about evil spirits who drew their power from nature but coming up blank. Usually, all spirits, evil or not, were attached to a single domain—a forest, a human household, or water—and he couldn't for the life of him remember any spirits who could cross from one element to another.

"I'll try to help you if I can, but I can't guarantee it will be enough to keep you and your companions out of harm's way," said Leshy, giving a dismissive wave to Damian. "Be on your way now, Brother in Element."

"Thank you." Damian inclined his head, pressing his fist to his chest. "I won't forget your kindness."

He left the clearing, Leshy's heavy gaze burning his back. As soon as the forest closed behind him, he switched to a run. Connecting to his element, he commanded nature to obey. The thickets spread apart, giving him way, and thick tree roots sank underground. As the feeling of the upcoming storm pressed heavily on his soul, he ran faster and faster, the ground trembling under his feet, responding to his emotional state.

Damian rushed into the clearing where he had left Cole and Dallas and zoomed through the barrier he had erected, just to find Cole sitting in front of the fire with a little twig in his hand, staring at the flames without blinking. Dallas was still sleeping as if there was no tomorrow.

"Dima—" Cole got up, turning to Damian, but he interrupted him with an impatient gesture.

"Wake up Dallas," he said, breathing hard. "We're leaving immediately."

Cole's eyes widened, but he didn't ask anything and shook the young hunter awake. Conjuring some water, Damian extinguished the fire, and a few minutes later, they started on the way across the forest, following the direction given by the magical apple and saucer.

Damian chose not to run but rather walk as fast as they

could, in fear of Dallas getting winded too fast running on the uneven terrain of the trail. He quickly explained why they had to leave in such a rush, and after that, they proceeded in silence, saving their strength.

He wasn't sure how long they had been walking, but according to the magical device, they were still far away from the wide valley lying on the border with the woods. The forest started to change around them, a few pines sprinkled among leafy trees here and there, and even though Damian kept wielding his element, making their walk easier, it seemed like the forest had no end.

Dammit... We are moving too slow...

Just as the troubling thought sprung up in his mind, the weather began to change. A cold wind rushed through the area, playing with the branches, showering them with leaves, and suddenly, silence—dead and heavy—enveloped them in its suffocating embrace. Then a flock of black birds rose in the air with ear-piercing screeches. They made a wide circle above them and flew in the direction of the valley, their shrieks echoing through the silent forest.

Damian came to a sharp halt and opened his other sight, quickly exploring the area. His arms dropped, and he bowed his head, his chest rising and falling with heavy breaths. In a matter of a few seconds, the temperature went down considerably, making Dallas shiver in his thin shirt, wrapping his arms around himself.

Damian met his brother's calm gaze and gave him a short nod. "Get ready," he said quietly. "Whatever Leshy warned me about, it's here." He moved his hand in an arch, a trail of orange light following his movement. "There's so much dark energy here that if this was happening in the human world, we'd be suffocating."

Without any additional words, Cole unsheathed his swords, and they responded to his magic, illuminating the area with a dim glimmer. As if replying to his move, the wind picked up, the trees trembling and bending down from powerful gusts. An even rustling noise broke the deafening silence coming from above. The amount of dark energy seemed to double, infused by an ungodly amount of demonic essence.

Damian glanced up, and his jaw dropped, the blood running cold in his veins. Hundreds of dark figures moved above them with considerable speed. Hanging from the branches, leaping from one branch to the next, climbing down the tree trunks, they looked like some freakish, four-legged spiders. Darkness partially concealed them, and Damian couldn't identify what they were, but one thing he knew for sure—they were demons.

"Dima, they have tails and horns," Cole whispered, holding his sword at the ready, "and their eyes glow a bright red."

"Tails and horns," Damian echoed, narrowing his eyes at the demonic mob circling above them, and a terrible realization assailed him. "Wait… Cole, can you see if they have hoofs instead of feet?"

Cole frowned, squinting his eyes. "Hard to say. They're too far and moving too fast, but I think you're right."

"Perun almighty, help us…" Damian exhaled, looking around the tiny clearing they stood in. "How much I wish we had brought some salt with us."

"Salt?" Dallas sheathed his ax and shrugged Zabava's backpack off his shoulders. "Ask and you shall receive." He reached into the backpack and pulled a cylindrical box of salt. "Iodized even. I hope that'll do."

He gave the box to Damian, then put the backpack on and tightened the straps, checking it to make sure he wouldn't lose it if he needed to fight.

"We'll find out soon," Damian murmured, grabbing the box out of Dallas' hands. He walked around the clearing, spilling a generous amount of salt on the grass to create a circle. "These demonic monkeys"—he pointed up, without taking his eyes off what he was doing—"are *cherti*... They're not large, but there is no such thing as just one of them. They always come in vast groups, as you can see. Nasty little creepers."

Throughout his years of serving as a Destiny Enforcer, Damian had had a few encounters with these demonic spirits, and every time, sending them back to the Slavic realm of spirits and demons presented a serious challenge. Evil to the core, they were masters of trickery and manipulation, and it was practically impossible to kill them. But never had he seen so many of them in one place.

Suddenly, the *cherti* stopped moving, as if following the silent command of an invisible master, and stared down at them, a carnivorous glimmer in their eyes. Then all of them moved a few feet down, their eyes shining like pieces of burning coal. They tilted their heads decorated by a pair of hooked horns, and Damian shuddered as their mouths stretched into a predatory sneer, displaying a set of small, sharp fangs.

"What's going on?" Dallas asked, his ax in his hands again. "Why did they stop hopping?"

"Their master is coming," Damian whispered, wondering why he was whispering. In the silence engulfing the forest, his soft voice sounded like thunder, anyway.

"Do you know who their master is?" asked Cole, his fingers gripping the hilts of his swords tighter.

"Yes, now I do, but I shouldn't say his name out loud. It will immediately bring him straight to us," replied Damian, probing the forest with his magical sight for the presence of other beings of magic. To his dismay, the *cherti,* with their massive amount of demonic essence, polluted the area so heavily that he couldn't detect anything other than their presence.

Cole chuckled mirthlessly. "Well, big bro, I think that choo-choo train has left the station." He pointed with his sword at something behind Damian's back. "You can say his name now, since he's already here."

Slowly, as if in some creepy nightmare, Damian turned around and cold perspiration covered his forehead. "Perun almighty," he exhaled. "When Leshy warned me, I knew it was going to be bad, but I had no idea how bad…"

"That's one big motherf—" Dallas cut himself off and raised his ax, nothing but cold determination reflected in his steel eyes.

CHAPTER 13

~ DAMIAN BLAKE ~

The forest bowed to the ferocious gusts of wind, the trees bending down to the ground. A giant monster moved through the woods toward them, his head and torso towering above the tallest trees. The earth trembled from his heavy steps, each tremor as powerful as the aftershock of a major earthquake. His face looked like that of an old man, a net of deep wrinkles visible even from this distance. The monster's long, jet-black hair fell down his shoulders in greasy tendrils, and although the wind was ravaging the area, neither his hair nor the disheveled rags covering his enormous body were affected. Two large horns grew from his temples, curving back over his head, and his eyes glowed with a malignant red glimmer.

"An *anchutka*," Damian exhaled, involuntarily taking a step backward, cold sweat dripping down his back.

Even though he had heard enough horror stories about *anchutkas,* the stories had never been told by those who had met the dark Slavic spirit personally. The people who had been unfortunate to come across one of them had never survived to tell the tale. The *anchutkas* were the embodiment of evil, having only one goal—kill, destroy, and extinguish any speck of light.

They could change their appearance at will, and by the time a person realized who they were facing, it was too late to do anything. It was impossible to kill them with a mortal weapon, and what gave the *anchutkas* a serious advantage was that unlike the rest of the evil spirits, they weren't bound to a single element, moving as easily in water as on land.

As soon as Damian said the monster's name, the *anchutka* stilled, and a carnivorous smile stretched his lipless mouth, exposing terrifying fangs. He opened his maw wider, a web of saliva glistening in the moonlight stretching between his teeth, and a deafening roar escaped his throat. The wind picked up the blood-curdling sound, and the echo amplified it tenfold, carrying it into the darkest corners of the forest. The roar morphed into an ominous cackle, and the *cherti* supported their master with their high-pitched snickering, hopping up and down on their branches.

A strange sensation washed over Damian, and he gasped, doubling up, feeling as if someone had punched him in the gut. It didn't take him long to realize what had just happened, and the startling revelation made his heart thunder desperately against his ribcage. He straightened with effort and snapped his fingers, wondering if he could still teleport them back to the Lady Gatekeeper's house, but as he expected, that was no longer an option.

"The *anchutka* is not working alone. Someone just cast a spell, grounding everyone in the area. I was hoping we could run for it, even if it would throw us off course by days, but I can't teleport..." Damian squared his shoulders and drew a deep breath, exchanging a quick look with Cole and Dallas. "We have no choice but to stand our ground here," he said in a fast whisper, his glowing daggers materializing in his hands. "I don't think the *cherti* can cross into the salt circle, but it's not going to stop the *anchutka*."

"What is the point of running?" Cole shrugged nonchalantly,

watching the *anchutka* as the demonic spirit uprooted a massive tree, throwing it out of his way. "If someone hired this monster to kill us, it'll find us in any place of any world."

"True," Damian agreed, "but I was hoping to delay the meeting."

The anchutka pointed at Damian, an expression of deep loathing distorting his ugly features. "Prepare to die, Child of Earth," he roared and proceeded forward, uprooting and breaking trees as if they were nothing but tiny twigs. He halted a few yards from them, staring down with icy contempt, and then cocked his head, a horrid snarl curving his mouth.

"No, seriously, Child of Earth," he rasped, placing his massive fists on his hips. "The way my master spoke of you, I thought you were something special, dangerous even." He pointed at the circle of salt and gave a loud guffaw. "A salt circle? Who do you think I am, you ignorant boy?"

He held out his hand, his yellow, broken nails morphing into razor-sharp claws. A blast of wind escaped his disgustingly filthy palm, easily blowing all the salt away, outbursts of wild laughter following every next gust. The *anchutka* took one more step, and now he was so close that Damian could see his entire giant body between the trees. Not surprisingly, he had a long tail ending in an arrowhead-like point and hoofs, like that of a goat, instead of feet.

"One more step and he's going to be right in the middle of our clearing," Dallas whispered, his voice cold and emotionless.

Damian didn't get a chance to reply as a gale blasted through the forest, but it wasn't produced by the *anchutka*. An earsplitting ruckus followed the wind, something knocking, clapping and screeching, the sound coming from all directions at once, magnified by a long-lasting echo.

Cole groaned, pressing his fists to his ears, his sensitive hearing hurt by the loudness of the noise. Damian spun around, and his eyebrows rose. Leshy stood across from the monster, towering over his domain, standing just as tall as the evil spirit.

"Why don't you try intimidating someone your own size, asshole!" Leshy shouted, pointing at the monster, the winds dancing and swirling around him.

"Leshy," the *anchutka* growled, his eyes ablaze with the flames of hatred.

"Anchutka," Leshy replied flatly, raising a large wooden club to his shoulder.

The *cherti* started to jump from tree to tree again, excitement making them look like a bunch of freakish monkeys from Hell even more. The *anchutka* pointed at them and shouted, "You take care of these three. You know the orders!"

Without much care whether his demonic army acted on his command, the *anchutka* bolted toward Leshy, one of his hoofs stepping on the clearing right next to Damian. The Master of the Forest replied with a hair-raising roar, meeting him halfway. The two giants collided in a deadly embrace just a few yards away from them. Their shouts and growls rose over the forest, overpowering the cacophony of deafening noises following Leshy, and the howling of the increasing gale force wind. Stormy clouds gathered over their heads, obscuring the light of the moon and stars, and the earth shook violently with every step they took.

With a deafening ruckus, the *anchutka* kept uprooting the trees, slamming them at Leshy as he aimed at his head. The screen of dust, leaves and splinters of wood rose into the midnight sky, obscuring the deadly confrontation between the two legendary monsters unfolding before their eyes.

The elemental energy of Earth mixed in with the demonic essence increased significantly, sending Damian's magical senses into a wild frenzy, and only now, he detected a powerful circle of a dark enchantment surrounding the immediate area. Since he still had the use of his magic and elemental power, he was positive it wasn't the God's snare. Besides, the area was too large for that. However, he had no doubts this was the spell that had prevented him from teleporting, locking him inside the forest.

A heartbeat later, all hell broke loose, and Damian had no time to dwell on it. With blaring screeches, the *cherti* rushed down from the trees. Like a dirty, stinky avalanche, they flooded the entire clearing, surrounding them from every direction, dropping on their heads and shoulders directly from the branches. The black swirls of demonic essence wrapped around him, suffocating him with the unbearable stench of sulfur. There was nowhere to run and no air to breathe.

Damian spun in place, trying to rip the revolting monsters off his shoulders. Their sharp claws sunk deep into his arms, tearing his skin into bloody shreds, but he didn't care. His glowing daggers sliced through the tiny demons, severing their limbs, cutting their heads off, piercing their hairy bodies. It seemed like there was no end to them, and the more he killed, the more demons came to replace the fallen.

Extremely strong and fast for such small demonic entities, the *cherti* overwhelmed him by sheer numbers, forcing him to his knees. In the shifting ocean of the evil mob, he tried to find Cole or Dallas, but couldn't see anything. He heard the sound of Cole's swords hissing through the air somewhere close by, and through their connection, he could sense his brother's emotions, and that told him he was still alive. But he had no idea if Dallas was still standing.

"*Ignius!*" Cole's desperate voice broke through the clamor of the fight, and a wall of fire rose on Damian's left.

"No..." Damian whispered, sweat mixed in with blood running down his face, flooding his eyes. "Cole, no! The *cherty* dwell in fire! *Incanto Comlium!*" He pointed his dagger at the blazing barrier, trying to break the spell his brother cast.

The fire began to dwindle, and for a moment, he could see

Cole and Dallas still fighting, but it was too late. The ground shook violently, and a deep fracture split the clearing in two, leaving him separated from them. Sinister flares of crimson light erupted from the fracture, illuminating the area, and the deadly energy of the Dark Nav started to sip through the crack.

"No…" Damian froze in place despite at least a dozen demons hanging on him.

He stared at the growing fracture with horror, thousands of uncontrollable thoughts rushing through his mind. He needed to close the entry to the Dark Nav. The energy of the Nav would feed on his and Cole's magic, rendering them helpless while increasing the strength of the demons. But what was even scarier was that it would provide the *anchutka* with more power.

Damian took a deep breath and channeled all the elemental energy he could gather from nature. As his entire body lit up with a bright orange light, he redirected all his power toward the slowly growing crack in the ground, commanding his element to close it.

He felt the resistance of the demonic essence, and he increased the flow of his elemental energy. His body arched, and the muscles on his arms and chest bulged from the unimaginable strain, sweat running down his back. A strangled scream escaped his tightly pressed lips as he tapped into his internal resources, adding the magic of the Destiny Enforcer into the mix. The fracture stopped growing, but it wasn't closing, and he started to feel the incapacitating influence of the Dark Nav.

His legs trembled, and he dropped to his knees, weakness engulfing him like a toxic cloud. With his blurry vision, he saw something dark and sinister rising from the crack. The fire ignited brighter, smoldering heat enveloping him, and he could no longer see his brother.

"*Cole,*" he moaned through their link, but he didn't get a response. Struggling to rise to his feet, he shouted out loud, "Cole! Dallas!"

No one answered his call.

A cold, crippling fear spread through him, numbing him from the inside. He could still hear the clamor of the battle between the *anchutka* and Leshy, but he could see nothing. The *cherti* forced him down, twisting his arms behind his back, and he had no strength to fight them.

One of the demons seized his head, pushing his face into the dirt. He jerked, gasping for air, but couldn't get rid of its iron grip. As his vision turned red and his lungs began to burn, someone's strong arm yanked him to his feet. Loud thunder boomed over the forest. The ground shook again, and the crack started to close a lot faster than he could ever do it. A powerful gale rushed through the clearing, swirling into a tornado funnel. It picked up every single demon, sending all of them flying into the chasm. By the time the access to the Dark Nav was closed completely, all the *cherti* were gone—each and every one of them.

"Cole! Dallas!" Damian spun around, searching the clearing, but the screen of smoke, dust and debris obscured his vision. A tiny serpent of panic slithered its way into his soul, making his heart beat somewhere in his throat, but he squashed it, determined to keep his mind clear.

Silence engulfed the night forest. The *anchutka* was gone, and he couldn't find Leshy anywhere. When the dust finally settled, Damian found himself standing alone in the clearing scorched by the flames—real and demonic. Feeling exhausted physically and magically, he slid to the ground and bent forward, rubbing his temples. He cleared his mind and isolated everything unrelated to Cole, focusing only on their connection.

"Cole, where are you? Please tell me you survived this... mess..."

His brother didn't answer his call, but through their blood bond, he could feel his presence. It wasn't strong, but it was there, and that meant Cole was alive. All Damian could do now was hope that Dallas was with him, and both were safe. The thought gave him the small boost of energy he needed, and with a moan of pain, he forced himself to get up and look around again. A dark shadow moved among the trees, and a massive black bear holding a gigantic ax stepped into the clearing. Damian gasped, taking a step back involuntarily, but the bear raised its massive paw in an apparent peaceful gesture.

"Greetings, Earthling. I come in peace," he growled, but then tittered, and a veil of green and orange sparkles enveloped him.

When the sparkles disappeared, Damian saw a slender young man standing in front of him. His golden-blond curls cascaded to his shoulders, and his large blue eyes stared at Damian with unconcealed curiosity. He was dressed in ordinary jeans and a T-shirt, but Damian knew he was anything but ordinary. The man didn't try to conceal his energy signature, and his godly powers, in combination with the elemental energy of Earth, were wrapping and flowing around him in soft waves.

"Svyatobor," Damian whispered and inclined his head in a respectful bow, greeting the Slavic god of Nature.

"Commander Damian Blake," Svyatobor replied, a kind smile dancing on his sensual lips. "It's nice to finally meet you in person, Child of Earth." He lowered himself to the ground and rested his back against a tree, gesturing for Damian to join him.

Feeling at the end of his rope, Damian didn't object and sat down next to him, wrapping his arms around his bent legs. His every muscle responded with aches and pains, and he shifted, trying to find a better position, but to no avail.

"I was preoccupied at the moment and couldn't be here myself, so I had Leshy deliver my message to you and protect you while you were in his forest. As soon as I felt your distress, I dropped everything I was doing and came here. I'm sorry it took me so long to break through, Commander," the god of Nature said quietly. "But someone had erected a nasty barrier outside this clearing, and it took me a while to bring it down."

He looked at Damian, sympathy in his aquamarine eyes. "I could have spared you so much pain."

Damian glanced down at his arms resting powerlessly on his lap. Deep welts left by demonic claws were still bleeding. His blood-soaked shirt was shredded, and his chest and stomach were covered in scratches, bite marks and bruises. He just shrugged weakly, dropping his head.

"I can control physical pain," he replied, his voice void of emotions.

"That wasn't the pain I was referring to," Svyatobor objected, placing his hand over his heart. "I can feel it, you know. I'm the god of Nature, and you're a Child of Earth. There is nothing you can hide from me."

Damian nodded, his lips forming the semblance of a smile. "I know." He sighed, feeling numb and hollow. "I wasn't trying to hide anything. I just—" He cut himself off, shaking his head. "In that fight, I lost my brother and my friend. I'm sure Cole is alive. I would've known if he wasn't. But I have no idea what happened to Dallas."

"Your brother is an ancient vampire." Svyatobor glanced at him sideways. "He can hold his own. Your friend, however, is a different story, but from what I understand, it's not his destiny to perish in this forest." He waved his hand around his domain. "Soon, Dallas will find himself at a crossroads, and he's the only one who can choose his path."

"Ahh… Svyatobor," Damian exhaled with a sigh, "can you spare me the riddles? What are you talking about?"

"I can't tell you, and as a Destiny Enforcer, you should know why that is," replied Svyatobor, tones of reproach surfacing in his voice. "There's one thing about Dallas that I *can* tell you, though. Being a human hunter was never his destiny."

"I guess that confirms he's still alive," Damian murmured, pulling down on his shirt as he attempted to cover at least some of his wounds from the touch of the cool night air. "Better than nothing." He pushed himself away from the tree and hissed as pain spiked through him.

"Lie down," Svyatobor commanded in a no-nonsense tone, and when Damian didn't move, he seized his arm and pulled him closer, leaning his back against his chest. "When your god commands, you obey." He chuckled, shaking his head, and added, sounding softer, "Just stay still and let me heal you, Commander."

The god of Nature placed his hand over Damian's forehead, and his power washed over him, taking the pain away almost at once. Weakness assailed him, and he groaned, closing his eyes. As Svyatobor kept circulating his healing power through him, all his wounds stopped bleeding and closed. Then he shifted Damian slightly, resting his back against the tree, and let go.

"Thank you," Damian whispered, feeling dizzy and faint. "How did you know?"

"Know what?" Svyatobor asked.

"A few things," Damian replied. "That I would be traveling through the Land of Dreams, for one. Destiny Enforcers are not common guests in magical nexuses."

Svyatobor averted his gaze, a vibe of discomfort surrounding him almost palpable. "I had quite a peculiar and very demanding messenger who wouldn't take no for an answer... Someone told me that you're going to be here, as well as to expect some serious troubles to follow you," he said at length, avoiding Damian's gaze.

"Who sent the messenger?"

"Sorry, I can't tell you that. When the time comes, I'm sure you'll find out." Svyatobor raised his face, his blue eyes pleading with him not to push the matter. "But I'm glad he did. I'm the god of Nature, and as a Child of Earth, you're my brother in element, Damian. I will always do everything I can to protect you." He spread his arms a little, a lopsided smile making him look even younger and a lot more human.

"Thank you," said Damian, wondering who this mysterious person could be, but he knew asking Svyatobor about it was pointless, so he left it alone.

"What are you going to do now?"

"I'll find Cole and Dallas," Damian replied flatly, not even noticing his fingers rubbing the edge of his bracelet. "After that, I'll continue with my mission."

"That's what I thought," Svyatobor murmured, staring into the woods. "Do you know where he is?"

Damian shook his head slowly, agonizing pain gripping at his heart at the mere idea of losing Cole again. He swallowed, pushing the troubling thought away. Then he looked at the god of Nature, meeting the calm gaze of his bright eyes.

"Do you think I'm cursed, Svyatobor?" he asked after a short pause, shocked by how weak and raspy his voice sounded. "Is it possible?"

Svyatobor's eyes shone brighter, and Damian held his breath, feeling as if the god of Nature was reading his soul.

"You're marked by the Beast. I can see it..." He moved his hand over the scar on Damian's face without actually touching it. "But you're not cursed." Svyatobor looked away and the light of his power slowly vanished from his eyes. "Why would you ask that?"

Damian frowned, pinching the bridge of his nose, but then ran his fingers through his hair, covering his scar, and shook his head.

"I'm sorry," he whispered, his throat tight. "I'm just tired, I think... Tired of fighting this endless battle... losing everyone I ever loved and not being able to do a damn thing to stop it from happening..." His voice broke, and he exhaled, looking anywhere but at the god of Nature. "I knew this mission was going to be dangerous. I should have never brought Cole with me. And what was I thinking, letting a human boy tag along? How could I make such an unforgivable, stupid... stupid goddamn mistake!" He slammed his fist against the ground and bit his lip.

Svyatobor rose to his feet and looked up at the sky. He waved his hand, and the wind picked up, blowing away the stormy clouds. The moonlight washed over the clearing, touching everything with its cold, silvery light. Bracing himself against the tree, Damian got up too, a strenuous groan breaking through his tightly pressed lips.

"You're not cursed, Damian. We all make mistakes. We fail and fall. It's how we rise that makes all the difference in the world. I've seen the best warriors lose their battles because they gave up hope just one step away from victory. Don't be one of them." Svyatobor placed his hand on Damian's shoulder and snapped his fingers.

As the clearing spun around him, swimming in nauseating waves, Damian gasped, holding on to Svyatobor's arm for dear life. When he felt the firm ground under his feet, he swayed and staggered a step forward, but Svyatobor steadied him. Once the dizziness of teleportation passed, Damian opened his eyes and looked around. They stood on a border between the forest and an endless valley. As far as he could see, only rolling hills covered in tall grass spread for miles ahead.

"You know Leshy didn't kill the *anchutka* that had been sent after you," Svyatobor said, releasing Damian's shoulder. "He vanished as soon as I broke the barrier."

"I figured." Damian lifted his shoulders in a half-shrug. "They're not easy to kill. But even if Leshy succeeded, I'm sure whoever hired the *anchutka* has quite a few other monsters at their beck and call."

Svyatobor nodded, his large eyes filled with a strange longing. Then he turned back to Damian, and a barely noticeable smile curved his lips.

"I must go, but now that you're outside the forest, you should be as safe as you can be within the magical nexus.

Anchutkas don't love open spaces. They're a lot more powerful in the woods and lakes or rivers, so I don't think he'll dare attack you here. But if you ever need my help, don't hesitate to summon me." He glanced back at the forest. "There are only two living Children of Earth in all the worlds... Be safe, my young brother, and keep fighting."

Before Damian could say anything, the god of Nature snapped his fingers and vanished, leaving a trail of green and orange sparks in his wake.

Damian waited until the last sparkle dissipated and then sat down, staring at the horizon. It was still dark, but somewhere behind the tallest hill, the sky turned slightly gray—a sure sign of the approaching dawn. He tried to call his brother through their blood bond but received no reply, just like before.

He held out his hand, whispering a spell, and the silver saucer with the golden apple materialized in his palm. He placed them on the ground and said the enchantment in Russian, asking the magical device to show him his brother.

The apple moved, circling the edge of the saucer, and ripples spread across its surface. When they subsided, a dark, empty room appeared before him. The image zoomed in, and he saw Cole's face. With his eyes closed and his lips slightly parted, he appeared to be either unconscious or sleeping, but he was alive, and that was all that was important.

"Show me Dallas," Damian whispered, brushing the apple with his fingertip, and added, "Don't you dare show me the city in Texas. I wish to see the young hunter with that name."

The ripples rushed across the surface, showing him another dark room. Dallas lay sprawled on a dirty hardwood floor. His clothes were ripped, and blood trickled slowly from the cuts and welts left by the claws of the demons. His chest was moving, rising and falling with even breaths, and Damian exhaled with relief. Both were alive.

"Show me where my brother and Dallas are," he whispered, touching the apple with his finger.

The image in the saucer changed, and he saw an old castle on top of a hill, damaged either by people or by time and elements. A partially demolished stone wall surrounded it, and the gates were wide open. As far as he could see, there was no one guarding the wall, and he couldn't help but wonder if guards weren't needed because of some kind of magical protection, which turned the large castle into an impenetrable fortress.

"I need directions," he muttered, touching the apple again.

Once a map of the terrain appeared on the surface of the saucer, he studied it for a few seconds, committing everything to memory. Then he murmured the same spell, making the magical device vanish, and got up.

"Hang in there, little bro. I'll find you, no matter what," he whispered, staring at the horizon. "Even if I have to go to the end of the world."

CHAPTER 14

~ COLE ADAMS ~

Cole regained consciousness but didn't open his eyes, sharpening his other senses instead. He wasn't sure how much time had passed since he was brought here, but if whoever held him captive was watching him, he wanted them to think he was still out for a little while longer.

Cold air brushed his chest and stomach, making him suspect that either his shirt was too damaged to cover his body, or it was completely gone. He didn't detect the tightness of his back scabbard, and the thought that someone could have taken his swords sent chills down his spine. His skin was burning painfully, as if he had his entire torso and arms covered in third-degree burns, and he hated to even think about what could've caused that. An odor of mold and dirt lingered in the air, making him wonder if he was in some kind of basement or a dungeon.

The last thing he recalled was the fight in the forest. He remembered conjuring the fire, and the horror imprinted on his brother's face, but after that, everything went blank.

Dallas...

Cole strained his hearing, and somewhere far in the

distance, he detected a weak heartbeat. A human heart was thudding slowly and evenly like that of a sleeping person, but Cole wasn't sure if it was Dallas or the person who had captured him. He knew for sure it wasn't Damian's heart. He could recognize his brother's heartbeat out of thousands.

"*Dima...*" Cole reached out to his brother through their bond but received no answer, their connection feeble, almost nonexistent.

How is it possible? Only extremely powerful magic can sever a blood bond. Like Donna Luna's magic... An old memory surfaced in his mind, bringing forth a chilling sense of dread.

Cole opened his eyes, his gaze falling on a high, dirty ceiling covered in thin fractures and decorated by old spiderwebs. Carefully, he moved his head from side to side and realized with relief he was absolutely alone in a spacious room. His first assumption was wrong, though. He wasn't in a basement or a cellar. He lay on the hardwood floor of a large chamber that undoubtedly had seen much better days. The tall windows were concealed by filthy rags, but they were dense enough to prevent any light from coming inside, so he had no way of approximating the time of day.

Once beautiful wallpaper with golden ornaments was now shrouded by a thick layer of dust and cobwebs, its former splendor lost forever. Peeling off at the edges, it hung in dirty ribbons, exposing the mold-infested wall beneath. The hardwood floor lost its shine, looking dull and mucky, wooden boards warped and cracked in a few places. Five massive, rusty hooks embedded into the ceiling above him suggested that at some point a large bed with a canopy had been here, but now it was gone, and the room was devoid of any kind of furniture.

He tried to push himself up, but a weakness the likes of which he hadn't felt since before he was turned flooded him, and he fell back, hitting his head against the ground. His vision blurred, his stomach heaved, and he felt as if he was ready to throw up.

"What the fuck..." he moaned, the burning pain increasing with his every move. *I'm a vampire. Vampires don't get nauseous...*

Cole lifted his head slowly and glanced down, finding that even this small movement cost him serious effort. His entire torso was draped in a silver net, thin chains wrapping tightly around his body. Silver manacles were locked on his wrists, and although they weren't connected to anything, the effect of the silver on his body was enough to keep him more or less immobilized. His skin was raw and blistered in places where the chains came in direct contact with it. With a strenuous groan, he lifted his arm and touched his neck just to find the slick surface of a narrow silver collar under his fingertips.

As the room started to swim in nauseating circles, he bowed his head and shut his eyes, feeling like he was on a ship in the middle of a stormy sea.

The silver explains the weakness and the pain, but it doesn't explain the sickness, he thought. He had experienced the effects of silver more than once in his lifetime. He had been tortured and even injected with it before. But never had he felt like this—sick, feeble, and despondent.

Something clicked, and a door opened with a mournful squeak. A wave of vampiric essence touched Cole's senses, and he opened his eyes, expecting to see a vampire. A woman stood in the wide doorway, dressed in a long robe so thin it barely left anything to the imagination. Her chestnut hair wasn't styled, falling all the way to the small of her back in thick strands. She had pale skin characteristic to vampires, and her eyes shone a bright scarlet through the slits of the mask that covered two-thirds of her face.

She met his gaze, and her lips, adorned by a layer of red lipstick, curved into an arrogant sneer. Cole stared at her face, exploring the part he could see. He remembered her seductive smile, her sensual mouth and the chin with a small dimple in the middle. He had known her a long time ago. As realization dawned on him, he moaned and turned away.

I killed her with my own hands. I saw her bleeding out in that dark alley back in Paris. How is she a vampire?

"Hello, Nicolas," she said in French. Her voice had always been soft and musical, but now that she was turned, it was even more alluring than before. "Don't try to ignore me. You have no such luxury, my darling."

Cole didn't reply. The woman sauntered closer, the folds of her robe opening with her every step, exposing her long legs. She halted, looking down at him for a short while, exploring every detail of his face and body with her glowing eyes. Then she lowered to her knees and seized his chin, forcing him to face her. Too sick to fight her, Cole cracked his eyelids open and looked at her.

"You can take your mask off," he whispered, noticing that even moving his lips was coming with an effort. "There is no reason for this ridiculous masquerade. I know who you are, Eloise. What I don't know is how the hell you are still alive and a vampire to boot when I slit your throat myself?"

"I'm touched, darling. You still remember me." Eloise laughed, her melodic laughter hurting his ears like microphone feedback. She pulled the mask off, throwing it on the floor, and lowered herself slightly in a curtsy filled with mockery. Now that she was a vampire, she was even more attractive than he remembered, but the twisted lifestyle she had led for years reflected on her features. While she was undeniably beautiful, the set of her lips and the menacing glimmer in her scarlet eyes revealed her natural proclivity to evil. In addition, she had the pretentious posture of a person who got used to all her commands being obeyed without a moment's hesitation, no questions asked.

"Cut the crap, Eloise. What am I doing here? What do you

want?" Cole growled, but his growl morphed into a painful groan as she pressed the chains tighter to his chest, holding them with her gloved hand.

She snickered, the expression of arrogance making her tender features look ugly and sinister. "You killed me, all right." She seized his collar and yanked him closer, her eyes now only a few inches away from his. "What you didn't know was that at the moment when you cut my throat, I had more vampire blood in my system than human." She let go of him, and he sank back heavily. "So, like it or not, you are my maker, love."

Cold laughter bubbled up in Cole's chest, a frosty, uneven smile curving his lips. "No, darling, I'm not your maker. The low-life vamp who donated his blood to you is. You're old enough as a vampire. You should know how it works by now."

"Oh, I know that." Eloise waved her hand, dismissing the matter. "But since you were the one who ended my miserable human existence, I prefer to think of you as my maker."

"I'd rather die," Cole muttered, closing his eyes.

Eloise cackled again. "Trust me, if it was my choice, you would've been dead the very moment you were delivered here, but I'm just doing my benefactor's bidding, and he wants you alive and well tamed." She looked away, the expression of disdain on her face replaced by scorching fury. "I'll be honest with you. For centuries I lived and breathed vengeance, dreaming day and night about turning you into a pile of hot ashes, but your maker made sure to cover your tracks well. No matter how hard I tried, I couldn't find you anywhere."

She pressed heavily on Cole's chest, burning him with the silver. He clenched his teeth, refusing to give her the satisfaction of hearing him scream. She let go and cocked her head, staring at him with undiluted loathing.

"What changed?" Cole asked, even though he didn't give a damn, but the longer she talked, the more time he had to figure out what was going on and find his way out of this predicament.

"I met my master," she continued airily after a brief pause, strange tones of longing in her voice. "He showed me that revenge on someone like you is not worth it. You're beneath me..." She shrugged with a cocky flick of her wrist. "In case you still haven't discovered it, power is the only thing that's worth fighting for, my darling."

She moved her fingers over his cheek, tracing the shape of his jaw, and it took all of his resolve not to jerk his head away from her touch.

"Power?" He cocked his eyebrows, unable to conceal his disgust. "You have no honor, no dignity, no self-respect." He huffed, a corner of his lips lifting, forming a crooked smile. "What kind of power can someone like you have, except for the power to kiss the ass of your so-called benefactor?" he said, his voice filled with derision. "I also wonder what you had to do to get the power you're talking about."

"You're right. The road to power is not easy, and quite often, it is paved with indignities, but the result is well worth it." Eloise leaned forward and seized his collar again, lifting his head off the ground. "As far as what kind of power..." She cackled, moving so close that her lips brushed his earlobe as she spoke. "As you can see, right now, I have the power over you, so I suggest you be a good boy and do as you're told."

"Or what? You're going to torture me with silver?" He spread his arms. "Be my guest. You said it yourself—your master wants me alive. You can't kill me."

"Oh, yeah, he does want you alive and restrained, but he's not going to be here for a few days." She got up, glowering down at him with contempt. "In the meantime, I can fully enjoy your company."

She continued talking, but Cole barely listened to her, his mind set on her last words. It was going to be a while before her master would arrive here. A lot could happen by then. He didn't doubt for a moment that his brother wouldn't rest until he found him, and these few days were giving Damian a chance to do that.

I have to find Dallas and my swords... I wish I could get her to tell me who her master is...

"Are you listening to me, Nicolas?"

Eloise's furious voice sounded above him, and a hard slap across his cheek followed, sending him into the next bout of nausea. His body convulsed, and he pressed his hands to his stomach, doubling up.

"It's amazing," she whispered, forcing him to turn to her again.

"What is?"

"The effect this strange collar and manacles have on you," she replied, carefully running her fingertips over the silver bands on his wrists. "When I touch them with my bare hand, the only thing I feel is the burn of the silver. But you..." Her voice trailed off, and she shook her head, an expression of sincere bewilderment on her face. "It disabled you completely, turning you into nothing more than a helpless, sickly human. My master told me it would happen like this, but he didn't explain why."

Cole remained silent, a disarray of thoughts crowding his mind, but none of them gave him an answer to what these strange restraints were and why they affected him in such an unusual way.

"Anyway." Eloise sprung up to her feet, brushing down her dress. "I intend to enjoy your company while my master is away." She twirled her hand at him. "Get up."

Completely ignoring her, Cole shut his eyes and focused on dealing with the weakness.

"You will obey me, Nicolas," she hissed, tones of anger creeping up into her voice. "Or you will regret your little rebellion dearly."

He glanced at her, feeling numb and tired. "Do what you want with me, but I'm not going to come to heel."

"We'll see about that." A malignant smile stretched her bright red lips, and she sauntered her way out of the room, sending him one more ominous stare from the doorway.

Cole hoped she'd leave him alone for at least a few minutes, giving him a chance to think in peace, but she returned almost immediately, dragging another man with her. His arms were shackled, and a thick chain was attached to his restraints. She yanked the chain, propelling him forward as if he was a useless rag doll, and he dropped to the floor next to Cole.

"Cole," he moaned, both happiness and horror reflected in his steel eyes. Dallas scrambled to his knees, reaching for him, but Eloise pulled on his chain, holding him back.

Cole glanced at the young man, quickly assessing his state, and his silent heart jolted with pain. Besides the cuts and welts Dallas had sustained during the fight with the demons, new bruises decorated his face, and his left eye was swollen shut. His shirt was gone, and blood was still trickling from the puncture wounds of a vampire bite on his neck and his arm. His entire body was trembling, and Cole wasn't sure whether it was the result of cold, fear, or blood loss.

"Dallas," he said quietly. "Hang in there, my friend. You're going to be all right."

Eloise laughed. "Don't make promises you can't keep, my dear."

She seized a handful of Dallas' hair, yanking his head back, and her long fangs extended as she brushed her lips over the pulsing vein on his neck. Dallas' eyes moved to the side as he sent a murderous glare to her, but he gritted his teeth and said nothing. She raised her face and gave Cole an arched stare.

"Now, darling, get up, or watch me drain the last drop of blood out of your boy toy." Her smile grew more sinister, and she waved her hand at Cole. "Do it fast, Nicolas. Patience is not my virtue, as you know."

"Cole, don't bow to her…" Dallas reached for him, the chain

attached to his wrists falling to the floor with a loud clatter. "She can do whatever she wants with me. I don't care…"

"How sweet," Eloise sang, grazing Dallas' neck with her fangs. She opened her mouth wider, as if ready to bite, but Cole raised his arm, stopping her.

With a low groan, he pushed himself up and stilled, swaying, trying to deal with his physical condition. She didn't rush him, watching his struggles with a contemptuous smile. Clenching his teeth, he was able to get to his knees, but when he tried to rise to his feet, he had no strength.

Eloise cackled, pure delight in her laughter. "Stay on your knees, darling. Your position satisfies me."

She released Dallas and approached Cole, her long fingers threading through his curls. Lifting his chin, she bent down and kissed him, forcing his lips apart with her tongue. The strong smell of her perfume and the artificial taste of her sticky lipstick invaded his senses, awakening the gag reflex he hadn't felt since he was human. When she pulled away, he wiped his lips and looked at the bright red smudges on his hand with disgust.

"Tell me, Nicolas," she asked, peering down at him. "Who is this young man to you?" She switched her attention to Dallas, narrowing her eyes at him. "Even though a vampires' sexuality is flexible, I don't remember you lusting after boys. Ever. So, who is he to you?"

"Isn't it obvious?" Cole sent a veiled gaze to Dallas, silently pleading with him to go with the flow. "He's my human companion, Eloise," he said quietly. "I'm too old, and the hunt lost its thrill for me a long time ago. At my age, I don't need a lot of blood to sustain myself, and he gives me everything I require."

"Is that so?" She seized Dallas by the scruff of his neck and pushed him into Cole's arms. "Go ahead, feed. I want to see you do it." Her tongue moved over her lip, and she bit it lightly, her gaze getting fogged. "If you remember me, you probably recall that I enjoy watching almost as much as doing…"

With stiff fingers, Cole pulled Dallas into his chest, noticing a haunted look settling in his eyes. But when he wrapped his arm across Dallas' stomach to hold him still, the young man tilted his head, exposing his neck for him, and gave him an easy smile.

"Do it, master," he said, his voice calm and soft. He lifted his arm, encircling Cole's neck to force his face down. "Everything is as usual. Nothing is different."

Cole winced inwardly but lowered his head and carefully touched Dallas' warm skin with his lips. The young man's muscles tensed, and Cole could hear his heart thudding in desperate bursts against his ribcage, but he didn't pull away. With a soft hiss, Cole extended his fangs and sunk them into his flesh, making sure to infuse his bite with as much vampiric essence as he could to suppress the pain. Dallas sucked in a sharp breath, and his entire body shuddered, but as the effect of the vampire bite spread through him, he relaxed, leaning heavily against Cole's chest. His arm dropped to the floor with a dull thud, and he moaned, his breathing quickening.

As the hot blood filled Cole's mouth, he cursed himself silently for doing it to Dallas. Carefully, he raised his eyes, watching Eloise through the strands of his hair. She looked almost ecstatic, her hand pressed to her chest, her lips parted, her eyes drunk with desire.

He pretended to drink, trying to take as little blood as possible, and soon pulled away, gently lowering Dallas on the floor next to himself. Then he brought his own hand to his mouth and punctured the tip of a finger with his fang. Without much care for whether Eloise would mind him doing it, he smeared his blood over the puncture wounds on Dallas' neck and arm, instantly healing him. The young man moaned and opened the eye that wasn't swollen, a drunk smile playing on his lips.

Eloise stepped closer and lowered herself to her knees in front of Cole. "When you two are together, it's a sight to behold... Quite enjoyable, I must say..." She wiped a drop of blood off Cole's chin and licked it off her finger with the tip of her tongue. "I think next time I'll join—"

Suddenly, she cut herself off and rose to her feet, listening to something intently. Then she glanced at Cole with regret in her eyes. "I guess joining is going to have to wait," she said coldly. "I'll see you in a few, darling." She turned on her heels and walked out the door, locking it.

* * *

As soon as the sound of her steps disappeared, Cole dropped flat on his back, a soft moan escaping his lips. Despite the fact that he didn't take a lot of blood from Dallas, it still had been enough to give him back some of his strength despite the effect the silver chains and collar had on him. With remorse twisting his soul, he turned his face toward Dallas, meeting the warm gaze of his gray eyes.

"Dallas, I'm so sorry," he whispered. "You know I would never—"

Dallas chuckled weakly, interrupting him, still looking a little drunk. "Of course, I know that. Just like I would never call you *'master'*, or anyone else for that matter, but I couldn't let her torture you..." He closed his eyes and swallowed, visibly fighting the intoxicating effects of the vampire bite. "Can I ask you something?" He sounded uncomfortable and shy, but when Cole nodded, he continued, "You're not the first vampire who bit me, you know... But"—a flush crept up his cheeks, and he cleared his throat awkwardly—"I never felt like this when the other vamps did that. I'm so sorry, but there is something about your bite that made me... and I promise, I don't... No, seriously, Cole, I—"

Watching his blush turned brighter, Cole laughed, but his laughter morphed into a moan as his stomach turned again.

"Ohhh... Dallas, don't make me laugh. It makes the nausea so much worse," he muttered as he watched his young friend squirm under his gaze. He sobered up quickly and continued, "The other vamps didn't care about how you felt or if their bite hurt you. I couldn't do it to you..." He paused, averting his eyes. "The idea of taking your blood was hard enough. I didn't want you to be in pain. What you feel is the effect of a true vampire bite. Unfortunately, it's sexually arousing, and in many cases, quite addictive. The way your body reacted was absolutely normal, and you have nothing to be ashamed of. I'm sorry I had to do it to you."

"Jesus Christ..." Dallas exhaled, scrambling into a sitting position. He rested his back against the wall, gazing down at Cole. "Is that why most of the victims don't fight vampires when they bite them?"

Cole nodded. "Yes, it takes away any resolve and desire to fight," he whispered, old memories of days long gone flashing before his eyes. He glanced at the door, hoping that whatever kept Eloise busy would keep her away for as long as possible. "I've never asked you, Dallas, but how old are you?"

Dallas' eyes crinkled at the corners. "You didn't check my paperwork when you hired me?"

"No, I was a little pissed at you, to be honest."

"Sorry," Dallas said, but there was nothing apologetic in his humorous gaze. "I'm twenty-eight. Well, almost. If I make it through the next two weeks, I'll be twenty-eight."

"Lord almighty!" Cole pushed himself up to his elbows, readjusting his position to see his young friend better. "You're but a child."

"That depends on who you ask." Dallas helped him sit up, resting his back against the wall. "From a human point of view,

I'm a mature adult, but compared to you, Ruslan and your brother, I'm a single-cell organism."

"Right you are." Cole smiled, shaking his head. "For someone so young, you are quite a skilled fighter. How long have you been training?"

Dallas glanced at him and turned away, his gaze growing distant.

"Most of my life, I guess," he whispered, his blood-stained fingers tugging at the hem of his shirt. "As a child, I was bullied a lot… For my age, I was a short and scrawny boy with no parents to protect me." He rubbed the back of his neck, the chain on his wrists clinking with his move. "At the time, learning martial arts seemed to be the only way I could protect myself… or maybe I just needed enough confidence to stand up to the bullies. Since I didn't have anyone who cared to send me to a martial arts school, I started to train on my own by watching videos and different tutorials online. Luckily, nowadays, you can find everything you need on the internet." He smiled at Cole, the sadness in his gaze sending a wave of warmth through Cole's heart. "When I was finally on my own and found my first job, I joined a martial arts school, and proceeded with formal training."

"How about the programming?" Cole asked, looking at his friend with respect. "Did you put yourself through college to get your Master's?"

Dallas nodded. "I studied, taking as many classes as I could while working as a night guard to pay for my education and living. It took me longer, and it wasn't easy, but I'm glad I did it. Once I graduated and got my first job as a software developer, I never looked back… Well, at least financially."

He fell silent, and Cole didn't ask anything else, remorse clawing at his heart. "Dammit, kid," he said at length. "Why did you insist on going with us? You are young, smart and strong-minded. You have your entire human life ahead of you…" He pressed his lips into a firm line, muscle twitching in his jaw. "My brother and I are a thousand years old. We've lived hundreds of lives and seen more than one person can handle. Besides, Damian is a Destiny Enforcer. He has no choice but to do what he does. You had a choice to stay home and be safe, to live a normal life. Why did you have to choose pain?"

"You're right. Maybe Damian didn't have a choice," Dallas replied, fidgeting with the rusty links of his chain, "but you did. You also could have stayed back with your maker. Why did you go?"

"Because Damian is my only brother, my flesh and blood." Cole glanced at Dallas sideways. "We stand together no matter what. Always. If Damian died…" His voice cracked and faded into silence. He looked toward the door, his hand clutching at his silver-wrapped chest, but he barely noticed the pain of the burns. "I don't think I want to live in this world if my brother is not in it. I would never forgive myself if I stayed behind and something happened to him. Besides, it's about River, Luc and Jamie. The lives of my friends are at stake, and I'll be damned if I do nothing to save them."

Dallas nodded slowly, staring down at his chained hands. "I know it sounds weird probably, because I met you just a few months ago," he said after a short pause, "but for the first time in my life, I realized what it feels like to have a family and people who care about you. I lived alone for years without knowing what I was missing." He raised his face, meeting Cole's gaze. "You, Damian and Ruslan are *my* family, even if you don't consider me yours, and I would do anything to keep you safe…" He bit his lip, lowering his eyes.

Cole didn't say anything, a thick lump stuck in his throat. Dallas' lips twitched a little as he observed his reaction.

"You think I didn't notice what you two were doing when we traveled across the forest?" A wide grin appeared on Dallas' face, twinkles of humor igniting in his eyes. "Every time when we stopped for the night, you and Damian each took a shift guarding our camp, but you never woke me up, allowing me to sleep a full six hours."

"You're human," Cole replied with a shrug. "You needed it more than us." He threw a reproachful glance at Dallas and laughed softly, pushing him on his shoulder. "Dammit, boy, just lay down and get some rest now. Something tells me that soon you're not going to have this option."

Cole folded his arms across his chest and closed his eyes, willing for the floor beneath him to stop swimming and wobbling. The soft jingle of the chain told him that Dallas lay down, and a few minutes later, his heartbeat slowed down, and his breathing became even. Despite the nonstop pain in his tortured body, little by little, Cole drifted off to sleep.

CHAPTER 15

~ DAMIAN BLAKE ~

Damian didn't pay attention to how long he'd been walking across the valley. The scenery remained the same, and a narrow path that was weaving and circling around the hills seemed to be endless. He didn't stop for the night or even for a short break, halting once in a while only to check the directions with the magical device the Lady Gatekeeper had left for him. Since Dallas had Zabava's backpack on him when he disappeared, Damian had nothing to eat, but he didn't feel the hunger, his mind focused on one thing only—finding Cole and Dallas as soon as possible.

By the time the last rays of the setting sun touched the land, Damian climbed on top of a hill and observed his surroundings. From this elevated position, he noticed a small village positioned at the edge of the valley, backing into another forest. He lowered himself to the ground and stared at the peaceful view unfolding before him. For the first time since Cole disappeared, he felt how truly worn out he was. Exhausted by the fight with the demons and by an over thirty-hour walk, he could barely feel his feet. And the magical exhaustion wasn't doing him any favors either.

"You have to take a break, Commander," a high-pitched voice squeaked next to him, causing Damian to flinch and snap in the direction of the sound. A German Shepherd puppy sat by his side, a wide, doggish grin splitting his face.

"Zhulik! You need to stop sneaking up on people like this," he grumbled, stroking the pup's thick fur.

"Sneaking up? Hardly." Zhulik snorted, covering his eyes with his paw. "You're so drained that a crash of rhinos could run right by you, and you wouldn't even notice."

"I'm surprised I can still stand upright," Damian muttered, staring straight ahead. "Where were you when I was fighting the demons? God knows, I could have used your help then."

"Sorry, I was a bit preoccupied from the moment you decided to visit the Land of Dreams despite your orders," Zhulik growled, pushing him on his side a little stronger than Damian liked. "Anyway, while you were dancing with the itsy-bitsy demons, I was playing messenger-boy, delivering a message about your desperate situation to Svyatobor."

"Oh," Damian mumbled, not fully processing everything the gargoyle said. "My gratitude…"

Zhulik sighed, shaking his head. "Tonight, you must get at least a few hours of sleep, and you have to eat something before you continue."

"I can't," Damian objected. He stared in the direction of the village, wondering if he could make it there. "I don't know what happened to Cole and Dallas, and every minute can make a difference."

"Yeah, right." Zhulik rolled his eyes, cocking his head. "A lot of good you'll do to your brother if you're exhausted to the point where you can't lift a finger." He pointed forward with his paw and gave Damian a meaningful stare. "You can see the first house at the edge of the valley, right?"

"Yes, so what?" Damian shrugged and winced as his aching muscles responded to his move.

"We're in a magical nexus, so you don't need to worry about exposing the World of Magic," Zhulik continued, sounding almost serene. "It's another hour's worth of walking there, I believe. Don't waste time and teleport."

"Fine," Damian muttered and snapped his fingers. The world jerked and tilted, and dizziness assailed him. But when he could see clearly again, he was still sitting on top of the same hill, Zhulik staring at him with sarcasm in his glowing eyes.

"Like I said." The puppy waved his paw dismissively. "The proof of the pudding is in the eating, Commander." The air around Zhulik shimmered with azure sparkles, and the dog vanished, replaced by a massive stone gargoyle in his natural form. He pushed Damian on his shoulder, gesturing at his own back. "Climb up. I'll take us there in a jiffy."

Damian scrambled to his feet with a laborious groan and climbed up on the gargoyle's back. Lying flat, he wrapped his arms around Zhulik's thick neck, pressing his cheek against his cold stone hide.

"Close your eyes and hold on to me as tight as you can, Commander," Zhulik said, sounding a bit grumpy. "And if you utter a single word to anyone that I let you ride on my back, I'll kill you myself."

"You will not," Damian whispered, his eyelids suddenly so heavy that he couldn't keep his eyes open.

"Probably not, but that's not the point," Zhulik grumbled, tones of humor surfacing in his voice. "Hold on."

The hill vanished from beneath him, and for a split second, Damian felt as if he was hanging in midair, supported by nothing. Then he hit the ground hard with his head and back, and everything went blank.

* * *

"Open your eyes, young man." Someone shook him gently, and a light slap on his cheek followed.

He groaned and cracked his eyelids open to see an old woman leaning over him, an expression of concern reflected on her weather-beaten face. She grabbed his arms and endeavored to pull him up, but quickly gave up and sat back on her heels, tucking the strand of her gray hair under her flowery kerchief.

"You're a little too..." She stopped mid-sentence as if looking for a better word and shook her head, pursing her lips. Her eyes, too bright and youthful for her age, crinkled at the corners. "You're a bit too heavy for me, son. Can you get up on your own?"

Damian pushed himself into a sitting position and rubbed the back of his head, cursing the dull headache and the exhaustion. With the help of the old woman, he rose to his feet and halted, swaying a little. He stood at the edge of the village he had seen from the hilltop, in front of the first house. Night had descended upon the land, and it was hard to see farther than a few hundred yards, but the place seemed to be small—no more than a dozen homes.

The woman's gaze moved up and down his body as if sizing him up, and an appreciative smile brought forth a net of thin wrinkles on her face. "You're a big boy, aren't you?" she murmured, opening the gate for him. "Please, come in. You fell off your horse and hit your head. Let me check your wounds first, and then I'll get you some food and let you rest before you continue on your journey."

"A horse?" Damian mumbled, flabbergasted, just now noticing a giant black stallion nibbling on the grass a few feet away by the fence. *"Goddammit, Zhulik! Did you have to turn into such a tall horse and throw me off to boot?"*

"Hehehehe." Zhulik's laughter sounded in his mind. *"Seemed like a good idea at the time. And I didn't throw you off. You did that all by yourself, so stop blaming everyone around you for your own*

failures." The stallion shook his head, his long mane flying in rich waves. *"You'll thank me later, Commander."*

"Thank you, ma'am." Damian turned toward the woman, inclining his head in a respectful bow.

He followed the old lady inside but halted in the doorway, carefully observing the large room illuminated by a single candle sitting in the middle of a small table. To his surprise, the house was cold, a smell of dust lingering in the air as if no one had lived here for a while. Two doors stood ajar, one leading into a bedroom and the second one into a kitchen, which seemed to be as dark and cold as the rest of her home.

"Ma'am, eh?" The woman gestured at a chair, turning to him. "Take a seat," she said, her voice sounding cold and commanding, "and before we start, do explain to me what a Destiny Enforcer is doing in the Land of Dreams unannounced."

Damian's jaw dropped as he stared at the old woman in shock.

"Destiny Enforcers have the right to visit any magical nexus if it's necessary to carry out their mission," he said, lowering himself onto a chair. "We can't be anywhere near the Isle Buyan, though. That's the only limitation we have."

"Two rules which you have broken without thinking twice. You do not have a Destiny Council assigned mission because I would've been notified, and you have been so close to the World Tree that I can still detect the traces of its magical energy on your skin." The woman leaned closer to him across the table, her eyes igniting with a bright blue light. "Explain yourself at once." She straightened, folding her arms. "Or by the gods, I will force you to do so." She waved her hand, and the yellow glimmer of a cloaking spell filled the room. "Now!"

A powerful wave of her magical energy wrapped around Damian, turning the pain in his head into scorching, liquid anguish. He groaned, squeezing his temples with his hands, and bent forward, nearly hitting the tabletop with his forehead. The pain seemed familiar, reminding him of the sensation he had felt every time Magnus yanked him out of the human world into the Destiny Council Realm, but magnified tenfold.

He tried to fight her brutal mind-intrusion, but all his efforts were to no avail. Even though he didn't think she was more powerful than him, somehow, she managed to tap into the only element of his magic that made him subservient to the Destiny Council—the part of his soul that had been fused with the Board of Destiny.

Damian raised his eyes at her, his vision blurry from pain. "Please..." he groaned, his chest shuddering with shallow breaths as he struggled to breathe. "I can't... please..."

She released her magical grip on his mind and rose to her feet, bracing her hands against the table. Damian moaned and fell back in his chair, gasping for air, his eyes still watering.

"That was just a little taste of what I can do to you should you get smart with me, Enforcer. Speak now," she demanded, leaning forward. "I don't have patience for your kind."

"My lady..." He got up and swayed, grabbing the edge of the table to stay upright. Then he let go carefully and inclined his head, pressing his fist to his chest. "My lady, Vasilisa the Wise, guardian of the Sacred Garden, daughter of the mighty Black Voron."

As he stated her name and proper title, she cocked her head slightly, an expression of surprise changing her hard face. Then she flicked her wrist, gesturing for him to proceed. "Your name and title, Enforcer."

"I'm Commander Damian Blake, Shadow Enforcer to Lord Magnus," he introduced himself, carefully gauging her reaction. "You're right. I'm not here on an official assignment. But although this mission is deeply personal to me, I believe the outcome will benefit not only the people I care about but everyone who stands on the side of Light."

"Personal?" she hollered, slamming her fist against the table, nearly extinguishing the candle. "How dare you lie to me? Who do you think I am?"

With a shake of his head, Damian raised his hands, staggering a step backward. She snapped her fingers, and the air around her shimmered with bright blue sparkles emitting an eye-watering light. Once the light dissipated, the old lady was gone, replaced by a young woman dressed in ancient Russian armor, a short sword in her hand. Her long blonde hair was styled in two braids, which snaked down her chest all the way to her waist, and her electric-blue eyes shone with rising anger.

"My lady, please, let me explain—"

"Destiny Enforcers do not have anything personal," she shouted, interrupting him, resting the tip of her sword at the hollow of his throat. "When a person assumes the mantel of an Enforcer, they relinquish all their personal possessions and sever all ties with the world of humans. Besides that, their emotions are stripped, at least partially. There can be nothing personal in your miserable life, Blake."

Damian spread his arms but then dropped them and shook his head, having no energy for anything else.

"Would you let me speak?" he asked quietly, bracing himself for pain. "Or do you prefer to answer your own questions, Vasilisa the Wise?"

She fell silent, blinking at him furiously, but lowered her sword. "Fine. Speak."

"I don't have any personal possessions, but this mission is personal to me," Damian said so softly that she had to lean forward to be closer to him. "I'm a Destiny Enforcer with centuries of experience under my belt, but my heart is not empty." He averted his gaze, an already familiar, suffocating wave of internal torment squeezing his throat, making it hard to breathe. "I have no idea why I am like this... not like the other Enforcers, but it is what it is."

In his usual frank and concise manner, he told her everything that had happened to him since the fight under the Old Ladoga fortress, and why he was in the Land of Dreams, breaking direct orders and every rule he could think of. This time, she didn't interrupt him, but as he proceeded with his story, the flames of anger vanished from her blue eyes and her features softened. When he finished, she approached him and craned her neck, gazing at him with unconcealed curiosity. Reaching up, she moved her fingers over his cheek, pushing his hair out of his face.

"You're right... I've never seen an Enforcer like you... To be completely honest with you, I haven't seen many normal people like you either," she whispered, dropping her hand. "So, you're risking everything to save the lives of two Wardens who are your friends and a human woman with whom you're in love. How very loyal of you... how romantic..."

"I'm not in lo—" Vasilisa chuckled, rolling her eyes, and he cut himself off, averting his gaze. "Yes, my lady. Loyal and romantic—it's me."

"But what shocked me the most in your story was the part about your brother," she mused, ignoring the tones of sarcasm in his voice. She sat down, her chainmail clinking with her every move. "Your younger brother is an ancient vampire—the very thing you've been taught to hate and destroy—yet you walked for over thirty hours without stop, stretching yourself to the limit, just to find him faster so you could save his undead life?"

"Yes, my lady," Damian replied, a dull ache spreading in his chest at the thought of his brother and Dallas. "Cole is not an ordinary vampire, and he's my only brother. I would walk to the edge of the earth to see him safe."

She cursed in old Russian, leaning sideways against the table, and a chain of emotions flashed across her face so fast he couldn't distinguish any of them. Then she sighed and gestured for him to sit down. He lowered himself heavily onto a chair, feeling at the end of his rope.

"Fine," she muttered after a short while. "You convinced me. I will help you save your brother, and then we'll talk about your friends when you're in a more... um... agreeable state of mind." She drummed her fingers against the table. "Now, tell me where your precious vamp is."

Damian channeled his magic, but it took him a while to gather enough of it to summon the magical device. Then he placed the saucer and the apple on the table and touched it, asking to show him Cole's location. Vasilisa's eyes widened for a moment, but she didn't say anything and switched her attention to the saucer, observing the view of a half-demolished wall surrounding a castle reflected in its surface.

"I know this city." She glanced at Damian, disbelief written all over her face. "If I didn't fully trust that this ancient magical device would show me the correct location of your brother, I would have never believed it."

"What is this place?" asked Damian, an expectation of more trouble coiling in the pit of his stomach.

"The former City of Gold," she whispered. "Or what's left of it after the Ancient Master of Power, Mrak Delar, was done with his vengeance on the late King Alexander. It happened quite a while back, about"—she twirled her wrist, her gaze growing distant—"five or six years ago, I believe. As a Destiny Enforcer, you surely heard the story."

"No, my lady," Damian replied, thinking back to those days. "At the time, I was under the 'no one' status, so I wasn't in touch with anyone in the Destiny Council realm."

Her eyebrows rose, her mouth shaping the letter 'O'. "Wait," she breathed, leaning closer to him. "I think I know who you truly are, Commander Blake. I've heard about a Gypsy Witch and a Destiny Enforcer, and their legendary love story. That was you, wasn't it?" She got up slowly, looking down at him with unconcealed interest. "Dmitri Chernov. That's your true name, isn't it? And your brother is Nikolai Chernov, presently Cole Adams—the King of the Arizona Vampire Court."

"Yes, my lady."

"Heaven and Earth…" she exhaled, scratching the back of her head, but then sat down and continued, "Anyway, as you're aware, there are three large kingdoms in the Land of Dreams, governed by three sisters. The Kingdom of Copper is ruled by Queen Anna. Her sister, Queen Olga, takes care of the Kingdom of Silver, but the Kingdom of Gold was taken over by King Alexander, an evil tyrant. It's a long story, but I'll make it short since time is of the essence. In his infinite hubris and stupidity, King Alexander went against Master Mrak Delar, and that was the last thing he did. The Ancient Master of Power killed the evil king. The army, led by his friends, breached the walls surrounding the castle, and the city fell."

She tapped the saucer with her finger, gazing down at the view, and bit her lip.

"What happened after?" Damian asked. "Who's in charge of the Kingdom of Gold now?"

"Queen Lada, the youngest of sisters," Vasilisa replied. "But she chose not to restore the original capital. She believed the walls of the old city were infused with the blood, pain and suffering of her people, and she didn't want any part of it. With the help of her other siblings, she built a new City of Gold at the opposite end of her kingdom and has left the old castle unoccupied for all these years. But it seems like now, someone found a use for it." She readjusted her long, thick braids, a shadow of unease darkening her features. "If your brother is held in the old castle, it's not going to be easy to break him out. The place is still a formidable fortress, despite the damage. Besides, you know the City of Gold is miles away from here, don't you?"

"I don't care how far it is. As I said, I'll walk to the end of the world, and I'll take this fortress apart brick by brick if I have to," Damian replied, looking at her with cold determination.

"Is that before or after you fall off your horse?" She raised her eyebrows, mockery in her blue eyes. "Mighty warrior my ass."

"You're right." Damian got up and walked toward the window. He halted there and crossed his arms behind his back, staring at the dark village street outside. "I'm injured, exhausted physically, and drained magically. You exercising your control over me didn't do me any favors either… But I'll do what I can with whatever I have left in me."

She shrugged. "I did what I had to do. The Land of Dreams is my domain, and I don't like uninvited visitors from the Destiny Council realm."

Damian didn't reply, staring out the window. As he noticed the black stallion pacing in front of the house, he brushed his hand over his tattoo, calling to his gargoyle. *"Zhulik, come inside, please."*

With a light pop, the gargoyle materialized next to him in his true form. He turned toward Vasilisa, and a warning growl rumbled in his stone chest. She tilted her head, and her gaze darted from Zhulik to Damian, one corner of her lips lifting.

"You're full of surprises, Enforcer," she muttered dryly. "You have a gargoyle bound to you?"

"My gargoyle is free to leave any time he wishes," Damian objected, placing his hand on Zhulik's head. "He's my friend, not my servant." Zhulik shifted closer to him and sat down with a heavy thud, pressing his side against his leg, but the growl died down in his chest.

Vasilisa pursed her lips, her gaze darting from Damian to Zhulik as she carefully approached them. She opened a small leather bag attached to her belt and pulled out a vial with a clear liquid inside. Keeping an eye on the gargoyle, she offered it to Damian.

"Drink it, Commander," she said, shifting away from Zhulik as his lips curved in a silent snarl. Then she threw her hands up, for a moment looking like a desperate little girl. "You know it'll make him feel stronger. Why are you still growling at me?"

Zhulik snickered and winked at Damian. "I didn't like what she did to you earlier, Commander," he said, shifting from paw to paw, "but the potion is safe. You need your strength back, and you can't heal yourself at the moment. Drink it."

Damian took the vial and held his breath as its powerful magical energy spread through him. He uncorked it and brought it to his lips, gazing at Vasilisa over the rim of the bottle.

"Bottoms up." She gestured for him to proceed.

"I hope you are not going to turn me into a baby-goat," he muttered.

"Tempting," she murmured, "but not today."

"In that case, *za zdorovie*," he said the traditional Russian toast and swallowed the contents of the vial in one gulp.

For a heartbeat, nothing happened, but just when he thought it didn't work, a powerful burst of magical energy surged through him, energizing his every cell. His muscles tensed, and he threw his head back, a scream of joy escaping his lips. He collapsed to his knees, and his body arched, his wings expanding behind his back. The floor trembled under him as the energy of his element flooded his body. All the cuts and bruises started to close with incredible speed, his strength returning to him with every breath he took.

"Svarog almighty," Vasilisa whispered, carefully touching the black feathers of his wings with her fingertips, her eyes wide. "You're a Child of Earth."

Damian got up and rolled his shoulders, noticing that the soreness and weakness were gone. "At your service, ma'am," he said, a thin layer of sarcasm in his voice. Once his wings disappeared, he pressed his fist to his chest and inclined his head in a formal bow. "Thank you for your help, my lady."

"Are you mine to command?" she asked, giving him an arched stare, but since Damian remained silent, she continued, "We'll speak about that later. In the meantime, if you feel better, we should probably visit the City of Gold."

She placed her hand on Damian's shoulder and snapped her fingers, causing the room to spin around him. In the last moment, he felt a soft burning in his tattoo as the gargoyle merged into it, and everything disappeared in a swirl of colors.

CHAPTER 16

~ DAMIAN BLAKE ~

A gust of cold breeze rushed through the valley, howling in the partially demolished section of the wall. Standing on top of a tall hill, Damian could see the castle and a part of the abandoned city behind it. The houses stood dark and empty, some of them partly destroyed either by people or time and the unkind weather of the Kingdom of Gold.

The castle was just as gloomy, its facade wrapped in slithering vines and ivy, its massive double doors warped and broken as if someone had blasted them with a wrecking ball. The golden cupolas had lost their shine and were covered in strange green stains. Some of the intricate golden ornaments that used to decorate its walls were coated in a thick layer of dirt.

"Do you feel it?" Vasilisa whispered, pointing at the castle.

Damian nodded. He didn't even need to use his other sight to know that a powerful shield of dark magical energy encircled the former City of Gold, following the perimeter of the wall. He pressed his palm against the tattoo on his arm.

"Zhulik, can you check what's going on?" he asked, and once the gargoyle materialized next to him, he squatted, placing his hand on his rocky shoulder. "Be careful, my friend, try not to set off any magical alarms."

He was expecting some kind of sarcastic comeback from Zhulik, but he just nodded and vanished with a soft pop. He returned a minute later, his widened eyes shining brighter than usual.

"Oh, Commander," he breathed, his wide chest shuddering with short breaths as if a solid-rock monster needed air to survive. "You shouldn't be going there." His gaze darted to Vasilisa, and he added, "And neither should you, Vasilisa, if you truly are wise."

Vasilisa threw a troubled look at Damian, disbelief clear on her face. "What did you see, gargoyle?" she asked, and a soft golden light wrapped around her body, following the flow of her dark red cloak.

"A powerful layer of wards and protection spells encapsulates the castle and a large area surrounding it into an enormous dome," replied Zhulik, speaking to Damian, stubbornly ignoring Vasilisa. "This magic is so intricate and complex that it couldn't have been cast by a regular wizard or even a Master of the Dark Arts. Only a god with incredible power could've erected such a potent defense line."

Moving slowly like in an overpowering nightmare, Damian turned back to the city and scanned it with his other sight, sending some of his elemental energy toward his eyes to reinforce it. Just as Zhulik said, a dome of magical energy encapsulated the castle, glowing with a soft purple light. Thin lines ran up the contraption, meeting somewhere high above the tallest tower. The space between the lines was infested with thousands of tiny runes and sigils, but none of them looked familiar to him.

"Perun almighty," he whispered, cold sweat covering his forehead.

"Do you think your brother is still alive?" Vasilisa's voice broke the troubling train of his thoughts.

Damian closed his eyes, opening his mind to the connection with his brother. *"Cole... Nikolai..."* His call disappeared into nothing. But even though Cole didn't reply, Damian could feel their weak link somewhere far in the back of his mind, like a dying flame of a candle.

"He's alive," he whispered. "I can't communicate with him because something blocks our blood bond, but I would have known if he was dead."

"Something?" Vasilisa chuckled mirthlessly, pointing at the dome of magical energy. "These runes can sever any psychic link, even as powerful as a blood bond between a thousand-year-old vamp and his human companion..." She glanced at Damian and shrugged. "Even if the companion is not very human."

"Zhulik thinks these wards were conjured by a god," said Damian, unable to take his eyes off the glyphs glowing dimly in the surrounding darkness.

"Not just any god." Vasilisa stepped closer to Damian, her left hand landing on the pommel of her sword. "One of the old ones—an ancient god—if I am not mistaken. Even I'm not familiar with these runes..."

Damian switched his attention to the magical barrier, slowly searching its surface for anything that could help him find a weak point but finding none.

"The old ones... The great ancient power... What if the elusive master who stands behind Koschei and Donna Luna... What if... He has always wanted to capture Cole alive... What if... what if..."

The thoughts danced in his mind, tripping over each other, and he couldn't focus on anything helpful. As his eyes kept moving from side to side, up and down, checking every single glowing symbol, desperate to find a way to his brother, one of the runes drew his attention. Just like everything else, he didn't know what it was, yet there was something familiar about it, and the more he looked at it, the more he was positive he knew what it was.

"Vasilisa," he called, lowering to one knee. He grabbed a small twig and drew the rune on a small patch of sand. "This rune... this is not a rune at all, is it?"

"Why—," she started to say, but cut herself off, lowering to her knees next to him. "You're right." She glanced up at him, her finger tracing the shape of the symbol. "It's not a rune, and if I remove a few of the lines..." She quickly erased a few elements of the design and sat back on her heels, gazing at him with a question in her eyes.

"I've seen it before... Maybe not a hundred percent the exact symbol but something very similar," he muttered. "It happened when one of my missions took me to the Welsh Otherworld."

He stared at the rune, old memories emerging in his mind, calming down the storm of thoughts. He remembered that mission. It took place shortly before he and Cossack were attacked in the Carpathian Mountains by the Hutsuls covenant, and he lost his memories. He recalled how much Magnus didn't want him to take the Otherworld assignment, but Lord Ulrich Aramir—the Head of the High Council at the time—insisted on Damian and his team taking care of the situation themselves, and Magnus didn't have enough power to object.

"Gwyn ap Nudd," he whispered. "I remember seeing this symbol glowing on the door into Gwyn's palace in the Otherworld." He looked at Vasilisa, noticing the shocked expression on her face. "You know Gwyn is one of the old ones. A long time ago, he was partially stripped of his godly powers, though."

She nodded slowly, her fingers fidgeting with her braid. "Despite his reputation, Gwyn would never stand on the side of Darkness," she said quietly. "He couldn't have done it."

"Agreed," Damian muttered, his focus back on the wards. Now that he saw the symbol, he could easily find it again, and as he looked at it, another familiar glyph drew his attention. "What the hell?" He leaned forward a little, narrowing his eyes. "I'll be damned…"

"What do you see?" Vasilisa asked, squeezing his elbow.

Damian took a twig and added two more symbols to the drawing, one on either side of it. Staring at the picture in disbelief, he shook his head, his hand rising slowly toward the rune branded on his shoulder.

"Does it look to you like these three symbols are connected into one, creating a large monogram?" he asked, his throat dry.

She nodded.

"I have no idea what the symbol on the right represents, but I know this one," he whispered.

Carefully, he erased a few lines of the design and bit his lip, his mind still refusing to accept and process the reality. He pressed his palm over his brand, sending a touch of his magical energy through it, and the rune of the Shadow Enforcer lit up with a soft, white light. In the middle of it, a small image glowed slightly brighter, closely resembling the glyph he drew in the sand.

Vasilisa gasped, her fingers brushing over the Shadow Enforcer's rune on his shoulder. "What does this sign mean?"

"Lord Magnus," Damian whispered. "It's his symbol. I'm his Shadow Enforcer, so my brand carries a small part of it, too."

"Is he—"

"No, never." Damian straightened, brushing sand off his knee. "I can't say that I always understand and agree with what Magnus is doing, but I know whatever he's doing, he does it for the good of the realm… all realms. His soul is not dark, Vasilisa."

She glanced at him, the crease between her eyebrows becoming deeper. "How about the third symbol?" she asked, switching her attention to the magical dome. "Do you know what it represents?"

Damian shook his head. "No idea. I've never seen it before."

THE SHADOW CURSE

He moved his hand up, ready to rake it through his hair in a habitual move, but then froze with his fingers digging into his scalp as a crazy thought rushed through his mind.

"Vasilisa," he whispered, a raspiness in his voice making him clear his throat. "I'm going to try something, and you're going to think I'm insane, but this is the only thing I can think of at this moment. If I am wrong, I will activate the wards."

Vasilisa shrugged, slight twinkles of humor igniting in her eyes. "Look at it this way, Enforcer. We're fresh out of choices here, so if your idea won't work, we'll have to use brute force, anyway. At this point, who cares if you activate this monstrosity of wards? Go for it. A crazy idea is better than nothing."

Damian raised his hand, ready to teleport, but then lowered it and turned toward her. "Vasilisa," he said quietly. "I don't know how the wards will react if I activate them accidentally. If something happens to me, promise me you will get Cole and Dallas out of there and take them to safety."

She stared at him intently for a few long seconds, a fleeting shadow crossing her face, turning it harder. "You have my word, Enforcer," she said finally. "I'll do everything in my power to save your brother and your friend."

He gave her a curt nod and turned to his gargoyle. "Stay with Vasilisa, Zhulik," he said softly. "If something goes wrong, take care of Cole for me."

The gargoyle dropped his head and shifted from paw to paw, now looking like a sad puppy. "As you wish, Commander," he muttered, not meeting his eyes.

Without saying anything else, Damian snapped his fingers and vanished from the hill. He materialized a few feet away from the magical dome and carefully approached it, trying to keep his magical energy under control. It didn't take him long to find the three symbols he was looking for.

He pressed his hand to his throat, his heart thudding heavily in his chest. "It's now or never," he whispered to himself. Channeling his Destiny Enforcer's magic, he placed his palm over the brand on his shoulder and opened his connection with the Board of Destiny. As its powerful magical energy surged through him, he collected as much as he could in his right hand and carefully touched the symbol representing Magnus on the dome.

"Please, Magnus, just this one time..." His thought faded as he wasn't sure what he was asking Magnus to do in his silent prayer.

Holding his breath, he sent a powerful blast of his magical energy through the symbol, commanding the wards to unlock. The symbol lit up brighter under his touch and the entire contraption started to vibrate, producing a low buzzing noise. A wave of white light spread through it, traveling like ripples on the surface of a lake. The purple glimmer of the lines and runes turned white, infused with his magic. The buzz grew higher and higher, finally morphing into a single high-pitched tone. The sound rang through the dark valley, echoing through the ghostly city, and then gradually died down.

A dark hole materialized in the place where Damian had touched the dome, and within a few seconds, the entire contraption vanished, leaving behind just a few dimly glowing sparks that were slowly falling to the ground, dissipating on their way down.

Damian released a ragged breath, staggering an unsteady step back as he glanced over his shoulder at Vasilisa. He had expected anything but that, and judging by the stupefied expression on Vasilisa's face, she hadn't expected it either. She stood on the hilltop, staring intently at the city, her right hand still rested on the pommel of her sword.

"Cole..." Now that the wards were down, Damian probed his link with his brother carefully. *"Nikolai, please say something..."*

"Dima?" Cole's voice sounded weak and shaky in his mind, and an overwhelming wave of emotions flooded their connec-

tion—happiness, longing, fear, remorse. *"Dima! Where are you? Are you okay?"*

"I'm here, little bro," he replied, projecting the image of his surroundings through their link. *"I'm coming for you..."*

"Alkonost was right, Dima. My past has caught up with me..." Cole's voice trembled and disappeared. *"Dallas is with me, but our situation is... I'm disabled by some strange restraints that make me weaker than a sickly human. Severe blood loss debilitated Dallas, and he's in no condition to fight either. It's Eloise who holds us prisoners in this castle, but it's not her who wields the magic. I don't know who her master is, but he is on the way here, bro, and I don't think I'll survive—"*

"I believe he's an old god," Damian replied. *"Try not to do anything to provoke Eloise, little bro. Do whatever she wants from you, just lie low and give me a few minutes to figure it out. I'll get you out of there before he comes."*

"Dima, I'm sorry, but this is the end..." A wave of warmth infused with deep despair rushed through their connection. *"I wish I could see you one more time before—"*

"Don't say that!" Damian's heart halted in his chest, pain and fear twisting his gut. *"Nikolai! Please! Just a few more minutes, brother mine."*

The answer never came.

Damian stared at the tall wall surrounding the castle, his chest shuddering with short breaths as he couldn't fill his lungs with oxygen. Noticing dirty swirls of a fog-like substance materializing right next to the demolished part of the wall, he forced himself to calm down and focus on the task at hand. Gradually, the fog became thicker and darker, taking on a solid shape, and soon a dense line of monsters armed to the teeth with swords, axes, and other weapons stepped out of the shadows. A menacing army of demons in their natural form stood between him and his brother, their eyes glowing with an ominous purple glimmer. The next gust of wind brought the suffocating stench of sulfur and the reek of demonic essence.

With a light pop, Vasilisa materialized next to him, placing her hand on his shoulder. "Damian, all these monsters"—she moved her hand from side to side, pointing at the dark wall of the demonic army—"are demons from different demonic realms. No way you and I can fight them and live to tell the tale."

"I know," he whispered, numbness spreading through his chest.

"We need help," she continued, squeezing his shoulder. "We need purifying Fire, a lot of it, which neither you nor I wield, but I know someone who does."

"I can use the purifying light of Creation," Damian replied without taking his eyes off the demonic army.

"Come on, Damian," she whispered, her voice almost pleading with him. "Give me fifteen minutes."

"Go…"

She stepped in front of him, blocking the view of the wall. "Don't do something stupid, Enforcer. Wait for my return." She seized his arms and shook him slightly. "Swear to me that you'll wait."

He looked down at her, and a sad smile touched his lips. "I can't promise you that, my lady, but I can promise something else," he said quietly. "You see this castle?" He pointed over her shoulder. "My brother is in there, and he doesn't have fifteen minutes. A bunch of low-life demonic assholes is all that stands between us." His smile turned into a dark, ferocious snarl. "I swear to you, I'll kill them all or die trying."

She bit her lip, a deep frown settling on her face hardened by many battles. "Hold your ground for as long as you can, Commander. I'll be back as soon as possible with the help we need." She snapped her fingers and vanished.

Damian glanced at Zhulik, meeting his blazing gaze. "It's up to us now," he muttered, channeling his magic. "Are you ready, my friend?"

A dangerous growl sounded in the gargoyle's chest in reply. Damian laughed—a dark and ominous sound he didn't recognize as his own—and rushed toward the wall, summoning his daggers as he went. The gargoyle ran by his side, growing in size with every step he took, until he was as tall as a horse.

The demons roared, and the amount of demonic essence they emitted tripled. As they charged toward them, the ground trembled. Deep cracks materialized around them, flames and dark smoke rising from within, and Damian knew Mother Earth couldn't tolerate these demonic abominations, despising them as much as he did. He channeled the light of Creation through his daggers, entwining it with the elemental energy of Earth.

Before the first demon reached him, Damian came to a sharp halt and spread his arms, a single word escaping his lips, *"Illucious…"*

A powerful blast wave of purifying energy expanded around him, rushing in all directions. It washed over the few demons nearest to him. They howled in pain and twirled in place, their terrifying limbs flailing, their malformed bodies set ablaze. The rest of them, however, kept running forward, quickly surrounding him. He spun in place, his glowing daggers charged with elemental energy and the light of Creation spreading death and destruction with every move he made.

Zhulik rushed through the mob of demons like a steamroller, his stone hide impervious to their claws, fangs, as well as to their blades. In no time, the air was filled with the reek of demonic goo, fumes of sulfur and the stench of demonic essence. The bangs of weapons, the roars and growls, the profanities shouted in different tongues, and the cries of pain and anger turned into a nonstop blaring ruckus.

The demons assailed Damian from every direction, closing

over him like a disgusting tidal wave. Although he could still parry their massive blades, a few of them managed to slash his back and arms with their claws. With all-consuming fury catalyzed by adrenalin rushing through him, he barely even acknowledged the pain. He swung his daggers, decapitating the abomination in front of him. A fountain of demonic goo washed over him, nearly suffocating him with its stench, but he didn't stop, cutting and punching his way toward the broken wall.

"*Exitius!*" he shouted, his magically magnified voice rising over the cacophony of the battle.

As the blast wave of his spell expanded around him, it pushed the lines of demons away from him, giving him an opportunity to take a breath and regroup. Sweat mixed in with blood ran down his face, flooding his eyes, and he wiped it off with the back of his hand. He was almost there... Another few dozen monsters, and he'd be at the wall. Zhulik materialized next to him, his rocky side pressing against Damian's arm. The gargoyle lowered his head and growled—the sound so deadly and fierce that the demons shuddered, a cloud of whispers rising over them.

"Damian!" A female voice magnified by magic boomed above him, causing him to raise his head and hold his breath in awe. A large group of wyverns was quickly approaching from the valley, their powerful wings cutting through the air with a loud hissing noise. Vasilisa rode the wyvern upfront, a sword in her hand. "Take cover, Commander!"

"*Praecidio Amnia,*" Damian whispered, and then channeled more of his magic, moving his hand in a circular motion above his head. "*Praecidio Amnia Circula Archni.*"

As the powerful shield of his protective magic surrounded him, he dropped to his knees, wrapping his arms over his head. Zhulik stepped closer, towering over him, and one more magical barrier, conjured by the gargoyle, manifested over him.

Wyverns barged into the area, flooding it with so much fire that the valley turned into a scorching inferno in a matter of a few heartbeats. The lines of the demonic army trembled. Furious shouts and cries rose to the dark sky together with the clouds of dark smoke. The stench of burned flesh became unbearable, and in combination with the reek of demonic essence, it polluted the air to the point where Damian had a hard time breathing, gasping for air with his mouth open.

Soon, smoke and fire obscured his vision completely, and he lowered his head as much as he could, silently praying for his shield to hold. Soon after, the screams and roars of demons dwindled into complete silence. The heat and smoke dissipated, and Damian was finally able to breathe. Carefully, he straightened and looked around.

The demonic army was gone, hungry flames devouring the last remaining bodies, turning them into puddles of slime. The wyverns landed. Vasilisa dismounted and headed toward him, her sword still in her hand.

"Cole, are you there?" Damian reached out to his brother but received no verbal response. A wave of despair rushed through their connection, nearly crippling him. *"Nikolai..."*

He sprung to his feet and darted toward the opening in the wall, jumping over the slowly disintegrating bodies of demons, weapons and cracks in the ground. Without looking back, he vaulted over the wall and dropped into a crouching stance on the other side, surveying the area.

CHAPTER 17

~ COLE ADAMS ~

Cole woke up with a start and jolted upright, immediately regretting such a sharp move. Debilitating weakness intensified by severe nausea hit him like a sledgehammer, and he doubled up, pressing his hands to his stomach. After a few endless seconds, he started to feel better and allowed himself to straighten his back, stretching his shoulders carefully. Looking around, he tried to determine what had ripped him out of his sleep but couldn't find anything that would make any sense.

The castle stood gloomy and silent, and Dallas lay sprawled on the floor by his side. Cole observed the young man, dread spreading through him. Dallas' suntanned face was beyond pale, appearing almost yellow. Dark shadows were etched under his tightly shut eyes, and his parted lips were dry and colorless. He moaned in his sleep and turned his head to the side, exposing his neck where a thin blue vein pulsed weakly under his skin. His hand rose to his chest, his fingers trembling slightly over a few deep welts and cuts left by demon's claws.

Cole narrowed his eyes and frowned, noticing that the wounds on Dallas' body looked red and inflamed, a slight odor of decay exuding from them. He placed his palm over the young man's forehead, feeling the heat emitted by his body even before he touched him. As soon as his hand came in contact with Dallas' skin, the hunter cracked his eyelids open and jerked away from his touch, his arms rising into a defensive position.

"Shh." Cole brought his finger to his lips, gesturing for Dallas to calm down. "It's just me. Don't be alarmed."

Dallas exhaled with relief and relaxed, resting his back against the wall, his arms wrapping around his bent legs.

"What time is it?" he asked, his teeth chattering a little.

"I don't know," Cole replied, wishing he still had a shirt so he could give it to Dallas.

The cold never bothered him. Since he was a child, he got used to tolerating the discomforts of chilly weather, rain and snow, and right now, being a vampire, he wasn't sensitive to low temperatures at all. Dallas, however, looked like he was freezing.

"Something woke me up," Cole continued, "but I have no idea what it was." He took in Dallas' appearance once more, registering a feverish glimmer in his eyes. "Dallas, be honest with me, please. How are you feeling? Are you okay?"

"I am—," he started but didn't finish the statement, lowering his gaze. "I feel a little off. It's probably nothing. Just the blood loss. That bitch fed on me a few times while you were unconscious. She didn't take a lot of blood, but still..." He shrugged and winced, his hand jerking up to the welts on his chest.

Cole shook his head. "I believe I'm old enough to recognize when a human runs a fever," he said quietly. "I think some of your wounds are infected."

"I don't have a fever," Dallas grumbled, wrapping his arms around his unclad torso. "Your hands are icy cold, and it's freezing here."

Cole was about to reply when a fluctuation in the magical energy field drew his attention. He wasn't experienced enough to know what had created the spike, but he was positive it was somewhere very close to the castle, and somehow, it felt familiar. He tried to get up but was too weak and fell back, closing his eyes as the room danced around him in nauseating waves.

"Dallas," he whispered, motioning with his chin toward the tightly draped window. "See if you can find out what's going on outside, please."

Dallas got up, his moves slow and laborious. The long chain attached to his manacles fell to the floor with a loud clatter, causing him to sway and check his balance. Barely moving his feet, he made his way to the window. It took him a while to rip off the corner of the rag covering it. Once he was done, he rose on his tiptoes and peered outside.

"What do you see?" Cole whispered, leaning forward slightly.

"It's dark," Dallas murmured. "I see a tall wall…" He glanced back at Cole, his eyes widened in disbelief. "I swear it looks like a friggin' medieval fortress—battlements, watchtowers and all…"

"We're in the Land of Dreams." Cole chuckled. "I wouldn't be surprised if we are in some sort of abandoned castle. What else do you see?"

"Light… Purple, white and a little bit of orange…" Dallas narrowed his eyes, staring into the night. "The white light seems to be devouring the purple one."

"Dima…" Cole jerked forward, forgetting about his condition, but then moaned and fell back. A high-pitched tone rang outside, growing stronger and stronger, becoming too much for Cole's sensitive hearing. He groaned, pressing his hands to his ears, but the sound dwindled soon, once again replaced by silence. "Anything else, Dallas?"

Dallas turned back to the window but didn't get a chance to look. The door opened with a loud bang, and Eloise rushed into the room, moving a lot faster than any human could. She seized Dallas' neck and lifted him off the ground as if he were a little kitten and not a fully grown man. He didn't fight her, hanging limply in her strong grip, his tortured gaze never leaving Cole's eyes.

"Yes, Dallas," she said snidely, turning him slightly to see his face. "Anything else you'd like to share with us?"

"Eloise, let him go," Cole hissed, anger rising within him, followed by the feeling of his own helplessness.

"As you wish, darling." She cackled and threw Dallas down, placing considerable strength into her move.

He hit the floor hard and slid a few feet across the warped hardwood panels until Cole caught him. He pulled Dallas up, leaning his back against the wall, and spread his left arm over the young man as if that could help him protect his friend from what was coming. Dallas' head rolled to the side, falling on Cole's shoulder. His chest, however, was shuddering with short breaths, suggesting that he wasn't dead but unconscious. Since there was absolutely nothing he could do to stop Eloise, Cole froze in place and watched her intently as she sauntered her way to him.

"I have news for you, Nicolas," she said flatly, her scarlet eyes glowering at Cole with disdain. "My master is coming to collect you. He should be here in less than thirty minutes…" Her voice faded, and she glanced toward the partially unveiled window. "A lot earlier than I expected, I must say." She turned back to him and seized his chin, her long fingernails digging into his skin, drawing blood. "I was hoping to have quality time with you, but oh, well."

"Your master?" Cole laughed softly. "You mean some insignificant, itsy-bitsy dark wizard, a Master of the Dark Arts at the most?"

"Itsy-bitsy dark wizard?" Her grip became stronger, and he groaned as she forced his head backward, pressing him against the wall. "Is that what you think?" She lowered her face and kissed him hard, drawing blood from his bottom lip. Then she pulled back a little and hissed into his ear, "Tell me if you still think he's insignificant after he's done with you." She unlocked her fingers, wiping her hand on her dress with an expression of disgust.

"If he was something major, a god, for instance, why would he need you? Even though your lips seem to be permanently attached to his ass, he wouldn't tolerate a lowlife vamp hanging around his godly realm." Cole flicked an eyebrow, the corners of his mouth lifting. "As far as I know, vampires are still not allowed in any realms of the gods."

"Agh!" she huffed, jumping to her feet. "If you must know, he's not just a major deity. He's older and more powerful than all the gods of the existing pantheons put together."

"So, your master is one of the old ones..." Cole whispered more to himself than to Eloise, goosebumps rising on his arms at the mere thought of facing someone like that.

"Tuh-duh!" she sang, lowering herself into a curtsy filled with mockery. "He's almost here, darling, much closer than I expected. I can feel his presence. Another few minutes and I'll see him again." She twirled in place, pure elation lighting up her face. Then she stopped and raised her hand, closing her eyes. "Do you hear that?"

Cole sharpened his senses, and a low humming noise touched his hearing. He wasn't sure what it was, but the magical energy around the castle spiked stronger than before, and the amount of demonic essence rose to unimaginable heights.

"You feel it too, don't you?" Eloise continued talking, a maniacal glimmer in her eyes, but he didn't listen to her as Damian's strong voice sounded in his mind, reaching to him through their blood bond.

Cole's soul twisted with longing and remorse, the warmth and concern coming from his brother making everything so much harder. Just as he had expected, Damian was here—he would never abandon him. Yet he was too late. Damian was begging him to be careful, promising to be with him in just a few minutes, but time was something Cole no longer had.

"Dima, I'm sorry, but this is the end..." he whispered, his eyes on Eloise as she reached into the pocket of her silky robe and produced a large syringe with a long needle. The barrel of the syringe was filled with a thick, silvery liquid, and he didn't have to guess what it was. *"I wish I could see you one more time before—"* Cole blocked the communication link with his brother, not wanting Damian to feel his true emotions or his pain. With numbness suffusing his chest, he focused on Eloise.

"You can't kill me," he said, trying to sound calm and indifferent. "Your great and powerful master wants me alive." He tilted his head a little, his lips forming an icy smile. "I believe he's been looking for me for centuries. I don't think he'll be pleased with you if he finds a pile of ashes instead."

An expression of unadulterated fury distorted her face, and a loud hiss erupted from her mouth. She seized Cole's hair, yanking his head back, the hand with the syringe lingering inches above his chest.

"You're right," she seethed, her grip on his hair becoming tighter. "I can't kill you. But my master never said he wanted you alive and well. He just wanted you alive, and this was always our plan B, in case we couldn't tame you." She let go of him and pulled away a little, spreading her shoulders. "What this is going to do to you is worse than death. It will cripple you, making you suffer for the rest of your immortal life."

Her eyes lit up with a carnivorous scarlet glow, and her lips curled in a feral snarl. A loud scream tore from her mouth as she raised her arms over her head, holding the syringe with both hands as if it were a dagger. In the short moment when Cole followed her movement with his eyes, an understanding of what she was about to do to him sent chills through his body, locking his every muscle. The feeling of his own weakness and helplessness tormented his soul, making the situation so much worse. He didn't move and didn't try to reason with her, watching intently as she started to lower her arms.

Time slowed down, and the silence surrounding him became absolute, as if all sound ceased to exist.

All of a sudden, Dallas' arm wrapped around his shoulder, forcing him down. He threw himself over Cole, covering his chest with his body, and pushed him against the floor with his weight. Unable to stop the momentum, Eloise hissed like a poisonous serpent, and the needle penetrated Dallas' back, sliding between his ribs. The silvery substance entered his lung, and Dallas screamed as if someone was tearing his beating heart out of his chest. His body shuddered, and his face contorted by unimaginable pain. Tears glistened in his bloodshot eyes as he let go and fell heavily on top of Cole, unconscious.

"NO!" A terrible howl of anger and grief escaped Cole's lips. At the same time, the sound returned to the room, flooding it with the terrifying cacophony of a battle unfolding outside.

Eloise jumped to her feet, leaving the syringe in Dallas' back, and rushed toward the window. She peeked outside and cursed in French. Pressing her hand to her chest, she kept muttering something, but her voice was swallowed by the noise. The red flares of fire reflected on her face, making her look ominous, her lips forming the same words over and over.

"He is almost here..."

Cole had no doubt she meant her master, and silently, he prayed to his brother, who wasn't a god, but at this moment, Damian was the only god he believed in.

"Dima..." he called through their blood bond, but Damian didn't answer.

The ruckus of the battle dwindled, and the silence that enveloped the room was interrupted only by Dallas' strained breathing. Eloise marched back to Cole and stood over him, a chain of emotions rushing through her face, none of them promising anything good.

"I don't care," she hissed, talking to someone who wasn't in the room, a psychotic glimmer igniting in her wide-open eyes. Then she stomped her foot and shouted at the top of her lungs, "I don't care what you want anymore! Your plans didn't work, so I'm going through with mine!" She reached into a pocket hidden between the folds of her robe and produced a sharp wooden stake.

Carefully, Cole moved Dallas, placing him on the cold floor, and pushed himself into a sitting position with a strenuous groan, drawing a circle with his finger over his heart, his fingertip blistering at the touch of the silver chains.

"Go ahead," he said, shocked by how flat he sounded. "Do it. Kill me."

Eloise raised her arm, ready to strike him, when the floor trembled. She staggered back but didn't fall, her fingers with long claws wrapped tightly around the stake. The tremors became stronger, accompanied by a low grinding noise, and soon the entire building was shaking and wobbling like a house of cards.

A shower of dust fell off the ceiling, and a web of deep cracks spread in all directions. Then, with a thunderous racket, the whole front wall separated from the building and fell to the quaking ground with a deafening boom, raising a cloud of sand and debris in the air. Eloise squealed and stumbled away from an enormous hole, nearly falling, horror replacing the expression of anger on her face.

When the dust settled down, Cole saw the dark shape of a man supported by two giant black wings hovering in front of the opening. He moved forward and stepped on the floor, folding his wings, his every step sending more tremors through the castle. His orange eyes ignited with undiluted fury as his gaze fell on Cole, but before Cole could say anything, Damian's infuriated eyes bore into Eloise.

Throughout his life, Cole had seen his brother in different

situations. He had seen him angry and hurt, happy and sad, but never had he seen him like this. Covered in blood and black slime from head to toe, the man standing before him looked like a terrifying beast. The massive muscles of his shoulders and chest tensed as he spread his arms, causing the building to rock violently again.

"You…" His magically magnified deep voice boomed like thunder. "You dare threaten my brother?"

Eloise moaned in fear, raising her arms in a pleading gesture, but Damian barely paid attention. The silvery snake of his whip hissed through the air and wrapped tightly around her neck. She cried out as silver burned her skin and dropped the stake, her fingers grasping at the whip spasmodically.

"Please…" she wheezed, stretching her hand to Damian, begging for mercy.

Damian laughed, his white teeth bright against his dirty face, but there was no humor in his laughter, only deadly determination. Without warning, he yanked his whip back. The silver blades attached to the tip of the thong cut through Eloise's neck, decapitating her. For a moment, she stood swaying slightly, then her head fell off her shoulders, and her body collapsed, turning into ash before it hit the ground.

Cole stared at his brother, unable to take his eyes off. "You found me… *brat moi…*" The words rolled off his tongue before he could stop them.

A visible shudder rushed through Damian's body, and a deep sound—something between a moan and a growl—rumbled in his throat. He covered the distance between them in a few long strides and dropped to his knees in front of him, pulling him into a tight embrace. Cole rested his head against his brother's shoulder, unable to lift his arms, just now realizing how truly stretched he had been all this time.

"I will always find you, brother mine," Damian whispered, burying his face in Cole's matted hair.

CHAPTER 18

~ DAMIAN BLAKE ~

Damian let go of Cole and leaned over Dallas, carefully exploring him with his magical sight. The young man was still alive, his chest moving with short, laborious breaths. His eyes were opened, and a red, bubbling liquid coated his pale lips. He looked at Damian without blinking but couldn't say a word, silently begging him for help. Damian sat back on his heels and pressed the back of his hand to his mouth, thoughts—one scarier than the next—rushing through his mind.

"I feel the malignant presence of gray stones energy in his body. I'll try, but I don't think I can heal him, Cole. The gray stones will absorb the healing energy of Earth," he projected to his brother through their blood bond. *"Goddammit... It's my fault. My mistake... When Destiny Enforcers make mistakes, people die..."*

"Dallas saved my life, big bro." Cole's voice sounded in his mind. *"This injection was intended for me, and it would have crippled me for the rest of my existence."*

Damian took Dallas' hand into his, giving it a gentle squeeze. "Hang in there, my friend," he whispered, not sure if the young hunter could hear him. "I'll come up with something to help you..."

He turned back to Cole and seized the chains wrapped around his torso, ripping them off with his bare hands. Cole cried out, his fingers morphing into claws in response to the pain, his fangs extending, but he didn't move until the last piece of silver fell to the floor with a jarring clatter. Damian reached for the collar on his neck, but as soon as his fingertips came in contact with it, he hissed and yanked his hand back.

"That fucking monster," he muttered, his hands balling into fists. "The collar and manacles also have elements of the gray stones in them. If she wasn't—"

Damian cut himself off, slowly rising to his feet. The building trembled slightly, continuous tremors running through the walls and floors. A deep grinding noise filled the room, as if every stone, block and brick the castle was built of started to move and shift, and a cloud of dust fell from the ceiling. The amount of magical energy in the area increased significantly. It invaded his senses, overwhelming them, and he felt like his very skin was on fire. He spun back to face Cole, sweat beading his forehead.

"Can you stand up?" he asked. Lowering to one knee next to Dallas, he lifted him and got up with a strenuous groan, just now beginning to feel the true extent of his exhaustion.

Cole tried to get up, but after a few fruitless attempts, he fell back and shook his head, his shoulders slumped.

"Zhulik," Damian called, readjusting Dallas' position to shift his weight to his left arm. As the gargoyle materialized next to him, he approached Cole and pulled him up to his feet, supporting him with his shoulder. "Zhulik, I need you to give my brother a ride." He threw an apologetic gaze at the gargoyle, and added, "Please, my friend. I can't carry them both."

"Fine," Zhulik grumbled and lowered himself to the floor with a heavy thud. Sending a passive-aggressive glance to Cole, he motioned with his paw. "What are you waiting for? Get on."

With Damian's help, Cole climbed on Zhulik's back and

leaned forward, wrapping his arms around his massive neck. Suddenly, the door into the room flew open, and Vasilisa ran inside, her red cloak billowing behind her. Waving her hand, she opened a portal as she went.

"We're leaving!" she yelled, pointing at the vortex rotating with bright cerulean sparks. "Now! Now! NOW!"

"Zhulik, go!" Damian shouted, and walked through the portal, following the gargoyle and Vasilisa.

As the whirling blue mass started to close behind him, he glanced back and saw the darkness flooding the room. The silhouette of a tall man with glowing silvery-white eyes stepped into view, and a holler of unadulterated fury rattled the building.

* * *

THEY WALKED out of the portal, and Damian halted, observing his surroundings in awe. He stood in a small clearing encircled by a beautiful garden, the freshness of the night air embracing him with its coolness. The tall trees and underbrush were decorated by light orbs and twinkling, multicolored lights, creating a mysterious, semi-dark environment. A narrow cobblestone path led away from the clearing, disappearing into the shrubbery. An ancient apple tree grew in the middle of the opening, its branches weighed down by golden apples nearly touching a water well positioned right next to it.

Damian bent down and lowered Dallas on the soft grass, quickly checking his vitals. The young man was still alive, but his eyes were closed, and his breathing was so shallow that his chest was barely moving. Cole slid from Zhulik's back with a soft groan, falling on the ground inches away from Dallas. The gargoyle shook his head, staring at Cole, but then made his way to Damian and sat down next to him.

"Commander, you need to take the collar and manacles off

your brother," he said quietly, changing from his natural form into a dog. "This despicable device is draining him. He's in a lot of pain."

"I know," Damian whispered. "I'm not sure how. Anyone with magic is vulnerable to the effect of the gray stones. The collar will drain my strength and magical energy as soon as I touch it."

He squatted next to Cole and brushed his fingers over his cheek, pushing his unruly curls out of his face while searching his memories for anything that could help him to disable the gray stones.

"So, let me get this straight..."

Vasilisa's voice sounded behind him, and he got up, turning around to face her. She stood in front of the well, her arms folded over her chest. Cole's scabbard with both swords lay on the ground next to her feet, and Zabava's backpack was thrown over her shoulder. She met his gaze, and a sarcastic smile touched her full lips.

"You disobeyed the direct order of the Head of the Destiny Council," she proceeded, narrowing her eyes at him. "Then, once you entered the Land of Dreams, you broke a bunch of rules despite the severe consequences you'll be facing once all this is over. You risked everything to save the lives of your friends and the woman you love." She chuckled, but her gaze remained cold and steady. "But instead of helping them, you lost another soul—a young human to boot, and you put your brother through unimaginable torture." She bowed mockingly, spreading her arms. "Congratulations, Commander. You're by far the worst Destiny Enforcer I've ever met."

"You're right about that. I am not the best Enforcer out there who blindly obeys all the commands. However, there is one thing you're wrong about, Vasilisa the Wise." Damian averted his eyes, anguish settling in his soul like a heavy load. "I did all that to save the people I love, but that was only a part of the mission. Koschei the Deathless is responsible for all the pain and suffering, and I'm not going to stop until I find his death and put an end to his existence, ridding the world of this despicable evil." He raised his eyes, meeting her hard gaze calmly. "And that is the second part of my mission."

"Oh, wow!" She gave him an arched stare filled with sarcasm, clapping her gloved hands slowly. "You should be a motivational speaker, Commander. What an Academy Awards worthy performance." She tittered, her every word overflowing with mockery. She cut her laughter abruptly and took a step closer to him. "Judging by everything I've seen so far, Koschei is out of your league, Enforcer. He's smarter, a lot more powerful, and he has alliances you can only dream of."

Damian bit his lip and shook his head, forcing himself not to say something he would regret later. "What do you want from me, Vasilisa?" he asked instead, stifling a sigh.

She approached Cole and squatted next to him, carefully moving her palm over the collar on his neck. Then she turned to Dallas and placed her hand over his chest, chanting quietly. A soft white light cloaked her entire arm, and Dallas moaned, his body arching slightly under her touch.

"Curious," she whispered, removing her hand and rising. "Can you explain to me, Commander, why the dust of the gray stones affects your brother so severely? He's a vampire, is he not?"

"Yes, he is," Damian replied calmly, but everything inside him stretched to the limit.

"The gray stones react only to magical and elemental energies, and the more powerful the person is, the stronger and more painful the effect of the stones is on them," she proceeded. "I do believe vampires are undead, which means they can't wield any energy of life, including magic. So please, Commander, enlighten me."

Damian dropped his head, but she didn't let him. Seizing his chin, she forced him to look at her.

"Speak," she hissed through gritted teeth.

"My brother is a vampire, but he can wield magic," Damian said so softly that she had to lean forward to be closer to him. "I told you he was special. I didn't lie then, and I'm not lying now."

"I see," she murmured, her gaze darting from Cole to his swords and finally settling on Damian. "Let me ask you, Commander. What would you do to save the life of this young"—she narrowed her eyes at Dallas, a corner of her mouth lifting—"very young man? What are you willing to sacrifice to see the gray stone jewelry off your brother's neck?"

Damian swallowed hard, his throat constricted. He wasn't sure what Vasilisa had in mind, but he was positive it couldn't be anything good for him.

"Let me make it easier for you, Enforcer." Vasilisa pulled her long braids upfront, her fingers playing with one of them absentmindedly. "Number one—I can save the human. Number two—I have the tools that can take the collar and manacles off your brother. And if that is not enough, here is your number three. I know how to restore your friends' souls." She stared down at Damian, holding out three extended fingers, her eyebrows raised. "The question is, what are you willing to give me in return?"

Damian shook his head, bitter laughter rising in his chest. "Just tell me what you want me to do, and I'll do it if I can," he said. "I'm a Destiny Enforcer, a glorified slave of the Destiny Council. My life is not my own."

"Your fealty," she said icily, stepping closer to him.

"I can't give it to you. Like I said, my life is not mine to give —" A strangled moan followed by a wheeze interrupted him, and he turned toward Dallas. His eyes were tightly shut, and his face was contorted by pain, tremors running through his body.

"He'll be dead in the next five minutes." Vasilisa put her hands on her hips. "So, what is it going to be, Commander."

"Dammit, Vasilisa, why?" Damian exhaled. "You know full well I can't swear my fealty to you." Throwing his hands up, he fell silent for a brief moment. When he continued, his voice was quiet but firm. "I can promise you my obedience instead. If you save Dallas and my brother and tell me how I can restore the souls of my friends, three times I will come to your call, no questions asked. As long as your orders do not go against the Destiny Enforcer's code, I will obey your command."

For a moment, Vasilisa stood silently, rocking back and forth on her feet. "I think we have a deal, Enforcer," she said at length and waved her hand at Damian. "Now, let's see it. I need proof that you won't disappoint me when the time comes. Go ahead." She pointed down, her gesture causing Damian to wince inwardly.

"Dima, no... don't..." Cole's strained voice sounded in Damian's mind. Meeting his brother's haunted gaze, Damian lowered to one knee and pressed his fist to his chest, bowing his head.

"I'm yours to command," he whispered through tightly clenched teeth. "Three times, Lady Vasilisa. That's all you have."

"That's all I need for now," she said with a shrug. "You may rise."

She reached into her hip bag and pulled out two small vials. They were both filled with a clear liquid resembling water, but the one she held in her left hand emitted an unmistakable vibe of death, whereas the other one was glowing with the energy of life. She approached Dallas and lowered down next to him, a fleeting shadow of remorse crossing her features.

"Commander," she said without turning to him. "I need you to hold him. It's not going to be pretty."

Damian went to both knees above Dallas' head and pushed down on his shoulders, holding him firmly against the ground. The young man didn't react to his touch, wheezing accompanying every short breath he took. Vasilisa applied some pressure on his jaw, forcing it open, and positioned the vial emitting the energy of death to his lips.

"Here goes," she breathed and spilled the liquid into Dallas' mouth.

For a heartbeat, nothing happened. Then his Adam's apple moved as he swallowed, his eyes flew open, and a blood-curdling cry of pain tore from his lips. Dallas thrashed against Damian's grip, uncontrollable tremors making his body arch. A few seconds later, he relaxed and fell limply to the ground. The light vanished from his eyes, his pupils dilated as if he were staring into the abyss of death, and a soft breath escaped his tortured lungs.

"What did you do?" Damian whispered, looking at his young friend in horror. Pale and motionless, Dallas looked as dead as a doornail. "He looks like he—"

"We gave him the first elixir too late. So, for all intents and purposes, he's dead," Vasilisa interrupted him, bringing the second vial to Dallas' lips. "And if you don't stop asking me stupid questions, he will remain dead."

She tilted the vial, spilling its contents into Dallas' mouth. A mist, twinkling with bright white sparkles, surrounded his body, wrapping around him like a weightless cloak. For a moment, it lingered over him and then slowly dissipated without leaving a trace. Dallas took a deep breath, and his eyelashes fluttered, his eyeballs moving under his eyelids. Then, with a quiet moan, he opened his eyes and looked up into the dark sky. His gaze traveled to the side, searching the clearing, and Damian gasped, noticing a soft silvery glimmer in his gray eyes.

"Damian," he whispered, struggling to get into a sitting position. "What happened? Where am I?"

Damian helped him sit up, carefully supporting him until he was sure Dallas could sit on his own.

"What is the last thing you remember, hunter?" Vasilisa asked, squatting in front of him.

Dallas' glowing eyes went distant as he scratched the back of his head. "Some old castle," he mumbled. "A French vamp torturing Cole, trying to inject him with something that looked like liquid silver."

His gaze moved to Cole, and a strangled gasp broke from his lips, a chain of emotions rushing across his face in a matter of a few seconds—starting with horror and morphing into deep sorrow. He scrambled to his knees and crawled on all fours closer to Cole, grabbing his hand, but once Cole opened his eyes and smiled faintly, he exhaled in relief.

"So, that deadly concoction was meant for you, Nikolai Chernov?" Vasilisa lowered herself onto the grass, her bright eyes observing Dallas and Cole with blunt curiosity.

"Yes, my lady," Cole replied. "Do you know what was in it?"

"I do," Vasilisa replied airily, opening her hip bag again, but didn't add anything else. She peered inside, her arm going a lot deeper into it than the size of the bag should've allowed for. After shuffling there for a while, she finally pulled out a tool that looked like a wire cutter. "Care to do the honors?" She turned to Damian, offering it to him.

He took the cutter, and as soon as his fingers wrapped around it, a vibe of its powerful magical energy touched his senses. He approached his brother, kneeling next to him.

"It's going to hurt like hell," he said, moving Cole's right arm away from his body.

"Do it." Cole chuckled mirthlessly. "I'll take any pain compared to the way I feel right now."

Damian positioned the cutter, making sure the manacle was between its jaws, and took a deep breath before squeezing the handles. The cutting edge went through the silver like a hot knife through butter, and the bracelet fell off. A violent tremor rushed through Cole's body, and he screamed, throwing his head back. Damian dropped the cutter and wrapped his arms around his brother, pulling him to his chest.

"Nikolai, I'm sorry... I'm so sorry, little bro..." He kept whispering in Cole's ear, sweat running down his face, plastering the long, uneven strands of his hair to his cheeks. He held him until he stopped convulsing and moaned, lifting his free arm to tap Damian's shoulder.

Damian placed him on the ground and took his left arm into his, his hand trembling slightly. "Cole—," he started, but his voice broke, and he bit his lip.

"Do it, Dima." Cole smiled weakly and closed his eyes. "Do it fast."

"Goddammit, little bro... Why are you making me hurt you..." Damian squeezed the handles, cutting the second manacle off Cole's wrist, and as a terrible cry of pain tore from his lips, Damian embraced him, holding him until the worst was over.

Placing Cole back on the ground, Damian stared at the silver band on his neck, his hand with the cutter shaking. He knew what was going to happen once he cut the collar, and while he realized it was in Cole's best interest to remove it as soon as possible, he couldn't bring himself to inflict so much pain on his brother.

"Damian..."

Feeling a soft touch to his shoulder, Damian lifted his face to see Vasilisa standing next to him, a mix of respect and surprise changing her features.

"Let me do it, Commander," she said, not without tones of kindness in her voice. She kneeled by his side and pried the cutter out of his unbending fingers. Then she patted his arm and added, "Hold him, for it's going to be bad."

Damian sat down and pulled Cole up, leaning his back against his chest, making sure his head rested on his shoulder. Vasilisa positioned the cutter's jaws on the collar and, without warning, squeezed the handles. As soon as the collar fell to the ground, Cole's eyes widened, and bloody tears ran down his cheeks. He thrashed violently in Damian's arms, and a howl of pain rang through the garden, echoing endlessly between the trees.

Vasilisa placed her palms flat onto Cole's chest, muttering something under her breath. The light of her magical energy wrapped around him, and little by little, he relaxed, leaning heavily against Damian's chest. She removed her hands and sat back, shaking her head slowly, her palm clasped over her mouth.

"A Destiny Enforcer with a soul and a vampire with magic," she murmured, and Damian wasn't sure if she spoke to him or herself. "Are there any other surprises you and your brother harbor, Commander Blake?"

"Actually, quite a few," Damian replied, watching his brother's ashen face intently.

Cole's eyeballs moved, and his eyelids cracked open, his eyes glowing a hungry scarlet through the narrow openings. Turning his head away from Damian, he shifted in his arms and swallowed hard, closing his eyes again, and it was visible he was fighting the call of his relentless thirst.

"You need to feed to restore your strength, brother." Damian forced his head up and placed his arm closer to Cole's lips. "Do it."

"I'm not taking yours to restore mine," Cole objected, but his fangs extended despite his visible efforts, and he grunted, annoyance prominent in his voice. His eyes darted toward Dallas as the hunter rose to his feet, swaying slightly, and he added, glowering at him, "I'm definitely not biting you ever again."

"I wasn't offering." Dallas shrugged and approached Vasilisa, bowing to her in the best traditions of the World of Magic. "My lady, would you be so kind as to return my backpack to me, please?"

Vasilisa's jaw dropped, her golden eyebrows rising, but she took the backpack off and gave it to Dallas. He opened it and reached inside, muttering something under his breath. He produced a blood bag and headed toward Cole, throwing the backpack straps over his shoulders as he went.

Cole grabbed the blood bag and was about to rip it open with his fangs, but then stilled, his eyes gliding from one face to the next, a vibe of discomfort lingering around him. Vasilisa huffed, gazing heavenward.

"Feed." She waved at Cole in a dismissive gesture. "Do I look like a delicate flower to you, vamp? I've seen a vampire feed more times than I can count."

Cole turned paler than he was before, if it was possible, but lowered his head and ripped the bag with his fangs. Damian stepped between Cole and Vasilisa, shielding him from her cold eyes.

"My lady, thank you for restoring Dallas and freeing my brother," he said, inclining his head. "But now, I need you to fulfill the last part of your promise." She raised her eyebrows, her heavy gaze burning through him. "What do I need to do to restore my friends' souls?"

"Oh, that…" Vasilisa muttered, a semblance of disappointment in her voice.

She walked away and halted by the well, bracing her hands against its edge. Leaning down, she looked inside, and her eyes ignited with a brilliant blue glimmer as she started to chant softly under her breath. A weightless mist rose above the well, stretching its wispy tendril into the sky, and a scent of ozone permeated the air, entwining with the fragrance of greenery and damp dirt.

Slowly she raised her hands, keeping her palms up over the well. The mist engulfed her, and when it dissipated a few seconds later, she was holding two flasks. One of them was silver, with delicate ornaments engraved on its sides. The second one was solid black, and it looked like it was carved out of large obsidian, its surface glistening with the reflected light of the moon.

With a cold smile playing on her lips, Vasilisa made her way to Damian, offering the flasks to him. He took them, feeling the powerful magical energy they were emanating. Just like when she healed Dallas, the dark flask exuded the energy of death, whereas the silver one was surrounded by the energy of life.

"How do I use them?" Damian asked, scanning both bottles with his second sight.

"The same way I did when I healed and revived Dallas," she replied, her finger tracing the shape of the obsidian flask. "The black one has the Water of Death and the silver one is filled with the Water of Life. Do you know how they work?"

Damian nodded. During his initial training, he had been taught how to use these two magical elixirs, but until now, he had never come across them, and it didn't surprise him in the slightest. His eyes darted toward the well and the apple tree growing over it. The Sacred Garden of the Land of Dreams was the only place where the magical Waters existed, and Vasilisa the Wise guarded them with her immortal life.

"The Water of Death can heal any physical damage, closing all wounds—even if they are fatal—instantaneously," said Damian. "The Water of Life can bring back the dead."

"Exactly." Vasilisa inclined her head approvingly. "If you remember, I gave Dallas the Water of Death first, and it removed the deadly concoction from his body, healing his failing internal organs as well as external wounds. After that, I gave him the Water of Life, and it revived him." Her eyes darted to Dallas, and a strange light ignited in their depth, causing the hunter to wince, but she switched her attention to Damian momentarily and continued. "Did you see how small the vials were?" Damian nodded. "That's all you need. You'll have to mix just a few drops of each elixir with about two tablespoons of water and give them to your friends. But for the elixirs to work, you must free their souls first."

"How do I do that if I don't even know where and how Koschei stored them?" Damian sighed. Feeling too drained, he lowered himself to the grass next to Cole, resting his arms atop his bent legs.

She stared down at him, twinkles of sarcasm dancing in her eyes. "There is a spell that can find and free a human soul, no matter where it's hidden," she continued. "Unfortunately for you, I don't know it." As Damian dropped his head, she seized his hair, forcing him to look back up at her. "Just because I don't know it, it doesn't mean I can't help you, Enforcer. I know someone who has this sacred knowledge, and from what I gathered from your story, you were going to see her, anyway. After all, she's the only person in the Land of Dreams who knows everything there is to know about Koschei and his death."

"Lady Sineglazka," muttered Damian, cringing inwardly.

Vasilisa's lips twitched. "I see. Why do I have a feeling you're not fond of the idea of meeting with her?" She waved her hand almost immediately, stopping him from answering. "No need for a long-winded explanation. I don't give a damn. Sineglazka despises your kind. So, if you want to find Koschei's death and get the spell that will set your friends' souls free, get ready to beg and grovel, Enforcer, or she'll squash you like a bug." She snickered, tilting her head. "I, for one, can't wait to see you two together. Wouldn't miss it for the world."

"We've met before," Damian muttered, looking anywhere but at Vasilisa. "Anyway, go ahead and summon her. I'll deal with her."

"Can hardly wait." A shimmering, bluish mist swirled around her as Vasilisa channeled her magic.

She raised her hand to draw a summoning rune, and Damian

stiffened, bracing himself for what was coming, his heart beating somewhere in his knees. He locked and unlocked his fingers at his sides, feeling how clammy his palms were. Lady Sineglazka, the only niece of Baba Yaga, was a powerful ancient mage and a skilled warrior unlike any other. No one really knew which master she served, but one thing Damian knew for sure—it wasn't the High Council, since her dislike of the Destiny Enforcers, or anyone connected with the Destiny Council Realm, was legendary.

"My lady, wait." Dallas raised his hand to attract Vasilisa's attention, and she halted, half-turning to him.

Damian swallowed and took a ragged breath, forcing the memories of his last meeting with this cold and merciless woman to the back of his mind. He needed to calm down and think clearly. The destiny of those he loved, and a lot more than that, depended on his ability to reason with her. Dallas smiled at him, encouragement in his glowing eyes, and Damian gave him a grateful nod, realizing that his friend was giving him another minute to gather his thoughts and get ready.

"Before you summon Lady Sineglazka, may I ask you a question?" Dallas continued with an elegant bow, which made Damian wonder how this young modern man was able to adapt to the archaic ways of the World of Magic so easily and use them in such a natural way as if he lived with it for centuries.

Vasilisa approached Dallas and took his hand, pulling him closer. She peered into his eyes, and just now Damian noticed they were still glowing with the strange silvery light.

"I like him," she said, turning to Cole. "I think I'll keep him. I wanted to have a manservant in my Sacred Garden for quite some time. He'll do perfectly well for what I need."

"He's human." Cole got up, stepping closer to them. "From what I know, humans cannot stay in the Land of Dreams for a prolonged period of time."

"You're right about that." Vasilisa chuckled, patting Dallas on his cheek. "But our young friend here is no longer human. He crossed the veil before I could revive him, so when the Water of Life brought him back, he received some enhancements. Since humans can't return from the other side, that was the only way."

"Enhancements?" Dallas echoed her, all color draining from his face. "I hope I'm not going to grow a pair of horns or a tail."

"Not likely." She shrugged nonchalantly. "But you do have magic now, so if you serve me well and say pretty please, I may actually teach you how to use it in my spare time."

Dallas bowed to her again, but this time Damian noticed a carefully suppressed nervousness in his moves. "As enticing as your offer sounds, my lady, I have to respectfully decline. Cole saved my life, and my loyalty lies with him."

She regarded him with interest, the expression on her face that of a person observing a rare and exotic animal in a zoo. "Fine, your loss," she said at length. "What was your question?"

"What did Eloise inject me with?" Dallas asked. "You said you knew what was in the syringe."

"A very rare substance," she replied, sending a veiled gaze to Damian. "To be honest, I had no idea someone still knew how to brew it." She paused while Damian and Cole exchanged a troubled look. "It was an amalgam, but not a mundane one. A mix of mercury with silver kept in a liquid state by the dust of the gray stones and a powerful incantation. An amalgam like that can cripple an immortal being—even a deity—forever. Brewing it wasn't an easy task, and it required knowledge of the Dark Arts as well as skills in alchemy, so in the old days, it was used only if someone needed to disable a god."

The silence that enveloped the clearing was so heavy that Damian could hear water splashing inside the well. Vasilisa's eyes darted from Dallas to Cole and then settled back on Damian. Without saying anything else, she drew a rune, using her magic, and placed her hand over it, whispering a summoning spell.

A cold breeze rushed through the clearing, and the twinkling lights and orbs started to move faster, shining brighter. A chain of tremors ran through the ground, and a portal rotating with deep blue sparkles opened in the place where Vasilisa had drawn the rune.

Damian channeled his magic, ready to summon his daggers if needed. Cole extended his arm in the direction of his swords lying next to the well, and they vanished just to reappear in his hands. His eyes lit up with the magical energy he was wielding, and the stones in the pommels of his swords ignited with a bright light.

"Svarog almighty..." Vasilisa pressed her hand to her chest, unable to take her eyes off Cole. "You are... *the Godslayer...*"

CHAPTER 19

~ DAMIAN BLAKE ~

"Cole, suppress your magical energy!" Damian seized his brother's arm, pulling him closer. "Trust me, *brat moi*. You need to keep your cool no matter what happens next." Then he turned to Vasilisa, barely able to breathe. "Vasilisa, please, say nothing about Cole."

She moved her fingers across her lips. "My lips are sealed, Commander, but Sineglazka will see right through him, whether I say anything or keep my mouth shut."

"It's okay," Damian replied, watching the rotation of the portal becoming faster. "I'll deal with it if I have to."

"Can't wait to see you doing it," she muttered and stepped closer to the portal, a wide smile lighting up her face.

A cloud of aquamarine mist erupted from the portal, and a tall woman appeared in the clearing. Damian held his breath, having forgotten how truly tall Lady Sineglazka was.

Towering at least an inch taller than Damian, she presented a sight to behold. Her shoulder-length straight hair fell to the dark-brown pauldrons, framing the perfect oval of her face. With her thin lips pressed into a firm line and her thick eyebrows, which were a lot darker than her golden-blonde hair, she wasn't beautiful by modern standards. Her features were too hard and chiseled for a woman, most likely the result of many battles she had faced in her long, immortal life. Her muscled frame, clad in leather armor, appeared even broader in the shoulders than Damian remembered, and if someone was crazy enough to underestimate her on a battlefield, no doubt that would be the last thing they would ever do.

Sineglazka gazed down at Vasilisa with warmth in her unnaturally bright aquamarine eyes, and there was something awkward in the way the corners of her mouth lifted, giving the impression that smiling didn't come naturally to her.

"Vasilisa, darling, I'm so glad to see you." Sineglazka embraced Vasilisa, whose slender body disappeared in the bearhug of the warrior-mage. She pulled away momentarily and bent her knees slightly to look closer at her friend. "As happy as I am to be here, I must say your summoning call came quite unexpected."

Before Vasilisa could reply, Sineglazka straightened and looked around. Her unsettling eyes halted on Dallas, making him suck in a sharp breath and stagger a step back. Then she regarded Cole, and a deep frown settled on her unyielding face, but she said nothing, switching her attention to Damian.

As soon as her eyes bore into him, her magical energy spiked around her. The nostrils of her straight nose flared, and her breathing quickened, the breastplate of her armor moving up and down.

Oh, shit... Damian raised his arms to show her he was unarmed and meant no harm, but his move didn't produce the desired effect.

In one giant step, Sineglazka closed the distance between them, and her fingers wrapped around Damian's throat, lifting him a few inches off the ground with ease, as if he wasn't a six-foot-four man. He didn't try to fight her, holding his arms down.

"Sin, stop!" Vasilisa yelled, grabbing Lady Sineglazka's arm. "Release him, please. These men are in the Sacred Garden because I brought them here."

"What?" The mage looked over her shoulder, her eyebrows rising. "You willingly allowed a vampire and a Destiny Enforcer into the Sacred Garden?"

"Yes, and I had a good reason for it," Vasilisa replied, caressing her arm gently. "You need to hear him out, Sin."

"I need nothing! And you should know better, Vasilisa. I do not associate with the likes of him." Sineglazka turned to Damian and shook her head slowly, her lips curved in disgust. "And out of thousands of Destiny Enforcers, you had to pick this one? Magnus' favorite messenger boy?"

"You know me, Sin. I can't stand Enforcers, but this is a special case. This man is not a messenger boy." Vasilisa sighed. "He's a Commander and Magnus' Shadow Enforcer."

Sineglazka squeezed her fingers tighter, eliciting a strangled groan of pain from Damian. Cole took a step forward involuntarily, his arm reaching back to his sheathed swords, but Vasilisa gave him a barely visible shake no, and he froze in place.

The mage's eyes flashed toward Cole, and an ominous smile crossed her face. "Take another step, vamp, and I'll dust you before you can say *'blood'*."

She lifted Damian a little higher just to slam him down with her full strength. He hit the ground hard with his back and gasped for air, struggling to breathe as his diaphragm spasmed. Without much care, she turned him to his side and brushed her fingers over his upper arm, sending some of her magic through him. As the Shadow Enforcer rune lit up on his skin, she stared at it in disbelief for a moment. Then she pushed Damian, turning him to his back, and placed her knee on his chest, pinning him to the ground. He groaned but didn't move, staring straight up at her.

Dallas approached her and lowered to one knee, inclining

his head in a bow. "My lady," he said softly. "I beg you to let my friend speak. He is a Destiny Enforcer, but his mission is not commanded by the Destiny Council."

"Destiny Enforcers have no friends, boy," Sin muttered and looked up at Vasilisa. "Who is this human child?"

Vasilisa didn't reply, gesturing for Dallas to proceed.

"This one has," Dallas objected softly. "I, for one, consider myself blessed to have him as a friend."

Sineglazka leaned across Damian, almost crushing his ribcage with her considerable weight. She seized Dallas' chin and peered deeply into his eyes.

"Human you are not, but you are quite new to all this," she murmured and moved her knee off Damian.

He groaned softly but remained in the same position, carefully watching her every move. The warrior-mage got up and approached Cole. She looked down into his eyes, and the energy of her magic wrapped around him. A soft hiss of pain escaped his parted lips and his fangs extended, his hands clenching into fists.

"A vampire with magic," she whispered in disbelief. Her gaze darted to Cole's swords, and she threw a glance filled with bewilderment at Vasilisa.

"Please, listen to this child, Sin, and let the Enforcer speak." Vasilisa approached her friend, taking her hand. "Maybe he's young, but he speaks the truth. Commander Damian Blake a.k.a. Dmitri Chernov is here to save the people he loves, but also he and you have an enemy in common."

"You're kidding me, right? An Enforcer with love in his heart, eh?" Sineglazka glowered down at Vasilisa. "And the next thing you're gonna tell me is that the sun rises in the west and sets in the east?"

She chuckled darkly but seized Damian's neck again and yanked him to his knees. Grabbing a handful of his hair, she jerked his head back, her eyes halting on the scar crossing his face.

"So, who is that enemy in common?" She raised an eyebrow, folding her arms. "Let's hear it then. Must be a fascinating story you have, Enforcer. Until today, I didn't believe Vasilisa to be a gullible girl."

"Koschei the Deathless," Damian croaked and cleared his throat. "This is the enemy we have in common, and I came here in hopes of receiving some information about the whereabouts of his death." He got up, squaring his shoulders.

"Who told you that you may rise?" Sineglazka gave him an icy once-over and turned to Vasilisa. "Does he know that while he's in the Land of Dreams, we both can control him?" When Vasilisa nodded, she returned her attention to Damian. "I can twist you into a pretzel, and there is absolutely nothing you can do to stop me."

"Go ahead." Damian spread his arms with an indifferent shrug. "If bullying me makes you feel better about yourself, go for it. But I'm done kneeling and begging. You're either going to help us without the attitude, or this conversation is over, and my friends and I are leaving. It's your choice, Lady Sineglazka."

Vasilisa's jaw dropped as she stared at Damian in shock. For a moment, the mage remained silent, but then she slapped her hands on her leather-clad thighs and burst out laughing. "Feisty little Enforcer, aren't yah?"

"That's something new," Damian muttered, catching Cole's amused gaze. "No one ever called me that yet."

"Fine, since my best friend is begging me to give you a chance, I relent. Tell me what you need, and I'll see if I can help you."

Sineglazka lowered herself to the grass, adjusting her long sword, and gestured for Damian to take a seat. He sat down in front of her, crossing his legs. It didn't take him long to explain to her why he was here and what he was looking for. Once he finished, for a while, she didn't say a word, and a heavy pause engulfed the clearing. Then she ran her fingers through her hair, throwing it off her face, and shook her head with a deep sigh.

"To be honest, I still can't wrap my mind around the fact that you can care about anything other than your mission," she whispered, but there was no more mockery or derision in her voice, just sadness and a touch of genuine surprise. "Do you mind if I check the sincerity of your words, Enforcer?"

She held out her hands, and Damian put his hands in hers, feeling the roughness of calluses on her wide palms. "If reading my soul will help you make a decision, do what you must."

It wasn't the first soul reading Damian had to suffer through, but never had he felt like this. As soon as Sineglazka's magic invaded his mind, the pain that spiked through him was so sharp, he felt as if his head were about to explode. He groaned, clenching his jaw so hard his teeth squeaked. In the beginning, he tried to block all his memories and thoughts associated with Cole, but as she proceeded with the reading, he could no longer maintain the walls he had erected. A deep shudder ran through him, and he screamed, unable to control the agony.

"Dima!"

Somewhere in the depth of his tormented mind, he heard his brother's voice filled with concern and fear. He felt Cole's hands on his shoulders, and then the world around him went black. When he came to, he found himself in his brother's arms, Dallas kneeling by his side. Both Vasilisa and Sineglazka stood in front of him, conversing about something quietly.

"Are you finally back, Enforcer? I must say your mind is a terrifying place, and with everything that's weighing on your soul at this moment, I don't envy you." With a soft chuckle, the mage squatted before him, offering him a piece of parchment, and for a brief second, he saw a mix of warmth and sadness suffusing her features. Damian took it, still feeling weak and dizzy, and she continued, "Don't worry, Commander, your secrets are safe with me. Nothing of what I have seen in your past and found in your soul will ever be revealed to anyone else."

"Thank you, my lady," he whispered and swallowed with effort, his vocal cords painfully sore. He unfolded the parchment and stared at the words written in Dragon tongue, and even though he knew this ancient language well enough, he couldn't recognize this enchantment.

"This is the spell you need to free the souls of the Wardens and your lady. Once you read it and give your friends both magical elixirs, they'll be healed, and their souls will be restored. However, you must not waste your time and do it as soon as you can, for the longer their bodies are away from their souls, the harder it will be to restore them. As it is, they have been separated from their souls too long already, so they won't wake up right away. They will need time to recover from such a terrible injury," Sineglazka continued, her face turning hard once again. "Heed my advice, Enforcer. Forget about Koschei. Go home and take care of those you love."

She fell silent, exchanging a heavy look with Vasilisa. Then she sighed and squatted in front of him.

"Listen to me, child." The mage reached forward and brushed his cheek with her fingers, a tender gesture he hadn't expected from her. "Do not go after Koschei, for you will lose everything you hold dear to your heart, including your life."

"I will lose everything if I don't kill him," Damian replied, his throat tight. "He won't stop until everyone I love is dead. He said it himself on numerous occasions, and so far, he gave me no reason to doubt his promise."

"Or perhaps he won't stop until you and your brother submit to his master? Have you ever considered that this could be his true goal? To push both of you into a tight corner where you have no other options but to bow down to him?" Sineglazka asked. "Everything I've read in your soul leads to this mysterious person. He's the Beast Master, who marked you with Darkness, Koschei's and Donna Luna's master and an unknown old deity, whose powers seem to be greater than anything I have ever seen. I hate to be the bearer of bad news, but killing Koschei the Deathless will not solve your problems."

"We can never submit to Darkness," said Cole, squeezing Damian's shoulder as if asking for his support.

Sin's lips twitched as she glanced at him. "You *are* the Darkness, vampire. It's in your nature, even though you are touched by the Light. Why do you think the old one is so adamant about capturing you first? You'll be easier to convert than your brother, but he"—she pointed at Damian—"will follow you to Hell and beyond, to the Dark Nav and into Peklo, and to the end of all worlds. He'll die, sell his soul, do whatever it takes to save you, and your formidable adversary is counting on that."

"I will never switch sides. Not if I can help it," Cole muttered, but dropped his head, averting his gaze.

"Damian, listen to me carefully." Sineglazka placed her rough palm over his hand, and he braced himself for truly bad news. "Even if you find Koschei's death, there is a big chance you still won't be able to kill him. His death is hidden in a needle, but breaking it is prone to unknown dangers and shouldn't be done in the realm of humans. Trust me... If it were so easy, don't you think I would have done it myself a long time ago?" She shook her head, pursing her lips. "Are you sure you want to risk your life and the existence of your brother for a battle you will very likely lose?"

A bitter smile touched Damian's lips before he could stop it. "What do you propose I do, Lady Sineglazka? Bend my knee before the old one who's as evil as they come? Submit and pray that he spare the people I love? How about the rest of the world? The world I swore to protect and serve when I accepted the mantel of a Destiny Enforcer?"

"I see," she whispered, her gaze moving to Cole and then to Dallas. She got up and approached the young hunter. "Dallas, that's your name, right?"

"Yes, my lady," Dallas replied calmly, but his shoulders went up a little, his muscles tense.

"These two"—Sineglazka pointed at Cole and then at Damian—"are bound by blood, their past and powerful ancient magic. They will always stand together, no matter how deadly the situation is. But you..." She placed her hand on Dallas' shoulder, giving him a light nod. "You don't have to. Take Vasilisa's offer and stay here, in the Land of Dreams. She'll show you the world you've never dreamed of being part of. You just received the two most precious gifts—your life and magic—don't waste them on a mission that is bound to fail. The brothers have no choice, but you do, child. Please, choose wisely."

Dallas smiled, sending a veiled glance in Cole's direction. "Thank you, my lady." He inclined his head in a bow. "But I've made my choice a long time ago, the moment when Cole carried me out of a burning building, saving my life while risking his own."

"I see," she murmured again. "Let's do it then."

She stepped back and raised her arms, spreading them wide above her head while chanting something softly. The air shimmered with misty blue sparkles and when the mist vanished, Damian saw an image of a city. The mage moved her arm, and the view changed, showing him an old mansion that looked like a partially demolished fortress surrounded by an unkept garden, a river and an old church.

"Perun almighty," Damian exhaled, his right hand reaching for the bracelet on his left wrist of its own accord.

"I assume you are familiar with this place, Commander?" Vasilisa asked.

"Yes," Damian replied. "This is the village of Gus-Zhelezny in Russia. I recognize the Eagle's Nest estate. This place is—"

"Cursed?" the mage offered, her voice rising. "What did you expect, Enforcer? That Koschei would hide his death at a local supermarket?"

"No, of course not." Damian rubbed his forehead, old memories flooding his mind. "I've been there a long time ago, when the Eagle's Nest was thriving, and Andrey Batashov was at the top of his career."

"Then you know where you need to look for the chest." Sineglazka waved her hand and the view of the old estate vanished.

"The chest?" Cole asked, a slightly confused expression on his face.

"Yes, the chest," Sineglazka replied with a dismissive wave of her hand. "Koschei's death lies in the tip of a needle. The needle is hidden in an egg. The egg is in a duck, and the duck is in a rabbit. He locks the rabbit inside an enchanted chest that cannot be found by magic or discovered by the human eye. The only reason I can find it is because a long time ago, during one of my confrontations with Koschei, I was able to touch it, leaving traces of my magical energy on it."

"Whoa..." Dallas exhaled, his eyes wide with wonderment. "That's complicated. Needle, egg, duck, rabbit, chest."

"You have a lot to learn, boy. Start by reading Slavic lore and fairy tales." Vasilisa chuckled, giving him a light tap on his shoulder. "You'll see that there is never anything easy or straightforward there."

Damian bowed his head, pressing his fist to his chest. "Lady Sineglazka, Vasilisa the Wise," he said, raising his face, "thank you for your assistance. Now that I have everything I need and the location of Koschei's death, we should be on our way."

"Don't thank us, Enforcer," the warrior-mage huffed, one

corner of her mouth lifting into a crooked smile. "Unfortunately, I set you on the path of self-destruction."

"Godspeed, Commander." Vasilisa flicked her wrist, and a powerful wave of her magic rushed across the area, quickly disappearing into the woods. "I unlocked the Garden so you can teleport or open a portal straight from here," she said, slightly inclining her head. "If you survive, we may meet again sooner than you think."

Thinking back to the promise he gave Vasilisa, Damian suppressed a sigh and waved his hand, opening a portal into the realm of humans. He waited for Cole and Dallas to walk through the whirling sparkles and then followed them without looking back.

CHAPTER 20

~ DAMIAN BLAKE ~

Damian stepped out from the portal onto the steps of the Brown's Estate and shivered like from the gust of an icy wind. He was accustomed to teleporting to Paradise Manor, and the thought of River's desperate state and the building he used to call home in ruins made him crumble inside.

He halted, quickly observing the surroundings and checking the property for any supernatural presence. The sky was still dark, but far on the horizon, the soft glow of the approaching dawn touched the tips of the purple mountains. He inhaled a lungful of cold desert air, finally dropping his tense shoulders.

Dallas stopped by the door and turned around, leaning his back against it. "Is that how all your missions go?" he asked, and even though twinkles of humor were dancing in his gray eyes, his face looked ashen with exhaustion.

"Pretty much," Cole murmured with a half-shrug. "I warned you—the World of Magic brings nothing but pain, loss and suffering."

"You're probably right, but I'm still glad I know about its existence, and now that I have my own magic, maybe one of you could—" Dallas cut himself off as Damian ran up the steps and halted before him.

Gazing down at the young man, Damian could barely breathe as memories of recent events flashed through his mind. He seized his shoulders and pulled him into a quick embrace, ruffling the hair on the back of his head the way he used to do to Cole.

"You're still just a boy. Enjoy living a normal life without monsters hunting you from the shadows," he whispered. As he unlocked his arms, he caught an expression of shock on Dallas' face and added, "Thank you for taking the proverbial bullet for my brother back there."

"You both would have done the same for me and more," Dallas replied, sounding so assured in this fact, as if other options didn't exist. "And it was just a syringe, not a bullet." He shrugged, something close to disappointment sounding in his voice, and Damian couldn't help but smile.

"I promise when this mess is over, I'll assess your abilities and teach you combat magic myself, Dallas," Damian said, pulling the door open. "But until then, you're staying home and helping Ruslan with the affairs of the Court or anything else he needs you to do."

"Hold on, hold on." Dallas made a time-out sign with his hand, circling Damian to step in front of him. "Are you saying I'm not going with you and Cole to that Gus-whatchamacallit village to look for Koschei's death?"

"No, you're not." Damian folded his arms, pressing his lips into a straight line. "You're not ready for this. God knows you weren't ready for the trip to the Land of Dreams, either. I can't take the chance of losing you again."

Dallas blinked at him a few times, throwing his hands up. "But Damian—"

"This conversation is over," Damian cut him off. "You want to learn combat magic, the first thing you need to learn is how to obey orders."

"Yeah, right." Dallas headed inside the house, sending a veiled glance filled with sarcasm to Damian as he passed him. "What kind of lesson was that? Do as I say not as I do?"

Damian exchanged a quick look with Cole, and both burst out laughing.

"I heard that," Damian murmured, following him into the hallway.

Cole caught up with Dallas and gave him a light push on his side. "Trust me, Dallas," he whispered loud enough for Damian to hear. "When my brother says that the conversation is over, you better leave it alone. You're not going to like what follows if you don't." He chuckled, escaping into the living room before Damian could reach him.

Ruslan sat in a wide leather armchair in front of a TV with his arms folded over his stomach. He wasn't wearing a shirt, and his hair wasn't pulled into a ponytail as he always had it, the long strands falling to his bare shoulders and chest. A movie was playing, but he didn't look like he was paying any attention to it, his angled eyes distant and foggy. As soon as they walked into the room, his gaze came into focus, and he froze, his attentive eyes taking in their appearance, one at the time.

"Father..." Cole crossed the room and kneeled in front of his maker, resting his forehead against his knees.

Ruslan rose heavily, hauling Cole up with him, and gave him a quick hug before pulling away to look at him. "You're okay... you're back," he whispered, sounding as if he was talking to himself. "You are all home."

He glanced at Damian and closed his eyes briefly, relief visible in the set of his wide shoulders. But as his gaze halted on Dallas, his eyebrows rose, and his jaw dropped.

"What happened to that little troublemaker?" he asked, tilting his head. "He was nothing but a human pain in my neck when he left, but now he seems to be a magical pain in my neck. Why is that, son?"

"Because he saved my life at the cost of his," replied Cole.

"Explain, please." Ruslan waved at the couch, gesturing for everyone to sit down.

Feeling too drained to tell the entire story from the beginning again, Damian allowed Cole to take over. Unlike him, Cole liked to produce an effect on his listeners. His speech was eloquent and clear, his natural elegance and charm taking over as soon as he started talking. When it came to the moment where Damian broke into the castle, Damian couldn't help but laugh, scratching the back of his head.

"Is that how I look through your eyes?" he asked, choking on laughter. "A terrifying, winged beast?"

"My story, my point of view," Cole replied, trying to keep a straight face. "I tell it as I see it."

Damian raised his hands in a peaceful gesture, and Cole proceeded. When he finally finished, Ruslan got up and approached Dallas, placing his hand on the young man's shoulder.

"Welcome to the club," he said, sounding absolutely serious. "I'm sure you'll have plenty of time to regret it later." Then he turned to Damian, hooking his thumbs over his wide leather belt. "What's your next step, Dmitri?"

"I need to clean up and get dressed first." Damian got up, his hands brushing down his bare chest and ripped pants soaked with blood and demonic slime. "Then I go to the hospital and restore River, Luc and Jamie. If I ever want to see them alive, I must do it as soon as possible."

"Uh-huh…" For a heartbeat, Ruslan just stood there, drilling Damian with his heavy gaze. Then he switched his attention to Cole, looking at him over Damian's shoulder. "Son, why don't you and Dallas retire to your rooms. You both look like you need a good shower and some sleep." Before Cole could protest, he waved his hand, gesturing at the exit. "Please, give me and Commander Blake the room. I want to speak with him uninterrupted."

"Commander Blake? Uh-oh," Cole murmured, a vibe of unease lingering over him, but he didn't add anything else and walked out the door, pulling Dallas with him despite his feeble resistance.

As soon as they were gone, Ruslan turned to Damian, folding his arms. "So, you're planning to do it alone then, Commander."

It wasn't a question. He said it with so much conviction that Damian had no choice but to nod, having nothing else to say. Ruslan walked back to his chair and lowered himself onto it, his moves slow and heavy, as if the ancient vampire could experience the exhaustion.

"May I ask why?" Ruslan gestured at an armchair across from himself, inviting Damian to take a seat.

Damian sat down, rubbing the back of his neck. When he raised his gaze at Ruslan, dark, undiluted anguish stared at him from the vampire's eyes.

"I saw Dallas dying in Cole's arms, and the way Cole reacted to his death just—" Damian didn't finish and swallowed, his throat painfully dry. "I watched my brother suffer from the effect of the gray stones magic." He looked down at his hands covered in dirt and the brown splatters of dried-out blood, slowly shaking his head. "I can't do it, Ruslan. I can endure any pain myself, no matter how bad. But when Cole is hurt, I can't take it." He met Ruslan's gaze, finding no understanding there. "Don't you get it? He's my emotional attachment, my only true weakness, and going after someone as powerful and merciless as Koschei, I can't afford it." He thought for a moment and added, his voice barely audible, "Even Lady Sineglazka warned me about that…"

"I see." Ruslan leaned back in his chair, crossing his legs at the knee. "And what do you think is going to happen to your brother if you die? Do you seriously believe he'll be able to keep living while blaming himself for not being there for you? Asking himself over and over if you would still have been alive if he had been there to watch your back?" His eyes ignited a terrifying red as he folded his arms, clenching his teeth. "Do you seriously think Nikolai will survive your death? Again..."

"Ruslan—," Damian started, but Ruslan got up, interrupting him with a sharp move of his hand.

He made his way to the window and halted there, squinting his eyes at the bright rays of the rising sun.

"He probably didn't tell you... but since that memorable battle in August of nine hundred ninety-six when I turned Nikolai until a few years ago, your brother never stopped looking for you, Dmitri," Ruslan said without turning around. "To my surprise, when I turned him, he accepted his new status relatively easily, quickly adapting to the new lifestyle he had to lead being a vampire. But from the first moment when I allowed him to walk among humans on his own, all he did was look for you. He checked every square inch of the battlefield, hoping to find either your body or proof that you had survived..."

His voice trailed away, and he finally turned around, resting his back against the wall. Damian stared at him dumbstruck by the unconcealed anguish in the old vampire's eyes.

"As soon as the opportunity presented itself, I left Kievan Rus, taking Nikolai with me in the hopes that physical distance and time would heal his wounds," Ruslan continued, his hands clenched in front of him. "We traveled across Europe, Asia and the Middle East, visiting different countries and cities, but no matter where I took him, Nikolai never stopped searching for you.

"Anything he wanted, any crazy idea he had—Luciano and I made it happen, but a thousand years later, he still carried the belief in his heart that you were alive, never stopping his fruitless search. Nikolai is a force of nature, at least he appears to be. With time, he learned to be more careful, diplomatic and evasive, as you probably noticed, but I could always detect that well-hidden layer of pain..." He paused, a muscle twitching in his jaw. "When you found him in that dirty, fleabag hotel, you didn't just save him from the kidnappers... You gave him his life back." He approached Damian, his fingers lingering over his cheek without touching him. "Don't take it away from him again, my boy. Let your brother stand by your side."

"Ruslan," Damian whispered, unable to speak louder. "This mission is not sanctioned by the Destiny Council, so I don't have their support. I'm on my own. Koschei the Deathless is not easy prey, but it is his master that truly terrifies me..." Damian bit his lip, thinking back to the massive man with glowing eyes he had seen in the City of Gold. "He's one of the old ones, an ancient god. Are you sure you wish Cole to go with me?"

"I want you to know—I love my son more than life itself," Ruslan replied. "But the answer to your question is still yes. You will not go to the hospital alone. I lived long enough to realize that as soon as you say the enchantment Lady Sineglazka has given you, Koschei's magic, which holds your friends' souls imprisoned, will be broken. I'm sure the Master of the Dark Arts, as ancient and skillful as Koschei, will know as soon as it happens. Don't tell me this is not true."

"It's true," Damian replied. "The moment I free their souls, the clock will start ticking. Time will be working against me, and I'll have to move fast."

"Exactly as I thought," Ruslan murmured. "You were planning to teleport to Gus-Zhelezny straight from the hospital."

"Yes, sir. That was my plan." Damian got up, feeling as if the weight he'd been carrying for the last few days just tripled.

"Was?"

"Yes, was," he replied quietly. "I'll do as you wish, my lord, even though your desires go against my better judgment." He bowed stiffly and walked out the door, heading toward Cole's room.

* * *

DAMIAN HALTED in front of the entrance into Cole's bedroom and raised his hand to knock, but then dropped his arm, nibbling on his lip. He wasn't sure how long he stood in the semi-dark hallway, exploring the designs on the carpet absent-mindedly. It could have been just a second or a few minutes. Then he took a deep breath, knocked on the door and pushed it open without waiting for Cole's invitation.

The bedroom was dark. A thin line of yellow light crossed the floor, escaping the bathroom through the slightly cracked door. The sound of running water suggested his brother was in the shower, so Damian decided to wait for him here. He glanced at the bed, thinking about how much he wished to lie down, but then assessed his half-ripped, dirty pants and decided against it. With a low groan, he lowered himself to the carpet and rested his back against the bed, closing his eyes.

He didn't fall asleep, his mind lingering somewhere on the border between consciousness and the state of a dream. When Cole shut down the shower and walked out into the room, toweling his body, he opened his eyes but quickly averted his gaze.

"I'm sure you've seen a naked man before, a couple or three times." Cole winked, wrapping his towel around his hips. He opened his closet, but before getting dressed, he turned to Damian. "What did you decide?" he asked, his fingers pulling at a long thread on the edge of the towel. "Are you still planning to quietly leave me behind, thinking I'm not smart enough to figure out your plans?"

"Was I that obvious?" Damian glanced at his brother from under the strands of his tangled hair.

"Duh."

Cole rolled his eyes, grabbing black jeans and a T-shirt out of his closet. He got dressed quickly and sat down on the bed next to Damian. Sending a veiled glance to Cole, Damian leaned to the side, placing his head against his brother's knee, and closed his eyes.

Cole threaded his fingers through his brother's hair, his hand trembling slightly. Then he grabbed the long strand on the front and gave it a good yank. "Don't you ever think that you can leave me behind without saying a word, as though I'm a little child."

"Ouch... To me, you always are..." Damian mumbled faintly. "Give me a moment then. I'll go grab a quick shower, change and we'll be on the way."

He got up and glanced at his brother, his hand clutching at his throat of its own accord. The heavy load he'd been carrying in his soul since Koschei's attack on the Warden's bookshop just got heavier, leaving a constant, dull ache in his chest. Then, without saying another word, he turned on his heels and walked out the door.

CHAPTER 21

~ DAMIAN BLAKE ~

Damian stood in the entrance hall of the Brown's Estate, waiting for Cole to say his farewells to Ruslan and Dallas. He smiled at them, trying to project calmness and self-assurance, but everything inside him was stretched like a guitar string. He didn't like long goodbyes, and as a Destiny Enforcer, he never needed them. When an order was issued, he just got up and left, jumping straight into the thick of things.

Here, however, everything was different, and watching his brother promise Ruslan and Dallas that he'd see them soon sent chills down his back for some reason. Catching his gaze, Cole approached him, his fingers squeezing the handle of the leather case where he stored his swords and scabbard.

Giving a reassuring nod to Ruslan and Dallas, Damian placed his hand on Cole's shoulder and snapped his fingers, trying not to think about anything except for what lay ahead.

*　*　*

They materialized behind a large dumpster in the alley at the back of the hospital. Damian glanced around, making sure no one had noticed their arrival, but since the area appeared blissfully empty, he channeled some of his magic and drew a rune on the wall. Placing his palm over it, he connected his Shadow Enforcer rune to it and said a summoning spell, calling for Cossack.

With a light pop, Cossack manifested next to him almost immediately. He still wore his illusion, looking like one of the hospital workers, but Damian could see his true appearance through it.

"Dmitri," he whispered, even though they were alone. "Please, tell me you have the cure." He took a step closer, his eyes pleading.

"I have the cure," Damian replied. "What's wrong, my friend? Has anything changed?"

Cossack nodded and dropped his head, his arms hanging limply along his body. "They're dying, Dima," he whispered. "I know nothing about modern medicine, but the doctors said their organs are starting to fail, and it's a matter of hours before..." His voice faded into silence, and he looked away, a deep line etched between his eyebrows.

"Adrian, I have everything we need to save them," Damian said, squeezing his arms reassuringly. "I need you to take all three of them into a single room and then teleport us there. Can you do it?"

Cossack raised his eyes, his face resuming his usual emotionless hardness. "Yes, Commander. Give me a few minutes."

He snapped his fingers and vanished, leaving Cole and Damian alone in the empty alley.

"Dammit," Damian mumbled, turning to his brother.

Thousands of thoughts rushed through his mind, but he stopped himself from imagining worst case scenarios, counting the seconds to Cossack's return. Cole remained silent too, his face cold in that eerie vampire's way, but Damian knew him well enough to recognize the same deep concern he felt in his brother's thoughts. He slid down to the ground by the wall and stretched his legs, dropping his arms on his lap. Cole squatted next to him and froze, his gaze fixed on something visible only to him.

It took Cossack less than fifteen minutes to return, but to Damian, it seemed like he had spent at least a few hours sitting on the cold asphalt. Cole got up first, grabbing his case with the swords, and offered him his free hand. Damian seized it and rose, feeling an unusual stiffness in all his muscles.

"Everything is ready, Commander," Cossack whispered. "We moved all three of them into a single room and cloaked it with a powerful concealment spell and an illusion. You can do whatever needs to be done."

"Thank you, my friend." Damian smiled at him, squaring his shoulders. "Let's do it."

Cossack placed his hands on Damian's and Cole's arms, and the alley spun around them, disappearing into the whirlpool of the teleportation process.

They manifested inside a hospital room, the distinct scent of antiseptics, soaps and cleaners leaving no doubt as to where they were. A slightly yellow light filling the room signified the presence of a powerful cloaking spell, and the familiar vibe of the Destiny Enforcers' magic touched Damian's senses. Three hospital beds were positioned next to each other, with a small table located on the side. Damian looked at Luc and Jamie, a wave of despair sweeping over him, but as his gaze fell on River's pale face and her copper hair fanned over the white hospital pillow, his heart stopped for a brief moment, tightness suffusing his chest.

He averted his eyes, forcing himself to focus on what he needed to do next. Making his way to the table, he pulled out the flasks with the two elixirs and the piece of parchment with the words of the enchantment.

"I need six small glasses or any kind of containers that can hold liquid," he said, looking around for anything suitable. Cossack walked out of the room and returned a few seconds later, carrying a rack with six clean test-tubes inside.

"Is that good enough?" he asked, placing the rack on the table in front of Damian.

"It'll do."

Damian took the tubes and filled them with tap water to what he thought would be equivalent to two tablespoons. Then he opened the obsidian flask with the Water of Death and put a few drops of it into three of the vials. Working like on autopilot, he grabbed the silver flask with the Water of Life and repeated the procedure with the remaining three tubes.

"Here is what we're going to do," he said, motioning for Cole and Cossack to approach the table. "As soon as I read the enchantment, Koschei will know we broke his curse, and from that point on, it's not going to be long before he comes after me, so we need to move fast, no matter what happens next."

"I understand, Commander." Cossack inclined his head.

"Go on. What do we have to do?" asked Cole.

Damian pulled out two vials with the Water of Death and gave them to Cole and Cossack, squeezing the third one in his fist.

"Cole, I need you to take care of Jamie while Cossack will heal Luc. I'll attend to River," Damian continued, his eyes darting from his brother to his friend. "After I finish the spell, you have to make sure they drink the elixir. From what I've seen, they may have a reaction to it. Once it's over, you must give them the second dose right away." He pointed at the remaining three vials and then looked up at his brother. "Cole, we'll be leaving as soon as we're done here, so you should probably put your scabbard with the swords on before we start."

Cole nodded. Carefully, he placed the vial with the Water of Death back in the rack, away from the other three tubes, and squatted next to his case. He opened it and took the scabbard out, putting it on with fast, habitual movements, and then sheathed his swords.

"Cossack." Damian touched his friend's shoulder. "Once we give them both elixirs, they're not going to wake up right away, so don't get alarmed. It may take a while." He glanced away, staring into the dark corner of the room, and stifled a sigh. "I wish I could be here when it happens, but I truly have no idea what we're going to be up against next and how long it'll take before I can come back…" His voice faded away, and he added in a hoarse whisper, "If we return at all."

"Commander—," Cossack started but cut himself off as he caught Damian's gaze.

"After we leave, take them back into their rooms and let the human doctors do their job," Damian continued quietly. "Be there for them when they finally awake… even if I can't."

Cossack swallowed, a shadow of concern and sadness clouding his features. "I'll make sure they're as comfortable as possible and that everything looks legit in the eyes of the human authorities," he said. Then he pressed his fist to his chest, inclining his head, and added, "I'm yours to command. Always."

"Let's do it then." Damian took the piece of parchment and walked toward River's bed, halting by her side, his heart beating heavily against his rib cage. He waited until Cole and Cossack were in position and then read the words of Dragon tongue, carefully pronouncing each one of them. He finished the spell by saying River's, Luc's and Jamie's names. Making a split-second decision, he added Gypsy's name, unsure if the enchantment would work on a cat the same as on people.

Just as he leaned over River to give her the Water of Death, the light flickered on and off, and a tremor ran across the floor. The glass in the window rattled, a vibration spreading through the walls. Suddenly, all the lights went off, and Damian wasn't sure if the power outage spread throughout the entire hospital, or if it was only affecting the area around him. As the quaking turned stronger, he had to grab the side rail of the bed to keep himself from falling. A soft golden glimmer ignited under the ceiling, illuminating the room, and the tremors subsided, the buzz of vibration morphing into a heavy silence.

The light flowed in gentle waves, its presence soothing and comforting to his stretched nerves. Slowly, it descended, concentrating over River, Luc and Jamie. For a heartbeat, it lingered over them and then moved down, gradually getting absorbed by their bodies.

"It worked," Damian exhaled, the realization that the spell had done its job restoring his friends' souls giving him the boost of energy he needed. He pressed on River's jaw to open her mouth and glanced sideways at his brother and Cossack. "The Water of Death. Now."

Cautiously, he spilled the liquid in her mouth and waited impatiently, searching her face with his eyes. Just like the last time, nothing happened at first. Then River swallowed hard, and a moan escaped her lips, quickly morphing into a piercing cry of pain. Her body arched and convulsed. Damian held her down, sweat running down his forehead as if it were his body tormented by the magical elixir.

A moment later, River relaxed and fell back on the bed, her chest moving slightly with shallow breaths. Damian let go and rushed back to the table to grab the second tube, in his peripheral vision noticing that Cole and Cossack were ready too. Holding the vial with the Water of Life in his fist, he returned to River and nodded to them.

"Let's restore their life-force now." With these words, he leaned over River and gently pried her jaw open, spilling the elixir in her mouth. A sparkling mist surrounded her body, lingering over her like a beautiful, weightless cloak. Then it lowered and slowly dissipated, leaving a few glowing sparkles behind. River took a deep breath and relaxed, her breathing becoming deeper and more even, but as Damian expected, she didn't regain consciousness, remaining in what appeared to be a normal sleep.

He opened his magical sight and scanned her body, noticing with relief the soft golden shine of her human soul. Beautiful and warm, it flowed evenly throughout her entire being, uninterrupted by any evil magic. That told him she was whole and healthy again, and it was only a matter of time before she would wake up.

Damian leaned down and gently touched her forehead with his lips. "Return to me," he whispered and straightened. For a brief moment, he stood there, gazing down at her. Then he turned away and headed to Luc and then Jamie, quickly checking them with his other sight. Just like River, they were both restored, the light of their souls as bright and uninterrupted as ever.

He smiled, meeting Cole's and Cossack's concerned gazes. "It worked. They're back to normal." He thought for a moment, considering a few options, and then turned to his friend. "Cossack, there is one more favor I want to ask of you."

"You know I'll do anything for you." Cossack shrugged, a wide grin splitting his tired face. "What do you need?"

Damian grabbed both flasks and gave them to Cossack. "I believe there is still some elixir in both of these flasks," he said as Cossack took them. "If you get a chance, can you please teleport to Paradise Manor? If you remember, River's cat was affected by Koschei's curse as well. See if you can revive her too, okay?"

"But of course." Cossack chuckled, bowing. "What kind of Destiny Enforcer would I be if I didn't save the life of an innocent kitty?"

"Innocent, right." Cole snorted, gazing heavenward.

Not dignifying Cole's comment with a comeback, Damian approached him and placed his hand on his shoulder. "We must go now, my friend," he said to Cossack. "Be careful and make sure the Wardens and River are safe."

"Yes, Commander." Cossack pressed his fist to his chest in a habitual move. "What do you want me to tell the High Council?"

Damian stilled for a moment, thinking, but then waved his hand in a dismissive gesture. "Tell them nothing," he said quietly. "If they demand an answer, tell them you don't know anything, and if they want an explanation, they should ask me."

"But Commander—," Cossack started, but Damian shook his head, interrupting him.

"I'm not your Commander, Adrian," he said calmly. "I'm your friend, and I'm the one who disobeyed my orders. You shouldn't be responsible for my misdoings."

Before Cossack could say anything else, Damian snapped his fingers, and the hospital room spun around him in swirls of colors.

CHAPTER 22

~ DAMIAN BLAKE ~

"Where are we?" Cole turned around slowly, his hand brushing over the rough surface of a seven-meter red-brick wall.

A fresh evening breeze rushed through the area, playing with the tree branches and rustling through the overgrown shrubbery. The smell of greenery, wet trunks and the damp ground came with it, bringing back some old memories, and Damian stiffened, trying not to think about what lay beneath his feet.

"The Eagle's Nest Estate in Gus-Zhelezny, Russia," Damian muttered through gritted teeth. "Back in the eighteenth century, this place used to belong to a successful industrialist, Andrey Batashov, also known as the Iron King."

"Is everything still the way you remember?" Cole asked, glancing at his brother with curiosity.

Damian closed his eyes as he probed the estate with his second sight as far as he could reach. The presence of dark magical energy touched his senses, and he groaned, staggering away from the wall involuntarily.

"More or less," he murmured, his hands clenching into fists

of their own accord. "What you see is the mere shadow of what it used to be... But it's still just as ghastly and cold now as it was back then."

Cole closed his eyes and stilled, listening to something intently. "I sense death," he whispered at length. "Death and darkness."

Damian exhaled, a deep shudder rushing through him. "I'm not surprised. There are plenty of both here. This giant estate is located over miles upon miles of underground catacombs." He channeled his elemental energy and moved his arm parallel to the ground, probing the area beneath for as deep as he could see. "I can feel them... the passages and hollow spaces... They are still here, and only the gods know what kinds of dark secrets are buried under this land."

Damian looked at his brother, silent anger slowly rising within him, threatening to spill.

"What happened here?" Cole asked quietly.

"I didn't witness the actual events, but the local legend has it that Andrey Batashov had a mint hidden in these passages, printing gold and silver coins," Damian replied. "At the end of the eighteenth century, to hide his illegal activity from the emperor's inspectors, he gave the order to gather all the workers who operated the mint in a large underground basement, and then he flooded everything, allegedly killing close to three hundred people instantly." Damian paused, staring at the dark park behind the wall, tightness spreading through his chest. "I don't know if it's true, but the presence of death that you're feeling could be—" He cut himself off, nibbling on his lip.

"Ghosts?" Cole asked. "The unrest spirits of the workers?"

Damian shrugged with a slow shake of his head. "Who knows? Anything is possible, but that's not what bothers me..." He fell silent, his skin crawling with the presence of malignant energy. "This place is overflowing with dark magic... It's everywhere..." he said, gesturing at the estate. "Some kind of spell that has been cast here a while ago but is still active today... More than one, actually. I don't think it's wards or alarms, but I have no idea what it is." He took a deep breath, a corner of his mouth lifting into a humorless, crooked smile. "Get ready, little bro. Most likely, we'll find what we're looking for... with interest."

"Bring it on," Cole muttered icily, his eyes narrowing.

Damian tapped his brother's shoulder, motioning for him to follow, and headed toward the demolished part of the wall. Just to be on the safe side, he checked the area one more time, and since the path seemed clear, he easily hopped over the wall, landing on the other side. Following him, Cole vaulted over it, barely touching the bricks with his fingertips, and landed soundlessly on the ground, graceful and fluid like a dancer.

Many years had passed since Damian was here last, but he still remembered his way around this blood-chilling place as if he was here just yesterday. Time and the events of the last century had taken their toll on the Eagle's Nest, and the estate lost its former splendor, the once beautiful park and gardens standing wild and unkept. Trying to produce as little noise as possible, he headed among tall linden trees toward a narrow alley, which cut across the park all the way from the main gates to the house.

"I believe Andrey Batashov had some help when he flooded his mint," Damian whispered, glancing back at his brother, "and if Lady Sineglazka is right about the location of Koschei's death, he must be the one who helped Batashov with this task. I'm sure Koschei used the opportunity to store his magical chest here, in one of the cellars under the Eagle's Nest."

"This place is endless," Cole muttered, falling into step with him. "Where do we even start looking for one small chest? It's like searching for a needle in a haystack"

"I have some ideas." Damian shrugged. "Allegedly, someone discovered a root cellar under the estate. When he explored it, he found an entrance into one of the underground passages. However"—Damian glanced at his brother sideways, giving him a pointed stare—"the door was sealed, and when they tried to open it, they were assailed by such overwhelming fear that they dropped everything and ran out of the cellar, screaming. Sounds familiar?"

"Sounds like a turn-away spell," Cole murmured.

"My thoughts exactly," Damian agreed. "Why would a Master of the Dark Arts as powerful and experienced as Koschei place such a potent turn-away spell on a sealed door of an empty cellar if he wasn't trying to hide something behind it?"

Cole nodded but didn't add anything else. They walked in silence until they reached the edge of the park. Damian halted, observing the massive two-story building of the Eagle's Nest. The paint and drywall were gone in places, exposing large blemishes of red brickwork. Patches of grass and low shrubbery grew over the white stone steps leading toward the main entrance, and thin vines of ivy slithered up four tall, iron columns supporting a wide portico that had replaced a spacious balcony that used to be in its place. The old house stood dark and silent, and Damian stifled a sigh of relief, positive the house was absolutely empty—at least he couldn't detect any human presence either inside or outside.

Lowering to one knee, he closed his eyes and took a deep breath, surrendering to his element. With his magical sight, he could see the flow of dark magic as it polluted the bright glimmer of the elemental energy of Earth, leaving dirty splatters and holes in it. The darkness became thicker and more potent toward the other side of the house, pulsing and throbbing in one place like a disgusting black blob. As he focused on it, his heart rate picked up, and sweat covered his forehead. For a brief second, his thoughts scrambled, and his vision turned blurry, only one desire clear in his mind—the need to run and never return here.

"Dima, what's going on?" Cole's troubled voice sounded next to him, and Damian exhaled, just now realizing he had been holding his breath all this time.

"Dammit," he muttered, biting his lip. "I'm afraid this turn-away spell is going to give us some serious grief."

"You can sense it from here?" Cole asked, his eyebrows rising.

"Yes," Damian whispered, getting to his feet. "Let's go, and if you feel the need to run, fight it."

As he circled the building, the weather started to deteriorate quickly, dark clouds gathering above their heads, diminishing the last light of the setting sun. Damian glanced up and shook his head, wondering if some spells Koschei cast over the estate could alarm him of their presence after all, or if it was just a regular thunderstorm rolling in.

"There are no coincidences in the World of Magic," Cole murmured, as if hearing Damian's thoughts, his eyes focused on the bright zigzag of lightning slicing the sky.

The thunder rolled over the building with such overwhelming ferocity that the old house shook as though in fear, the sound bouncing from tree to tree in the park for what seemed like forever.

"Perun almighty," Damian exhaled, picking up the pace.

He walked along the side of the building until he found a narrow indentation with a stone staircase leading down toward a low opening. The walls here had no paint or drywall left, a web of thin fractures and cracks cutting across the red brickwork. The door was gone, and piles of rubble and debris were scattered all over the floor.

Damian shuddered, bracing himself for the upcoming bout of claustrophobia. Then, without slowing down, he ran down the steps and crossed the threshold. The influence of the turn-away spell increased significantly here, and he groaned, fighting the desire to leave. Cole came to a sharp halt, and his eyes widened, a shadow of fear crossing his features. Turning to his brother, Damian seized his wrist and pulled him closer.

"Fight it, goddammit!" he hissed into his ear, pushing him forward. "Since when are you afraid of anything?"

Cole shook his head like a person who just woke up from a terrible nightmare and clenched his teeth, but moved forward nevertheless, stepping heavily on the littered floor. Following the flow of the turn-away spell, Damian crossed the room and halted in front of another doorway. Just like before, the actual door was missing, so he didn't stop and proceeded down the steps leading farther into the basement.

The descent was short, and soon he found himself standing in a completely dark chamber. Channeling some of his magic, he conjured a few light orbs and sent them flying up and ahead. An unsteady bluish light reflected in the arched ceiling, illuminating a wide cellar. Rusty pipes ran along the wall, disappearing into it, and old ropes and shreds of isolation hung like the web of a giant spider. The floor was littered with pieces of wooden boards, crumbled bricks and chunks of concrete, and the smell of mold and decay permeated the cold air, entwining with the reek of dark magic.

At the opposite end of the cellar, he noticed a small door reinforced by an iron frame. It was tightly shut, and the handle was broken, with only a tiny hole remaining in its place. As soon as Damian took a step toward it, a slight buzzing noise touched his hearing, and he felt as if the air itself started to vibrate, its light tremors grazing his skin. The influence of the turn-away spell increased further, and he groaned, gritting his teeth, fighting the need to run. Glancing over his shoulder, he saw Cole standing right behind him, his face drained of what little color he used to have.

"Pull yourself together, brother, for it's going to get only worse from here on," Damian whispered, connecting with his magic. The connection didn't come immediately, but he was able to accumulate some of the magical energy in his hands. Focusing on the door, he held out his hands and said, "*Recludius.*"

Nothing happened.

Damian groaned, locking and unlocking his fingers as he fought the crippling influence of the dark spell. Channeling more of his magic came with effort, but he managed to gather enough and redirect it toward the door, whispering another spell, "*Exitius.*"

The loud bang rolled across the cellar, disappearing into the depths of the catacombs, but the entrance stood unaffected. For the next few minutes, Damian tried everything he could think of, starting with different spells and finishing with brute force, but all his efforts were to no avail. Finally, he gave up and stepped away, sweat running down his face, his chest shuddering with strained breaths. Between using so much of his magic and fighting the constant pressure of the turn-away spell amplified by the increasing effects of claustrophobia, he couldn't keep at it for much longer.

Staring at the locked door, a desperate thought crossed his mind. He connected with his element and opened his other sight, reinforcing it with the elemental energy of Earth. But once he explored the door and the area around it, he shook his head and let go—the entire cellar was infused with the same magical energy that kept the entrance sealed.

"Dammit... Koschei's magic seems to be stronger than I expected, if it is his magic in the first place, which I doubt, to be honest. I thought I could remove this section of the wall, but I'm afraid this whole wing of the building might collapse." He massaged his shoulder, considering all his options, and then turned to Cole. "There is one more way we can do it, but it'll take a lot of my physical strength and magic." He pointed at the exit out of the cellar and gestured for Cole to follow. "Let's go. We need to get back outside."

They crossed the chamber and made their way up the narrow staircase. Despite the burning desire to run, Damian walked slowly, following Cole, trying to preserve his strength. As soon as they stepped inside the front room, a loud bang sounded behind them, causing Damian to flinch and spin around. The doorway they had used a moment ago was tightly shut by a solid iron door, even though he was positive this door hadn't existed when they came here.

Before Damian realized what was happening, the entrance door, which hadn't been there just a few minutes ago, closed with another loud bang, and complete darkness enveloped the chamber, spiking up his relentless claustrophobia. A soft male voice whispered a spell, conjuring a few light orbs, and as a shimmering blue light illuminated the limited space in the middle of the room, he saw a group of men standing in front of them, shoulder to shoulder.

"Just ten of them," Cole projected, using their blood bond, *"but in the confinements of this tiny room, we'll be at a serious disadvantage. So, if you have a plan, now would be a great time to share it, bro."*

"Before you do something ill-advised, Commander Blake, I would suggest hearing me out." A tall man dressed in black pants and a shirt stepped forward, and his eyes ignited with a deep purple glow, betraying his supernatural identity. As Damian tensed, carefully channeling his magic toward his hands, the man chuckled, slowly shaking his head with a reproachful smile. "Please, don't do it, Commander. Being as old as you are, both you and your brother should be experienced enough to know that your magic is partially blocked by my spell, and in such a tight space, you have no chance of winning a physical confrontation. You're outmanned and outgunned, so to speak." He cocked his head a little, gesturing at his men. "Let's talk like civilized people, shall we?"

Damian exchanged a quick look with Cole and then raked

his hand through his hair, pushing the sweat-soaked strands away from his eyes.

"Who are you and what do you want?" he asked icily, folding his arms.

"Smart choice." The man chuckled again, but there was a strange nervousness in his laughter this time. "My name is of no consequence to you. All you need to know is that we're here to escort you to our master. He just wants to speak with you and your brother before Koschei has an opportunity to put his hands on you. A peaceful negotiation, in a manner of speaking. Come with us, and no one will get hurt."

"Uh-huh," Damian muttered, turning to Cole. "Do you think all dark wizards attend the same school of magic? Every time I meet one of them, I hear the same threat. It's as if they're reading from a notebook or something."

A slightly sarcastic smile touched Cole's lips as he took a leisurely step forward, his face calm and emotionless. "And if we don't go with you? What are you going to do then?" he asked, raising his eyebrows.

"Well," the man mused, a soft glimmer of his magical energy, which he didn't bother to conceal, rising around him in fluid waves. "I wouldn't recommend that at all because things might get a lot less pleasant in that case."

He held out his fist, slowly unlocking his fingers one at a time, and a purple energy orb materialized in the palm of his hand, electrical discharges crackling around it. A second man separated from the crowd, stepping forward, his eyes glowing with the purple light of his magic. The rest of the team remained in the shadows, but a thin metallic sound touched Damian's sensitive hearing, suggesting some of them unsheathed their blades, getting ready to attack.

Cole reached up for his sword, but Damian seized his arm, stopping him. Turning to the dark wizard, he took another step forward, now standing only a couple of feet away from him.

"Before we make our decision, may I ask the name of your master?" he asked.

"I'm sorry, Commander." The man smiled and squeezed his fingers, making the energy orb vanish. "But I'm not at liberty to disclose this information to you."

"Cole, get ready to fight," Damian projected, carefully regarding his opponents. *"Two men upfront are dark wizards. Leave them to me. Even though my magic is partially suppressed, I have enough to take care of them. The rest of the team seems to be—"*

"Shifters," Cole muttered, wrinkling his nose. *"They have a distinct stench about them. I got it."*

"So, what is it going to be, Commander?" the man asked, his gaze shifting from Damian to Cole and back. "Trust me, you have no choice but to go with us, and I truly prefer the no violence approach."

"Ready?" Damian projected, his eyes focused on two dark wizards.

"Always," Cole replied, his smile growing wider and darker.

Damian took another step forward, extending his hand to the man. "Let's do it then."

The dark wizard smiled and took it. As soon as their hands connected, a pair of handcuffs, shining with a brilliant white light, materialized in Damian's left hand, and he locked them around the man's wrists so fast that his opponent barely realized what had just happened to him. As the Destiny cuffs started to drain his magic, the wizard cried out and dropped to his knees, pain contorting his features.

The second wizard growled and spun toward Damian, channeling his magic, but Damian was ready. In one step, he closed the distance between them and seized the man's throat with his left hand, lifting him off the ground. As the man groaned, grasping at Damian's arm, the second pair of Destiny cuffs appeared in his right hand. With fast and precise moves,

Damian locked the shining manacles around his opponent's wrists and threw him on the floor.

Once the Destiny cuffs completed their deadly job, draining all magical energy out of the wizards, the doors blocking both entrances vanished, and the spell they cast to suppress Damian's magic dissipated. A low growl rose over the team of shifters, and the air around them shimmered as a few of them began to transform, but neither Cole nor Damian waited to give them the chance to finish the transformation.

"*Exitius*," Damian shouted, anger fueling his magic, and a wave of enormous power rushed forward. It impacted the group of shifters and lifted them off the ground easily, as if all these brawny men had no weight whatsoever. It smashed them against the wall with a dull thud, and a web of fractures spread toward the ceiling, pieces of remaining drywall falling off to reveal red bricks beneath it.

The shifters dropped into a helpless heap of bodies and flailing limbs, their cries of pain, strangled coughs and groans filling the air. Their weapons fell to the ground with a loud clatter, and while three of them still endeavored to scramble to their feet, the rest remained sprawled, seemingly unconscious.

Damian didn't wait for them to recover, channeling more of his magic toward his hands, but Cole was faster. Moving as swift as it was possible in the limited space of the cellar, he closed the distance between him and the shifters in a flash and swung his swords, decapitating the first man in his way. The other two cowered away from him in terror, raising their arms in a defensive gesture. Silent and deadly, Cole spun around, and his blades whistled through the air, leaving two more headless bodies in their wake.

Trusting his brother to deal with the remaining shifters, Damian lowered to one knee next to the dark wizards, a dagger shining with a brilliant light materializing in his hand. One of the men was unconscious, but the wizard who had spoken with him in the beginning was awake, staring at him calmly. Now that his magic was gone, he looked a lot older. Deep wrinkles crossed his forehead and gathered around his tightly pressed mouth, his short hair turning silvery white before Damian's eyes.

"Are you going to kill us, Commander?" he muttered, his voice so hoarse and strained that Damian had a hard time making out his words.

"Yes," he replied coldly. "My brother and I have unfinished business here, and I'm not in the habit of leaving behind enemies who can strike me in the back."

A pained grimace crossed the man's face as he nodded. "I understand. I probably would do the same if I were you," he whispered, sounding too calm for a man who was about to die. "But before you do that, I wanted you to know that it was never in my plans to kill you or your brother. We had strict orders to bring you both alive. As I said before, my master wants to speak with you."

"I'm sure he does," Damian replied dryly. "I'm also sure that one day he will speak with us, but it's not gonna happen until I say so." He rested his arm with the dagger atop his knee, looking at the wizard with cold interest. "Your master has been trying to catch us for quite some time already, but I still have no idea why he needs us so desperately that he goes through all sorts of troubles to capture us alive. Wouldn't it be easier to just kill us and be done with that?"

The man chuckled. "Koschei the Deathless believes it would be easier and a lot more effective."

"Curious," Damian muttered. "Tell me what you know, and I may spare your life."

"Why do you think I'm so comfortable speaking with you, huh?" The man huffed and closed his eyes with a shallow sigh. "That's because I know nothing of any importance. Ancient gods don't hold someone like me in confidence," he added after a short pause. "I'm just a sword for hire who took a job to make some quick cash. You need to speak with Koschei the Deathless or Azazel if you want any valuable information. But as I said before, Koschei and my master don't always see eye to eye when it comes to you and your brother."

Feeling a light touch on his shoulder, Damian raised his eyes and found Cole standing next to him, his blades dripping with fresh blood.

"We should get going before someone else gets in our way." Cole picked up an old rag off the floor and wiped his swords before placing them in his back scabbard.

Damian nodded and switched his attention to the dark wizard. "How many of you are out there?" he asked.

"Out there?" The man's lips twitched, forming a crooked smile. "You mean in the Eagle's Nest or in general?"

"Both," Damian replied.

"We were the only team sent here, as far as I know," he answered. "But it doesn't mean Koschei doesn't have his own agenda." He snickered, his eyes darting from Damian to the other dark wizard lying next to him. "In general—there are thousands of those who serve our master, worshiping him above all gods, old and new. He's a great ancient power unlike anything I've ever seen, and no one in their right mind would contest his supremacy in the World of Magic. Not even the Destiny Council..." Sparkles of excitement ignited in his fading eyes as he met Damian's unemotional gaze. "Trust me, Commander, when he sets his mind on something, there is nothing in this world or any other world that can stop him. Spare yourself the pain and suffering and come with me now, for sooner or later, you *will* bend your knee before him."

"Maybe, but not today." Damian placed his hands on the Destiny cuffs restraining the wizards and whispered a short spell. The white light emitted by the cuffs grew brighter, and when it dwindled, both dark wizards were gone.

"What did you do with them?" Cole asked, offering Damian his hand.

Making his dagger vanish, Damian got up and brushed the dirt off his pants. "I sent them to a Destiny Council holding facility," he muttered, his mind still on the words the wizard said to him. "When we're done here, I intend to speak with both of them again."

"Great ancient power... Supremacy," Cole whispered, echoing Damian's thought. "Did it sound familiar to you—"

"Like a part of that goddamn prophecy?" Damian smiled mirthlessly. "Yes, it did. Sired by the great ancient power, blah-blah-blah..." He put his hand on his brother's shoulder, directing him toward the exit. "Unless this prophecy is about someone else, it's the biggest bag of bullshit I've ever heard. We were sired by some drunken peasant who died before you were born, and our mother followed him shortly after. End of story."

They walked out of the cellar, and Damian inhaled a lungfull of air, feeling better in the wide-open space. Connecting with his element, he explored the area under the house and sighed with relief—seemingly, only one major corridor led in the direction of the chamber sealed by Koschei's spell, and he could follow it all the way into the part of the park that had been called the terrible garden when Batashov was still alive.

"I can see where this passage leads," Damian whispered, pointing toward the park. "I know where we need to go."

A few large drops of water fell on his shoulders, then a few more followed, and within a few seconds, frigid rain was heavily pounding the metal roof of the house, its drumming turning into a continuous hum. Damian raised his face, frowning as the bright zigzag of lightning split the dark sky. Thunder boomed almost immediately, and an icy gust of wind followed, causing him to shiver in his wet shirt.

"Silly me," Cole muttered, shaking his head. "I thought it couldn't get any worse."

Damian chuckled, giving Cole a light tap on his shoulder. "You're a vampire, remember? Impervious to cold. Start behaving like one."

"Haha." Cole rolled his eyes. "If I was behaving like a vampire, I'd be drinking your blood now."

"Is that before or after I turn you into a pile of ashes, Dracula junior?" Damian laughed softly, pushing Cole in the direction of the dark park.

"Doofus," Cole grumbled, but then a wide grin split his face, and he threw his wet hair away from his eyes. "Let's go already, before you catch a cold or something."

Keeping the connection with his element open, Damian followed the direction of the underground passage into the park. Soon, the rain increased, turning into an icy downpour, and the thunderstorm kept ravaging the area, the continuous flashing of the lightning bolts morphing into a nonstop light show.

After a short while, the underground corridor merged into a spacious chamber. Standing above the ground, Damian couldn't say for sure what this area was. However, the accumulation of the dark magical energy in this place was so high that he had no doubt it was the place they needed.

He halted and raised his arm, stopping his brother. They stood at the edge of a wide clearing, surrounded by tall linden trees and thick shrubbery. The center of the space was barren of any greenery, and the wet ground stood out like a dark, sore thumb. The next lightning forked through the sky, illuminating the clearing, and Damian held his breath, staggering backward until his back hit a tree.

Cole gasped, pointing forward, his eyes widening in horror. "What the hell was that?" he hissed, reaching for his sword.

CHAPTER 23

~ DAMIAN BLAKE ~

Damian looked in the direction his brother was pointing, and shivers ran down his back. As the next lightning flashed through the sky, everything changed before his eyes. Gone were the narrow paths, unattended park and barren clearing. A beautiful garden surrounded by well-trimmed shrubbery and tall trees spread out before him as far as he could see. Soft music flowed in the night, the sound of voices and laughter touching his ears.

The thunder rumbled above his head, and Damian flinched, taking his eyes off the unusual view for just a moment. When he looked back, the vision was gone, and the cold rain kept beating the tall, wild grass and overgrown bushes. He opened his magical sight but still didn't see anything different. The same thick layer of dark energy slithered over the ground, flowing around him and Cole in dirty swirls.

"What the fuck is going on here?" he mumbled under his breath, slowly turning around.

The lightning bolt crossed the sky, and a few more joined it, illuminating the area again. The music and voices returned, and a slight odor of ozone touched his nostrils.

"Dima!" Cole yelped, his voice ringing with terror.

In the unsteady light of the thunderstorm, he saw a tall pole erected in the middle of the clearing. A half-naked man with shoulder-length black hair was strung up at the pole, his wrists attached to it with a heavy iron chain. Another man stood behind him, holding a bullwhip in his hands. While they looked real enough, a strange pale glow surrounded their bodies, and as Damian narrowed his eyes, staring at them, he noticed that they weren't quite corporeal, coming in and out of focus with every next flare of lightning.

"Dima, tell me the truth, *brat moi*," Cole whispered in his ear, seizing his arm above the elbow. "When you were here the last time, did they capture and flog you in the terrible garden?"

"What?" Damian glanced at his brother in shock. "No, of course not. I was here for a short time, and I left as soon as I was done with my business. Why would you—"

He didn't finish his statement and took a step forward without realizing he was doing it, his eyes glued to the man attached to the pole. Getting into position, the executioner swung the whip, and the leather thong bit into the man's bare back, eliciting a strangled cry of pain out of him. Blood streamed down from a deep welt, and in the next flare of lightning, Damian saw a set of old scars disfiguring the prisoner's back, running from his shoulders down to his waist.

The whip hissed through the air again and again. The man screamed and thrashed, pulling against his restraints. His head tilted back and to the side, and now Damian could see a small part of his face deformed by a scar cutting from his hairline down to the middle of his cheek.

"So many men were flogged to death in the terrible garden in those days, but I swear, I was never one of them," Damian whispered, cold sweat dripping down his face, mixing with the frosty rainwater. "God knows I've been flogged more than once in my life, but never in this terrible place. I don't understand…"

After the next lash, the man at the pole stopped screaming and hung limply, supported by the chain. His head tilted back all the way, his long hair partially concealing the gruesome view of his mangled back.

"Dima, the prisoner looks like you, down to the scars on his back and face... It *is* you... but if you were never punished here, it can't be..." Cole stared at the unconscious man, his hands clenched into tight fists. "It's not spirits or phantoms or apparitions. I think it's an illusion, a message..."

Immediately after Cole said that, the man with the whip approached the prisoner and seized a handful of his hair, moving his head to the side as far as he could without breaking his neck to allow them to see his face, as if he wanted them to know how much the man at the pole looked like Damian. Then he let go and slowly turned around.

Even from such a close proximity, Damian couldn't see the executioner's face clearly. His eyes were glowing with a blinding silver-white light, and the rest of his features were indistinguishable because of that. He was tall, at least seven feet, if not more, his black hair framing his face in soft waves. As he dropped the whip and spread his massive shoulders, Damian sucked in a sharp breath.

"The Beast Master," he hissed, his chest shuddering with quick breaths.

The glow of the man's eyes dimmed just a little, and a wide smile crossed his face as he started to morph, changing his shape into that of a terrifying monster. Once the transformation was completed, he spun around and slashed the prisoner's back with his horrid claws, ripping it to shreds. A choked scream broke from Damian's lips as if it were him strung up at the pole and not an apparition that looked like him.

Glowing mist rose around the prisoner, and when it dissipated, a woman with long, black hair hung in restraints in his place. Her body was covered in terrifying wounds, blood streaming down her back and face, and she appeared dead, her lifeless, faded eyes looking into the sky. The mist wrapped around her again as the next transformation began, the color of her hair changing to copper, brilliant red sparkles dancing in it with each flare of lightning.

Damian stood frozen in place, staring at the ghastly scene without blinking, his hand clutching at his throat. The lightning bolts kept illuminating the park, their constant flashes making the blood-chilling view even more terrifying, and the thunder rolled in continuous heavy outbursts in contrast to the soft music flowing through the air. A thin metallic sound managed to break through the cacophony of the storm, partially ripping Damian out of his strange stupor. With a sword in his hand, Cole zoomed through the clearing, the flares of light bouncing off his blade and his wet clothes.

He reached the man with the glowing eyes and swung his weapon, cutting his body from his shoulder to his groin. The red stone ignited brighter in the pommel of his sword, and wisps of dark smoke followed his move. The executioner dissipated, leaving behind a few ghostly, phosphoric lights that vanished soon after. The entire view swayed and flowed and was gone a moment later.

Cole sheathed his sword and returned to Damian. He put his hand on the back of Damian's head and pulled him closer, resting his forehead against his brother's, rainwater running in icy rivulets down their faces.

"Dima, it was just a cruel illusion," Cole whispered, pulling away. "None of it was real, and it's over now." He let go of his hair and slapped his wet cheek gently.

"I know. I'm sorry, I just—" Damian closed his eyes and swallowed hard. "I just want to understand who conjured this image and what kind of message they were trying to convey. It makes no sense." He dropped his head, wiping water off his face. "Did you recognize who the executioner was?"

Cole shook his head. "When I approached him, the image became blurry and faded." He readjusted the straps of his scabbard and ran his hand through his hair to push the soaked strands away from his eyes. "You heard the dark wizard back there. Koschei and his master don't see eye to eye when it comes to our wellbeing." A slightly sarcastic grin touched his lips, showing off the tips of his fangs. "Maybe the old one is trying to warn you about Koschei's intentions? Or vice versa?"

"If they can't find common ground, why do they work together in the first place? The old gods are more powerful than any Master of the Dark Arts, and they are not known for their patience. Why does he keep Koschei around if the ancient sorcerer openly goes against his wishes, trying to kill us any opportunity he gets?" Damian took a deep breath and focused on connecting with his element. "This question has been driving me crazy for quite some time."

"Indeed…" Cole muttered, poking the wet dirt with the tip of his boot. "What worries me is that until we find the answer to this question and figure out what they want with us, we're at their mercy, flying blind in a constantly reactive mode."

"Fine, let's be proactive then and do what we came here to do. I'm not going to break my head trying to guess the twisted intentions of two evil bastards." A dark smile touched Damian's lips as he headed toward the center of the clearing. He halted there and opened himself to the flow of the elemental energy of Earth. "Think about it. If we get Koschei out of the picture, we don't have to worry about him contradicting his ancient master and all the questions associated with him. All we need to do is find out why the old one wants us at his disposal and his plans. Maybe we'll sit down and have a nice chat with him after all."

He glanced at his brother over his shoulder and winked, trying to project calm determination while not really feeling it. He wasn't sure why, but he never told Cole what bothered him the most. Since he got a closer look at the ancient deity back in the City of Gold, he couldn't get rid of the nagging feeling that he had seen him somewhere already. It wasn't his face—throughout all the close encounters, Damian had never seen his features clearly.

It was his eyes, or rather the light they were emitting. That blinding white glow he got used to seeing in Magnus' gaze whenever the Head of the Destiny Council was angry. All members of the High Council had the same powerful magic that lit up their gazes like the high beam headlights of a truck, turning their eye color into that unnerving silvery shade.

Dammit, Magnus, he thought, focusing on the underground chamber. *If Cole and I survive this ordeal, you better have some answers for me, old man.*

"Hold on to something, brother," Damian murmured. "Here goes nothing."

The ground shook, responding to his command, and a low grinding noise rose in the air. First, a narrow fracture split the earth, running across the clearing. As Damian poured more of his elemental energy into it, it grew wider and deeper, pieces of dirt and small rocks sliding inside. Soon, the top layer of dirt was gone, and the rough surface of brickwork became visible through the hole. Damian didn't stop. Lowering to one knee, he buried his fingers into the ground at the edge of the opening. His wet shirt stretched tightly over the bulging muscles of his shoulders, back and chest as he fought the resistance of the stonework.

With a loud crack, the masonry finally gave in, pieces of bricks and cement falling inside an underground chamber. Once the opening became big enough for him and Cole to pass through, Damian let go of his element and got up, his chest shuddering with laborious breaths. The rain seemed to increase, mercilessly pelting him with icy streams. He wiped his face, staring down into the dark abyss of the chasm he created.

"Ready?" he asked Cole, and when his brother gave him a short nod, he added, "I'm going first. Wait until I call you."

Damian stepped off the edge of the chasm and dropped inside. A moment later, he landed on the balls of his feet and rolled over his shoulder to break the long fall, rising back up with ease. Whispering a quick spell, he summoned a few light orbs and observed his surroundings. Unlike other areas of the underground catacombs that he had seen so far, this large chamber seemed spared by time and elements. The stonework remained whole, as if it was never flooded. An old machine was positioned at the other end of the room, and it looked as if just yesterday it was used to strike coins.

He opened his other sight and scanned the room, noticing the layer of dark magic. It flowed uninterrupted along the perimeter, getting heavier toward a small table located by the wall. Other than that, the chamber seemed to be void of any kind of presence—magical or mundane.

Damian glanced up at the hole in the ceiling and massaged his shoulder, cursing the pieces of bricks and concrete scattered on the floor. The rainwater dripped through the opening, gathering into puddles under his feet.

Cole, he reached out to his brother through their blood bond. *You can come—*

Before he finished his statement, Cole landed softly next to him and halted, looking around. A soft hiss escaped his lips as his fangs extended, and his eyes lit up with the scarlet glow of his vampiric essence.

"Let's do what we came here to do and be on our way," he whispered, his last words getting swallowed by the next outburst of thunder.

"Why?" Damian spun around but didn't notice anything alarming. "Do you sense something I don't?"

"Death and darkness," Cole replied in a whisper. "Just like everywhere else in this estate but magnified tenfold."

Damian couldn't help but survey the area once more before heading across the chamber toward the table. He halted a step away from it and moved his hand in a wide arch, whispering a revealment spell. The air in front of him shimmered, and a thin glass-like layer of his magic materialized before him.

"I'll be damned," Cole whispered, peering through the layer of spell over Damian's shoulder.

An intricately crafted oak chest sat in the middle of the table, the flickering glimmer of the light orbs reflecting in the gold ornaments decorating it, sparkling in the rubies embedded into its hasp latch. It was locked by a small padlock that seemed too delicate to stop anyone from breaking in. The already familiar energy signature of Koschei touched Damian's senses, and he clenched his teeth, fighting the desire to break the chest into tiny, wooden splinters.

"Is that it?" Cole asked, disbelief in his voice. "This padlock is so flimsy I can break it by simply touching it. Don't you think Koschei would have picked something a bit sturdier to keep his death protected?"

"Yeah, it's his chest, alright." Damian scanned the box with his second sight and frowned, his lips curving into a grim smile. An already familiar combination of three glyphs entwined with each other glowed over the padlock. "The lock is purely decorative. His magic protects it. Look…" He moved the layer of the revealment spell closer to the chest and channeled more of his magical energy into it. "You see these three interwoven symbols? This is what keeps the chest protected. I want to say it's some form of protection magic, but before a few days ago, I hadn't ever seen wards like this. Luckily, now I know how to unlock this magical monogram." Damian reached for the chest but then pulled his hand back, staring at it in doubt. "If by some great miracle Koschei still doesn't know we are here, as soon as I touch this chest, he'll find out."

Cole unsheathed both swords and jerked his chin at the

chest. "That's what we came for, so we don't have a choice on the matter. Go for it."

Damian directed some of his Destiny Enforcer magic toward his hand and brushed his fingertips over the Shadow Enforcer's rune on his shoulder. Whispering a quick spell, he reached toward the monogram and touched the symbol that represented Magnus, channeling his magic through it.

Once his fingers came in contact with the wards, they responded with a low buzz, the air around the chest shimmering and vibrating. The glyphs started to grow, their shine increasing every next second. The noise magnified, turning into a high-pitched tone that filled every nook and cranny of the chamber. Cole groaned, bending his knees, his arms rising of their own accord as the sound became unbearably loud for his vampire hearing.

Damian pressed his hands to his ears, staggering a step back. The note trembled somewhere above his head and then died as suddenly as it had started, replaced by a deafening bang of thunder. The symbols flashed one last time and dissipated, leaving just a few sparkles behind.

The howling of wind filled the chamber, and it seemed as though the storm was now raging not only on the surface, but in the underground catacombs as well. A bolt of lightning struck through the hole in the ceiling and impacted the floor a few feet away from them, raising a cloud of dirt and debris in the air. Thunder boomed almost at the same time. Koschei's magical energy signature lingering around the chest became stronger, as if some other incantations were activated the moment the wards were broken.

"Get the chest and let's get the hell out of here," Cole shouted, raising his voice over the cacophony of the storm. "If we have to fight Koschei, I prefer to do it above ground."

Damian rushed toward the box to grab it, but as soon as he touched it, something clicked, and the padlock vanished in swirls of gray smoke. The lid flipped open, and before he or Cole could do anything, a large black rabbit hopped out of it. The animal landed on the floor and halted there, rising on its hind legs, its ears flat against its back.

"The needle is inside an egg. The egg is inside a duck. The duck is inside a—," Damian started to recount the words of Lady Sineglazka, but cut himself off and pointed at the animal, shouting, "Cole, get the goddamn rabbit!"

As soon as Cole made a move toward it, the furball took off at a speed no normal rabbit could muster. Cole cursed and dropped his swords, bolting after it. The rabbit ran around the chamber, making zigzags, sharp turns, hopping against the walls. Cole added to his speed, and in no time both turned into blurry streaks. Cursing Koschei and his creative way of hiding his death, Damian jumped on the table, trying to keep out of his brother's way.

A heartbeat later, Cole came to a screeching halt next to the table. He crouched, his left arm braced against the floor, his glowing eyes moving from side to side as he watched the rabbit bouncing around the room. In this pose, with his lip curled in a snarl, he looked like a ferocious beast, waiting to strike his prey. Suddenly, he threw his right arm forward, and when he straightened, he held the struggling rabbit by the scruff of its neck. He bent down, reaching for his sword when the animal vanished from his hand with a soft popping sound, and a duck flew up toward the hole in the ceiling, its wings beating loudly through the air.

"Fuck!" Damian roared and spread his wings. Pushing off the table, he took off, following the duck through the opening to the surface.

As the hell storm tormented the park, the constant flashing of lightning blinded him for a moment. The wind was so powerful that he had a hard time keeping in the air, and its howls sounded like that of a hungry monster. The rain deteriorated to a torrential downpour, slashing at him as he tried to find the black duck in the dark sky. As the next lightning illuminated the sky, he noticed the shadowy silhouette of the bird moving higher and higher with each flap of its wings.

Cursing under his breath, Damian flew after it, feeling his element slowly abandoning him the farther he rose above the ground. Weakness enveloped him, reminding him that if he went any higher, he would sever his connection with Earth completely, losing his magic, his strength, and his immortality, and that wasn't something he could afford to risk.

In a last-ditch effort, he summoned his dagger and propelled it at the duck with all the strength he had, infusing it with his magic. The shiny blade zoomed through the stormy sky and found its victim. The duck screeched and started to fall, disappearing from view for a brief moment. Damian waited for it to come into view and rushed after it. He stretched his arm, ready to grab the dead bird, when it vanished in a cloud of sparkling purple mist, leaving a golden egg behind.

He missed catching it by no more than an inch, and an infuriated scream broke from his lips. Folding his wings behind his back, he outstretched his arm and streamlined his body, his eyes never leaving the small golden egg. Falling faster and faster, he reached as far as he could, and his fingers finally wrapped around the egg just a few yards above the clearing. Realizing that he had no time to open his wings and break his fall, he snapped his fingers and vanished from the sky, teleporting into the underground chamber.

Damian manifested next to Cole, dropping on the cold floor. With a low groan, he scrambled to his knees and bent forward, propping his hands against his lap, his chest rising and falling with heavy breaths, water running down his face and body. Answering the silent question in his brother's eyes, he lifted his right arm, showing him the egg.

Taking the hand Cole offered, Damian rose to his feet and

looked down at the egg, expecting it to vanish like the rest of the subjects in Koschei's chest, but it just lay in his palm, the shimmering light of the orbs reflecting in its smooth surface.

"Should we break it?" Cole asked. He reached for the egg, but then dropped his hand, shaking his head.

"Yes, but not here," Damian replied. "Like you said, if we have to face Koschei, we shouldn't do it in a small underground chamber."

He moved closer to Cole, ready to teleport them out of here when the ground shook with such strength, he had to take a step back to keep his balance. The icy wind rushed through the room and a lightning bolt forked inside, hitting the floor. Thunder rumbled, bouncing from the walls to the ceiling and disappearing in the clamor of the storm outside. Koschei's energy flooded the area, pressing on Damian's senses, and his magically amplified voice boomed louder than the thunderstorm.

"How dare you, puny Enforcer?" Koschei's voice was coming from every direction at once, and a heavy wave of dark magic surrounded Damian, restraining him. He glanced at his brother just to find that he was in an even worse situation, the glowing ropes of Koschei's spell wrapped tightly around his arms and torso.

Damian connected to his magic, trying to break Koschei's restraints, but he was too drained by the previous events, and all his efforts brought no results. A toxic purple mist rose from the ground, invading every square inch of the room, and Damian coughed, struggling to fill his lungs with oxygen. He swayed and dropped to his knees, lingering at the edge of consciousness. With his blurred vision, he saw Cole lying on the dirty floor, his entire body now wrapped in the ropes of magical energy.

The purple mist covered him like a frosty blanket, sending tremors down his still struggling body, and at that very moment, he knew there was nothing he could do to stop what was coming from happening. When he noticed strange inclusions glowing with greenish phosphoric light breaking the mist, he wasn't sure his dimming mind wasn't playing tricks on him. But the inclusions grew larger and shone brighter, devouring the mist. The temperature in the chamber dropped so low, he couldn't stop shivering in his wet clothes. The hold of Koschei's magic lightened up, and finally, he was able to take a lungful of air.

Dark shadows materialized in the mist. A large group of people surrounded him and Cole in a tight circle, their unsteady forms flickering and fading in and out, an unmistakable vibe of death coming from them. A man separated from the crowd and approached him, his entire body glowing with a soft phosphoric light.

"Leave now... We can't hold him much longer..." His voice sounded in Damian's mind. "Slay the monster who killed us all..."

With tremendous effort, Damian seized his brother's arm and snapped his fingers. As the chamber spun around him in nauseating circles of the teleportation process, he saw the ghosts vanishing, and Koschei's dark shape manifesting in the room. His bony arm reached for Damian, but the sorcerer was too late to stop them.

As darkness embraced him, a holler of unadulterated fury reached Damian's ears, and his lips quirked up in a smile. For the first time since all this started, Koschei was no longer ahead of him.

CHAPTER 24

~ DAMIAN BLAKE ~

They materialized on a mountain plateau overlooking the Sonoran Desert and a small lake hidden among rocky cliffs and large boulders. The sun in zenith showered Damian with much-needed warmth and light, and he turned on his back, trying to stop himself from shivering. Glancing to the side, he saw his brother lying next to him, and he sighed with relief.

"Cole," he called to him, his teeth chattering a little.

Cole moved his head slightly, a faint smile dancing on his lips, his blue eyes sparkling with excitement. "We did it," he whispered, "didn't we?"

"We're alive, and we have Koschei's death." Damian pushed himself into a sitting position. He held out his hand, showing the small golden egg to his brother. Cole also sat up, gazing around with curiosity.

"Where are we?" He got up, squeezing water out of his shirt.

"At one of my safe points, not far from Tortilla Flat." Damian moved his shoulders carefully, feeling the nagging ache of exhaustion settling in his muscles. "I have a few of them in different areas of the desert. Here, we are under the cover of wards and protection spells. I conjured them myself, so they are powerful enough to give us a short reprieve and allow me to restore at least some of my elemental energy."

Damian lay back down and relaxed his buzzing muscles, welcoming the embrace of his element. As the healing energy of Earth surged through him, partially restoring his strength, he smiled blissfully and closed his eyes. A short while later, he cracked his eyelids open and took in his brother's appearance.

Cole sat at the edge of the cliff, with one leg dangling off it and the other pulled to his chest. The sunlight played with the stones embedded into the pommels of his swords, coloring his golden-blond hair with red and blue streaks. He looked relaxed and a little pensive, his arm resting leisurely atop his bent knee. With his crystal blue eyes gazing into the space above the lake, he reminded him of the time when they both were human, just normal boys, trying to survive the harsh reality of their lives.

Damian got up and stretched his arms, wincing from the touch of wet clothes to his body, and approached his brother, taking a knee by his side. Cole looked up at him, and a familiar, warm smile lit up his face. Damian ruffled his curls just the way he used to do when they were kids and placed his hand on his shoulder.

"Ready," he asked. "The break is over. It's time to go."

"Where?"

"Somewhere where the wards are a lot stronger than mine and can withhold any of Koschei's attacks." Damian got up and glanced at the view below, feeling cold and empty on the inside. "Before I crack this egg, I want to make sure nothing will interrupt us."

"I'm positive you don't mean Paradise Manor or my estate, because you won't risk bringing Koschei's attention to Ruslan and Dallas," Cole muttered, rising. "And you can't be going to the Destiny Council realm since I'm a vampire, and you are probably a *persona non grata* after disobeying all your orders. So where are we going, brother mine?"

Damian let out a harsh breath, and his shoulders slouched. "To the only person who can protect us, and whom I trust to let me complete my mission before turning me over to the High Council," he replied.

"Dima, but—," Cole began to say, his eyes widening with understanding.

Damian smiled at him, placing his hand on his brother's arm. "We have to finish what we started, little bro. I will gladly pay any consequences just to see all of you safe." He squeezed Cole's arm gently. "Trust me. This is the only way."

Before Cole could object, Damian snapped his fingers, and they vanished from the cliff.

* * *

THEY MANIFESTED in front of massive iron gates that blocked an entrance into a large property. A narrow asphalt road disappeared into a picturesque park, which concealed the enormous mansion of the Guardians HQ situated in the depth of the gardens, away from prying human eyes.

Damian approached a security monitor on the side of the road and placed his palm over the screen. As he channeled his Destiny Enforcer magic through it, the brand on his shoulder lit up with the bright white light of his magic.

Something clicked, and an indifferent male voice sounded through the speakers. "Identify yourself."

"I'm Commander Damian Blake, Shadow Enforcer to Lord Magnus, the Head of the Destiny Council," Damian replied, turning slightly to make his rune visible to the camera. Then he waved in Cole's direction. "This is Cole Adams, the King of the Arizona Vampire Court. We seek an audience with Archmage Allerton."

"A Destiny Enforcer in the company of a vamp?" The man tittered, disbelief blending with sarcasm in his words.

Something clicked again, and a different male voice sounded through the system. "Commander Blake, what is your business with the Archmage?"

"My mission is urgent, and I can't discuss it with anyone other than the Archmage." Damian stepped closer to the gates, allowing his eyes to ignite with a bright orange shine, and added through gritted teeth, "You're wasting my time, guard, and patience is not one of my virtues. If you know what's best for you, you'll let Quinn Allerton know about my arrival at once."

Something clicked, and the monitor went dark, but the gates remained locked, a layer of wards still glowing over them.

"Dammit!" Damian cursed, pinching the bridge of his nose. He took a deep breath, suppressing the rising wave of aggravation, and scanned the surrounding area with his other sight, wondering how long it would take for Koschei to detect either his presence or the energy signature of the golden egg now that he was outside the warded territory.

A metallic click was too jarring for his stretched nerves, causing him to wince and snap around. The gates jerked and began to open with a loud screeching noise. The screen lit up again, and the voice of the second guard sounded through the system.

"Commander Blake, we apologize for the delay," he said. "Archmage Allerton is expecting you in his office. He grants you permission to teleport from the grounds directly into his chambers."

Without waiting for another invitation, Damian stepped through the gateway, motioning for Cole to follow him. Once they crossed into the Guardians HQ property, the gates closed behind them, and the wards lit up again.

"Perun almighty, thank you," Damian whispered. He placed

his hand on Cole's shoulder and snapped his fingers, teleporting them directly into the Archmage's office.

As soon as they materialized in front of a large office-style desk, Quinn Allerton got up and inclined his head slightly, greeting them. Damian pressed his fist to his chest, relieved to see concern reflected on the Archmage's face.

"Commander Blake, Mr. Adams, what can I do for you?" Allerton said, gesturing for them to sit down. He pushed his spectacles down his nose a little and observed them over the rim of his glasses, his eyebrows rising. "Did you take a swim in the Chicago River?"

A guilty smile crossed Damian's face, and he spread his arms, looking down at his wet clothes. "No, sir," he said. "We were a lot closer to Gus River by the town of Gus-Zhelezny in Russia."

Allerton's jaw dropped, and for a moment, he just gaped at them, slowly shaking his head in disbelief. Then he threw his hands up and motioned at the chairs again.

"Heaven and Earth, Commander," he grumbled. "Sit your asses down, both of you, and start talking. I want to know exactly what kind of mess you two got yourselves into while you"—he pointed at Damian—"had strict orders to remain in Paradise Manor. When all this is over, the High Council will cut belts out of your back, Damian. You realize that, don't you?"

"And I will gladly take my shirt off and allow them to do it, assuming I survive what's coming," Damian said quietly, placing the golden egg on the table.

Allerton reached for the egg, his fingers trembling slightly, but then jerked his hand away, as if afraid it could burn him, and rose sharply, sending his chair rolling back until it hit the wall.

"Please tell me this is not what I think it is," he whispered, his face turning ashen.

"Judging by your reaction, it is exactly what you think it is," Damian replied calmly. "And this is the reason we are here."

"Goddammit, Commander!" Allerton hissed, heading toward the exit. "A little warning would have been nice!"

He walked out of the office and spoke with his guards in a hushed voice. Once both men scurried away, he returned and pulled his chair back to his desk, his sharp moves betraying his nervousness. Lowering himself onto it, he leaned forward slightly.

"I just gave orders to reinforce all the wards and protection spells over the HQ property. While you remain under the cover of my wards, Koschei can't detect you or the egg," Allerton continued. "Now, start talking, Damian, before I change my mind and send you straight to one of the Destiny Council holding facilities."

"I'm sorry, sir." Damian exchanged a quick look with Cole. "We had no time to make calls or ask for permission to enter."

He told Allerton everything that had happened since the moment they saw him last in Paradise Manor. When he finished, the Archmage got up and started pacing the office, his lips moving as if he were repeating every word Damian had just told him. Then he stopped next to him and sighed, nibbling on his lip.

"Damian," he said, an unexpected softness in his voice. "Lady Sineglazka was right. If killing Koschei was as easy as breaking that legendary needle, she could have done it centuries ago. She's an ancient warrior-mage gifted with incredible power. You're a Destiny Enforcer and a Child of Earth, and I have no doubts about your abilities, but I dare say she's a lot more powerful than you..." He trailed off, and a deep crease crossed his forehead. "I do like you, Commander, and I don't want to see something unfortunate happen to you or your brother."

He stroked his beard, his eyes growing distant. Damian nodded and got up, numbness spreading through his chest.

"I understand, sir," he said calmly, taking the egg from the desk. "The safety of your Order and your academy is your utmost priority." He gestured for Cole to rise. "We'll be on our way."

Allerton made an impatient gesture with his hand, interrupting him. "You'll do no such thing, Commander. I can't let you do it on your own because that would mean your certain demise, as well as the true death for your brother. Since you came here seeking my help, I will provide you with my support as I promised a while ago," he said, taking the egg from Damian's hand. "But understand one thing. As the Archmage of the Guardians Order, I must report everything that's going on in the Guardians HQ to the High Council."

"I understand, sir." Damian inclined his head. "Do what you must."

Allerton waited for Damian and Cole to sit down and continued, "I also want you to know that Koschei the Deathless is not just a Master of the Dark Arts. Born at the time of creation, he used to be a dark god of the Nav, in his power equal to Chernobog and his twin brother. So, if you think it'll be easy to dispose of him, think again."

"I know," Damian replied.

"Dammit, Commander," Allerton muttered. "When Lord Magnus told me you were stubborn and insubordinate, he truly didn't do you justice with his choice of words."

"My apologies." Damian bowed his head to hide a wide grin crossing his face as he imagined the conversation between Allerton and Magnus.

The Archmage gazed heavenward and twirled his wrist. "In that case, why don't you do me the honor." Allerton offered him the golden egg, giving him a challenging look. "I can sense that the wards have been reinforced already, so you can go ahead and break it."

Damian took the egg, his fingers wrapping tightly around its slick shell. Squeezing it in his fist, he carefully knocked it against the edge of the table and froze in place, all his senses on high alert.

Nothing happened.

He peered at the egg, with shock realizing that not only did it not break, but its shiny surface didn't suffer even the tiniest crack either. Damian raised his hand with the egg and slammed it against the desk, this time applying all his physical strength while amplifying it with his magic. With a jarring noise, the table split in two, all the documents flying to the floor in a cascade of paper. The phone fell with a loud ding, pens and pencils rolling in all directions.

Damian looked at the egg again, and his jaw dropped. Its surface remained as flawless as ever, shining with reflected electric light.

"Holy shit," Cole murmured, scratching the back of his head. "What do we need to do to break it?"

Allerton chuckled, shoving his hands into the pockets of his pants. "It's true what they say... Who needs brains if you have the strength? Right, Commander?" He met Damian's flabbergasted gaze and burst out laughing, his kindhearted laugh dispelling the tension in the room. Then he turned toward Cole, and added through laughter, "You asked the correct question, Your Majesty."

"Oh, dammit." Damian facepalmed as realization dawned on him and then bowed to the Archmage, trying not to laugh. "Forgive my language, my lord. It's been an extremely long day—or few days, actually—and I think my brain needed a little jumpstart. I totally forgot that I wasn't cooking an omelet out of this egg."

Damian lowered the egg to the floor and kneeled, positioning his hands around it without touching it. He channeled his magic and the elemental power at the same time and started to chant, clearly pronouncing the words of the enchantment in Dragon tongue. Swirls of orange and white light emerged from his palms, tiny electrical discharges crackling around them. They entwined with each other and then encompassed the egg, lifting it a few inches above the ground.

It rose higher in the air, starting a clockwise rotation as Damian continued sending more of his magical energy through it. The lights in the office flickered and went off, only the glow of magic illuminating the room. As the complicated spell kept draining his energy, Damian's arms shook slightly, perspiration covering his forehead, but he didn't stop, tapping into his internal resources. Cole took a step closer to him, concern shadowing his features, but Allerton seized his elbow, slowly shaking his head.

Suddenly, the egg ceased its rotation and froze in midair. A thin, dark fracture marred its golden surface right in the middle. Damian stopped chanting and rose to his feet, breathing heavily as if he'd run a few miles. He moved his hand up, placing it under the egg. It lowered softly into his palm, and the glimmer surrounding it dwindled, submerging the office into complete darkness. Then the electric lights flickered again and turned back on. Damian exhaled and dropped onto a chair, staring at the cracked egg in shock.

"Congratulations, Commander. Not too many people can surprise me, but you certainly have." Allerton stepped behind him, placing his hands on Damian's shoulders, and leaned forward, observing the egg with curiosity. "I didn't think you were privy to such an ancient enchantment. Usually, Destiny Enforcers don't bother learning anything outside of combat magic. This unlocking spell is as old as Creation itself. Where did you learn it?"

Damian glanced back at him, a faint smile crossing his lips. "I'm not that different from other Enforcers, sir," he objected softly. "Combat magic is what I do best. But when I visited the Master of Kendral the last time, I told him about my plans, and he suggested using this spell if I ever find the egg with Koschei's death. Even though Master Alliandr taught me how to use it, he wasn't sure I would be able to execute it." He chuckled, wiping the sweat off his forehead with the back of his hand. "Now I know why. This spell drained the life out of me."

Allerton nodded, a thoughtful look settling in his attentive eyes.

"Hmm," he murmured as he circled the broken table to get his chair. He pulled it closer to Damian and sat down, crossing his legs at the knee. "To be honest, when you started to chant, I wanted to stop you. Just like Master Alliandr, I didn't think you had the kind of magic needed to execute it, and I didn't want to see you hurt." He smiled, a chain of crow's feet materializing around his eyes. "But then I changed my mind… It's not the first time I witness you doing something that logically you shouldn't be able to do. You and your brother are…" His voice trailed off, and he glanced at Cole, but then averted his gaze and continued so quietly that Damian wasn't sure if his last words were meant for his ears at all. "A magical paradox, if I've ever seen one…"

"We should probably open it and see what's hidden inside," Cole suggested.

"Damian, did Master Alliandr teach you how to destroy the needle by any chance?" Allerton asked. He pulled a handkerchief out of his jacket and took his glasses off, wiping them absentmindedly.

"No, he wasn't sure if any magic was needed to break the needle at all, but he was worried about possible consequences of doing it in the realm of humans," Damian replied. "I guess we'll find out now."

He held the egg in both hands and pressed on it along the line of the fracture. With a loud crack, it split open, and Damian sucked in a sharp breath, staring at the object that fell out of the eggshell in disbelief.

"Well," Cole mumbled, sounding a bit lost, "that doesn't look like a needle to me…"

CHAPTER 25

~ DAMIAN BLAKE ~

Damian stared at a small metal key with the numbers three-zero-one engraved on it, lying in the palm of his hand, and thousands of thoughts rushed through his mind at the same time. It wasn't a needle as everyone expected, and since the key didn't project any energy of magic whatsoever, he was positive it was as mundane as they came.

"This object has no magical properties." Allerton touched the key with the tip of his finger, furrowing his brow. "It looks just like any regular key."

"I beg to differ, my lord," Cole said with a wide grin splitting his face. "It has a pretty powerful protection magic." He lifted his shoulders in a half-shrug in reply to Damian's puzzled stare. "At least humans believe so."

"What do you mean?" asked Damian, checking it with his second sight just to be sure.

"If I am not mistaken," Cole continued, "this is a key to a safety deposit box. I'm not sure which bank it's from, but I have a safety deposit box in Phoenix Central, and my key looks just like this one."

"Perun almighty," Damian exhaled. "Are you saying Koschei hides his death in plain sight? In some mundane bank?"

"Why not?" Cole asked. "It's not the worst place to hide a magical artifact. No one will think about looking for something so dangerous and powerful in such a mundane establishment."

"Or it could be a trap," Damian objected. "Koschei knows I can't expose the World of Magic, and I won't let my brother do it either. He wants to put us in a position where we'll be defenseless without our magic."

"Agreed," Allerton muttered. "It is a trap." He reached for his handkerchief nervously but didn't wipe his glasses, squeezing it in his hands. "What do you want to do, Commander?"

Damian leaned heavily on the arm of his chair, staring out the window at the beautiful ocean of greenery surrounding the Guardians HQ.

"Something's gotta give," he whispered at length. Raising his eyes at Quinn Allerton, he read the silent agreement reflected on the Archmage's face. "Running is no longer an option, but even if it were, I refuse to live my life looking over my shoulder. People are getting hurt, Quinn"—he looked down at the tiled floor, numbness spreading through his chest, filling his limbs with lead—"people who are closest to me, and I can't have it. I won't forgive myself if..." He fell silent, unwilling to voice his fears.

"It's too dangerous, Commander." With a deep sigh, Allerton wiped his hands on the handkerchief and stuffed it back in his pocket. "Not only for you, Cole and your friends, but for everyone... for this world and all the other worlds. Just think about it. For some reason, an unknown ancient god wants you and Cole imprisoned or at his beck and call, which is even worse. Who knows why or what his goals are?"

"Exactly," Damian agreed. "We don't know, and it's about time we found out, because whatever he plans to do, it can't be anything good, and someone needs to be there to stop him when he makes his move. Might as well be me."

Allerton looked away, and a deep wrinkle appeared between his eyebrows, his lips pressed into a bitter line. Then he got up, straightening his pants, and turned to Damian.

"Give me the key," he said quietly, holding out his hand. "I'll scry for the location of the bank." Damian placed the key in his palm, and Allerton put it into the inside pocket of his jacket. "It's not going to take me long, but you both should consider staying a while longer to grab something to eat in the cafeteria and get some rest before you leave. You look like you need it." He thought for a moment before asking, "Damian, do you remember the room you and Jamie used the last time you visited the Guardians HQ?" Damian nodded, and Allerton continued with a slightly guilty look on his face. "It's still unoccupied. To be honest, I hoped Jamie would return to the Guardians Order, but he chose the mantel of the Wardens Brotherhood." A distant smile ghosted his lips as he turned to Cole and gave him a quick once-over. "I'll send a few blood bags to that room for you, Your Majesty, and some fresh clothes for both of you."

"Thank you, my lord," Cole inclined his head, a vibe of discomfort lingering over him, "but you don't have to address me as Your Majesty or Mr. Adams. Cole is just fine."

Allerton's smile grew warmer. "Sorry, Cole, old habits die hard." He switched his attention to Damian and waved in the direction of the gardens. "Damian, if you need to reconnect with your element, I can send one of my guards to escort you to a quiet place where you can spend a few minutes alone with nature."

"Much obliged." Damian got up heavily, thinking that he didn't need a few minutes but a full week in the middle of the desert, alone, doing nothing but his normal level of training, just to get back into shape. "I need it."

Allerton nodded and walked out the door, gesturing for them to wait.

* * *

BARELY PAYING any attention to where he was going, Damian followed the guard along the endless maze of pathways and trails. The park and gardens of the Guardians HQ were famous for their beauty and the rich collection of rare flowers, plants and trees. Being a Child of Earth, he would normally enjoy it, appreciating the magnificence of nature more than anyone else could, but today, his mind was far from all that. Deep in his thoughts, he nearly ran into the guard escorting him when he stopped.

"Commander Blake, this is the place Archmage Allerton asked me to show you." The guard opened the gate into the area of the gardens surrounded by a low iron fence. "We call it the Silent Garden. At this time, it's always empty, so you'll be alone there, and I'll remain here to make sure no one bothers your solitude."

"Thank you, sir." Damian smiled at the man absentmindedly and crossed inside, but then halted and turn around. "My brother may decide to join me. Please let him through if he shows up." As the guard opened his mouth to ask a question, he quickly added, "His name is Cole Adams. You'll recognize him easily because he's the only vampire in the Guardians HQ."

The guard bowed to him, a low ceremonious bow, a kind smile hiding under his thick facial hair. "As you wish, Commander."

As Damian walked through the Silent Garden, he started to understand the meaning of the name. The silence here seemed to be absolute, undisturbed even by the chirping of birds and bustle of insects, and Damian couldn't help but wonder if some kind of spell was cast over the area to keep it so quiet. The fresh scent of greenery, flowers and earth enveloped him, soothing his stretched nerves, and he finally dropped his tense shoulders, brushing his hand over the green leaves and flower petals as he passed them.

The paved path soon turned into a narrow trail which merged into a small opening surrounded by flowerbeds. There were no benches or anything else to sit on, so Damian made his way into the center of the clearing and pulled his wet shirt off before lowering himself on the ground, feeling the silky grass and cold, slightly damp dirt under his skin.

A moan of pleasure escaped his lips as his element embraced his drained, aching body, gently caressing his skin. He closed his eyes and let go, wiping his mind blank. He didn't want to think, and he was afraid to feel anything. All he wanted was a few minutes of peace.

He wasn't sure how long he spent in blissful oblivion. When a familiar vampiric energy signature touched his senses, his lips quirked up into a smile, but he didn't open his eyes.

"Nikolai," he whispered, tapping the ground next to him, inviting his brother to join.

Cole sat down by his side, and Damian finally cracked his eyelids open, glancing in his direction. He had changed into a fresh T-shirt and jeans, but he hadn't left the scabbard with his swords back in the room, and the leather straps crossed his wide chest.

"I met Allerton on my way here." Cole lay down on his side next to Damian, propping his cheek against his palm. "He found the bank."

"Did he tell you which bank it is?"

Cole nodded. "Phoenix Central," he replied without looking at him. "The same branch I use. That's why the key looked so familiar to me."

"Perfect," Damian murmured. "This is the first thing that has gone right in the last few days."

"How so?" Cole pushed himself up, supporting himself on his elbow to look at Damian.

"We can walk into the bank like any law-abiding citizen, and you can ask to check your safety deposit box..."

Cole chuckled. "I thought you may want to do that." He sobered up and shifted a little to readjust his position. "Are you sure going there in the daytime, when there are so many people around, is the best approach?"

"I'm not sure about anything, but I don't want to break into a bank in the middle of the night. Phoenix Central is a giant corporation, so I'm sure they have state-of-the-art security systems and guards in every corner, working day and night. As you know, my magic can't hide us from certain types of modern tech." Damian paused, going through all possible options in his mind. "I have enough problems with the High Council as it is, I don't need to add a bank robbery on top of everything else." Reading the doubt written all over Cole's face, he added, "We already suspect it could be a trap, and the fact that Koschei has a safety deposit box in the same branch as yours makes me think he got it after he waged the war against me. Day, night—what difference does it make?"

"We're speculating... It could be a trap or a dare, or maybe Koschei just decided to go mainstream and keep his countless treasures in a bank." Cole reached into his pocket and pulled out his phone. "But I'll be honest with you, as scary as Koschei is, his master terrifies me even more, and I'm not in a rush to meet him," he muttered, opening the list of favorite contacts.

"Neither am I, little bro... neither am I..." Damian murmured, a new thought emerging in his mind at his brother's words.

"I'm sorry, but I had about enough with all these mysteries. If it's possible, I'd like to know what we're about to walk into." Cole pressed the dial button, placing the call on speaker. The phone beeped a few times before a female voice answered it.

"Cole, where the hell have you been?" the woman asked, tones of displeasure in her voice. "I've been looking everywhere for you. I'm glad you left Ruslan in charge, but it would be helpful if—"

"Delia, hello, darling. I missed you too," Cole purred, interrupting her, an uneven smile playing on his lips as he stared into the depth of the garden. "I'll be back at Court sooner if you get some information for me."

"What kind of information?" Delia asked, a vibe of irritation still surging through the phone line.

"Do you still have your contact in the Phoenix Central Bank?"

"Yes," she replied. "What do you need?"

"I need to find out who owns safety deposit box number three-zero-one, and when they purchased it."

Something shuffled on the other side of the line and the sound of heels clicking on the tiled floor rang through the speakers before Delia came back online. "Give me a few minutes. I'll call you back," she promised and hung up the phone.

Cole lay down again, lowering his cellphone on the grass. Delia didn't make them wait long, and a shrill ring sounded in the silence of the garden just a short while later. Cole answered the call, placing it on speaker.

"I have your information," Delia said, her voice cold and demanding. "You better be at Court soon, and I expect some serious payment."

"Anything you wish, darling." An evil grin split Cole's face, his fingers tracing the edge of the device. "And as many times as you can handle."

Damian raised his eyebrows, but Cole just shook his head, wagging his finger at him.

"The safety deposit box in question belongs to one John Emrys, and he got this box a long time ago, in nineteen thirty-one, less than a year after this particular branch of Phoenix Central had been open. Since he got this box, he has never visited the bank again." Delia took a meaningful pause and then added, "Was that all you needed?"

"Yes, thank you," Cole said, the playfulness gone from his voice. "I owe you one, Delia."

"You owe me a lot more than one, King," she replied icily. "When you return, get ready to pay. Royally." She hung up the phone before Cole had a chance to say anything.

"Emrys? Can he be more obvious? The name he used literally means 'immortal'," Damian muttered, running his hand over his face. "Now I understand even less than before. In nineteen thirty-one, I was under the *no one* status. I wasn't even on Koschei's radar at the time, constantly on the run, hiding from monsters and from the Destiny Council." He looked at his brother, guessing what he was thinking by the expression on his face.

"Do you still think it's a trap?" Cole asked, echoing Damian's assumption. "Because I have no idea what to think anymore."

"And we're right back where we started from," Damian murmured. He sat up and turned to Cole, searching his calm face with his eyes. "Please, don't go with me, Nikolai. Just let me do it alone. Let me be your big brother just this one time and protect you."

Cole didn't say anything, looking anywhere but at him.

"Cole..." Damian nudged him on his side.

"Are you kidding me?" Cole shouted, jumping to his feet, his gaze burning with indignation. But then he just waved his hand and sat back down. He bent his knees, wrapping his arms around his legs, and turned away from him, just the way he used to do when they were kids.

"Fine, you're coming with me," Damian all but growled, channeling his magic. "I hope Koschei won't mind if I throw a wrench into his plans..."

He got up and drew a rune shining with the orange glow of his elemental power in the air. The communication window opened immediately, and a young man with black eyes and long, obsidian hair stepped into view.

"A little warning, bro," Cole whispered as he scrambled into a kneeling position and inclined his head in a bow.

"Master Alliandr," Damian greeted the Master of Kendral, pressing his fist to his chest.

"What can I do for you, Commander?" Alliandr asked, gesturing for Cole to rise.

Damian quickly explained the situation to him and filled him in on the details of his plan, catching Cole's flabbergasted glance. "I have the key that belongs to Koschei, but we both know that we shouldn't break the needle in the realm of humans. The consequences could be unpredictable. So, we'll have to take it elsewhere," he added at the end. "Would that be enough for you to perform the type of magic I need?"

"Your plan is bold and dangerous, Commander, but I expected something like this coming from you…" He paused, his gaze going slightly out of focus as he rubbed his chin. "The key to some mundane box which Koschei hasn't touched in years? I doubt it'll be enough, but I can try. Do you have a location rune for me?"

"No." Damian shook his head. "We're at the Guardians Order Headquarters in Chicago, and no one can teleport on their grounds without special privileges, but the Archmage gave me permission to use my portals if I have the need. So, if you conjure a location rune, I can open a portal for you."

Alliandr channeled his magical energy and quickly drew a rune shimmering with the quadruple colors of his power. Feeling a gentle touch of the runic magic to his mind, Damian zeroed in on it and waved his hand. A portal rotating with bright blue sparkles materialized next to him. Alliandr closed the communication window and a moment later, he walked out of the portal, halting next to Damian. A light breeze ruffled his long hair, throwing a few strands into his eyes, and he pushed them off impatiently, a soft smile touching his full lips. The sunlight bounced off a spherical ruby pendant on a delicate gold chain visible beneath his partially unbuttoned white shirt.

"Shall we?" He raised his eyebrows, his gaze moving from Cole to Damian.

Damian picked up his shirt and put it back on, shivering from the touch of the cold fabric to his skin, and then caught up with Cole and Alliandr. As they walked through the gardens, following the guard, Alliandr touched Damian's elbow, and a slightly shy smile graced his chiseled face, giving it an unusual softness.

"Commander," he said, a vibe of discomfort surrounding him, "there is something I want to ask you."

Damian glanced at him, wondering what could make this powerful young man feel so uneasy. "What is it, Master?"

"There is a chance I will have to…" His voice trailed away, and he cleared his throat. "I may need to break one of the major laws of the World of Magic to get you where you need to be. As a Commander of the Destiny Enforcers, you'll be obligated to bring me before the High Council for doing that, because if you don't, they will send other Enforcers after me."

"Then I guess we'll be sharing a cell in the Destiny Council's holding facility," Damian replied with a crooked smile, realizing which major law the young Master of Power was referring to. "I already lost count of how many rules I broke in the last few days. One more, one less—that's not going to tilt the scales for me, but for your sake, let's keep it as a last resort and try to avoid it, if possible."

* * *

The door into Allerton's office was wide open, two guards standing on either side of it. Quinn Allerton sat behind a new desk, the key lying in front of him as he was reading a large tome in a thick leather binding. As soon as Damian, Cole and Alliandr crossed the threshold, closing the door behind them, Allerton raised his face, looking at them over the rim of his glasses, and his lips parted, his eyes widening. He got up awkwardly, pushing his chair back, and bent down in a low ceremonial bow.

"Master of Kendral?" he mumbled, rising, his gaze darting from one person to the next. "But how...? Why?"

"Master Alliandr, please allow me to introduce Quinn Allerton, the Head of the Guardians Order," said Cole, gesturing at the Archmage.

"My lord, I've heard a lot about you but never had the honor of meeting you in person," said Alliandr, bowing slightly. "I wish I could spend more time in your establishment, but as you're well aware, I can't be away from Kendral for a prolonged period of time, so we should probably get to business." He pointed toward the desk. "May I see that key?"

The Archmage grabbed the key from the desk and offered it to Alliandr. The Master of Power took it carefully, placing it in the palm of his hand, and his eyes flooded with darkness as he channeled his quadruple power. A veil of multicolored sparkles wrapped around his arm, slithering up all the way to his shoulder, tiny lightning bolts sparkling in the air above him. The Master of Power placed his other hand over the key, channeling more of his power through it.

"His eyes," Cole projected to Damian through their blood bond, staring at Alliandr. *"I can never get used to seeing this blackness, no matter how many times I see it. He looks like a demon from urban fantasy TV shows."*

"Said the guy with chronic pink eye," Alliandr murmured,

throwing a veiled glance at Cole, but the corners of his lips lifted.

"Oops..." A wide grin crossed Cole's face. *"I had no idea you could intercept our communications through the blood bond."*

"I'm a Master of Power." Alliandr exhaled as he let go of his magic. *"Even I don't know the true extent of my power."* He closed his eyes and when he opened them again, they were his normal obsidian color, the whites looking bright next to the dark irises. Turning to Damian, he spread his arms. "I'm sorry, Commander, but as I expected, this key is not enough. I cannot summon the needle, using their shared energy bond. As much as I hoped to avoid visiting the bank, Plan A is a no go. We're going with Plan B."

"Plan B?" Allerton asked in a hoarse whisper, taking his glasses off. "Do I even want to know what it is?"

"Given that you're reporting directly to the High Council, probably not," replied Alliandr, passing the key to Damian.

Allerton turned to Damian and Cole, his face turning ashen. "Commander?" he said, his fingers squeezing his glasses until they broke, pieces of glass dropping to the floor. Since Damian remained silent, he took a step closer, reaching for him, but then his hand dropped, hanging limply at his side. "Damian, you're already in a world of trouble with your superiors. You must tell me what's going on."

"Master Alliandr is right. Plausible deniability, my lord. You can't be part of it." Damian met Allerton's terrified gaze, remorse clawing at his heart. "If I had a choice, I wouldn't have you involved in the first place, but unfortunately, I was out of options. I hope you can forgive—"

"There's nothing to forgive, Damian." Allerton sighed. "I hope you know what you're doing, though, because I'm not worried about myself. Only about the three of you. Please be careful and don't add anything to the growing list of your offenses, Commander. Incurring the wrath of the High Council could be just as dangerous to a Destiny Enforcer as to a Master of Power, and I wouldn't wish anyone to suffer through their trials."

"Been there, done that. Never again," murmured Alliandr, a dark shadow crossing his youthful features. "We'll be careful, my lord."

"Heaven and Earth," Allerton muttered through clenched teeth, approaching Cole. "Mr. Adams, I think you're the only one among you three who knows how to use a phone." He pulled a business card and a pen out of his pocket, quickly wrote a number on the back of it and gave it to Cole. "This is my personal cellphone number. Call me if you need my help." Then the Archmage held out his hand to Damian and added, "Godspeed, Commander. I hope to see you alive and not in Destiny cuffs once all this is over."

"My gratitude." Damian shook his hand, cringing inwardly as the thought of the Destiny Council's dungeons and their infamous Destiny cuffs crossed his mind. "We'll be leaving right away."

Allerton touched the hem of Damian's shirt and shook his head. "I have sent a fresh set of clothes for you to your room, in case you'd like to change before you leave. After that, you have my permission to teleport from anywhere in the Guardians HQ grounds."

Damian pressed his fist to his chest. "Thank you, my lord," he said, truly meaning it. "I'll get in touch if I—" He cut himself off and squared his shoulders. "I'll be in touch as soon as we're done."

He turned around and walked out of the room without looking back.

* * *

Walking briskly along the narrow corridors of the Guardians HQ, it didn't take Damian long to find his room. He pushed the wooden door open and bent down slightly as he crossed inside. Allerton was right. With nonexistent décor and only essential furnishing, the place was just the way he recalled it. He halted between beds, the old memory coming alive before his eyes.

"All this time I thought you literally meant that you're nobody." Jamie's voice sounded in his mind, and Damian's stomach twisted as he remembered his young friend the way he had seen him the last time—lying in a hospital bed, fighting for his life. He pressed his hand over his eyes, forcing himself not to think about it.

"I'll be right back," he said to Cole and Alliandr, grabbing the fresh clothes from the bed, and made his way to the washroom.

He changed quickly and glanced in the small mirror above the sink, barely recognizing the man staring back at him. Until now, he didn't realize how disheveled he looked with his skin covered in streams of dried dirt and his hair in disarray. Besides that, his face was gray with exhaustion, and for some reason, his scar stood out more than usual. He opened the faucet and washed his hands and face before heading back to the bedroom.

Alliandr sat on the only chair with his legs crossed at the knee. Cole was pacing the room, holding his phone to his ear. His swords were no longer in the scabbard behind his back but lay inside a new leather briefcase, undoubtedly provided by Quinn Allerton. The fit wasn't perfect, but it was good enough for him to carry his weapons without attracting any unwanted attention.

"Yes, Father," Cole spoke, tones of nervousness in his words. "That's exactly what we're going to do. You heard me right." He fell silent, listening to Ruslan, and even though Damian could hear Ruslan talking, he couldn't make out his words. Cole threw his free hand up, rolling his eyes. "Of course, I'll be careful. What do you think? And no, my crazy brother and I are not going to get Master Alliandr in trouble with the High Council." He massaged the back of his neck, looking like an annoyed teenager talking to his overprotective parent. "Yes, Father, we'll be at the bank in a few minutes, so please leave right away and drive fast. Time is of the essence." He hung up the phone, meeting Damian's gaze, and explained, sounding a little aggravated, "I don't have my key to the safety deposit box on me, and without it, we won't be able to enter the vault, so I asked Ruslan to bring it over."

Damian raised his arms, chuckling. "I wasn't questioning you, bro. I know nothing about banks and their vaults. The last time I had a safety deposit box was… ehhh"—he looked up, as if trying to remember—"never?"

He sat down on the bed, hiding his face in his hands. Taking a few deep breaths, he blocked everything not related to the mission, focusing only on what needed to be done. Feeling a light touch on his shoulder, he raised his head to see the Master of Power standing in front of him.

"Commander, you are not ready," he said, tilting his head a little, and since his eyes were darker than normal, Damian knew he was using his other sight. "I can see how drained magically you are. Your plan requires heavy use of magic from all of us. We'll fail if you go like this."

A weak smile touched Damian's lips before he could stop it. "Wouldn't be the first time for me."

"Failing or fighting with limited magical energy?" Alliandr gave him an arched stare, twinkles of humor in his eyes.

"Both." Damian laughed, rising. "I guess fighting on the verge of shutting down is part of being a Destiny Enforcer."

"Today, we can't take that chance." Before Damian could stop him, darkness flooded Alliandr's eyes. The air around him became thick with the amount of elemental energy he was wielding, and his hair fanned around his face. He seized Damian's shoulder, pulled him closer, and held out his hand, manifesting a large energy orb in his palm.

"Master—," Damian groaned, realizing what the young Master was planning to do, but when he tried to pull away, he couldn't move.

In one sharp move, Alliandr thrust the energy orb through his chest, muttering the words in Dragon tongue under his breath. The blast of elemental energy surged through Damian, reviving and energizing his every cell. He screamed, throwing his head back, his hands curling into fists, and for a brief moment, he felt like his heart stopped beating, pain and joy entwining within him. Cole gasped and rushed to his side, but the Master of Power raised his free hand, stopping him.

When Alliandr let go, Damian moaned and dropped to one knee, bowing his head. When he was finally able to fill his lungs with air, he got up, meeting Alliandr's humorous gaze.

"Now, I can see that you're ready." The Master of Power gave him another once-over and let go of his power, his eyes returning to their normal color. "Let's get it done, shall we?"

Cursing inwardly his subserviency to anyone who could wield the elemental energy of Earth or could manipulate the magic of the Board of Destiny, Damian placed his hands on Alliandr's and Cole's shoulders and teleported them out of the Guardians HQ.

CHAPTER 26

~ DAMIAN BLAKE ~

They materialized in an empty plaza in front of a vacant unit with a "For Lease" sign hanging on the door. It was close to four o'clock, but the sun was blasting from clear blue skies. In addition, the pavement emanated waves of heat, and a smell of overheated asphalt lingered in the air.

"Where are we?" asked Master Alliandr, looking around with curiosity.

"One of my teleportation spots," replied Damian, motioning toward the exit from the plaza. "It's almost four o'clock, and I didn't want to expose the World of Magic by manifesting out of thin air in the middle of a bank."

"Well…" Cole cleared his throat, biting his lip to stop himself from laughing. "I'm afraid some exposure is unavoidable." He jerked his chin toward Alliandr.

Dressed in a white shirt, tight leather pants and tall riding boots, he looked like a medieval prince or a knight, and his long black hair falling to the middle of his back just increased the resemblance. The sword sheathed at his belt wasn't helping the situation either.

"Dammit." Damian raked his hand through his hair as he

observed the Master of Power closely for the first time since he arrived. "We're only one block away from the bank. We'll be fine. Besides, humans will think he's an actor or LARPing... Humans always find a creative way to explain the unexplainable and feel good about it."

Alliandr chuckled. "I can conjure an illusion."

"No, don't waste your magical energy, Master. Something tells me you'll need it later," Cole objected, starting on his way toward the street. "Damian is right about humans."

They made it all the way to the intersection without any unwanted adventures, but as soon as they turned onto the main street, people started to notice them, staring at the young Master openly, turning around to do a double take once they passed him. The eyes of every woman on the street and some men were glued to him, following his every step. Alliandr visibly shuddered and bowed his head, allowing his long hair to partially conceal his face.

"Dammit..." Damian cursed quietly. "It's impossible for a Master of Power to walk the realm of humans unnoticed."

"I should have asked Master Mrak Delar how he deals with it," Alliandr whispered. "He takes care of all the affairs related to this world. I hardly ever visit it."

"As long as they just look, we'll be fine. Besides, we're almost there," said Cole. He turned into a large plaza, heading toward a tall beige building with signage displaying the name and logo of the bank attached to the facade.

In addition to the bank, a couple of large department stores, a few smaller shops and restaurants were located in the plaza, and at four o'clock, almost every parking spot was occupied. A few people stood on the marble steps in front of the glass doors leading into Phoenix Central, waiting to use the ATM.

"A vampire and a... er... wizard, I think... I don't feel any other supernatural presence in the area," said Alliandr, glancing at Cole. "Is this vamp one of your subjects?"

"My maker," Cole replied. Walking up the steps, he halted in front of Ruslan.

The ancient vampire took in his son's appearance, muscle twitching in his jaw. "Your key," he said quietly, offering it to him.

Cole took it, placing it in the pocket of his jeans, and passed something to Ruslan so fast that Damian couldn't see what it was. Dallas took a tentative step forward, but Ruslan seized his wrist, holding him in place. The young man blanched, and his pupils dilated, indicating that Ruslan's grip was a bit too tight, but he didn't say anything and didn't try to free himself. Ruslan gave his son a barely visible nod and headed down the steps, pulling Dallas with him.

As he passed Damian, he halted for the briefest moment, just enough to whisper, "Dallas and I will patrol the area around the bank. We're here if you need us."

He glanced at the Master of Power, his face remaining an emotionless mask, and walked away, circling the building.

Here goes... Damian pushed the door open, not sure what to expect, and crossed the threshold first. He halted in a spacious, glass-and-marble lobby, quickly surveying every square inch of the space and every person inside. Despite the fact that he couldn't detect anything magical, cold perspiration covered his forehead, goosebumps rising on his arms like from a touch of an icy breeze.

Alliandr stopped by his side. "Damian, I don't see anything abnormal here," he whispered.

"Neither do I," said Damian. "But for whatever reason, I feel —" He didn't finish his statement and stilled, probing the bank again, all his senses stretched to the maximum.

"Uneasy?" offered Alliandr. "Me too."

"Let's proceed with caution," Cole suggested and moved forward. He approached a woman in a bank uniform and smiled, turning on his charm of both the human and vampire variety.

"What can I do for you?" she asked, smiling back at him.

"I'd like to check my safety deposit box." Cole reached into his pocket for his wallet and showed her his ID and the key.

She peered at his ID and typed something on her computer. Her smile grew wider, her eyes igniting with adoration and curiosity as she realized who he was. She turned to him and pointed at a chair in the waiting area.

"Mr. Adams, please have a seat and someone will be with you momentarily," she sang, gently directing him toward a chair even though it wasn't necessary. "Is there anything I can get you while you're waiting?"

Alliandr looked at Damian, puzzled, and Damian couldn't help but chuckle, gazing heavenward.

"Don't ask," he muttered, making his way to Cole. "My brother is a sort of local celebrity here. Arizona's most eligible bachelor, and successful entrepreneur."

"And he's a vampire," said Alliandr, astonished.

"For the last thousand years or so. I guess modern humans are not as terrified of the undead as they used to be a few hundred years ago, thanks to popular TV shows and urban fantasy novels." Suppressing his laugher, Damian lowered himself onto a chair next to Cole, but he didn't have time to relax as an employee of the bank approached them.

"Mr. Adams, my name is Brian Cox," he introduced himself, gesturing at a door at the other end of the room. "Please, follow me." However, as Damian and Alliandr got up to join them, the man turned around and stopped them. "Unless you are renting this box jointly with Mr. Adams, I can't allow you to access it."

Cole stepped closer to him, staring directly into his eyes, and his vampiric essence spiked around him, making his eyes glow slightly.

"I believe my business partners are authorized to access the box," he said calmly, his deep voice wrapping around the man in soft waves. "Please, check your signature card."

The man's eyes widened, his jaw slack, but he looked down at the clipboard he was holding in his hand and smiled apologetically. "I'm sorry, Mr. Adams, you're absolutely right. Your business partners can come with us."

As they followed the employee across the floor, Damian sharpened all his senses, getting ready for a sudden attack, but even as they walked through the door into the secure bank vault, he still didn't detect anything out of the ordinary. The entire space of the room, floor to ceiling, was covered with hundreds of metal doors of different sizes. Besides the walls, a few towers filled with boxes were positioned in the middle of the room. Brian crossed the room and halted in front of the back wall, turning to Cole.

"Your key, Mr. Adams." He inserted his key into a keyhole and waited until Cole did the same. They turned the keys at the same time and the metal door opened, revealing a box behind it.

Cole pulled out the box, and Brian directed them to an adjoining room where he left them, closing the door behind himself. Damian looked around but didn't notice any cameras or any other security tech in this room. Quickly probing the vault with his other sight, he turned to Alliandr.

"There is no one in the actual vault," he said quietly. "I can see Brian and a few more humans standing outside the door." He channeled his magic and drew a wide circle over his head, whispering a few words in Dragon tongue. As the yellow glow of a cloaking spell engulfed all three of them, he continued, "It won't hide us from the motion detectors, but if there are cameras inside the vault, we will be invisible to them. All we need to do is find box number three-zero-one, and bring it here, so we can open it without being watched."

"I don't think there are any cameras there," Cole muttered. "My box is number three-four-nine. Since they're positioned in numeric order, I assume it won't be far away from Koschei's."

Damian opened the door and headed toward the wall where Cole's box was located. It didn't take him long to find what he needed. He redirected some of his magic toward his hand and moved his fingers over the door with the number three-zero-one engraved on it. A barely noticeable presence of magical energy reached his senses, and he let go. It wasn't a residue of an old spell. Neither was it a protection spell. A strange familiarity of this energy signature made him stay in place, a whirlwind of thoughts rushing through his mind.

"Perun almighty... It's here," he whispered, mostly to himself. Turning to his brother and the Master of Power, he repeated louder. "I believe we found it."

Master Alliandr touched the door with the tip of his index finger, sending a smidge of his magic through it, and whispered a short spell. "I conjured an illusion over this wall, so if there are any recording devices in this room, they won't register us opening the box." He extended his hand to Damian. "Let me do it, Commander," he said with a soft smile. "When it comes to combat magic, you're a lot more capable than I am. I need you and Cole to be ready in case something goes wrong once I open this door."

Damian gave him the key and stepped back, channeling his magic, ready to summon his daggers. Cole opened his briefcase and pulled out his swords. Quickly strapping the scabbard on, he sheathed his weapons and touched Alliandr's shoulder.

"We're all set, Master," he whispered, exchanging a quick look with Damian.

Alliandr inserted the key into the keyhole, turned it while touching the second one, and whispered a single word in Dragon tongue, *"Recludius..."*

The lock clicked, and the door opened easily. Carefully, he pulled the box out and headed toward the adjoining room.

Damian scanned the bank, but since everything remained peaceful and magic-free, he followed his brother and the Master of Power. Alliandr placed the box on the table and lifted the lid carefully, as if expecting a poisonous snake to strike from within.

A small wooden chest decorated with silver and gold ornaments lay inside the standard bank safety deposit box. It didn't appear locked, and as far as Damian could see, there were no wards or protection spells placed on it. The same weak energy signature he had detected earlier became more apparent now, its familiarity sending shivers down Damian's back.

"Too easy. After the hell Koschei put us through, I have a hard time believing that finding his death will be so... uneventful. It's too good to be true," he whispered, shaking his head. "Alliandr, do you sense the magical energy of this box? Do you know what it is?"

Alliandr frowned, his eyes turning darker. "I can sense it, but I have no idea what it is. I've never encountered anything like this before."

"It feels familiar, but I can't place my finger on what it is," Damian murmured.

"Should we open it?" asked Cole. "Maybe some things are easy because they're meant to be? All we have to do is destroy this needle, and then—tuh-duh, Koschei is dead. No need to break any laws or rules, no risk of facing the Destiny Council trial..."

"I wish it was so easy," Damian murmured, shaking his head. Nothing ever came easy for him. He had to shed sweat and blood for everything he had ever achieved in his life. "We can't break the needle here, anyway. It can be done only in a controlled environment."

Holding his breath, he removed the chest out of the box, freezing in place with his senses stretched to the limit. Since nothing changed, he lifted the lid carefully and peered inside.

On a bed of black silk lay a long golden needle, radiating a powerful vibe of magical energy. While its magic had the distinct signature of Koschei's energy signature, Damian could detect some other magic in it, the one he sensed before, and there was nothing dark about it. He reached for the needle, noticing that his fingers were trembling slightly, but Alliandr stopped him.

"Damian, I think I should do it," he said quietly. "If it is indeed a trap for you and Cole, it'll be attuned to your energy signatures, and we don't want to alarm Koschei ahead of time. Hopefully, the old sorcerer didn't expect that the Master of Power would get involved personally."

Damian lowered his hand, and Alliandr took the needle. As soon as his fingers came in contact with it, everything changed.

The lights in the room went off.

A deep tremor rushed through the floor of the bank and the walls trembled, a low metallic sound filling the air as every box started to vibrate within their compartments.

The door into the room flew open, hitting the wall with a clamorous bang. Brian appeared in the doorway. Dressed in a bank uniform, he looked the same as before, but his eyes glowed with a deep purple light. While he still had his human soul, its golden light was polluted by dark splatters of demonic essence. Damian staggered back, spreading his arms wide to shield Alliandr and Cole, and his daggers materialized in his hands.

The presence of demonic essence increased, flooding the room with its suffocating miasmas. Before long, the room was filled with people. The bank employees and customers stood shoulder to shoulder in front of them, leaving no space for them to move, let alone fight. Their eyes shone with the same purple light, but as Damian checked them with his other sight, he detected the glow of a human soul in every single one of them.

"They're all possessed but alive," Alliandr whispered,

confirming his observation, and staggered back, quickly placing the needle back in the box and shoving it in his pocket.

Brian stepped forward, and a malignant smile distorted his lips. "Commander Blake," he said, his unnatural purple eyes drilling into Damian. "As a Destiny Enforcer, you can't kill humans. With your brother—a vampire—so close to you, you can't use your purifying magic. If you think you can teleport, I'll be happy to disappoint you—you cannot do it either. Submit, and no one will get hurt."

Damian glanced over his shoulder at Alliandr, his eyes pleading. "Master, save my brother," he said in a quick whisper. Alliandr shook his head and opened his mouth to say something, but Damian interrupted him. "I know Cole can conjure his own shield, but it won't be potent enough to keep him safe in such close proximity. I also know you have the purifying Fire, but please, keep my brother alive, and I'll take care of the rest."

Ignoring Cole's feeble objections, Alliandr pushed him against the wall and braced his arms on either side of him, shielding him with his body. *"Praecidio Amnia,"* he hissed through clenched teeth, drawing a circle in the air over himself and Cole. *"Praecidio Amnia Circula Archni."*

Once sure his brother was safe, Damian turned to Brian. "Here you go again. The same threat over and over." He folded his arms, an uneven smile lifting a corner of his mouth. "Do I really have to go through that cheesy *'I'd-rather-die-than-give-up'* speech?"

Pure fury distorted Brian's face. The dirty, dark swirls of demonic essence rose over him and the mindless crowd standing behind him.

"Take him and the vampire!" he shouted, pointing at Damian. "Kill the Master of Power!"

The crowd of possessed people moved forward, and Damian knew he had to act fast, since there was no more space for doubts or choices.

"*Commander.*" The words sounded in his mind, making him flinch. Damian stilled for a moment as he recognized Quinn Allerton's voice. "*My mages are shielding the bank. Do what you need to do.*"

He had no time to think of how Allerton ended up here and why. Raising his daggers above his head, Damian crossed them sharply, sparks flying in the air as metal hit metal.

"*Illucious,*" he breathed, infusing the blades with the light of Creation.

A blinding white light filled every corner of the room, spreading around him like ripples on water. He heard Cole's cry of pain and a deep growl of the Master of Power as he struggled to maintain his shield. The stench of demonic essence increased, and dull thuds of bodies falling on the floor suggested that the purifying light of Creation was doing its job, expelling demonic energy from humans.

As the light dwindled, Damian observed the room in horror, trying to gather as much magic and elemental power as he could. Brian and the rest of his crew lay on the floor, unconscious. However, a dark smoke of demonic essence was seeping through the vents and under the door, filling the limited space. It hovered over people, invading their bodies again. One by one, people started to rise as if nothing had happened, their glowing eyes staring at him with icy hatred.

"*Ventius,*" Damian croaked, impacting the mob with a powerful gust of wind to prevent them from coming any closer, hoping that it would give him enough time to summon more purifying energy into his daggers. He coughed, suffocated by the reek of sulfur, and pressed his arm over his mouth and nose.

The front line fell on the back lines, pushing them backward, but more possessed people were forcing themselves in through the door, and soon everyone was back on their feet, stretching their arms toward Damian.

"*Illucious Amplio,*" Damian roared. Not only his blades but his entire body ignited with an eye-watering white light. As the light started to dissipate, he felt weakness suffusing his body, reminding him how taxing the purifying magic was and how much of his strength it required.

Meanwhile, the crowd was slowly rising again, angrier than ever. By this time, the demonic energy was so thick in the room, he could cut it with an ax. It seemed like the more purifying magic he used, the more potent the demonic essence became. He glanced back, meeting Alliandr's horrified gaze.

Damian opened himself to the flow of the Destiny Enforcer magic, taking on his true form. Spreading his wings, he shielded the Master of Power and his brother. "Alliandr, my magical batteries are quickly depleting. Can you try to open your portal or teleport? See if you and Cole can get out of here."

"I can't," Alliandr groaned. "I already tried... This entire building is blocked. You have to let me help you cleanse them."

"No." Damian met Alliandr's black eyes and shook his head. "If you drop your shield, Cole will die." He found Cole's eyes and swallowed hard, realizing what he might need to do if push came to shove. "I swear I will kill every single goddamn one of them before I let them put one finger on my brother."

Switching his attention to the demonically challenged mob, Damian stepped forward and spread his arms. Like an avalanche, the crowd enveloped him, crushing him with the weight of their bodies, tearing at his wings. He dropped to one knee, struggling to breathe.

"*Illucious*," he whispered, sending every scrap of magical energy he could gather into his blades.

From such a close distance, the purifying energy of Creation burned through the demonic essence, and people fell to the floor, unconscious. Damian raised his daggers again, his chest shuddering with laborious breaths. Towering over the crowd, he watched them closely as the next dose of demonic essence entered the room, slithering down in disgusting, stinky swirls, gathering over the fallen people by the entrance into the room.

I hope the gods can forgive me for what I am about to do...

Damian bent down and found Brian on top of the heap of bodies. Yanking him up, he raised his dagger, ready to strike, when a powerful blast of magical energy rushed through the room, hitting him in his chest. The impact was so powerful and so sudden that he couldn't keep on his feet, propelled backward into the wall.

The second wave of the same magic flooded the room with a dazzling light, making it impossible to see anything. Damian groaned, raising his arm to shield his vision. The new energy was soothing and warm, not an ounce of darkness in it. It enveloped him, gently caressing his skin, partially restoring his strength. Damian got up, in his peripheral vision noticing that Alliandr dropped the shield surrounding him, but still kept one around Cole.

With shock, Damian recognized the energy signature of this magic, but he couldn't find any reasonable explanation for its presence in the realm of humans. Unstoppable in its power and purity, the magic of the World Tree itself filled the space. Spreading in powerful waves, it destroyed any evil and darkness in its way.

Slowly, the light toned down, gathering along the walls and ceiling like a thick, glimmering shield, and now Damian could see the silhouette of a man in the doorway. The possessed people were lying on the floor, unconscious, and the swirls of demonic essence no longer polluted the air. The man took a few steps forward, carefully maneuvering between the bodies, and halted in the middle of the room. In his hands, he held a glowing object emanating the energy of the World Tree. Damian narrowed his eyes, trying to see through the shine.

"Cole," the man said, his voice shaking with strain.

"Dallas?" Cole stepped forward, but Master Alliandr held him back, conjuring a new, stronger shield around him.

"The demons are everywhere… Quinn Allerton and his mages are keeping them from exiting the building and possessing more humans," Dallas groaned. "This magic stops demonic essence from entering this room, but I don't think I can hold it back much longer. Ruslan told me what you were planning to do. I hope I can give you enough time to execute your plan."

His legs trembled, and he fell to one knee, but somehow, he managed to keep the magic of the World Tree flowing in soft, even waves. Damian approached Dallas, and now he could finally see the object in his hands. A feather—half white and half midnight blue—encapsulated in the dense orb of its own magical energy lingered above his palms.

"Oh, Dallas," Damian moaned, crumbling inside. "What have you done, my little brother…"

Dallas raised his blazing eyes, blood trickling from his nose. "I gave you the chance to kill the monster before he kills us all and destroys the world."

"Hang in for as long as you can, Dallas," Damian whispered, unable to speak any louder, his throat dry. "We'll be back for you, I swear." He patted his cheek gently, the way he would normally do to Cole. "Just survive, my friend, please…"

He got up, turning toward the Master of Power. "Alliandr, can you teleport or open a portal now since Dallas blocked the demonic essence?"

"No," replied the Master of Power.

"Fuck!" Damian hissed, wiping sweat off his forehead. "Does the needle have what you need to weave your magic?" Alliandr nodded, his black eyes still set on Dallas. "Desperate times, desperate measures. We're going with your plan. Do it now! We must move fast and return here, before Dallas…" His voice trailed off, and he swallowed hard, falling silent.

Holding the needle in his hand, the Master of Power stepped away from the wall and spread his arms, chanting softly in Dragon tongue. At first, his eyes flooded with blackness, but as he channeled more of his power, the darkness dissipated, giving place to the colors of different elemental energies. He rose a few inches above the floor, and his hair fanned, flowing as though lifted by a light breeze.

The floor trembled, and the entire building swayed, responding to his powerful magic. A storm gathered inside the room, dark clouds veiling the ceiling. Lightning forked through the air and thunder boomed, making Cole bend his knee, gazing up in awe. Damian stepped closer to his brother, seizing his elbow. He had always known Masters of Power were as powerful as any god, but never had he seen such a great and terrifying display of their mighty magic in action. Alliandr was wielding all four elements, commanding the forces of magic and nature with such ease, as if he were casting nothing more than a basic protection spell.

Suddenly, the Master of Power stopped chanting and struck the space before him with a fist. Without producing any sound, his arm went through the air as though it were a solid object, leaving a glowing hole in its wake.

Breathing hard, Alliandr lowered himself to the floor and pushed both hands through the small opening he had created. Applying all the magic he had and all his physical strength, he began to pull the edges of the rupture apart. The massive muscles of his arms rippled with strain, a thick pulsing vein crossed his forehead, and his strangled scream resounded through the room. After a short while, he let go and stared at the rip glowing with the multicolored energy of his power, sweat running down his face.

"Too small," he muttered, shaking his head. "I've already forgotten how hard it was to do it. I've never had to do it alone before."

Damian approached the tear and moved his fingers over its glowing edge. Since its energy didn't feel threatening, he seized one edge of it with both hands, shocked at how tangible it felt under his touch.

"Let's try it together," he said, giving a short nod to Alliandr.

"Sorry, Commander," Alliandr objected, suppressing a sigh. "You don't have what it takes to rip the fabric of reality. You have to be either a god or a Master of Power. No one else can do it."

"If it doesn't work, then we'll have to do something else, but at least let's give it a try first." Damian's lips twitched as he gave a pointed stare to the young Master.

Alliandr frowned but took the other side of the tear. "If you feel pain in your hands, you must let go at once, Commander."

"Will do." Damian nodded.

"On three…" Alliandr whispered, his eyes fixed on Damian.

He counted to three, and they connected with their magic at the same time. Pulling at the edge of the tear with all his strength, Damian channeled his Destiny Enforcer magic, assuming his true form, and added his elemental power into the mix. Applying all his strength, he pulled at the edge, and to his shock, it gave in. The tear grew wider and longer, and soon the opening was big enough for an adult man to go through.

Alliandr let go, staring at Damian in awe. "Impossible," he whispered.

Damian leaned down and braced his hands against his knees, taking a few deep breaths. "It worked. Everything else doesn't matter," he muttered, straightening, and gestured for Cole to approach. "We must go right away."

He waited until his brother and the Master of Power slipped through the tear and threw one last glance at Dallas. The young man was still in the same position, the orb with the feather shining as brightly as before, emitting the soft waves of protective magic, but Damian knew it was only a matter of time before he collapsed, and the demons would flood into the room again.

With his heart wrenched, Damian stepped through the tear to the other side and froze in place, staring around in astonishment.

"Oh, that is not what I expected..." he whispered, summoning his daggers.

CHAPTER 27

~ DAMIAN BLAKE ~

The icy wind howled and screeched, blowing between the tall peaks of black mountains. The sky frowned upon the barren, rocky land, electrical discharges flashing above the thick screen of clouds. Damian took in his surroundings, realizing that they stood on a large plateau enclosed by deep chasms and stiff cliffs leading into a bottomless void. Just a few hundred yards ahead of them, a massive castle stretched its tall ridge turrets with sharp spires toward the stormy sky. Its walls were constructed out of black material resembling obsidian, the gray ambient light reflecting dimly on its surface.

The castle didn't have a wall, which all things considered, was kind of useless. Apart from the owner of the place and a few of his closest allies, no one knew the location of the castle, and without powerful magic, nobody could reach it. Something dark and shifty slithered along the side of the building, and Damian squinted his eyes, trying to distinguish what it was.

"Looks like demonic essence," Cole said, pointing at the castle.

"It is," replied Alliandr, his voice raspier and deeper than normal. "Sorry, this is as close as I could get us to Koschei's stronghold."

Damian glanced at the Master of Power, and his stomach knotted. Alliandr looked drained not only of his magic but of his life force as well. Mutilating the fabric of reality was strictly forbidden and considered one of the highest offenses on the Destiny Council's blacklist. Luckily, not too many supernatural beings had what it took to perform this kind of magic, but even those who could do it paid for it dearly.

Unlike gods, Masters of Power weren't immortal, and their seemingly unlimited power was restricted by their fragile human bodies. The more magic and elemental powers they used, the faster they got drained, physically and magically, and the longer it took for them to restore their strength. And right now, Alliandr looked like he was ready to collapse.

The wintry air grazed Damian's skin, making him shiver in his thin clothes, and he tore his eyes away from the Master of Kendral, switching his attention back to the castle.

"I guess this is where we need to be," he said. "Since I can see the area in front of the main entrance, I can teleport us the rest of the way." As the next gust of wind brought the stench of sulfur, his mouth curved into a bitter smile. "Let's see what Koschei cooked up for us this time."

He placed his hands on Alliandr's and Cole's shoulders and gave them a short nod, teleporting to a small square in front of the palace. They materialized just a few yards away from a tall double door leading into the building. From up-close, the castle appeared even more sinister and intimidating. The constant flares of lightning reflecting in its jet-black facade in combination with the stench of sulfur, the area looked like a depiction of Hell or some other demonic underworldly realm.

Before they could take a step, the earth shook, and a deep fracture cut through the rocky ground, circling the building. A low grinding noise sounded from beneath as the chasm continued growing, now at least three yards wide. Swirls of gray smoke, illuminated by a dark red light, rose from it. Rocks kept sliding from the edge of it, flying down into the void, never reaching its bottom. The land blackened around it, fissures and cracks snaking through the rounded edges.

Damian took a few steps forward and peeked inside. A hole, shining with a bright scarlet light, gaped back at him from the abyss. He shuddered and staggered away from it as the debilitating energy of the Dark Nav washed over him.

"The gate into the Dark Nav," said Master Alliandr, halting by his side. "You can't teleport over it or open a portal. It's not going to be easy to cross it."

"Unless we find a way to close it, of course," Damian murmured, lowering to one knee. "Get ready."

Sensing the fluctuations in the magical energy field, he glanced around to make sure they were still alone. The landscape remained just as desolate and frigid as before, but he couldn't get rid of the feeling that someone was watching their every move. Perhaps it was just the closeness to the gates into the Dark Nav or the presence of a widespread demonic essence, or maybe it was his overly stretched nerves that played tricks on his mind. Damian took a deep breath, exhaling slowly, and opened himself to the flow of magic and elemental energy.

If Koschei is watching us, we better don't disappoint...

Placing his hands flat against the cold ground, he surrendered himself to his element, focusing on the giant chasm in front of him. He probed its edges and cursed quietly—with the energy of the Dark Nav making him weaker, he didn't have enough power to close it completely.

Slowly, he rose to his feet and moved away from the crippling influence of the Nav as far as he could. Then he spread his arms, trembling with strain, and the light surrounding him became so bright it illuminated the entire plaza. He threw his head back, his body arching. The earth groaned and shook violently, resisting his assault, but he didn't stop, channeling more and more of his power.

With a guttural growl, he ripped a giant block of black rock and lifted it in the air, his muscles burning from strain. Using all the resources he had, he moved it over the chasm, carefully turning it around, and then gently lowered it to the ground, creating a sturdy bridge. With sweat running down his face, Damian dropped to one knee, his chest rising and falling with heavy breaths, the orange light engulfing him gradually dwindling.

"Whoa..." Alliandr exhaled, staring at him in awe. "I must admit, wielding the element of Earth was never my strength, but Heaven and Earth, Commander... I've never seen anything like this done before—"

An ear-piercing screech sounded from above, interrupting him. The Master of Power fell silent with his mouth opened slightly as he sucked in a sharp breath, his eyes igniting a blazing red, flames dancing in their depth.

"Elemental Fire," whispered Cole. "I don't know why, but I can feel it all around me." He moved his hand, pale red swirls of elemental energy following his move, and the stones in the pommels of his swords lit up even though he didn't touch them.

Damian raised his eyes, searching the stormy sky, and the small hairs on the back of his neck stood on end. Flying high above their heads, a giant dragon-like creature circled over the castle, its wide leathery wings beating the air heavily.

"A dragon?" Cole asked, unsheathing his swords.

"I don't think so," Damian muttered. "A lot scarier than any dragon."

"Zmey Gorynych," said Alliandr, his eyes set on the creature circling above. "The size of a large dragon, impenetrable scales, and three heads that breathe fire."

"How do we kill it?" asked Cole.

"You don't," replied Damian. "You're a vampire. A light touch of a single flame from this monster will turn you into a pile of ashes." He spun around, searching for anything that Cole could use as cover, but found nothing. "You need to sit this one out, brother."

"Uh-huh," murmured Cole, and by the look in his eyes, Damian knew trying to talk him out of this fight was a waste of breath.

The second screech, louder and more ominous than the previous, filled the air as Zmey Gorynych dove down, descending sharply. At the same time, the amount of demonic energy rose to the next level, and as Damian looked toward the gates into the Dark Nav, he saw a grim shadow materializing within the gray swirls of smoke.

"Demons." Cole narrowed his glowing eyes, his fingers wrapping tightly around the grips of his swords. "If you don't want me to fight the three-headed moth, I'll take care of this little disturbance." He jerked his chin toward the rising wall of darkness.

Damian didn't get a chance to reply as a powerful blast of fire scorched the land just a short distance away from them.

"Cole, take cover," he shouted, spreading his wings. Rising just a few feet above the ground in fear of losing the connection with his element, he summoned his daggers, infusing them with his magical energy.

Hovering right above, the *zmey* glowered down at him, and Damian could swear, all three heads of the monster were snickering, flames dancing in their menacing eyes. The *zmey* swooshed his long tail and took a deep breath, getting ready for the next strike. He pulled all his heads back, and the scales on his chest lifted as he accumulated more fire in his lungs, a dim red glow encapsulating his massive body.

Damian didn't wait for the *zmey* to attack. "Alliandr!" he yelled, pointing at the beast.

"*Igneous Orbus,*" the Master of Power shouted, rising high above the ground.

An enormous fireball materialized in the palm of his hand, and he propelled it at the monster, infusing it with his magic. The fire hit the monster on his side, and he snapped one of his heads in Alliandr's direction, anger rising around him almost palpable.

"*Igneous Amplio,*" Alliandr hissed, and two powerful jets of fire escaped his palms, impacting the beast's wing and setting the tip of his tail ablaze.

The *zmey* squealed, not so much from pain but rather from annoyance, and turned his entire body toward the Master of Power. He opened all three of his maws, displaying terrifying fangs, each of them as long as Damian's dagger.

"Oh, shit," Alliandr mumbled, quickly conjuring a protective shield around himself, and Damian couldn't help but chuckle noticing the bewildered expression on his face.

The *zmey* breathed out, and three scorching streams of fire engulfed Alliandr, flowing over his shield, doing him no harm.

"*Aquamius,*" Alliandr roared, meeting the next fire blast with two jets of water. Fire and water collided with a deafening hiss, raising a cloud of hot steam in the air.

Using the opportunity, Damian flew closer to the left head of Zmey Gorynych and swung his sword, decapitating it. The head fell to the ground with a loud thud and rolled toward the chasm, its neck flailing around frantically, showering Damian with green, stinky slime.

"*Igneous!*" he shouted, trying to burn the headless neck, but the stump kept swaying in such a wide and chaotic manner that he missed it entirely.

Momentarily, the new head regenerated in place of the lost one, its eyes glowering at Damian with deadly intent. He pulled away, quickly going through all possible scenarios in his mind, but as the sound of metal hitting metal reached his ears, he glanced down, searching for Cole.

The gray smoke spread low over the ground, moving in shadowy waves, wrapping around the legs of a group of demons facing his brother. Cole stood before them, looking calm and relaxed, a dark smile exposing his fully extended fangs. As if feeling Damian's eyes on him, he looked up swiftly, and his smile grew wider, twinkles of excitement dancing in his gaze. One second, he was just standing there with his swords down, but the next moment, he was gone, his shining blades wreaking havoc among demons, leaving quickly decomposing bodies and puddles of reeking goo.

"Watch your back, brother mine," Damian whispered, switching his attention to the bigger problem.

Determined to keep the monster's attention away from Damian, Alliandr was attacking the *zmey*, giving him no opportunity to look around. Using Fire and Water, he drove the monster crazy with pain and annoyance. Forgetting about everything, Zmey Gorynych charged the Master of Power, assailing him with jets of fire while trying to strike him with his heads.

"Fuck no." Damian dove forward and seized the *zmey's* tail, yanking it with all the strength he had in him.

Damian knew he couldn't move the giant monster, but he wanted to give Alliandr a breather, and it worked. The *zmey* hissed indignantly and came to a screeching halt in midair, two heads out of three turning toward Damian. The monster sucked in a deep breath, his chest expanding, fiery flames breaking through his scales to the surface, and the position of his heads indicated he was planning to assail both of them at the same time.

Rising slightly higher, Damian dove straight down. His daggers whistled through the air, and one of the heads rolled down before it could release the next blast of fire. The headless neck stilled in midair, and a fountain of flames and sparks burst straight up, enveloping Damian with searing heat. Once the fire died down, he reached forward and seized the swaying neck, wrapping his arms and legs around it.

Thrown around like a ragged doll, he stretched up and pressed one of his blades to the place where a new head was about to form and hissed, "*Igneous.*" The blade went up in flames, instantly cauterizing the neck and stopping the head from regenerating. He let go and tried to get away from the monster to regroup when the second head struck, impacting him in the chest. He cried out, propelled a few feet backward, wrapping his wings around himself to soften the impact. Still, he hit the rocks hard, blacking out for a brief moment.

As soon as he came to, he pushed off the ground and went up in the air just in time to see Alliandr cutting one of the *zmey's* heads off. In the air, the Master of Power seemed to be a lot more comfortable and faster than Damian. As soon as the head fell, he conjured the purifying energy of Fire, cauterizing the wound immediately, and before the last head could strike him, he was away from its reach.

Zmey Gorynych screeched and huffed, releasing a cloud of smoke reeking of sulfur into their faces, causing both of them to cough and pull back. Damian's eyes watered, tears running down his face, and for a moment, he could see nothing, a burning pain exploding in his head. Dropping his daggers, he squeezed his head with his hands, his fingers digging into his scalp.

"Damian!" Alliandr's desperate scream ripped him out of his abyss of torment.

Suppressing the pain, Damian summoned his daggers and spread his wings, rising back up. Alliandr was on top of the *zmey's* long neck, his arms wrapped tightly around it just below the head. Zmey Gorynych swayed his last remaining head from side to side, trying to shake him off, but Alliandr held on to him for dear life, his hands glowing with the energy of Fire, burning through the monster's thick scales.

"Alliandr, let go!" Damian shouted.

Alliandr unlocked his arms, pulling away from the monster, leaving deep, bleeding gashes on the *zmey's* neck in the place where he had held it. Touching his bracelet, Damian turned it into a whip and swung it. The silver thong swished through the air and wrapped around the monster's neck. Damian pulled it back, channeling all his magic and power through the whip. The beast thrashed violently, but all his efforts were to no avail.

Alliandr's sword struck through the air, blazing like silver lightning. Its blade, made of pure *Ardenium* steel, cut through the scales, flesh and bone without effort. The last head dropped to the ground, hitting it with a dull thud. Damian leaned back, pulling his whip harder to stop the headless neck from thrashing, and a low groan escaped his lips.

The Master of Power held out his hand and shouted, "*Igneous Amplio!*" A blazing stream of scorching flames hit the *zmey's* neck before he could regenerate his last head. His wings flapped one last time, and the monster plunged down in a spiraling motion, his tail still pounding the rocky land.

"His heart is still beating!" Damian yelled. "We need to stop it."

They both zoomed down. Being closer to the ground, Damian landed first, feeling relieved to be back in his element, and ran toward Zmey Gorynych, holding his daggers in his hands. Cole was there before Damian or Alliandr could reach the monster. Moving at his full vampiric speed, he circled the beast, halting in front of him. Then he raised his arm and struck the *zmey's* chest with all his strength. As his sword slipped between his ribs, finding his still beating heart, the monster turned rigid, his tail stopped beating, and then went limp.

Cole didn't say a word, but his blade protruding from the monster's chest shone a bright red, and a heartbeat later, the entire body of Zmey Gorynych went up in flames so intense and hot that both Damian and Alliandr halted, raising their arms to shield their eyes. The fire encircled Cole, licking him, wrapping around his arms like silky, scarlet ribbons.

"Nikolai!" A howl of absolute horror broke from Damian's lips, his heart pounding heavily against his ribcage. Not fully realizing what he was doing, he sprinted toward his brother, everything inside him twisting with dread. But as he reached him, he couldn't believe his eyes. Cole walked out of the fire, absolutely unharmed, a few flames still dancing in the palm of his hand. He squeezed his fingers, extinguishing the flames, and raised his face, meeting Damian's bewildered gaze.

"Don't ask," he mumbled. "I have no idea."

"Dammit, bro..." Damian moaned, pressing his hand over his eyes. Then he wrapped his arms around Cole, pulling him into a short hug. "One day you'll be the end of me. Don't you ever do that again!"

"The fire was elemental in nature." The Master of Power seized Cole's chin, forcing his head up, and peered into his eyes. Cole grunted, grabbing Alliandr's wrist with his hand but didn't apply his full strength, patiently waiting for the Master to free him. Alliandr let go and exchanged a troubled look with Damian. "I can still sense it in him." He moved his fingers over Cole's chest without touching it and switched his attention back to him. "It's burning in your heart... You're a vampire... Your heart is silent. It's impossible. The purifying component of elemental Fire should've burned you from within, yet you're still alive."

Cole shook his head, spreading his arms a little. "When I was fighting the demons, I felt something..." He fell silent, his eyes darting back toward the chasm. "It was like a wave of heat, you know? Then my swords went up in flames, even though I didn't cast the spell..." He frowned, rubbing his forehead, leaving streaks of demonic goo on his skin. "Every single demon is dead, burned to ashes."

"Master, we'll figure it out later," Damian said, waving in the direction of the castle. "After all this is over, we'll visit you in Kendral and speak with Kal, the Elemental of Fire. But right now, we need to get away from the gates into the Nav. Its energy feeds on our magic, making us weaker the longer we spend here, and we're drained after the fight with the *zmey* already."

As soon as Damian stepped onto the uneven surface of the stone bridge he had created, the deadly influence of the Nav tripled, feeding on his magic and elemental energy like a hungry monster. Grinding his jaw, he kept moving forward without slowing down until his feet touched the ground on the other side. He waited until Cole and Alliandr made it across and headed up the steps toward the entrance into the castle.

Connecting with his magic, he opened his other sight, sensing the weakness dominating his body. To his surprise, the door wasn't locked or guarded by any spells or wards, and as far as he could see, there wasn't anything magical within the walls. Carefully, he put his hands on the doorknobs and pushed the doors open. They opened with a mournful squeak, and cold air smelling like mold and dirt burst outside.

Before going in, he glanced back at the glowing tear in the fabric of reality they had come through. It was still just as large, shining with all the colors of the rainbow, appearing even brighter against the gloomy backdrop. The longer they spent here, the harder it would be for Alliandr to fix it. He thought back to Dallas' desperate situation and stifled a sigh as a chilling realization flashed through his mind.

We're moving too slow... We won't be in time to save Dallas... Dammit... He cursed quietly, not sure if he was cursing himself or Koschei and his flunkies. *I can't think like this. I must focus or I'll fail again...*

Gesturing for his brother and the Master of Power to wait, he crossed the threshold, stepping into a dark, spacious lobby. Looking down, he saw his own reflection on the polished black marble floor. Above him, a giant chandelier hung from the tall, arched ceiling. Squinting his eyes, Damian sucked in a sharp breath. The chandelier was made from human bones, with skulls used as candle holders.

A wide staircase led to the second floor, and two dark hallways spread in opposite ways. Since Damian still couldn't detect any magical presence or Koschei's energy signature for that matter, he motioned for Cole and Alliandr to come in. As soon as they crossed inside, however, the door snapped shut behind them, and absolute darkness encompassed the lobby. A burst of magical energy, dark and sinister, surged in all directions, originating somewhere above them, and this time, Damian recognized the energy signature without guessing. A loud cackle sounded from the second floor, an echo bouncing it against the vaulted ceiling.

As the derisive laughter died down somewhere in the light-deprived hallways, a soft purple glow illuminated the lobby. Damian glanced in the direction of the light and swallowed hard, goosebumps rising on his arms. Written with Koschei's magic, a few words levitated in midair, shimmering with a bright purple glimmer.

Honey, I'm home...

CHAPTER 28

~ DAMIAN BLAKE ~

The next burst of dry, wild laughter sounded under the ceiling, and a few purple arrows materialized under the writing.

Alliandr shrugged, a weak smile tugging at his lips. "I consider it an invitation," he said calmly and headed toward the stairway, but his heavy, slightly unsteady steps betrayed his true state of exhaustion.

Damian glanced back at the locked main door, knowing without checking it with his magical sight that not only was it tightly shut, but it was also blocked by some kind of spell.

Perfect. He gestured with his chin at the second floor and glanced at Cole.

"This is it," he said, using their blood bond. *"This is what we've been waiting for—our one and only chance to stop this evil once and forever."*

Cole smiled, and the mix of excitement, worry and determination in his glowing eyes sent a bolt of electricity through Damian. They ran up the wide marble steps, catching up with the Master of Power at the top. The stairway ended at a large hall. It was also dark, exuding a vibe of doom and abandonment. Something clicked, the dry sound echoing under the tall ceiling, and the enormous chandelier turned on, glowing with a soft purple light, illuminating the area.

Just like in the lobby, the chandelier was made from human bones connected with thin gold chains, and the rays of purple light were shining from the eye sockets of the skulls. Each skull seemed to be filled with magical light orbs, but instead of shimmering with the usual blue light, they were beaming with the color of Koschei's magical energy.

The black marble floor reflected the glimmer of the orbs, and it seemed as if the entire room was drowning in Koschei's magic. The tall door at the other end of the hall opened with a high-pitched squeak, the dark doorway gaping at them like the black maw of a monster.

"Ready?" asked Alliandr, his left hand landing on the pommel of his sword.

"For a while." Damian turned to the young Master of Power, searching his face with his eyes. "Alliandr, are you sure you can still—"

Alliandr nodded, a muscle playing in his tightly pressed jaw. "I'll do what needs to be done, Commander."

They crossed the hall and stepped into an enormous throne room. Just like before, as soon as they walked in, the doors closed behind them with a loud bang, and a wave of magic swept across the floor, sealing the entrance. Damian expected it and bit his lip to stop a sardonic smile from making an appearance. With Cole and Alliandr on either side of him, he strolled toward the other end of the room, carefully observing his surroundings.

With its opulent grandeur, which sole purpose was to intimidate the visitors and make them feel small and insignificant, the throne room presented an unsettling and spine-tingling view. Tall columns were erected on both sides of the space, positioned along the walls. Looking as if they were roughly cut from the black rocks of this strange realm, they shone with gold embellishments, thin golden vines wrapping around them all the way from the bottom to the very top.

A few tall stained-glass windows lined up the walls, but with their dark glass and the gray light of the world outside, they barely produced any illumination. Most of the light came from the two chandeliers filled with purple light orbs.

A thick black carpet with golden swirls stretched from the entrance to the massive throne positioned on a tall dais. Seemingly, the throne was made from the same material as the columns, a few tall, mountain-like peaks decorating its back. While they were positioned randomly, there was something dark and dangerous about their looks. Just like everything around, the armrests of the throne and the tips of the peaks were embellished with gold. Instead of legs, the seat was supported by skulls, most of which were human, their blind sockets staring at Damian with warning.

Koschei sprawled leisurely on the throne, his legs spread wide, his right arm propped on the armrest. In his home realm, he looked different from the way Damian used to see him in the world of humans. While his face was covered in deep wrinkles and his skin was pale, it no longer resembled a skull wrapped in old parchment. A gold crown on his head glimmered in the unsteady light, the gemstones embedded into it sparkling dimly.

Clad in black leather armor and a fur-trimmed cloak with a gold clasp locked on his shoulder, he didn't look like a skeleton but rather like a massive warrior, and a long sword lying across his lap completed the resemblance.

As he watched Damian, Cole and Alliandr with his glowing eyes, a contemptuous smile curled his lipless mouth, a vibe of malignant excitement and carnivorous gluttony rising over him. He leaned forward, gripping the armrest with his fingers, waiting patiently for them to come closer.

"Hello, boys," Koschei said as soon as they stopped a few feet away from the throne. "Don't you think you should kneel in the presence of the king?" He arched his eyebrows, derision sparkling in his eyes.

"Not in your lifetime," Damian replied calmly.

"Aw, Commander Blake." Koschei snickered, leaning back in his chair, looking smugger than ever. "Even you can't be so stupid. Don't you see you're trapped here, completely at my mercy?"

"How sweet that you think so," Damian replied, folding his arms. "It's weird, but I was thinking the exact same thing. Go figure..."

"Aw, Damian, you're so cute with your overconfident bravado," Koschei continued. "No wonder the late Detective Evans fell for you."

Late Detective Evans? Damian held his breath, his mind working on overdrive. *Either he doesn't know we restored her soul, or she didn't... No! River can't be dead...*

Koschei slapped the armrests, giving a loud guffaw. He cut his laughter abruptly, his features turning arctic-cold. "You're locked in this castle, physically and magically. You are at my mercy. And even if by some very unlikely... great... ginormous miracle you manage to escape my realm with your lives, the Destiny Council will hunt you all down and prosecute you for mutilating the fabric of reality." His eyes halted on Alliandr, mockery radiating from him. "I believe Master Alliandr is personally acquainted with the trial room and the effect the Destiny Oath bracelets have on any being of magic. Don't you, Master?"

Alliandr smiled, his eyes flooding with the darkness of his power. "Do you see me worried about the Destiny Council?" he asked without skipping a beat.

"Do you remember that cage in the trial room, Master Alliandr?" Koschei continued as if he didn't hear him. "A wonderful torture device, I must say. I only wish I had one of those in my possession." A malignant smile stretched his lipless mouth, an ominous glimmer in his eyes igniting brighter as he waved his hand, dismissing the subject. "Anyway, your isolation in Kendral is quite annoying. I believe I owe you a little something, and I don't like to be indebted. But as much as I wanted to meet with you again face to face, I couldn't cross into your realm without your permission."

"To be honest, I'm a little surprised to hear you're so eager to meet, Koschei, since I don't think you'll fare any better this time than the last time when we met face to face, as you put it," replied Alliandr not without sarcasm in his voice.

Koschei crossed his legs, all but rolling his eyes, endless hubris prominent in his lazy moves. "If the Hollow Band couldn't keep me restrained, nothing else will. Moreover, I believe you used your Hollow Band to imprison poor Azazel. Am I right?" He cocked his head, an ugly, derisive grimace contorting his face. "In addition, last time you had quite a team with you—the dark Master of Power, the Fire Elemental and his Phoenix, the Child of Earth, and someone truly special to you— the young and beautiful Destiny Keeper. Am I right, Master?"

Alliandr didn't reply, but his entire body went rigid, the magical energy field spiking around him in response to his emotions.

Koschei leaned forward, propping his chin against his fist. "You're drained, Master," he proceeded, his eyes moving up and down Alliandr's body as if sizing him up. "I can sense that you're one step away from shutting down. As far as your team, you have a vampire and a Destiny Enforcer—good lads that are hard to kill, yet not nearly as powerful as your former team. And should I remind you again that you no longer have the Hollow Band to contain my magic?" He got up, towering over them with malice. "You three stand no chance against me."

He spread his arms, his fingernails elongating into claws, and the entire building vibrated as he channeled his powerful magic. He switched his attention to Damian and Cole, a deep frown accentuating his wrinkles.

"The old one was right," Koschei screeched, pointing his hooked finger first at Damian and then at Cole. "You and your brother cannot be killed. You're like a pair of goddamn cockroaches—you can survive a nuclear holocaust. No matter what kind of deadly monsters I throw in your path, you manage to slither your way out alive." He cackled, the sound so frosty and menacing that the blood froze in Damian's veins. "Unlike the old god, I strongly believe your death would resolve a lot of problems, but since it seems to be impossible, I relent. The old one will get what he wants. The only way to contain you two is to subdue you in such a way that you can no longer move, begging me to allow you to breathe."

Damian shrugged nonchalantly, cocking his head. "Your threats would have been a lot more effective, if we didn't have this..." He nodded to Alliandr.

The Master of Power held out his hand, and the golden needle manifested in his palm. He held it between his thumb and index finger, showing it to Koschei. The old sorcerer blanched and gasped, plastering an expression of horror on his face, but then a slow, menacing smile stretched his mouth, showing a set of yellow-brown teeth.

"Go ahead." He flicked his wrist without as much as a shadow of worry on his face. "Break it, Master. I dare you."

"Funny thing about that enormous Riders Library in Kendral," said Alliandr, sounding almost bored. "If you spend there long enough, you can find all sorts of interesting things." He took a pause, pinning Koschei with his dark gaze. "We know that breaking this needle will produce a magical energy blast more destructive than a powerful bomb."

He glanced at the needle in his hand, probing it with his fingertip. "Why do you think we worked so hard, breaking all the rules just to get you away from the human realm and trick you into coming after us to this desolate land? We realized if we had to face you in the world of humans, we wouldn't be able to kill you without losing millions of innocent lives in the process." Alliandr folded his massive frame into a ceremonial bow filled with mockery. "So, thank you for meeting us here, and for sealing this place with your magic. We couldn't have done it without you."

For a second, Koschei stared at the Master of Power, his mouth agape. Then he started to clap his hands slowly, his every clap echoing through the throne room, pressing on Damian's stretched nerves.

"Wow," he said, nodding approvingly. "What an unexpected maneuver..." Then he yawned demonstratively and twirled his wrist. "If you feel comfortable that you three can survive the blast, go ahead, break the needle. Make. My. Goddamn. Day." The last few words, he spoke slowly, spitting them out one at the time through gritted teeth, and Damian froze in place, a dark feeling of foreboding settling in his chest.

"Alliandr," he whispered, stretching his hand to him, but he was too late.

The Master of Power took the tip of the needle with his free hand and applied some pressure, trying to break it.

Damian gasped as the world suddenly tilted, and the throne room spun around him in sickening waves. Pain the likes of which he had never felt before consumed his entire being, and a holler of anguish rang through the room. He could hear it but couldn't recognize this harrowing sound as something his vocal cords could produce. Other sounds surfaced in his dimming mind, and he tried to focus on them, but to no avail.

"Alliandr, stop! You're killing him!"

Damian recognized this voice, and he reached for it—at least he thought he did. The pain ceased, just as abruptly as it began, leaving him weak and breathless, gasping for air. He cracked his eyelids open to find himself lying on the black carpet, Cole's arms wrapped tightly around him. As his gaze traveled toward the throne, he saw Koschei on all fours, struggling to get up, his gold crown lying on the floor before him. He finally managed to sit back on his heels and grabbed the crown, placing it on his head. His mouth twitched, a grimace of disdain changing his features.

"You didn't read about this one in your famous Riders Library, did yah, Master of Kendral?" he panted, wiping sweat off his brow. "Well, let me explain, boys." He rose to his feet with a groan, readjusting his armor and the scabbard with his sword. "A few months ago, I made a few small improvements to my needle." He caught Cole's flabbergasted gaze and cackled. "Yes, vampire. I can walk into any human establishment unnoticed, even into a bank. So, while you all were busy unraveling the mystery of the ring and saving the natural balance, the old one and I used the opportunity to invade the Destiny Council realm, killing every single soul we could find there. I used this rare occasion to fuse the deadly essence of my needle with the powerful magic of the Destiny Board."

He took a meaningful pause, watching Damian rise to his feet with Cole's help. Damian leaned heavily on his brother's shoulder, staring at the ancient Master of the Dark Arts with a mix of horror and loathing as a terrible revelation washed over him.

"Judging by the look on your face, Enforcer, you got my meaning, but let me explain to the rest of you," Koschei continued, touching his own chest, and then pointing at Damian. "My death equals the deaths of every single person bound to the Destiny Council realm. I'm not sure, but I believe this includes the High Council as well." He snickered as he pushed the gray strands of his hair away from his face and switched his attention to Alliandr. "So, Young Master, would you like to give it another try?" He gave Alliandr an arched stare. "Go ahead, kill me." Since Alliandr didn't move, he laughed again, spreading his arms. "What? You changed your mind?"

The expression of delight on his face morphed into a scowl of anger as he took a step closer, his glacial gaze darting from Damian to Cole.

"When all is said and done, I still outplayed you, meager Enforcer." Koschei's eyes ignited with a malignant glimmer as the carnivorous excitement took him over. "Yes, you're nothing but an insignificant Destiny Enforcer—expendable to your masters, one of many, a weak slave without a mind of your own," he seethed, droplets of saliva spraying from his mouth. Then he squared his shoulders, looking down at Damian with abhorrence. "As I mentioned at the beginning of our pleasant conversation, you *are* trapped here, completely at my mercy. If you and your brother accept your defeat and submit to me, I'll let Master Alliandr return to his realm alive. Make your choice, Commander Blake, and do choose wisely."

Damian dropped his head, thousands of thoughts flashing through his mind. All of them as terrifying as they were dangerous. At this point, however, he didn't have many options, and he was willing to give anything a try before surrendering himself and his brother to two powerful monsters. While he wasn't worried about his own life, he was afraid to even imagine what kind of consequences his submission could have for the world. There was a reason the old one was so desperate to capture them, and judging by all the events, this reason couldn't be anything good.

He wasn't willing to take this kind of risk. Not today. Not ever.

He opened himself to the blood bond with his brother, but instead of reaching to Cole, he spoke to the Master of Power.

"*Alliandr, can you hear me?*" he asked, feeling Cole's fingers squeezing his arm tighter.

"Yes. Speak." Alliandr didn't move, but his voice sounded loud and clear in his mind.

"Do you know any spell that can immobilize Koschei?"

"I think so. I can try," Alliandr replied, his voice not as self-assured as before. "Koschei is right. I'm drained, and even if my spell works, it'll give you no more than a few seconds."

"That's all I need." A dark smile crossed Damian's face. "I either succeed or I die. Fifty-fifty. I like my odds." He raised his face, his eyes settling on his brother. Cole gave him a barely visible nod, but his fingers trembled as he removed his hand from Damian's arm. Turning to Alliandr, Damian commanded, "Do it now."

Alliandr's eyes flooded with blackness as he connected with his full quadruple power. The castle shook, and the floor shuddered beneath their feet. The zigzag of a lightning bolt struck outside the windows, followed by a deafening boom of thunder. The frosty gale rushed through the throne room, pushing Koschei backward, pinning him to his throne, and bright flames broke through Alliandr's skin, dancing on his arms and shoulders.

He pointed at Koschei and shouted a few words in Dragon tongue. Koschei yelped, his wide-open eyes drowning in fear, his arms rising to shield his face of their own accord. The translucent silvery bubble of Alliandr's spell materialized around the sorcerer, and Koschei stilled inside, his face distorted by a silent howl.

"Now, Commander," Alliandr hissed through gritted teeth, perspiration glistening on his forehead.

Without waiting for a second invitation, Damian sprinted toward Koschei, praying that Alliandr's spell held long enough for him to do what needed to be done. The cuffs shining with brilliant white light materialized in his hand as he crossed inside the sphere of Alliandr's magic. Seizing Koschei's arm, he locked the Destiny cuffs on his wrists and backed away from him, turning to the Master of Power.

"Alliandr, it's over..." he exhaled, his arms still shaking from the strain and the burst of adrenalin surging through his system.

With a soft moan, Alliandr let go and swayed, nearly falling. A weak groan sounded behind Damian, making him turn around. Koschei was on his knees, his head bowed low. He lifted his face, and Damian cringed inwardly at the cold hatred in the ancient sorcerer's eyes.

"How dare you..." He struggled to get up but fell back down. As the debilitating power of the Destiny cuffs kept draining him of his magic, he moaned and dropped to his side, closing his eyes for a heartbeat. The spell he cast to seal all the doors in his castle vanished, and the purple light of the magical orbs dwindled, leaving them in a semi-dark throne room.

"Oh, I dare." Damian approached Koschei and squatted, seizing the hair on the back of his head, forcing him to look up. "Thank you for reminding me of who I am. Maybe I'm an expendable slave, but I can wield an extremely dangerous weapon that is unique to my subservient kind. The type of weapon that can bring down to their knees and restrain any being of magic, even as powerful as you are. I believe the Destiny cuffs are almost as effective as the Hollow Band. Am I right?" He brushed his fingers over the shining surface of the Destiny cuffs and got up. "You made sure I can't kill you, Koschei, but I can make sure you'll never harm anyone again." He shrugged. "The Destiny Council's dungeon can hold you powerless and restrained for the rest of your very long, immortal life. Enjoy the oblivion..."

He channeled his magic, getting ready to send Koschei to the Destiny Council realm, when Alliandr's soft voice sounded in his mind.

"Damian, stop," the Master of Power said. *"You can't do it. The Destiny Council has been compromised. If the old one could breach the security of the realm and enter unnoticed, he can do it again. Until we*

know how he did it the last time, the Destiny Council realm is no longer safe."

Damian exhaled, running his hand over his face, feeling the exhaustion with every bone in his body. *"What do you propose, Master?"*

"I believe Kendral is still secure," replied Alliandr. *"We'll keep Koschei restrained by the Destiny cuffs. In addition, I have quite the special dungeons in my realm that can contain any being of magic, even ones as powerful as Azazel or Koschei. Do you trust me, Damian?"*

Damian nodded.

Alliandr moved his hand parallel to the floor, muttering something under his breath, and a pile of thick iron chains materialized next to Koschei.

Koschei gasped, trying to cower back, but was too powerless to make a move. "Master," he moaned, "aren't the Destiny cuffs enough? You don't need to—"

"Yes, I do," Alliandr interrupted him, his voice void of emotions. "As I said, I did some light reading back in Kendral. According to lore, twelve iron chains are what is needed to truly restrain you, so forgive me if I don't take any chances."

He snapped his fingers, and the chains came to life. They slithered toward Koschei with a loud clatter and wrapped tightly around his ankles, neck and torso, pinning his arms to his sides. Koschei groaned, his eyes rolled back, and he fainted. Alliandr squatted next to him, quickly checking him with his other sight, and then waved his hand, opening a portal. With a strenuous groan, he lifted Koschei, throwing him over his shoulder, and turned to Damian.

"Commander, you and Cole need to return to the realm of humans," he said softly. "There is a chance you can still save your young friend." He bowed his head, releasing a shuddering breath. "I'll be back to fix the fabric of reality as soon as I send Koschei to the dungeon." He halted by the portal, and a faint smile graced his drained face. "If the Destiny Council wants to prosecute me for that, I'll stand the trial, but I want you to be the one to bring me in."

"Alliandr—," Damian started, but the young Master of Power raised his hand, stopping him, a shadow of vulnerability crossing his features.

"Don't let them send Moore after me, Damian. You owe me this much," he whispered, barely meeting Damian's eyes.

Dammit... Damian swallowed, numbness spreading through his chest. Then he raised his gaze at the powerful young man before him and pressed his fist to his chest. "I'm yours to command, Master," he said, his throat constricted. "I'll do as you wish…"

Slightly inclining his head, Alliandr walked through the portal, closing it behind himself.

CHAPTER 29

~ DAMIAN BLAKE ~

All this time, Damian didn't fully realize the pressure he was under. Only now, when he exited the castle, was he able to breathe freely for the first time in days. Now that the shadow of Koschei was no longer looming over him, he could finally relax, at least to a degree.

The demonic essence surrounding the castle was gone, leaving the late evening air crisp and fresh, and the gate into the Dark Nav was closed. The tear in the fabric of reality glowed with a soft colorful light in the distance, reminding him that even though he had completed his original mission, his troubles were far from over.

He placed his hand on Cole's shoulder and snapped his fingers, teleporting them to the glowing entrance into their world. Halting next to it, he turned to his brother, gesturing for him to go through, but Cole raised his hand, stopping him.

"Dima," he said, readjusting his scabbard, which seemed to become his nervous habit. "What did Alliandr mean when he said that we may still have enough time to save our young friend."

"Dallas," replied Damian, massaging his aching shoulder. "He was talking about Dallas."

"Why? Do you think the demons will be able to—"

"No, Cole. Demons have nothing to do with this," Damian said, wincing inwardly at how hoarse his voice sounded. "Back in the vault, Dallas saved us all but at a high price. He wielded powerful, ancient magic that was way above his pay grade. I'm afraid it may cost him his life."

"But why?"

Suppressing a sigh, Damian continued softly, "Think back to the lessons in magic I gave you. It takes time to learn how to channel your magic without depleting your internal resources, and the more powerful the magic you wield, the faster it drains you. You have to train your mind and body to know when to stop, to feel when you tap into your own life energy and stop before it's too late." He looked away, his thumb rubbing the edge of his bracelet. "Everything happened so fast, I didn't get a chance to train Dallas, to condition his body for the use of any kind of magic… let alone the all-consuming magic of the World Tree."

Cole froze in place, his blue eyes widening in fear. "No," he whispered. "How did he… It's impossible. Where did he…"

Damian pushed Cole gently toward the opening. "Every second we spend here talking, Dallas is burning out his life force to keep this entrance safe for us."

Cole nodded and stepped through the tear, disappearing on the other side. Damian threw one last glance at Koschei's castle and followed him.

* * *

AFTER THE DULL, gray light of Koschei's realm, the electrical lights of the bank vault seemed too bright for Damian's eyes. He blinked a few times, adjusting his vision, and then looked around. The room was still locked and sealed by the spell, but he could no longer detect any hostile presence. His gaze fell on Dallas, and a weight settled in his heart. The young man lay sprawled on the floor, his head resting on Ruslan's lap. His suntanned face was drained of color, and his sweat-soaked dark hair plastered to his forehead, accentuating the paleness of his skin. Ruslan's hand was stroking his shoulder mechanically, and Damian wasn't sure the ancient vampire realized he was doing that.

Quinn Allerton sat on a chair by the table with his arms resting on his lap. His head was bowed down, and he looked beyond tired. As soon as Cole and Damian appeared, he got up and exhaled with relief, pressing the heels of his hands to his eyes.

"Thank God you are alive," he breathed, reaching for his handkerchief even though he didn't have his glasses on. "The Master of Kendral is not with you?"

"He'll be here soon," replied Damian.

Ruslan rose to his feet, gently lowering Dallas' head to the floor. He halted in front of Cole, his mouth pressed into a straight line, and for a short moment, he just stood there, taking in every detail of his son's appearance.

"You are back," he said at length, sounding as if he still couldn't believe it. "Koschei?"

"We couldn't kill him," replied Damian, "but we took care of him. I don't think he'll ever see the light of day again."

In so many words, he told Allerton and Ruslan everything that had happened. When he finished, Allerton shook his head, shoving his hands into the pockets of his pants.

"Commander Blake, you did the right thing, but you'll pay dearly for it," he said quietly. "I know we're not children, so we are not going to discuss the unfairness of life." His lips twisted in a mirthless smile. "The High Council doesn't take disobedience lightly, but I'm not talking about you disobeying Lord

Magnus' orders." He pointed at the glowing tear and then threw his arms up in a desperate gesture. "Goddammit, Damian! Both you and Master Alliandr will face a trial for this, for there is no greater offense than the mutilation of the fabric of reality, and as a Destiny Enforcer you knew that."

"Of course, I knew that! But that was the only way. Even though Alliandr could sense the location of Koschei's realm, he was unable to open a portal or teleport there. If we faced Koschei in this world, the number of human casualties would have been devastating," Damian said quietly. "I did what I had to do to keep the humans safe and prevent the exposure of magic." Damian glanced at Dallas and then met Allerton's heavy gaze. "You don't need to report me or get involved in this, my lord. As soon as I take care of Dallas, I'll return to the Destiny Council realm and surrender myself to the High Council voluntarily. Master Alliandr has nothing to do with any of this."

A sad smile crossed Allerton's face. "I understand. You're trying to protect the Master of Kendral," he said, exchanging a quick look with Ruslan. "However, no one will believe that you could've done something like this on your own. You don't have the power."

"Yet it's true," Cole objected, meeting Allerton's eyes calmly. "I'll state it under an oath if I have to."

"You can't lie under the Destiny Oath, my child," Ruslan objected. "The Destiny Oath has powerful magic which prevents you from lying."

"Since I'll be telling the truth, I have nothing to worry about. My brother ripped the fabric of reality, and I saw it with my own eyes. I'll state it under the Destiny Oath, or a polygraph, or any other oath out there."

"A polygraph?" Allerton snorted in such an un-Archmage-like manner that Damian couldn't help but smile. "You're a vampire. You have no pulse or a heartbeat. A lot of good that would do."

"Whatever is going to happen to me is not important right now," Damian cut them off, wincing at how harsh and cold he sounded. "When the time comes, I'll face the consequences of my actions, but right now, I am worried only about Dallas."

He lowered to his knees next to Dallas and quickly explored him with his other sight. The young man was drained completely—no magical energy left in his body, but that wasn't the worst. The glow of his human soul and the energy of his life force was nearly gone too, and only a tiny flicker of light still lingered in his slowly beating heart.

I'm too late... He sat back on his heels, hiding his face in his hands, blaming himself for this entire situation. Feeling a light touch on his arm, he looked up and saw Archmage Allerton standing next to him.

"There is nothing you can do, Commander. He's dying. It's only a matter of a few hours," he said gently, lowering to one knee next to Damian. "The boy is a hero. He saved us all." He brushed his fingers over Dallas' pale cheek, stained with blood, his hand shaking slightly.

"How did it happen?" Damian asked through clenched teeth, forcing himself not to sound as harsh.

"He had that feather," Allerton replied with an apologetic shrug. "I have no idea how he came in possession of such a powerful magical artifact, but when he pulled it out of his pocket, I warned him..." The Archmage swallowed, and his lips quivered as he looked away, clasping his hand over his mouth. A moment later, he exhaled a ragged breath and continued, "I told him that he'd die, but the only thing he cared about was saving you and Cole."

"As soon as you three left, the demonic essence invaded the building, possessing every human in its way," said Ruslan. "A powerful dark magic locked and sealed the bank, and no matter what I tried, I couldn't break through. So, I did the only thing I could do to prevent the exposure of the World of Magic."

Ruslan glanced at Cole, and his forehead creased. "I called Archmage Allerton, using the business card Cole gave me. The Guardians mages were able to shadow the bank and prevent demons from possessing more people, but no matter what we tried, we still couldn't break in to help you."

"That was where Dallas stepped in," Allerton took over. "The magic of the World Tree burned through the shield of dark magic, allowing Dallas to get inside. It helped him to expel the demonic essence from the vault, but because he had to wield it in an ungodly amount and for a prolonged time, it also burned his life force."

Damian closed his eyes and connected with his element. It took him too long to gather a small amount of it in his hands, and he knew it wasn't nearly enough to perform healing magic.

"Damian, stop," Allerton said, putting his hand on Damian's arm. "The healing energy of Earth can't heal him, and even if it could, you are too drained to perform any kind of healing. There is nothing you can do. He's dying..." The Archmage shook his head, crestfallen. "I wish he listened to me when I told him not to do it..."

"I'm glad I didn't... and I would do all this again... if I could..." Dallas cracked his eyelids open, his fading gaze moving from Damian to Cole. "You are both alive... here... you did it..."

Cole lowered next to Dallas, placing his hand on his shoulder. "No, Dallas, you did it." He swallowed, red liquid gathering in the corners of his eyes.

Dallas unlocked his hand, and a feather—snow-white and midnight-blue—fell out of his stiff fingers. "Bird Alkonost told me that being a human hunter was never my destiny," he whispered, "and she was right. I knew I'd die... but when the magic of this feather started to whisper in my mind, telling me what needed to be done, I had no doubts... My life in exchange for yours?" He raised his eyes at Cole, his lips twitching slightly, and then added in a whisper, "For me, it wasn't a choice."

Cole bowed his head, and a large red drop fell on Dallas' chest. "My little brother... no... what did you do?" He pressed his hands to his face, rocking slightly, and his wide shoulders shuddered.

"Wait," said Damian as a sudden realization dawned on him. "I believe that wasn't what Bird Alkonost had in mind, Dallas." He looked at Ruslan and then at Allerton. "There is a way to save your life, sort of. Actually, a few ways, and this is the choice you need to make."

"What are you talking about, Commander?" Allerton frowned. "Don't do anything crazy. You're already a dead man walking."

"Then I have nothing to worry about, do I, Archmage? One more offense won't make it any worse," Damian replied calmly and turned toward Dallas. "Here are your choices, my friend, but I must warn you—none of them are particularly good. So, if you prefer to..." Damian swallowed hard, having a hard time saying the words out loud. "If you chose to leave this world and cross the veil, we'll respect your decision."

"What are the choices?" asked Dallas, and it seemed like every word he spoke came with more effort than the previous.

"As a Commander of the Destiny Enforcers, I'm authorized to offer you the mantel of a Destiny Enforcer," Damian said, his stomach twisting into a painful knot just from thinking about doing it to Dallas. "As soon as I bind your soul to the Board of Destiny, its powerful magic will restore your life force and enhance your magic, making you immortal. The drawback is that you'll be subservient to the Destiny Council. The initial training will be worse than hell, and they will partially suppress your emotions."

"What are my other choices?" asked Dallas, his face as calm as always.

"Either Cole or Ruslan can turn you," replied Damian,

sending a veiled gaze to his brother. "The drawback... You'll become the very thing you used to hunt and kill."

Dallas closed his eyes, and the Adam's apple in his neck jerked. "These are my only choices?" he asked, a layer of bitterness underlying his words. "Become a supernatural cop, enslaved by the terrifying High Council, or spend the rest of eternity on a liquid diet of blood, a helpless slave to the thirst."

"Welcome to the World of Magic, my boy," said Ruslan, a sad, kind smile on his face. "There is always someone who yanks your leash. But if it would make any difference, I will turn you myself, making you Cole's true brother. We'll teach you how to lead an almost normal lifestyle, and how to deal with the thirst." He took one knee next to Dallas, taking his hand. "I'm not going to lie. It'll take a few years before I'll be able to set you free into the world, and these few years of adjustment are not going to be easy."

Dallas nodded and bit his lip, his steel eyes sliding from one face to the next.

"There is one more option, Dallas," offered Damian. "I can summon Vasilisa the Wise. Possibly, the Water of Life can still restore your life force, but this time, she's not going to let you go. You'll spend the rest of your life serving her in the Sacred Gardens, and you'll never see any of us again." Carefully scanning Dallas' body with his other sight, he stifled a sigh. The young man was one step from crossing the veil. "You must choose now, my friend, before it's too late."

"Wow." Dallas chuckled weakly, glancing at Cole. "My choices suck royally, no pun intended." Then his gaze darted to Damian, and he nodded. "I'll go with you, Damian. I choose the mantel of the Destiny Enforcer." He looked at Cole and Ruslan, a vibe of guilt palpable around him. "Thank you, but drinking blood is not something I can ever get used to. Besides"—he lifted his shoulder in a weak half-shrug—"I just enjoy normal food."

Damian lifted Dallas carefully and straightened, holding him against his chest. "I guess I'll have to face the High Council earlier than I expected." A sad smile ghosted his lips as he looked at his brother. "I'll be fine, little bro. Not the first time for me. Take care of our friends and River. I wish I could be there for her, but…"

His voice trailed away, Koschei's words ringing in his mind —*late Detective Evans*. He didn't believe it. He refused to believe it. River was alive, even if she was still in her enchanted sleep. He would have known if she wasn't…

He caught Allerton's desperate gaze as the Archmage frowned, an expression of despair shadowing his features. "Damian, I'll speak with the High Council in your defense. I'll do everything in my power to help you."

"My deepest gratitude, sir, but I don't want you to get involved, endangering yourself." Damian inclined his head and then glanced at his brother, winking at him. "I'll see you soon, little bro."

He shifted Dallas' weight slightly toward his left arm and snapped his fingers, vanishing from the vault.

CHAPTER 30

~ DAMIAN BLAKE ~

Damian materialized in the semi-dark hallway in front of Magnus' office. The door was tightly shut, but he could sense Magnus' powerful energy signature emanating from behind it. He took a deep breath and raised his hand to knock, but the door opened silently before he could do it. Not expecting a warm welcome, he crossed the threshold and halted, his arms wrapping tighter around Dallas' unconscious body.

The Head of the Destiny Council stood behind his enormous desk, his eyes blazing with undiluted fury. He waved his hand, and the door snapped shut behind him with a loud bang. Damian froze in place, bracing himself for the display of Magnus' wrath, but he stood silent, his chest shuddering with furious breaths. It wasn't the first time Damian got Magnus hot under the collar, but it was the first time when the eye-watering brightness of his eyes sent chills down his spine.

"You," Magnus hissed after a long pause, and the walls of the office shook, responding to his anger. "How dare you! What you did—" He cut himself off, his eyes so bright that Damian had to avert his gaze.

Damian raised his face, carefully taking in Magnus' appearance. To his shock, through Magnus' display of righteous fury, he could sense something else. Something he wasn't accustomed to sensing from this powerful and terrifying man—fear.

"My lord, I know I disobeyed your commands, and I'll submit myself to your mercy and take any punishment willingly, but first—," Damian started, taking a tentative step toward him, but Magnus made an impatient gesture with his hand, interrupting him.

"This young man is dying," Magnus muttered, making his way around the desk toward Damian. "Why did you bring him here?"

"You're right, my lord. He's dying," Damian replied quietly. "This is Dallas Gray. He's the young wizard who saved us all, paying for it with his life force, and I offered him the mantel of a Destiny Enforcer."

Magnus shoved his hands in his pockets, squeezing his teeth so hard they squeaked. "Of course, I know what he did," he said, irritation still clear in his voice. "The amount of the World Tree magic he used was unprecedented. I could sense it from here. Anyone who has an ounce of magic in them could." He placed his hand over Dallas' chest, quickly scanning his body, and shook his head, dropping his arm. "Heaven and Earth, Commander! What's wrong with you? How could you let it happen?"

He channeled his magic and drew a rune in the air. Pressing his palm over it, he whispered a summoning spell. A few minutes later, someone knocked on the door.

"Come in," Magnus muttered, spreading his long robe apart to put his hands in the pockets of his pants.

"You summoned me, my lord." Ivor walked into the office and pressed his fist to his chest, bowing. "I'm yours to command."

"Learn how to address your superiors properly, Commander Blake," Magnus grumbled, flashing an angry glance at Damian.

Ivor's lips quirked up at the corners, and he quickly bowed his head lower to hide his face, but his shoulders shook in silent laughter. "What can I do for you, my lord?" he asked calmly once Magnus gestured for him to rise.

"This is Dallas Gray." Magnus pointed at the young man. "Effective immediately, he's accepted into the Destiny Enforcers' training program as an apprentice."

Ivor's jaw dropped, and he threw a bewildered glance in Damian's direction but didn't ask anything. "Yes, my lord."

"Normally, a Commander is supposed to bind the soul of his recruit to the Board of Destiny," continued Magnus, still speaking through gritted teeth, "but since Dallas' Commander happened to be the imbecile standing here, I need you to do me a favor, Ivor."

"Anything, my lord," replied Ivor, having a hard time keeping a straight face as he sent a veiled glance at Damian.

"Dallas is dying, and we don't have much time. Can you please initiate the binding ceremony immediately?" Magnus asked.

"Of course." Ivor took Dallas from Damian's arms, draping his body over his shoulder.

"I don't want Moore anywhere near this boy," Magnus continued with a sigh, "but I don't think Commander Blake will be available to train him in any foreseeable future. As soon as Adrian returns from his current assignment, I want him to take care of the training. In the meantime, you're responsible for Dallas Gray's initiation."

"Yes, my lord. I'll keep an eye on him and make sure he's well taken care of." Ivor inclined his head, ready to leave, but Damian seized his elbow, stopping him.

"Just one more favor, my lord," he said, barely meeting Magnus' eyes.

"I believe you're fresh out of favors, Commander," Magnus muttered, but then gazed heavenward. "What else do you want?"

"Keep his emotions intact, please," said Damian quietly. "He's a good man. Don't mutilate his personality."

"Yeah." Magnus huffed. "Apparently, you're an expert in mutilation." His eyes ignited brighter again, but he nodded to Ivor, gesturing for him to leave. As soon as Ivor walked out and closed the door behind himself, Magnus swung his arm and punched Damian in his jaw. Not expecting something like this, Damian gasped and collapsed, a burst of white light exploding in his head. He pressed his hand to his face and raised his watering eyes at Magnus, the metallic taste of blood filling his mouth.

"Why did you do it, Dmitri?" asked Magnus. He flicked his wrist, and a yellow glimmer of a cloaking spell enveloped his office. He lowered to his knees next to Damian and repeated his question, calmer this time. "Why did you do it? Speak freely, but I must know the truth. Why didn't you stay back in Paradise Manor?" It seemed as though this punch helped him let out some steam, and now he looked more tired than angry.

"How could I?" Damian scrambled into a sitting position, leaning his back against the wall, and wiped the blood off his lips with the back of his hand. "Magnus, you don't understand..." His voice shook, and he looked away from the pair of blazing eyes glaring at him with reproach.

"Then talk to me, my boy. Explain." Magnus changed his position and sat down next to Damian, rubbing the knuckles of his right hand.

"Luc and Jamie were dying," Damian whispered. "River was dying. Koschei went after Hawk and his pack. He killed every single vampire in Cole's Council, and he nearly killed his maker." He turned to Magnus with a shake of his head. "You didn't think Koschei was going to stop after killing those I loved, did you? An unspeakable evil like him never stops, every victory just catalyzing their hunger for blood and power." He dropped his head, his limbs tingling with fatigue. "I couldn't let him win, Magnus. I just"—he swallowed, his eyebrows pinched together—"I couldn't just sit and watch…"

His voice faded into silence, and for a few long seconds, he couldn't speak, a chaos of thoughts, wishes and regrets spiraling in his mind. Magnus didn't say anything, silently fidgeting with the ring of the member of the High Council, but a haunted expression settled in his eyes, dimming them down to a light silvery color.

"I understand you're not pleased with me disregarding your orders again, Magnus, but I had to do something before it was too late. I'm sorry, but I made my choice, and I stand by it," Damian continued, looking at the opposite wall shimmering with the yellow glimmer of the cloaking spell. "If you have to punish me for doing what I believed was right, not only for me but also for the realm I swore to defend, then do it." He extended his arms to Magnus, his hands locked into tight fists.

Magnus didn't move, peering at Damian's clenched hands. "So, you made this choice on your own. No one pressured you?" he whispered, his voice hoarse.

"Yes, I just said that. Except you, no one dares pressure me." Damian chuckled, but quickly sobered up, narrowing his eyes at Magnus, and repeated, "Yes, I chose my path on my own. Why?"

"How about your brother?"

"Cole? What does he have to do with Destiny Council affairs?" asked Damian, instantly alert.

"Just answer my questions, Dmitri."

"Cole chose to stand by my side, even though I did everything I could to keep him away from all this," replied Damian. "Despite him being a vampire, Cole always fights on the side of Light. Why, Magnus? What are you not telling me?"

"Many things," Magnus replied dryly. He got up with a low groan and headed toward his desk. He braced his fists against the desktop and leaned forward heavily, bowing his head.

Damian also rose to his feet and squared his shoulders, massaging his aching neck. "So, what now?"

"Now?" With one hand still resting on the desk, Magnus turned sideways, looking at Damian as if he had never seen him before. "Now, you will face the tribunal and Master Alliandr will stand trial for mutilating the fabric of reality. I'm not going to mention any other of your offenses, like using the magic of the lake hidden beneath Paradise Manor to revive an ancient vampire or promising your obedience to the Guardian of the Sacred Garden, but I can't cover up what you and the Master of Kendral did in that bank."

"No, my lord, please." Damian took a step forward, noticing a shocked expression on Magnus' face. "I'm not begging for myself, but for Alliandr. He had nothing to do with it. I'm the one who tore the fabric of reality, and I'll face the tribunal for that, but please, don't get him involved."

Magnus pursed his lips, tilting his head, and threw his arms up. "Do you even hear yourself, Dmitri? No one will believe you."

Damian frowned, giving Magnus a quick once-over. "Something tells me you believe I can do it, and my statement doesn't shock you at all," he said, folding his arms. "According to Quinn Allerton, neither my brother nor I should be able to open the door leading to the Sacred Lake under Paradise Manor, yet we both could. Why is that, Magnus?" He raised his eyebrows, staring at him quizzically. Since Magnus didn't reply and didn't change his position, Damian continued, "Why was it so important for you to know that Cole and I chose to go after Koschei of our own volition, huh? Was that a free will test or are you afraid to get blamed for our actions?"

Magnus's eyes widened for a split second, and he stilled, a muscle playing in his jaw. "I am not obligated to answer any of your questions, Commander," he said at length.

"I know you are not obligated to even listen to me. Who am

I? Just another Destiny Enforcer, a glorified slave. You could have snapped your fingers and sent me into the darkest dungeon of this realm," Damian replied, invading his personal space, and even though Magnus wasn't short, he towered over him at least a few inches. "But you didn't, did you?"

Magnus shook his head, raising his hands in a placating manner, but Damian didn't care anymore, pain and anger blending into an explosive concoction in him.

"How about this question…" he hissed, his voice shaking. "I had the pleasure of meeting an ancient god—an old one who works with Koschei. Riddle me this, Magnus… Why are his eyes shining just like yours? Can you answer that question?" He seized Magnus' arm, holding him in place, his fingers digging deep into his bicep. "I have another good one for you… Why do his wards have your sigil built into them? Why could I unlock his wards by channeling my own energy through *your* sigil? And why is this fucking old one so adamant about capturing me and my brother? Why would a powerful ancient deity, who is more powerful than Svarog, Odin and Zeus, want a Destiny Enforcer and a vampire? Please, enlighten me, my lord."

He slammed his hand against the desk, causing Magnus to flinch and shrink away from him.

"Answer. My. Questions!" He spat out one word at a time through gritted teeth, and with every word he said, Magnus turned a shade paler.

"Because…" he exhaled after a short pause and froze in place with his mouth open, staring at him without blinking. Then he dropped his head, pinching the bridge of his nose, and Damian knew he wasn't going to answer any of those questions.

Damian chuckled bitterly, staggering backward. "Thank you, Magnus. For a moment there, I was under the mistaken impression that you actually gave a fuck about me, but now I know better."

"I do care! Goddammit, Dmitri! I care too much, and it's

dangerous for both of us!" Magnus shouted, raising his face, desperation and anger entwining in his glowing eyes. "If I didn't care, why would I summon your gargoyle to send him to Svyatobor with a message? Yes, I was watching your every step as you were breaking all the laws and rules, traveling through the Land of Dreams! I could have stopped you and brought you here at any time, but I didn't, did I?" He stopped talking, his chest moving with hard breaths. "I was trying to warn you about the old one in the Eagle's Nest. He is the Beast Master who marked you, and he…" He didn't finish his sentence and turned away, burying his fingers into the mass of his graying hair.

Damian dropped his arms, staring at him in horror. "You know who he is," he whispered, unable to raise his voice any higher as the terrible realization constricted his throat. "He nearly crippled Cole and killed Dallas. He murdered my beloved Vita. He put me through unimaginable torture back then, and I nearly died from wounds without my healing power." His voice shook, and he turned away, covering his mouth with his hand.

"Dmitri, please, listen—"

"For five hundred years, Magnus!" Damian shouted, the floor shaking under his feet as he failed to control his power. "Five hundred years! I lived like a drifter, going from place to place, never settling down, running from you and monsters, but most importantly—from myself. I buried my heart and my soul in the same grave where Vita rests, and for centuries, I walked this earth like a shadow, dead and hollow on the inside." He pointed at Magnus, his entire body locked with rage and disappointment. "You manipulated the Board of Destiny for me to meet Sam Vetrov. You ordered me to remain in Paradise Manor when I could've returned to the Destiny Council realm, and that changed everything… You made me… feel, love, care… again… I didn't need it… I didn't want it…" His voice broke, and he swallowed, every word reverberating through his sore vocal cords. "Now I have people in my life... people whom I love more than life itself... You made me vulnerable to this monster."

"Dima, my boy, please... I just wanted you—"

"All this time you knew who the Beast Master was, and you didn't warn me," Damian whispered, turning around, this simple movement taking a lot more effort than it was supposed to.

"I swear I have no idea who he is!" Magnus yelled, his voice ringing on high tones. "I only have suspicions and guesses that are unsupported by any facts and cannot be verified." He pressed his fingers to his eyes and stilled for a heartbeat before lowering his hands. "I can't voice my suspicions because of what I think is impossible..." He spread his arms a little, looking tired and destroyed. "For the last few months, I tried to read his paths on the Board of Destiny almost every day, and every time, I came up with nothing. He's dead. He must be... Centuries ago, I saw him die with my own eyes..."

"I don't care how impossible you think it is. Give me his name," Damian hissed, anger slowly simmering down, emptiness taking its place.

Magnus raised both hands, taking a few deep breaths to calm down. "I swear you will have the name today and the answers to some of your questions when you return here. I want to do one more reading, just to make sure."

"Return? You're letting me go?" Damian mumbled, his hand rising to his throat of its own accord.

"No, I am not," replied Magnus, looking at his tightly clenched hands. "Every member of the High Council knows about what happened in the bank. You will be tried by the supreme tribunal of this realm for your crimes." He pinned Damian with a heavy gaze, but since he didn't react, Magnus continued, "I can't help you with that, but I believe I can help Master Alliandr."

Damian looked at him, his heart speeding up in his chest. "What do you need me to do?"

Magnus circled his desk and opened one of his drawers. After shuffling there for what seemed like forever, he pulled out a small glass orb. He placed it on the table and channeled his magic, his eyes ablaze once more. Gently, he positioned his hand over the orb and whispered a few words in Dragon tongue. A glowing, white mist filled the orb, sparkling dimly like fresh snow reflecting an electric light on a winter night. Momentarily, Magnus let go and offered the orb to Damian.

"I will teleport you to Kendral. You have an hour to deliver this orb to Master Alliandr," he said quietly. "He'll know what to do with it."

"Yes, my lord," Damian replied, taking the orb.

"Once you are done in Kendral, you must return here immediately and surrender yourself to the High Council," Magnus continued, his voice flat and even, as if he were reading from a phone book. "Am I clear, Commander?"

"Yes, my lord," Damian replied, but as Magnus reached for him to send him to Kendral, he took a step back, halting him. "I need an extra hour in addition to that."

"What for?" asked Magnus, frowning. "Don't you understand I'm already taking a chance by letting you go? I'm supposed to cuff you and send you to a holding cell where you're going to await your trial."

"Magnus, please." Damian looked away, his chest aching, numbness suffusing his limbs. With all his previous experience as a Destiny Enforcer, he knew full well that Magnus was already doing more than he should have by trying to keep Alliandr safe, yet he couldn't help it, hoping for one more favor. "Just one hour. I must know if River, Luc and Jamie survived." He dropped his head, biting his lip. "I want to see my brother one more time."

"Fine. One hour," Magnus said. "You have two hours to visit

Kendral and the world of humans. If you're not in my office in time, I'll have to bring you here by force. Am I clear, Commander Blake?"

"Thank you. I'll be here in time," Damian replied. He pressed his fist to his chest and inclined his head. "I'm yours to command."

"Oh, my boy…" Magnus whispered, barely audible, his hand lingering over Damian's cheek. "Please don't do anything crazy. Don't make it harder on both of us…"

Magnus touched Damian's forehead with two fingers, and the white office spun around him, quickly melting into the darkness.

CHAPTER 31

~ DAMIAN BLAKE ~

Damian materialized in a spacious chamber. Two tall windows were draped by heavy panels, which prevented any natural light from coming inside. The space was illuminated by the unsteady candlelight of a three-candle chandelier sitting on a small table at the opposite wall, and the smell of melted wax and the light scent of smoke lingered in the air. Alliandr and an unfamiliar older man sat by the table, looking through a bunch of documents. Alliandr's sword lay on a large four-poster bed, and everything looked calm and peaceful.

As soon as Damian appeared, they both turned in his direction. The older man jumped to his feet and unsheathed his sword, his fast and precise movements indicating he was a trained warrior and holding a weapon was a lot more comfortable for him than holding a pen. He wasn't tall, no more than five-foot-ten, and next to the tall and muscled Master of Power, he appeared even shorter than he was. He emanated a weak magical energy signature characteristic of a wizard, but it didn't seem to be developed well enough to be dangerous, suggesting that magic wasn't the main weapon in his arsenal.

"A Destiny Enforcer," the man hissed, stepping in front of

Alliandr. "Your kind is not welcome here. Leave, or I swear I'll make you regret ever crossing into this realm."

"Father." Alliandr chuckled softly, placing his hand on the man's shoulder. "Allow me to introduce Commander Damian Blake, my good friend." He pressed slightly on the man's arm, forcing him to lower his blade. "He's always welcome here, and I have been expecting his visit." Then he gestured at the man, turning to Damian. "This is my father, Randall."

"Nice meeting you, sir," said Damian, slightly inclining his head.

"Uh-huh." The man sheathed his sword, narrowing his honey-colored eyes at Damian, but then glanced back at his son and added, "You need to be more careful when choosing your friends, son. Are you sure he's not going to cause you any troubles?"

"I'm absolutely safe with Damian, Father. Please give us a few minutes," replied Alliandr.

Randall nodded and left the room, giving Damian another icy once-over on his way out.

"So, this is it, then?" asked Alliandr, gesturing for Damian to take a seat. "The Destiny Council wants me?"

"No. That is not why I am here," replied Damian, lowering himself onto the chair across from the Master of Power. "Your father is quite fierce in protecting you. I didn't notice any family resemblance, though." He glanced at the door as if Randall were still there.

"Randal is a high-ranking member of the Riders Order." A warm smile touched Alliandr's face. "He's not my biological father, but he raised me since I was just a baby, taking care of me, training, teaching and protecting me. He is the only father I've ever known, and he *is* my father in all the ways that matter." Alliandr's eyes grew distant and slightly foggy, like that of a person traveling down memory lane, and an unusual softness suffused his features, making him look younger.

"May I ask how old you are, Master Alliandr?" Damian asked, observing him with curiosity. "In human years, that is."

Alliandr raked his hand through the black mane of his hair as he got up and headed toward the window. He halted there and pulled a panel aside. The late evening view of a medieval city spread before him, the orange-red light of torches illuminating a large square before the palace. On one side, far beyond the city, tall mountains stretched their snow-covered peaks toward the sky, and the thick wall of a forest reached all the way to the edge of the populated area on the other side.

"I'm not immortal, and so far, my human years are equal to my magical years. Like all Masters of Power, I was born with the ability to wield all four elements and magic." Alliandr chuckled without taking his eyes off the view. "I'm thirty-four, Damian. Master Mrak Delar forfeited his power and the throne of Kendral to me when I was just twenty-five, which made me the youngest Master of Power in the history of Kendral." He walked back to the table and sat down. "Seems like all this happened just yesterday…" He met Damian's gaze and sighed, sadness shadowing his black eyes. "That is a long story, my friend, and maybe one day, we'll meet here again, so I can show you my world and tell you everything you want to know."

Damian nodded, wishing that one day was today, and he didn't have to deliver a message from the Head of the Destiny Council to the young Master. Shuddering inwardly, he reached in his pocket and brought up the orb shining with Magnus' magic.

"Magnus ordered me to deliver this message to you." Damian placed the orb on the table in front of Alliandr.

The Master of Power took it, holding it carefully between his thumb and middle finger. Then he covered it with his other hand and closed his eyes, the magical energy field around him spiking. The orb shone brighter, and the white mist within started to spin. As the rotation increased in speed, the brilliant glow intensified, and when the light finally dwindled, the orb was gone.

For a short while, Alliandr sat with his eyes closed, rubbing his forehead absentmindedly. Then he opened his eyes and looked at Damian, his eyebrows rising.

"Damian, you can't do it," he whispered, sounding hoarse. "I won't accept it, my friend. I can't let you take the fall for me."

"You have to." Damian got up and leaned forward slightly, propping his hands against the table. "I'm just a Destiny Enforcer. Like Koschei said—expendable, one of many. You're the Master of Kendral. Your realm needs you, and if it wasn't for me, you would never be in this situation in the first place."

Bowing his head, Alliandr pressed his hand to his chest, his fingers crumpling his white shirt, and his shoulders slumped.

"You're wrong," he said, barely audible. "You're not expendable, otherwise Lord Magnus wouldn't be sending this message to me."

He pulled a blank piece of paper out of a pile of documents and took a feather from the table. Dipping it into ink, he wrote a few words on the page and offered it to Damian. He took it and peered down at a spell written in Dragon tongue.

"What is it?" Damian asked, glancing up at Alliandr.

"This is the incantation you need to tear the fabric of reality," Alliandr explained, looking anywhere but at Damian. "Lord Magnus asked me to teach you how to do it in case you need to prove to the tribunal that you did it on your own. Memorize it."

"Do you think I can do it?" Damian reread the spell, committing it to memory.

"I don't know what to think," Alliandr replied, the corner of his mouth lifting just a touch. "I have seen you do it with me. Can you do it on your own? I have no idea. The simple answer should be a definitive no. You're a Destiny Enforcer and a powerful Child of Earth, but you don't have the power you need to perform a spell of this magnitude." He cocked his head a little, looking at Damian with interest. "There is nothing simple about you, is there, Commander?" He tapped Damian on the shoulder and added, "Please, tell Lord Magnus I'll do everything exactly as he told me."

"What did he ask you to do, Alliandr?" Damian asked, warning bells ringing in his mind.

"Sorry, I can't tell you." Alliandr sighed and offered him his hand. "Do you trust me, Damian?"

"Do I have a choice?" Damian locked his hand in a firm forearm handshake.

"No, not really." Alliandr smiled apologetically. "But it won't be the first time for you. What do they say about Destiny Enforcers? No mercy, no remorse, no regrets, no choice?" He sobered up quickly, looking out the window at the beautiful view of his realm. "I'm indebted to you, Damian, and I swear on my power, when the time comes, I'll do everything I can to help you."

"Thank you, Master," Damian replied. "I hope one day we'll meet again."

He waved his hand, opening a portal. Giving Alliandr a short wave goodbye, he stepped through the rotating mass of blue sparkles, wondering what he was about to find on the other side.

It was late evening when Damian stepped out of the portal onto the steps leading into the Brown's Estate. He sucked in a deep breath, enjoying the touch of the cool desert air to his skin, and pushed the door open. As always, it was unlocked, so he slipped into the darkness of the lobby, heading toward the library.

Before he went a few steps, an almost imperceptible movement of air brushed his face, and his brother appeared in front of him, blocking his way. His eyes darted to Damian's wrists, and his tense features relaxed just a little. Noticing that, Damian chuckled, shaking his head.

"If the High Council had me arrested, I wouldn't be standing here," he said, giving Cole a gentle tap on his shoulder. "No one can walk around in Destiny cuffs."

A slightly shy smile graced Cole's face. "I'm just happy to see you again," he said quietly. "I thought—" He cut himself off and looked away.

Damian frowned, annoyance flaring through him as he realized what was going on. "How long has it been since I left with Dallas?"

"Three days," Cole replied, looking at him with curiosity.

Dammit, Magnus... Why? He let out a harsh breath, trying not to think what the true reason behind Magnus manipulating the flow of time could be. "The time in the Destiny Council realm moves differently," he explained. "To me, it seems like only a few hours have passed."

Cole nodded, gesturing toward the library. "Would you like to come in?"

Damian shook his head. "I don't have time. Magnus gave me just one hour to settle my affairs here before I have to return to the Destiny Council realm to face the tribunal." He dropped his head, exploring the marble swirls on the tiles. "I wanted to see you one more time before—" He didn't finish his statement and bit his lip.

"Tribunal?" Cole repeated, his voice raspy. "Is that like a military tribunal?"

"Yes, something like that," replied Damian, unwilling to go into details. "A military tribunal on steroids. Don't worry, little bro. It'll take a long time, but I'll be all right. Eventually."

Cole nodded, but by the way his shoulders hunched, Damian knew he didn't believe one word he said. "Did Dallas survive?" he asked after a short pause.

"Yes. Magnus accepted him into the training program. I'm

not sure he'll ever be all right, but he's alive," replied Damian. "Did Luc, Jamie and River recover?"

Cole's face turned ashen, and the look of sympathy in his eyes made Damian's blood run cold.

"Dima," Cole started, taking a step closer, reaching for him.

"They're not dead," Damian whispered, staggering away from his brother's touch. "I would have known if they were. Magnus would've told me."

"They're not dead," Cole echoed him, his voice turning softer. "Luc and Jamie regained consciousness a few hours after you and I left the hospital. They completely recovered and are back to normal. Yesterday, Jamie stopped by, asking about you. He wanted to see you before leaving for the Wardens HQ in Paris. Both Luc and Jamie were summoned for questioning." He fell silent, fidgeting with the ring on his finger.

"And River?" Damian asked, not sure if he wanted to hear the answer to this question.

"River never woke up," Cole whispered, placing his hand on Damian's arm. "Dima, unlike Jamie and Luc, she's human. It may take her body a lot longer to recover. You know that, right?"

Damian nodded, unable to speak, his heart thudding in uneven bursts in his chest.

"Sam returned two days ago and took her home," Cole continued. "She's back in Paradise Manor now."

Damian nodded again, swallowing the thick lump in his throat. "I have to see her before I leave," he whispered.

"You should." Ruslan's deep voice sounded behind him, and Damian turned around to face him. The ancient vampire approached him, his eyes moving up and down his body as if checking him for injuries. "You should see her and talk to her," he continued gently. "She's in a magical coma, and her condition is unpredictable. River loves you, and the sound of your voice can make a difference. You never know..."

He offered his hand to Damian, and as Damian took it, Ruslan squeezed it tighter, giving him a reassuring nod.

"You will return, Dmitri," he said, and it wasn't a question. "Godspeed, my son."

Damian smiled. "I always do, Ruslan. Take care of my little brother."

He turned to Cole, the expression on his brother's face hollowing him out. Cole stepped closer, his arms dangling limply along his sides, and it seemed like even the smallest movement caused him physical pain. He raised his red-rimmed eyes, everything he felt written clearly on his face.

"I won't survive your death... not again..." Cole's voice touched Damian's mind, enveloping him with a wave of despair.

"It's not easy to kill me, little bro, and Magnus will never let it happen." He pulled Cole into an embrace, burying his fingers into the mass of curls on the back of his head. *"It may take time, but I swear on my power, we'll meet again, brother mine."*

"I'll take the Destiny Council realm apart brick by brick if I have to, and I'll fight to the end, but I'll never give up on you, *brat moi...*" Cole pulled away, meeting his eyes.

Damian stepped back, taking in his brother's appearance one more time. Then he gave a short nod to Ruslan and snapped his fingers, teleporting to Paradise Manor.

* * *

THE DAMAGE DONE to Paradise Manor by Koschei hadn't been taken care of yet, but the giant hole in the roof was covered with a blue tarp, and all the rubble and debris were gone. The broken cactus was also removed from the property, and only a short stump remained in its place. Moving slowly, as if the last strength had abandoned him after the conversation with Cole, Damian stepped across the doorless threshold. He walked through the foyer into the dark hallway on the right and headed toward River's bedroom.

The house appeared empty, his steps echoing loudly, amplified by the strange acoustics. He didn't bother checking the area for any supernatural presence, too drained to even think. As he neared the door into River's bedroom, he saw a man sitting next to it, his head bowed low, his fingers wrapped around the grip of his saber.

"Cossack," Damian called him, and his friend raised his face, warmth and sadness fusing in his gaze.

He got up and pressed his fist to his chest. "Commander," he said. "I was expecting your arrival. Lord Magnus spoke with me a short while ago."

"I'm sure he did," Damian muttered, placing his hand on the door handle. "As much as I like to see you, my friend, my time is limited." He cracked the door open, ready to go in, but Cossack placed his hand on his arm, stopping him.

"I know," Cossack said in a soft whisper. "Magnus told me everything." He looked away, stroking his long mustache automatically. "Do you know how long…" He didn't finish his question, but Damian understood him.

"I have no idea," he replied, stifling a sigh. "I don't know how long I'll have to wait for the trial. The sentence for what I did is—"

"Magnus will never let anything happen to you, Dima," Cossack interrupted him. "I don't know why, but everyone knows how deeply the Head of the Destiny Council is attached to his Shadow Enforcer. You'll be all right."

"I don't know if it's true, Cossack, and frankly, I don't care." Damian looked over his friend's shoulder into the darkness of the hallway. "This world is safe from Koschei… My job is done, and I'm done…" He pushed the door all the way open and stepped inside the bedroom, but halted in the doorway and added, without turning around, "I'm too tired, my friend. All I want now is a few minutes of peace with no one hunting me or the people I love." He smiled and closed the door behind himself quietly. "All I want is a few minutes without pain."

Most of the bedroom was submerged under the cloak of darkness, even the electric clock on the bedstand was turned off. The only source of light was a tiny plug-in night light under the window. River lay on the bed, covered with her favorite blanket, her beautiful copper hair cascading down her shoulders. Her chest was rising with even breaths, and she appeared to be asleep. Damian opened his other sight and quickly scanned her body. The energy of her human soul shone brightly, pulsing slightly with every beat of her heart. Even and healthy, it was unobstructed by a dark spell. Her body and soul were intact, yet she was still in a coma.

Feeling a light touch on his leg, he looked down and saw Gypsy. The cat stepped softly over his feet, rubbing her side against him. She raised her head and looked up at him, her round eyes shining with a phosphoric glimmer.

"Gypsy," he exhaled, bending down to pet her. "You're alive... awake..."

Gypsy rose on her hind legs, stretching her paws to him. He lifted her, cradling her to his chest, and stroked her thick fur gently.

"Why is River still asleep?" Gypsy's voice whispered in his mind. *"You're back. Wake her up, Sasquatch."*

"I'm not sure I can. I don't know how." Damian halted by the bed and lowered the cat next to River. Leaning forward, he brushed his fingers over her cheek, feeling the coolness of her skin under his fingertips. He straightened, gazing down at her, searching for any sign that could help him wake her up, but finding nothing helpful.

"Don't just stand there!" Gypsy hissed, her claws making an appearance. *"Do something! Anything! Kiss her, for crying out loud."*

Damian couldn't help but chuckle. "Sorry, Gypsy. I don't

think this is that kind of fairy tale. A true love's kiss isn't going to do it." He took River's hand and kissed her knuckles, gently lowering it back onto the blanket. Then he leaned down and planted a soft kiss on her forehead. She didn't react to his touch, remaining just as motionless as before.

"Or maybe you're not that good of a kisser," said Gypsy. Climbing under River's arm, Gypsy curled into a ball, covering her nose with her bushy tail. *"How disappointing…"*

Damian glanced at his watch and stifled a sigh—he had only thirty minutes left. He lowered himself to the floor and took River's arm, pulling it closer to the edge. Then he rested his cheek against her hand and closed his eyes, his mind blank, his heart bleeding slowly with silent torment.

I'm so sorry, River… It's my fault… I should have never walked into your life…

He wasn't sure how long he sat like this, numb and oblivious to everything around him, when the door opened, and Sam's voice, shaking with anger, ripped him out of his stupor.

"You…" The old hunter crossed the room and seized Damian's shirt, slightly lifting him off the floor. "How dare you show up here!" He shook him, his face clouded by sorrow and fury. "It's your fault she's dying. I curse the day I gave you a ride to Arizona. I should have left you on the side of the road."

"Sam—"

Sam swung his hand and connected his fist with Damian's jaw without holding back. Damian's head jerked to the side, white spots dancing in his vision, but he didn't move, his arms resting limply in his lap. Blood spilled between his lips, trickling down his chin, but he didn't try to wipe it.

"You're right. I deserve it," he whispered, not looking at Sam. "Don't worry. In another few minutes, I'll leave this world forever. You'll never see me again."

"You bet your ass you will," Sam growled, and Damian felt the icy touch of a gun barrel pressed to his forehead. "I know you're immortal, so a bullet is not gonna kill you, but it sure will hurt like hell."

"Do it." Damian closed his eyes, bracing himself for pain, when he felt a slight movement behind him, followed by the metallic click of a cocked firearm.

"Father." River's cold voice, filled with suppressed anger, sounded behind him. "Please, kindly stop pointing a loaded weapon at my boyfriend." Damian felt her hand landing on his shoulder, and he held his breath, barely able to believe it. "Father, lower your gun, or I swear to God, I will arrest you for domestic violence, assault with a deadly weapon and anything else I can think of."

Damian opened his eyes to find Sam's gun still pointing at him. Carefully, he looked back. Dressed in her favorite pajamas with pictures of Gypsy printed on it, River sat on the bed with her Glock in her hands, her brows snapped together.

"Some things never change," Damian muttered, raising his arms.

"Your boyfriend?" Sam's arm shook, and he lowered his weapon, his eyes darting from River to Damian and back.

River lowered her bare feet on the floor, her fingers finding their way into Damian's hair. "Yes, Father," she replied softly, pulling Damian's head back a little to see his face. "While I was sleeping, I heard Damian saying he was short on time. Actually, I heard everything that was going on around me since you brought me home." A shadow of sadness crossed her features as she switched her attention to Sam. "I'm happy to see you, Dad, but do you mind giving me a few minutes alone with Damian before he has to leave?"

Lowering her gun on the bed, she got up and hugged her father, giving him a soft kiss on his unshaven cheek. His arms wrapped tightly around her, and he closed his eyes, a tear slipping from under his tightly shut eyelids. After a moment, he pulled away, running his hand over his face. Throwing another heavy glance in Damian's direction, he turned around and walked out the door, closing it behind him.

River kneeled in front of Damian, taking his hands in hers. He stared at her, unable to take his eyes off her, still struggling to believe she was awake, here, with him.

"I'm your boyfriend?" he asked after a short while, a thin layer of sarcasm in his voice, and the corners of his lips quirked up.

"That's what *you* said." River shrugged nonchalantly, her thumbs caressing his skinned knuckles.

"I did? When did I say that?"

"In the hospital, when you brought me in."

River looked away and bit her lip, fidgeting with a strand of her hair. He raised his hand and seized her chin, gently forcing her to look at him. She smiled and took his hand, pressing her cheek against his palm.

"I can't explain how," she whispered, closing her eyes, "but for a while, I was with you. I saw everything you've been through. I heard your every word as if my soul was attached to you somehow... All the way until you returned to the hospital with those elixirs. After that, everything went blank, and I could hear or see nothing until my father brought me back to Paradise Manor..." She opened her eyes again, silent tears sliding off her copper eyelashes. "I know what you did for me. I will never forget it." She leaned forward and wrapped her arms around his neck, hiding her face in his shoulder. "I know it sounds childish, but I don't want you to leave..."

Damian didn't say anything. There was nothing to say, and they both knew it. Instead, he embraced her, pulling her into his chest. His gaze fell on his wristwatch, and his heart jerked painfully in his chest. He had only ten minutes left. He raised his hand and snapped his fingers, teleporting both of them to the front yard.

River gasped and then laughed bitterly through tears. "I can never get used to you doing that." She let go of him and looked around, her eyes widening. "Oh, wow. That's a lot of damage, and my handyman is about to take a leave of absence."

"I know. I'm sorry." He kneeled in front of the broken cactus and placed his hands on the ground on either side of the stump. Channeling his elemental power, he sent it toward his hands and looked at River over his shoulder. "I won't be able to fix your house, but there is something I want to do for you before I leave. Something for you to remember me by."

"Dima, you can't think like that—," she started to say, placing her hand on his shoulder, but he turned away, focusing on the task at hand. He didn't want to give her false hopes, just as much as he didn't want her to see his own helplessness and despair reflected on his face.

As he kept channeling the elemental energy of Earth, a small saguaro cactus broke through the ground. It grew quickly, stretching toward the dark sky, two arms sprouting from the trunk, spikes rising on its ribs. Damian glanced back at River and chuckled, noticing her wide-open eyes and parted lips. For a short while, it seemed like she forgot about everything, watching him wielding his power, her face alight with wonderment. And for this one short moment, she looked like a little girl who still believed in magic.

"How many arms do you want on your new cactus?" he asked, still smiling.

"Just two," she whispered, the girlish look of awe leaving her features, giving place to sadness. She touched his arm, her fingers sliding down his bicep. "That's all I need…"

Swallowing hard, Damian turned away from her. He made sure the cactus was strong enough and let go. As he started to rise, a dull pain began to build up somewhere behind his eyes, and he grunted, glancing at his wristwatch.

"My time is up," he said, approaching River. He pulled her into a gentle embrace, but she encircled his waist, pressing her entire body against his. He moaned, burying his face into her hair. "I'm sorry, River, but I have to go, or they will yank me out of here by force."

"Return to me?"

It was a half-statement, half-question, and there was so much hope and torment in her voice that his heart made a painful somersault in his chest. He dropped his head, pulling away from her. Then he took her hand and brought it up to his lips, closing his eyes as he kissed it.

"Don't wait for me, River," he whispered, unable to speak any louder, his throat constricted. "Your father was right. I want you to be happy, and I can't give that to you."

"For someone who's a thousand years old, wisdom is definitely not one of your powers, Commander Blake," she murmured, shaking her head. "My father was wrong. I bless the day when he took pity on you and gave you a ride to Arizona. I bless that moment when I saw you for the first time in my house—shy and awkward like a teenager." She waved at Paradise Manor without taking her gaze off him. "Paradise Manor is in ruins, but it's still your home if you want it." She pressed her hands to her eyes and when she lowered them, her eyes were dry. "I want you to know... No matter how long you're going to be away, a woman and a cat are always going to be waiting for you here."

As the headache intensified, he hugged her one more time, and whispered into her ear, "I must go now. Be happy for both of us."

Focusing on blocking the unbearable pain in his head, he waved his hand and opened a portal. Then without looking back, he stepped into the rotating mist.

Here goes... Abandon all hope...

EPILOGUE

* * *

~ Damian Blake ~
Destiny Council Realm.

Damian walked out of the portal and halted in front of the door into Magnus' office. He already knew what was going to happen, so he just wanted to get it over with and be done. Steeling his resolve, he knocked on the door and pushed it open without waiting for an invitation.

Magnus was pacing his office, his entire body glowing with the eye-watering light of his magic, and the white walls of the room seemed to reflect his light, making it brighter than usual. Noticing Damian, he halted and turned toward him, clasping his hands behind his back.

"You're here," he said, tones of disbelief in his voice.

"Why are you acting so surprised?" Damian shrugged, feeling too drained and indifferent to play Magnus' mind games. "Even if I didn't want to return, you turned the summoning call on, so I had no choice."

"A summoning call?" Magnus furrowed his brow. "I didn't cast a summoning spell for you. I'm not going to lie. I was worried about you, Dmitri, but I didn't summon you. I trusted your word."

"Well, someone did." Damian walked up to the desk and grabbed the back of a chair, leaning on it.

"Dammit," Magnus muttered. "It could only be Miranda or Dorian. I'll speak with them after we're done here."

Damian nodded, but at this point, he didn't really care about the rest of the High Council and their motives.

"Are you going to say you didn't manipulate the flow of my time, either?" he asked quietly, glaring at Magnus from under his hair. "I spent here an hour at most, but three days passed in the realm of humans. Why is that, Magnus?"

A light smile appeared on Magnus' face, relaxing his tense features. "I'll take credit for that," he said, putting his hand into the pocket of his pants. "I hoped it worked the way I intended, and you had a chance to speak with Detective Evans before leaving the human world. If I hadn't manipulated the flow of time, she would've been in a coma when you visited her."

Damian froze in place and blinked a few times, staring at Magnus incredulously. "Thank you," he managed to say once he got over the shock. "I was there when she woke up, and I had about ten minutes with her before I had to leave."

"I'm glad to hear that, my child." Magnus shuffled from foot to foot, the vibe of discomfort around him becoming thicker. "As much as I hate to do it to you, it's time." He touched his desk, and a pair of glowing handcuffs materialized on it. "You know the procedures, Dmitri, so you should know how it works. I'm supposed to summon Commander Moore to escort you to your holding cell, where you will remain until the trial. However, given the circumstances, I'm not going to give Moore the satisfaction of seeing you down. I'll do it myself."

"That's very kind of you, my lord." Damian bowed slightly,

unable to conceal the layer of sarcasm in his words. Then he stepped away from the chair, crossing his arms behind his back. "I'm afraid the holding cell will have to wait a few more minutes. I believe you owe me an explanation. You promised to answer at least a few of my questions."

Magnus stilled in place, his eyes darting from Damian to the Destiny cuffs, his eyebrows snapping together.

"Fine, I'll try to answer some of your questions if I can," he said at length, but the barely noticeable tones of nervousness in his voice didn't escape Damian's heightened senses. "Since one of the members of the High Council has issued a summoning call for you, I must follow the procedures and cuff you in case they come here, looking for you."

"Do what you must." Damian held out his arms. "I have no choice but to trust you to keep your word."

Magnus pointed at one of the chairs. "Sit down, Dmitri. I don't want to see you collapse."

With a cold chuckle, Damian sat down, an uneven smile lifting a corner of his mouth. "I'm yours to command, I guess."

Magnus took the Destiny cuffs and approached him, taking his hand, but hesitated for a split second, a haunted look darkening his unnerving silvery eyes. Then, in one swift motion, he locked the cuffs around both of Damian's wrists.

Damian cried out and bent forward, feeling as if someone had punched him in the gut—nauseous and gasping for air. A searing pain crippled his body, clouding his mind, and he shuddered, weakness engulfing him as the cuffs kept draining whatever little magic and elemental power he still had in him, leaving him dazed and weak. The white room tilted as he started to slip to the side, but Magnus' strong hands steadied him, holding him in place.

For a moment, he blacked out, but a gentle slap on his cheek brought him back, and he cracked his eyelids open just a little, exhaling with a soft moan.

"I'm so sorry I have to do it to you, my boy," Magnus whispered with a pained expression on his face, as if it were him who suffered the effects of the Destiny cuffs. "But I must keep all the procedures to a T now, so when the time comes for you to face the tribunal, I can speak in your defense."

"Never mind that," Damian whispered, too weak to even move his lips. "Tell me about the ancient one. Why do his eyes shine with the same magic as yours? Why does he use your personal sigil to lock his wards? Are you somehow connected with him?"

Magnus expelled a ragged breath, his eyes widening momentarily. "There aren't many old gods who still roam this realm," he replied after a short pause. "As much as the Destiny Council wanted to register all of them in our archives, it proved to be an impossible task. Powerful and elusive, they're hard to find, and once their identity is compromised, they immediately take on a new one, becoming invisible again."

"What you are saying is that you won't answer any questions related to the old one," Damian murmured, unable to contain his aggravation. "Nice try."

"I don't know who he is. I can only guess, and in our line of work, assumptions and guesses can be deadly," Magnus replied quietly. "Don't you think I would tell you if I knew for sure? All I'm trying to do is keep you and your brother safe."

"Yeah, I can see that," Damian murmured, staring at the glowing cuffs on his wrists. "Forgive me if I have a hard time believing your words at this moment. If you cared so much about Cole's and my wellbeing, you would have told me who we're dealing with a long time ago. Without understanding why the old god wants us at his disposal, we're sitting ducks."

"I thought that was clear from the get-go. He wants you because of the prophecy." Magnus bit his lip, staring at the perfectly white wall of his office. "When Ruslan turned Cole, he brought the prophecy to life. He created the Darkness touched by the Light. But it was the Beast Master who activated the ancient prophecy and set both your destinies in motion. By marking you with the Darkness, he started an unavoidable chain of events."

Magnus grabbed a glass of water from his desk and took a sip. Watching him, Damian huffed quietly, shaking his head in disbelief. It appeared as though Magnus had known about the prophecy for centuries, but he neglected to say anything to him.

"Obviously," Magnus continued, placing the glass back on the table, "the old one thought that with you being a Destiny Enforcer, you would be easy to find and control. What he didn't count on was your infinite hardheadedness and constant disobedience." Magnus chuckled, twinkles of humor igniting in his eyes, but they were gone as quickly as they appeared. "He also didn't count on you giving up most of your magic and disappearing. So, from the moment you assumed the *no one* status, your energy signature changed drastically, and he lost you for at least five hundred years."

"What about Cole?" Damian asked through gritted teeth.

"Oh, your brother is a completely different story. As an ancient vampire, Cole seemed to be a low-hanging fruit. So, when the old one lost you, he decided to go after your brother, hoping that he would be able to find and convert Cole to his side a lot faster," replied Magnus, stroking his beard. "But just like you, Cole caught him off guard by choosing the side of Light every time… To be honest, even I have a hard time figuring out Cole's true supernatural identity."

"He's a vamp." Damian snorted, looking heavenward. "What's so hard to figure out?"

"It takes a loving and overly protective big brother not to see the reality." A warm, slightly mocking smile touched Magnus' lips. "Yes, Cole is a vampire, but he has magic and elemental power. So, his supernatural identity, as well as his energy signature is not only complicated but also quite unique."

Damian jerked in his seat but moaned and fell back as the next bout of weakness enveloped him. "I don't understand—"

"Don't make any sharp moves, my child. The more you move, the more the Destiny cuffs feed on your energy." Magnus placed his hand on Damian's shoulder, gently holding him down. "We both know Cole can wield magic, but I believe recently, you witnessed him embracing one of the elements—Fire, to be precise. That makes everything related to Cole even more paradoxical since the purifying element of Fire energy is fatal to the undead."

Damian nodded. "When I saw the fire engulf him, I thought it was the end for us both…" Damian's voice trailed off, and he exhaled a strained breath, the memory of Cole killing Zmey Gorynych still fresh in his mind. "But then he just walked out of the fire with flames dancing on his arms and shoulders as if he were a Fire Salamander or a Phoenix. Unharmed. Neither I nor Master Alliandr had any explanation for that."

"Perhaps he's a Child of Fire—a Fire Salamander or a Phoenix or some other type," Magnus murmured, his eyes turning slightly foggy. "The element of Fire is different from other elements. Many humans are born with the Fire in their hearts, but their powers are never awakened, and they live their entire life and die without ever knowing what they truly were. Cole's vampirism was supposed to destroy any magic or elemental power in him, but for some reason, it didn't happen. I believe something came to pass that awakened the Fire in him."

"If I ever see the light of day again, I am taking him to Kendral to speak with the Great Salamander," Damian muttered, frowning.

"Good idea. Kal is the only one who can tell what Cole truly is," replied Magnus. "Even though the tribunal cannot be avoided, I'll make sure you'll be cleared of all charges during the trial, Dmitri. I'll never let anything happen to you, my child, especially since you've done everything that had to be done.

Now that we're speaking freely, I must admit that my order to stand down was nothing more than a test of your free will. I wanted to know that when the time comes, you and your brother will do the right thing no matter what."

"Excuse me?" Damian mumbled, giving Magnus a bewildered stare. "When the time comes? What the hell are you talking about, Magnus?"

"Nothing you need to worry about now—"

"You have known me for over a thousand years," Damian continued as if he hadn't heard him, a weak wave of anger rising within him. "You've seen me bleed and die to fulfill my duty, and you still had the need to test my free will? To make sure I would choose the side of the Light?"

Magnus grunted, breaking their eye contact. "Just like you, I did what I had to do," he muttered. "I wasn't testing you as much as I was testing your brother." He pinned Damian with his pale eyes, pressing his lips into a straight line. "Magic or not, he's a vampire—darkness is in his nature, and I needed to know that when push comes to shove, you both will remain loyal."

"I hope you're happy with your test results." Damian shifted a little but fell back in his chair again, a groan of anger escaping his lips. "I swear to God, Magnus, the only thing I want right now is to tear you limb from limb with my own hands, for letting me go on such a dangerous mission unsupported and for endangering my brother's life. If you ever pull something like this again—"

Magnus chuckled humorlessly. "I guess I did the right thing by restraining you before we started this conversation." Then he narrowed his eyes, leaning forward slightly. "Unsupported? Hardly. As I mentioned before, I was watching you every step of the way, ready to step in at any moment."

"Much obliged." Damian clenched his teeth, barely able to breathe with powerless fury. The Destiny cuffs ignited brighter, their influence on him increasing, and he doubled up in pain.

"Once this trial is over, I'm fucking done with your bullshit... serving you... ahhh..." He groaned, his stomach twisting with nausea.

"Dmitri, you must calm down." Magnus seized his shoulders, holding him in place. Suddenly, he stilled, listening to something intently. "Dorian and Miranda are on the way here. I can sense their presence... We have just a few minutes before they knock on the door. Please calm down because—"

"Calm down?" Damian laughed—a menacing sound filled with pain he barely recognized as his own. "I'm extremely calm. You can take me to my holding cell now because this conversation is fucking over."

"Dmitri—"

"Unless you are ready to tell me who this ancient god is and how he is connected to you, I said this conversation is over," Damian hissed through gritted teeth, fighting the hold of the Destiny cuffs.

"I can't—"

"Then I'm done with you and with the Destiny Council." Gathering all his strength, Damian leaned heavily on the armrest, trying to get up, but his knees buckled, and he fell to the floor, the chair sliding away from him.

"What did you just say?" Magnus asked, looking down at him in shock.

"What don't you understand, Magnus?" Damian whispered, feeling at the end of his rope. "By not telling me the truth, you're setting me up for failure in the worst possible way. Whether or not I work for the Destiny Council, the old one is not going to stop searching for me, and sooner or later, I will have to face him." With an arduous effort, he lifted his arm, reaching up to Magnus, and the Head of the Destiny Council took his hand, lowering to his knees next to him.

"I'm sorry, my child," he whispered, hiding his face in his free hand. "I'm so sorry."

"Don't be sorry, Magnus. Help me instead! The old one's wards had a monogram comprised of three sigils. One of them was yours. The second one belonged to Gwyn ap Nudd. I didn't recognize the last one, and that tells me it represented him," Damian croaked, every word taking an effort. "Gwyn ap Nudd used to be a member of the High Council. Does it mean this ancient deity once was a part of the Destiny Council as well? His eyes look like yours and Gwyn's…" He raised his gaze at Magnus, pleading with him. "Please, Magnus, I'm begging you to tell me the truth. You know I'm loyal to you. I'll keep everything you say between us."

"Are you sure?" asked Magnus, sounding mortified. "Are you hundred percent positive the two sigils out of three belonged to me and Gwyn ap Nudd?"

Damian nodded, Magnus' reaction sending chills down his spine. "I can recognize your sigil with my eyes closed. After all, you branded me with it."

"Impossible… Oh, God, no…" Magnus whispered, his fingers gripping at Damian's hand harder.

"No—I'm wrong?" asked Damian. "Or no—you can't tell me."

"No, I don't know what to tell you." Magnus clasped his hand over his mouth. "I don't know how to—"

"Fine," Damian said, closing his eyes faintly, taking a short pause. "Then tell me why I could disarm his wards by channeling my own energy through your sigil?"

"You could do it because of who and what you are…" Magnus whispered, his face turning ashen. He glanced around, listening to something only he could hear. Then he looked down at Damian, remorse and warmth fighting for a place in his eyes. "The prophecy is only one reason the old one is searching for you and Cole." He fell silent, his chest moving with quick breaths, perspiration glistening on his forehead.

"I'm just a Destiny Enforcer and a Child of Earth, and my

brother is a vampire and maybe—big maybe—a Child of Fire," Damian whispered. "This makes no sense."

"God help me," Magnus whispered, sounding as if he was talking to himself, but his hand holding Damian's shook, betraying his internal turmoil. "Oh, my boy, I didn't ever want you to find out... especially not like this. I was sure it would never come to this..."

"Find out what?"

"Both you and your brother are so much more than what you think." A weak smile touched Magnus' lips. "I was hoping that becoming a Destiny Enforcer would hide your true energy signature, just like vampirism took care of Cole's, but I was wrong... Cole's magic and powers are breaking through despite what he is, and your true powers are manifesting faster than I could ever expect. This was why you could unlock the sealed door into the magical cave beneath Paradise Manor. This was the reason I believed you when you said you could tear the fabric of reality on your own." Magnus fell silent, breathing hard as if he just finished running a marathon. When he spoke again, his voice was so raspy that Damian had a hard time making out his words. "And because of that, the ancient god wants both of you under his thumb."

"What am I?" Damian managed to whisper, goosebumps covering his arms.

Magnus reached down, brushing his hair off his face, tears brimming his glowing eyes. "Dmitri, you and Nikolai are—"

A loud bang of enormous power exploded in the room, causing Magnus to gasp and fall forward, shielding Damian with his body. The entire building shook, and the floor quaked, a grinding sound filling the air. A brilliant white light flooded the office, making it impossible to see anything. At the same time, an invisible force seized Damian, yanking him from under Magnus, throwing him against the opposite wall.

He fell to the floor, a helpless heap of flesh and bones,

drained by the Destiny cuffs and subdued by the unknown dark magic. As an unbearable pain ripped him from inside, he screamed, thrashing and twisting within the hold of a hostile spell. A chain of strange images rushed through his mind, and there was nothing he could do to stop it. Some of them looked familiar, but some he saw for the first time, unable to register the meaning of any of them.

"Magnus…" Damian groaned, not sure if he was asking for help or wanted to know if the Head of the Destiny Council was still alive.

The blinding light dwindled a little, and laughter, dark and sinister, rose over the clamor of the quake. A man—no less than seven feet tall—with shining white eyes approached Damian and kicked him in the stomach. Damian coughed and flipped to his side, curling in on himself, but the man seized his throat, raising him in the air. Even though the man's face was inches away from Damian, he still couldn't distinguish his features, the blinding light of his eyes making it impossible. Damian hung limply, gasping for air.

"The old one…" he wheezed.

"Yeees-s-s, clever boy… I'm one of the old ones." The ancient deity laughed again, cocking his head. "As far as I can see, the summons I issued for you worked." He shrugged playfully. "Now… Say 'Uncle', little Enforcer," he said snidely as he squeezed Damian's throat harder, his voice wrapping around him like the deadly embrace of a poisonous serpent.

Damian jerked helplessly in his firm grip, the last drops of his life force slowly abandoning him, and he knew it was the end. With the Destiny cuffs severing his connection with his element, he was no longer immortal. He searched for Magnus but couldn't see him anywhere.

"Cole, can you hear me? Run, brother mine… run as far as you can and hide…" he reached out to Cole but received no response. The

place in his mind where he used to feel the connection with his brother was terrifyingly empty.

Suddenly, a second flair of white light blinded him, and when his vision cleared, he saw two giant men with blazing white eyes facing each other.

"Let! Him! Go!" Magnus' voice, magnified tenfold, thundered through the room, but Damian couldn't recognize him in the terrifying giant standing a few feet away from him.

"Or what?" The ancient god snickered, turning Damian a little to see his face. "One move of my fingers, and your precious Shadow is dead as a doornail. With this commendable decor on his wrists, I believe his immortality is gone. So, what are you going to do, Head of the Destiny Council? Sacrifice your little boy? It's been thousands of years since I received the last human sacrifice in my name, so I wouldn't mind if you do."

The light vanished from Magnus' eyes, and even though he didn't return to his normal form, he looked tired and resigned. Slowly, he bent one knee, pressing his fist to his chest.

"Magnus, no," Damian moaned. "Don't—" The old one dug his fingers deeper into his throat, drawing blood, and Damian fell silent, his mind barely registering the horror of the situation unfolding before him.

"I accept that as your submission." With a malignant glimmer in his eyes, the ancient deity lowered Damian to the floor in front of the Head of the Destiny Council and stepped back. "Say your goodbyes, for you'll never see him again."

Magnus looked down at Damian, nothing but warmth in his gaze. "Remember, you're more than what you think of yourself, my boy." He stifled a sigh. "Many years ago, I swore that I would never let anything happen to you, Dmitri, and I intend to keep my promise." He rose to his feet, towering as tall as the ancient deity. "You won. I'm yours to command, *brat moi…*"

"Let's end it once and for all, little brother." The old god seized Magnus' arm and snapped his fingers, vanishing from the office.

As soon as they were gone, the quake ceased. The door into Magnus' office flew open. Dorian and Miranda ran inside, accompanied by a few Destiny Enforcers. They shouted something, their eyes blazing like that of the ancient god. Dorian dropped to his knees next to Damian, checking him for injuries, screaming and shaking him. He removed the Destiny cuffs off Damian's wrists, and as his magic and power flooded him to the brim, his body arched weakly, but he fell back to the floor, unable to move.

"Commander Blake, can you hear me? What happened here? Where is Magnus?" Dorian shook him again, lifting him off the floor a little.

Damian could hear him, but he couldn't say a word. Like in an infinite loop, his mind kept replaying every detail of what had happened here just a few minutes ago step by step, Magnus' voice still echoing in his ears.

"I'm yours to command, brat moi*..."*

Brother mine...

EXCERPT

Read on for an excerpt from
N.M. Thorn's new book
The Shadow Enforcer Book 6:

* * *

~ Cole Adams~
Phoenix, Arizona

Everything was the same.

Yet everything felt different.

Cole stood on the rooftop of a three-story apartment building, looking down at the neighborhood. A chilly breeze rushed through the area, and the sides of his trench coat billowed in the wind, exposing two swords sheathed on his belt. A loose strand of his long, golden hair fell over his eyes, and he pushed it away, tucking it behind his ear in a habitual move. Over the course of the last six months, his hair had grown longer, but he didn't bother with his usual haircut, pulling it back into a ponytail like Ruslan.

Although the temperature was unusually low, nearing thirty-five degrees, the cold didn't trouble him. His undivided attention was set on the area below. A group of two- and three-story buildings surrounded a spacious, well-manicured yard illuminated by streetlights and some early Christmas decorations. Paver walkways wrapped around the shiny rectangle of a swimming pool, the tall leaves of palm trees reflecting in its mirror-like water.

He channeled his magic and closed his eyes, probing the empty courtyard with his senses. Even though he didn't possess the other sight, he could detect the presence of magic and the fluctuations in the magical energy field. When it came to identifying different types of magical and elemental energies, he wasn't as perceptive as Damian, but right now, he had no doubt. The apartment building was flooded with some type of dark magical energy.

"Son, I can see you from a mile away. Not only does your blond hair reflect the electric lights, but your eyes shine like a pair of brake lights, too." Ruslan's voice filled with humor sounded in his earpiece, and Cole couldn't help it, the corners of his mouth lifting.

"I'm not trying to hide, Father," he replied quietly, touching his throat mic. "I'm trying to identify what kind of beastie we're dealing with."

"So, I was right?" River's voice sounded through their communication system. "There is a beastie, after all?"

"You're always right, Lady River," Ruslan agreed, his voice sad and distant.

"Since we lost Damian, it seems like Arizona has become the epicenter of everything creepy and supernatural. The last six months have been nothing but a struggle. I wish he were—" River's voice trailed off, silence engulfing the midnight neighborhood.

Cole clutched his throat, his fingers nearly ripping the belt of the throat mic off. Six months had passed from the moment Damian returned to the Destiny Council realm, and since then, he hadn't heard from him. Their blood bond wasn't functioning, and neither Luc nor Jamie could find out anything from their superiors. It was as if his brother had ceased to exist.

"Cole, focus." Ruslan's voice rang in Cole's ears like an alarm bell, breaking his troubling train of thoughts. "Look down."

Cole glanced down, and his hand lowered to the pommel of his sword. Slithering between the shrubbery, following along the walkways, swirling around the tree trunks, a gray fog rose over the entire area of the courtyard, slowly accumulating in the center of the courtyard by the pool.

"River," he whispered, keeping his eyes on the fog. "Do you have the area blocked?"

"Yes. We have a police line surrounding the complex," River replied. "What's going on, Cole?"

"Not sure yet." Cole stepped closer to the edge of the roof, leaning over it a little. "I'll let you know as soon as I find out. Keep your people back and don't let humans in."

The fog gathered by the pool, slowly swirling in a counter-clockwise motion, rising higher and increasing in density with every passing second, and shortly after, the dark silhouettes of twelve women in long, flowing dresses materialized within it.

"I've seen something like this before," Cole whispered, pressing his finger to his mic. "It's like some weird déjà vu."

"Not a déjà vu." Ruslan's disembodied voice echoed Cole's thoughts. "We encountered something like this a few months ago."

"The demonic spirits of the night." Cole's hand slipped down from the pommel of his sword, his fingers wrapping around the grip. "*Nochnitsas...*" Ruslan didn't reply, but Cole knew he was right in his assessment. "Ruslan, we need to stop them. Hundreds of children live in this apartment complex. They'll feed on the energy of their souls, making them sick."

"We need iron." Ruslan's husky voice was so quiet that even Cole had to strain to hear him.

"I don't need iron, but you do," Cole replied, unsheathing his swords.

"Wait for me. There are twelve of them there."

Cole looked down and froze in place, a sense of foreboding growing stronger within him. Twelve *nochnitsas* stood in a circle, their arms raised, their long, black hair flowing in the frosty breeze. A blob of dark mist formed in the center of their circle, occasional sanguine sparkles igniting inside of it. They kept swaying slightly from side to side, the sound of their monotone voices melting with the rustling of the trees. As they continued to chant, the fog expanded around them, long, slithering tendrils reaching under the doors and through the windows.

"Father, we can't wait. Find something you can use and join me." Without waiting for Ruslan's response, Cole stepped off the roof.

He dropped three floors down and landed softly and soundlessly on one knee, his swords in his hands. Quickly rising, he looked down, noticing gray swirls of fog wrapped around his feet, creeping up his heavy motorcycle boots. As soon as the tendrils touched the fabric of his jeans, they turned into a black, sticky substance. Slowly, it kept progressing up, sending waves of dark magical energy through him. His throat spasmed, and to his shock, for a moment, he felt as if he experienced a heart attack. Dizziness assailed him, clouding his mind. Pain and numbness spread through his chest, and he groaned, staggering backward until he hit the wall of the building.

"Hell no. I'm a vampire. I don't need to breathe, and my heart is not beating. You're barking up the wrong tree, midnight bitches," he muttered, focusing on his magic.

As it came in an unrelenting wave of heat, the dark substance retreated from him, and his mind cleared. He took a tentative step forward, noticing that the fog pulled away from his feet, swirling around his legs without touching him. His lips twitched as he channeled more of his magic, sending it toward his blades. Moving swiftly and stealthily, he ran toward the *nochnitsas*. Busy chanting, they didn't notice his approach until it was too late.

He swung his swords in cross-motion, the *Ardenium* steel cutting through two of the demonic spirits in front of him. The *nochnitsas* hissed, a grimace of pain contorting their tender faces, and their bodies started to disintegrate into swirls of gray fog. The rest of them stopped chanting and turned to him, their eyes glowing with a sinister purple light, staring at him with undiluted hatred.

"A vampire..." one of them whispered, her musical voice trembling with fury.

"... he's not," the second one took over.

"He has a heart..."

"...and a soul..."

They kept talking, whispering, hissing, their smoky voices intertwining in his head, clouding his mind. He groaned, struggling to hold on to his swords, his magic slowly abandoning his body.

"Bad for him..."

"Good for us..."

Oh, shit... Shake it off... The thought surfaced in Cole's mind, barely breaking through the fog of the *nochnitsas'* magic, but even though he could think more or less clearly now, his body felt numb, his movements slow and heavy like that of a person locked in a night terror. *I haven't had a dream since I was turned. I can't... Neither can I have a nightmare.*

Spreading his arms, he roared, his vocal cords vibrating with strain, and his scream resonated through the midnight neighborhood. His magic came to life, invigorating his every muscle, expelling the suffocating influence of the nightmarish creatures before him. His well-trained body responded to the command of his mind, and his deadly blades hissed through the air, wreaking havoc among the monsters.

They danced out of his way, their moves gracious and fluid despite the expression of horror and fury distorting their beautiful, pale faces. The wind picked up, its icy touch grazing Cole's skin, lifting the sides of his trench coat. Even though Cole moved at his full speed, they somehow managed to follow his every step, and in an instant, they surrounded him, their billowing dresses and hair partially obscuring his view.

He spun in place, his blades leaving swirls of dark smoke behind as they cut into the *nochnitsas'* willowy bodies when an intense pain spiraled through him, nearly bringing him to his knees. He cried out, dropping his swords. His fingers tore at his chest, blood trickling from under his claws, and for a brief second, he felt as if his heart was about to explode.

Cole looked down, and a soft groan escaped his lips. One of the *nochnitsas* stood next to him, her arm penetrating his side, disappearing into his chest.

"He does have a heart..." the *nochnitsa* said, his mind, hazed by the pain, barely registering her words.

"Yes, he does!" A deep male voice sounded like the boom of thunder. "And you know what else he has?" An iron rod whistled through the air, eliciting a scream of horror and torment out of the demonic spirits, and Ruslan stepped into view, his eyes blazing with the scarlet light of vampiric essence, his terrifying fangs fully extended. He swung his iron rod again, turning the *nochnitsa*, whose fingers were wrapped around Cole's heart, into a cloud of smoke. "He has his father..."

Cole moaned in relief and collapsed to his knees, giving himself a short moment to regroup. Finding his blades, he rose again and sprang into action. The *nochnitsas* hissed and hollered, trying to avoid his powerful strikes and Ruslan's relentless attacks. They spun and twirled, the wind that followed them forming into howling twisters. Fighting the assault of the freezing gale, Cole and Ruslan refused to slow down, their every move fast and precise, and a few seconds later, the last demonic spirit of the night was gone, leaving behind the stench of demonic essence and dirty swirls of fog.

Cole lowered his swords, but Ruslan shook his head, pointing with the iron rod toward the swimming pool.

"We're not done, son," he said, speaking in an undertone.

A blob of black mist sparkling with crimson inclusions slowly rotated there, snake-like tendrils sprouting from it in every direction. They slithered over the ground and floated through the air, creating a thin net of dark magical energy all around their focal point. Quiet and ominous, they stretched toward the buildings, entering every single apartment at once, and strangled moans and cries of pain reached Cole's sensitive hearing.

The rotation of the blob halted abruptly, and a dark shadow manifested in its depth, moving and shifting within it. A crack, glowing with a bright scarlet light, materialized on its surface, and brilliant rays of light burst through it. The mist dissipated, and when the light dwindled, an old hag stepped forward, a wide sneer exposing her toothless red gums. The dark red skin of her face was covered in deep wrinkles, creases and spots, and her eyes glowed with a sinister red glimmer. The yellowish glow of streetlights bounced against her bald head, and even though the wind was gone, her red clothes flowed around her, long red ribbons twirling in a nonstop, chaotic motion.

She sauntered toward them, her moves slow and fluid but steady, like that of a person confident in their power. As her ghastly eyes swept over the apartment complex, her mouth stretched into a spine-chilling smile. Ruslan seized Cole's arm, yanking him back, and pressed his finger to his mic, whatever little color he had draining from his face.

"River," he said, his voice ringing with urgency. "Pull your people as far away from the building as you can and make sure no one crosses the police lines, not even emergency vehicles. I'll let you know once we're done, but you may need to call the CDC and alert them about a possible outbreak of—"

"Ruslan, what's going on?" River asked, interrupting him, deep concern in her voice. "Who—"

"Pestilence..." Ruslan finished his statement, his eyes never leaving the red monster in front of him. "But not one of the Four Horsemen... A lot older and more terrifying than any of the Horsemen."

"Pestilence? The Four Horsemen are real?" River's bewildered voice rang through the communication system, but Ruslan didn't reply.

The hag came to a halt and tilted her head a little, the net of her tendrils swaying and pulsing as they spread wider. "This old leech does have some brains." She pointed at Ruslan with her deformed, wrinkled finger, her smile turning into a horrendous grimace. "Say my name, bloodsucker. I dare you..."

"*Lihoradka*... Evil incarnate... One of twelve cursed sisters, condemned to torture and kill people till the end of eternity," Ruslan replied calmly, stepping in front of Cole to shield him. "My guess you are *Ogneya*, also known as *Goryachka*—the Fever."

"Is there a way to get rid of her?" Cole whispered so quietly that only the overly heightened hearing of the old vampire could catch his words.

"Heat or purifying Fire... We have neither..."

"Go figure? A smart ancient leech." *Ogneya* cackled. "I have no interest in you. You're already dead so you're useless to me."

She barely flicked her wrist, but an invisible force lifted Ruslan in the air, propelling him a few feet back. At the same time, her other arm struck forward, and she seized Cole's neck, pulling him closer. Ruslan hit the walkway hard but hopped to his feet almost immediately, bolting back to Cole. He wasn't fast enough. *Ogneya* squeezed her fingers, moving Cole so close to her face that he could smell the stench of her foul breath. Debilitating weakness spread through him, making him feel like a sickly human child with a high fever.

"You *are* a vampire, little one, aren't yah?" she screeched, forcing his lips apart with her bony fingers to check his fangs. "Yet you're brimming with the energy of life." She cocked her head, pinning him with her burning gaze. "How is that possible?"

Cole grabbed her skinny wrist with both hands, but to his dismay, he couldn't free himself from her iron grip, his weak fingers barely holding on to her. Ruslan seized her arm and tried to pull her away from Cole. His massive body arched, and the muscles on his arms rippled, but *Ogneya* just cackled, completely ignoring him.

"Let's see what makes you tick, little vamp." *Ogneya* pulled her free arm back and struck Cole's chest, her hand penetrating his rib cage as if he were incorporeal.

Cole froze, his eye widening in shock as an excruciating pain took hold of him, twisting him into a screaming, thrashing heap of flesh and bones. Heat the likes of which he had never felt before invaded his body, and he felt as if he was burning up from the inside.

"*Heat or purifying Fire. We have neither...*" Ruslan's words surfaced in his feverish mind, and he held on to the thought, fighting the influence of the monster with everything he had in his mind and body.

A strangled growl rumbled in his chest as a second wave of heat rushed through him. This one, however, didn't cripple him. On the contrary, it gave him energy, boosting his strength. Small flames burst through the skin of his hands, and *Ogneya* squealed, an expression of horror making her ugly face look even scarier than before.

He screamed as a burst of magical energy followed the surge

of the fire, his voice ringing with pure joy. Powerful and unstoppable, the elemental energy of Fire took him over, and two giant wings expanded behind his back, every flaming feather glowing a bright scarlet, emitting fountains of sparks. Ruslan fell back, raising his arm to shield his face as he stared at his son in awe.

Cole extended his arms, and his swords materialized in his hands, their blades on fire. *Ogneya* staggered back, her tendrils shrinking as she focused all her power on Cole. The red ribbons that he thought were part of her clothes moved forward, wrapping around him, pinning his arms to his torso. He threw his head back, laughing, feeling liquid fire rushing through him, and his entire body went up in flames, burning the ribbons as if they were made of paper.

Ogneya raised her arm, ready to snap her fingers, but Cole was faster. In the time shorter than a heartbeat, he swung his blazing sword, and it went through the ancient monster's body, cutting her in half. Her deafening screech rang through the neighborhood, and she exploded into a fountain of black and red sparkles. They fell all around him, quickly dissipating on their way down. Her tendrils vanished, and silence engulfed the apartment complex.

Cole's fingers unlocked, and his swords dropped to the ground with a metallic clang. He glanced over his shoulder at his flaming wings and then raised his hands, staring at the small flames dancing on his arms.

"Heaven and Earth." Ruslan got up but stood back, keeping his distance from the fire.

"Father, what's happening to me?" Cole whispered and dropped to his knees, wrapping his arms around himself. The light of the streetlights and twinkling sparkles of Christmas decorations spun around him in a crazy carousel, and then everything went dark.

TEASER: THE BURNS FIRE

(THE FIRE SALAMANDER CHRONICLES BOOK 1)

~ Zane Burns, a.k.a. Gunz ~
Modern Day, South Florida

The restaurant was nothing special, just another tiny hole-in-the-wall located on one of the countless South Florida canals. There wasn't anything noteworthy about its limited menu either. The only thing special about this place was its relaxed atmosphere. The restaurant had an open porch with three tables facing the canal. But the regulars were never sitting on the porch. They preferred to stay inside, leaving the romantic view to tourists and lovey-dovey couples.

Gunz had discovered this place shortly after he moved to South Florida, and since then he had become one of the regulars, visiting the restaurant at least a couple of times a week. He liked the laid-back atmosphere and easy-going crowd. It was a place where he allowed himself to relax and drop his guard. To a degree.

The inside room of the restaurant wasn't big, just a few tables and a bar. A big screen TV was hanging on the wall behind the bar, next to a few shelves with liquor. The air was infused with the smell of alcohol and fried food, and a heavy curtain of cigarette smoke was hanging under the ceiling. The room was relatively dark. Out of six wall lights only three were on, but no one ever asked to turn up the light.

Gunz walked through the room, quickly surveying every corner, and sat down at the bar. Tonight, besides a few regulars, there was no one new. A pretty young woman in her mid-twenties approached him right away. Here, she was everything—the owner of the restaurant, a bartender, a waitress—all-in-one, cross-functional queen of *Missi's Kitchen*.

"Usual, Mr. Burns?" she asked, smiling at him. Her skin, the color of dark chocolate, was smooth like silk and her large gray eyes framed with thick black eyelashes looked unnaturally bright on her face. Her long black hair was braided into countless thin braids and pulled into a ponytail on the back of her head, calling attention to her elegant neck.

"Yes, Missi, thank you," said Gunz.

She put three small shot glasses on the bar table in front of him and filled them with vodka. "I'll be back with your food in a moment," she told him, heading toward the kitchen door.

"Take your time, Missi," muttered Gunz, picking up the first shot glass. "I'm not in any rush tonight." He took a deep breath and downed the vodka without flinching. Placing the empty shot glass on the table, he exhaled and closed his eyes, enjoying the feeling of the harsh burning liquid rushing down his throat.

For a few minutes, he sat quietly staring at the TV. It was set to the local news channel, but he didn't listen to the news, his thoughts far away. Then he sighed and picked up the second shot glass. He gulped the vodka and put the empty glass next to the first one.

"Hard day, Mr. Burns?" asked Missi, placing a plate with a burger and steaming pile of french fries in front of him. "You seem to look broodier than usual."

TEASER: THE BURNS FIRE

Gunz smiled. He picked up a hot french fry with his fingers and nibbled on it. "You could say so," he said finally. "Just one of those days... This day a couple of years ago, I lost... someone."

"Your friend?" asked Missi, gazing at him with sympathy in her bright eyes.

"Yeah... friend. Vladislav Kirilenko," he replied absentmindedly, taking the next burning-hot fry from his plate. "I lost him to the world of magic. He's never coming back."

"*The World of Magic*," she repeated in disbelief, her eyebrows rising. "What is that? A fantasy novel? There is no such thing as magic. You're making fun of me, Mr. Burns." She shook her head, a soft smile tugging at her full lips.

Gunz smiled tiredly and picked up the last shot glass, squeezing it in his fist. "Third one for the fallen," he murmured and drank it quickly, returning the empty glass to Missi. "You know, Missi, I've been coming to your restaurant for over a year. Don't you think it's time you stop calling me *Mr. Burns*? I don't think I'm that much older than you. You know that you can call me Zane, or even Gunz, if you prefer to use my nickname."

"I know. I don't like nicknames. You're a man, not a pet," she said lightly, taking away the empty shot glasses and wiping the tabletop with a white towel. "Zane Burns..." She pronounced his name slowly, like she was sizing it up. "Sounds good, but I prefer to call you Mr. Burns. For some reason, it seems to fit you better."

Gunz felt someone's hand on his elbow and a hardly noticeable wave of magical energy swept through him. He snapped his head to the right and found a fake blonde sitting next to him. She was devouring him with her eyes, her lipstick-enhanced lips stretched in a sensual smile. Her hand unceremoniously traveled up his arm, following the shape of his biceps, and stopped at his shoulder.

"Yum," she said, gently probing him with her magic. "I'll call you anything you want, hon."

Gunz gave her a frosty once-over, turning his senses up. He had no doubt that she was something other than human. Her fingers softly massaged his shoulder, sending a stronger wave of magical energy through him. For a moment, his mind became clouded with desire and his body responded to her salacious magic with more eagerness than he expected.

Succubus, concluded Gunz, channeling the Fire, burning the poison of her magic out of his body. Her hand traveled down his arm, landing on his inner thigh. He seized her wrist, prying it off his leg and sent some fire toward his hand. Her skin blistered like from the touch of a hot stove, and she yelped in pain.

"Who are you? What are you?" she whimpered, trying to free herself from his smoldering grip, but he didn't let her go.

Gunz glanced around, making sure that no one, including Missi, was watching. "I'm a man who is not looking for company," he growled, sending some fire toward his eyes. The bright flames went up in the depths of his eyes, and she gasped. "Especially not the company of your kind." He released her wrist, observing red spots of burns and blisters on her skin. "Leave this place and forget about its existence. You understand?"

She nodded, fear making her every move jerky, and rushed out of the restaurant, nursing her burnt wrist. Gunz sighed, releasing the Fire, and turned back to the bar.

"Hey, Missi," he called and waited a moment as she appeared from the kitchen. "Can I have everything to go, please? And one more before I leave." He pointed at the bottle of Russian vodka that he usually ordered.

She put a shot glass on the bar table and filled it with vodka. "That's unusual," she murmured, her hands quickly packaging the burger and fries into a take-out box. "You never drink more than three shots."

A lopsided smile crossed his face, making a single dimple

TEASER: THE BURNS FIRE

appear on one of his cheeks. "I know. Usually three shots are my limit, but today I felt like I needed more." He downed the vodka and got up, grabbing the take-out box.

Missi shook her head, checking him with concern. "Do you want me to call you a cab?"

"Thank you, Missi. I'll walk. Take care." He nodded to her and walked out of the restaurant.

* * *

Gunz walked away from the restaurant and turned into a dark alley. He stopped and rubbed his forehead tiredly. *Maybe Missi was right. I didn't need that fourth shot,* he thought, his lips forming an uneven smile. It had been a while since he felt drunk and right now the world around him seemed to be unsteady. Possibly it was a combination of vodka with the residuals of the succubus magic. He surveyed the alley carefully to make sure that no one could see him and once satisfied, he waved his hand, unfolding the fire curtain of a portal.

He walked through the fire and ended up in the backyard of his house in Coral Springs. The house wasn't really his. It belonged to his friend, but she was away and wasn't planning to come back any time soon. In the meantime, Gunz had the full use of her house. Dizziness assailed him as he took a step forward. He chuckled and sat down heavily on the steps in front of the back door.

He closed his eyes and leaned his back against the door of the house, still feeling a little buzzed. He was about to get up when he felt a soft touch to his leg. Gunz looked down and noticed a small kitten. It couldn't have been more than a month old. The kitten was trying to climb on his lap, its tiny sharp claws catching the hard fabric of his jeans.

"Oh, hello, little buddy. What are you doing here?" said Gunz. He put the take-out box on the steps and gently picked up the kitten, holding it in his hands. The kitten turned on his engine, purring loudly, and licked his hand. Gunz laughed, gently stroking the kitten's thick gray fur with his fingers. "You found the wrong man, little buddy. I'm a dog person—give me a giant German Shepherd any day. Well, occasionally, I don't mind dealing with lizards. But cats…"

The kitten ignored his statement and climbed up his shirt, settling on his shoulder. He meowed into his ear and poked his cheek with his wet nose. Gunz petted the kitten, leaving him sitting on his shoulder, and picked up the take-out box. "Well, you're taking your life in your own paws, buddy… but if you're sure that you want to adopt a man like me then let's get going." He unlocked the door and walked into the kitchen.

Inside, Gunz put the kitten on the floor and opened the refrigerator. He poured some milk in a small bowl and placed it in front of him.

"Sorry, little buddy, I don't have any cat food or litter for you"—he quickly glanced at the wall clock that was showing past one in the morning—"and it's too late for shopping. I'll buy everything you need first thing in the morning."

The kitten ignored him, preoccupied with his milk. Gunz squatted next to him and softly stroked his back. The kitten moved closer to his bowl and growled defensively. Gunz laughed, rising. "I think I'll call you Mishka in honor of my good friend. You sure remind me of him."

He left the kitten in the kitchen and walked to the living room. His body was buzzing with the exhaustion of this endless day and the incident with the succubus didn't sit well with him. Missi's restaurant was normally free of supernatural visitors. He was probably the only one. And the succubus' behavior seemed a bit odd too. Until he used his power, she didn't sense the creature of magic in him. Something didn't feel right.

His cell phone rang, making him flinch. He pulled it out and

TEASER: THE BURNS FIRE

looked at the display. Jim. *One o'clock in the morning? That can't be good.* He clicked the green button, answering the call.

"Hello, Jim," he said and fell silent for a few seconds, listening to Jim. "You want me to come over now? Can it wait till morning?"

He lowered the phone down for a moment and sighed, bringing the shouting device back to his ear.

"No, I'm not drunk. Just a little—" Jim interrupted him urgently, obviously not pleased, and Gunz fell silent again, listening to his boss. "Yes, sir, I know the consequences of losing control of my power, and I assure you, I'm in complete control."

Gunz lowered himself onto the couch, rubbing the stubble on his chin tiredly.

"Yes, sir, I know that my job doesn't have weekends and days off," he said, hoping to calm Jim down. "I'm sorry, sir, I needed to unwind a little… I'm not drunk…"

He had been working with Agent Andrews for over a year and he had never heard him talking like this to him. Something serious was going on.

"Yes, sir, I know what Code Shadow means… I understand the urgency of the situation… No, sir. You don't need to summon me."

Jim didn't have magic and he couldn't use summoning spells, but his partner, Angelique, could. She was a witch and a seer. Gunz hated when they used summoning spells to call him. The persistent pull of the summoning spell on his mind was driving him crazy, giving him a pounding headache afterwards.

"I prefer not to drive right now, so I'll open my portal to your office right away, if you don't mind… Yes, sir, to Angelique's office… I'll see you both in a few minutes."

Gunz hung up the phone and shook his head, biting his lip. Code Shadow. It meant an abnormally high level of supernatural activity, endangering civilian lives. Since he started to work with the secret division of the FBI, dealing with supernatural occurrences, it was the first time that Code Shadow was officially issued.

"Fire Salamander—go," he muttered to himself and waved his hand, opening the fire portal into Angelique's office.

* * *

Get your copy of The Burns Fire Online Today!

DEAR READER

Thank you so much for reading The Shadow Curse. I hope you enjoyed the book and will join Damian Blake's next adventure in the sixth book of the series.

If you would like to stay up-to-date on the latest information about new releases, special offers, and more, sign up for my mailing list and get a FREE novella—www.nmthorn.com.

For more information follow me on
Facebook (www.facebook.com/nmthornauthor)
Instagram (www.instagram.com/nmthornauthor)
Or visit my website www.nmthorn.com

Join N.M Thorn's readers group to meet other readers, discuss the novels and the characters, get updates and do anything else related to the series.
www.facebook.com/groups/authornmthorn

BEFORE YOU GO...

Your reviews mean the world to me and are greatly appreciated. If you enjoyed the Shadow Curse, please take a few minutes to leave a review. It doesn't have to be long. It can be just a few words or stars rating.

Please help spread the word by taking this small extra step and leave your review on Amazon and/or Goodreads.

ALSO BY N. M. THORN

The Fire Salamander Chronicles
The Burns Path (Prequel Novella Book 0 - for my subscribers)
The Burns Fire - Book 1
The Burns War - Book 2
The Burns Defiance - Book 3
The Burns Codex - Book 4
The Burns Enigma - Book 5
The Burns Destiny - Book 6

* * *

The Shadow Enforcer Series
The Shadow Enforcer - Book 1
The Shadow Deception - Book 2
The Shadow Paradox - Book 3
The Shadow Storm - Book 4
The Shadow Curse - Book 5

ABOUT THE AUTHOR

N.M. Thorn currently lives in South Florida with her husband and son. Owner of a digital marketing agency by day and a writer by night, she loves spending her times creating new worlds, paranormal planes of existence and anything that could be described as supernatural.

When she is not busy working with everything digital or exploring fantasy worlds, she enjoys spending time with her family, reading, painting and practicing martial arts.

If you would like to share your thoughts, ideas or just send N.M. Thorn a message about the Fire Salamander world, feel free to contact her at: nmthornauthor@gmail.com

- facebook.com/nmthornauthor
- instagram.com/nmthornauthor
- amazon.com/N-M-Thorn/e/B07MY9JZMB
- bookbub.com/authors/n-m-thorn

Printed in Great Britain
by Amazon